The Minister Primarily

A Novel

John Oliver Killens

HARPER LARGE PRINT

An Imprint of HarperCollins*Publishers*

THE MINISTER PRIMARILY. Copyright © 2021 by The Grace Killens Revocable Trust, Inc. All rights reserved. Printed in the United States of America. No part of this book may be used or reproduced in any manner whatsoever without written permission except in the case of brief quotations embodied in critical articles and reviews. For information, address HarperCollins Publishers, 195 Broadway, New York, NY 10007.

HarperCollins books may be purchased for educational, business, or sales promotional use. For information, please e-mail the Special Markets Department at SPsales@harpercollins.com.

Foreword, "John Oliver Killens: The Real and The Fake" © Ishmael Reed

FIRST HARPER LARGE PRINT EDITION

ISBN: 978-0-06-309068-2

Library of Congress Cataloging-in-Publication Data is available upon request.

21 22 23 24 25   LSC   10 9 8 7 6 5 4 3 2 1

My father passed away without leaving a dedication for this novel. On his behalf, I am including the following dedication that I think my father would be pleased with:

To Georgia Killens, my great-great-grandmother Granny (seven years old when freedom was declared). She would say to my father, "Ah lord honey, the half ain't never been told." With that challenge he would tell part of that other half.

—*Barbara Killens Rivera*
Brooklyn, New York

Foreword

John Oliver Killens:
The Real and The Fake

O ne of the memorable moments from the Water-gate hearings occurred when Georgia's then-senator Herman Talmadge, an old-time primitive Southern demagogue and segregationist, said, "In Georgia a man's home is his castle."[1] Contrast this with one of the most powerful, ghastly, and shocking scenes in American literature. It occurs in John O. Killens's

---

1 "Where is the check on the chief executive's power as to where that power begins and ends, that is what I am trying to determine," Talmadge said. "Do you remember when we were in law school we studied a famous principle of law that came from England, and also is well known in this country, that no matter how humble a man's cottage is that even the king of England cannot enter without his consent?"

first novel, *Youngblood*. Joe Youngblood is one of the passengers on a train that is taking Black southerners to the North. Armed White men board the train and kidnap the Black passengers. When a young Black man objects on the grounds that the passengers are American citizens, he is brutalized:

> The rifle went off. The explosion temporarily deafened Joe. The Young Negro slumped down in the aisle, his right arm a shattered, bloody mass at the elbow. Joe jumped from his seat. The cracker with the mustache looked up at him. "See what I mean," he said to Joe, motioning with his rifle towards the young Negro. "Had to shoot one of the youngest and strongest bucks in the group. Won' no needer that neither—" He turned to a couple of his men. "Git him offa here fore he bleed up the train. Won't no call for that at all and Mr. Buck ain't gon like it. See how bad education is for niggers?"

The Black passengers who were en route to the North are put to work on the Buck plantation, where a defiant Black man like Youngblood is repeatedly beaten for his impudence. With this scene, Killens demonstrates the power that Black writers of his generation possessed. With his depiction of a South as hell for Blacks, a sentiment echoed by the poet Sterling Brown, where mobs could drag any Black person from his home and lynch him, and rape his female relatives, Talmadge's remark demonstrated the different worlds in which southern Blacks and southern Whites resided. In those days, a writer could contradict a White man, no matter how powerful, and be provided with space to do it. This was a time before Black Power became safe enough to appear on the cover of fashion magazines with models drawn from the "Generation Hamilton."

The novel was one of the weapons, not only to be used to reveal truths that mainstream audiences found uncomfortable. Killens and his contemporaries and friends John A. Williams, William Demby, William Gardner Smith, and Charles Harris, all World War II veterans, also annoyed the New York literary establishment by exposing the racism that existed in the armed forces, which contradicted the propaganda line coming from above that the war had been fought to end fascism, when racism is one of the most important components of fascism. In Killens's classic *And Then We Heard the Thunder*, a Black soldier becomes so fed up with the racist treatment that he receives from White soldiers and officers that he welcomes a Japanese attack on his encampment.

The character's name is Geoffrey Grant. A self-proclaimed Black Nationalist from New York City, he's given the standard Black Nationalist speeches:

> "You goddamn ignorant bawstards! The Japanese are fighting for your freedom and your dignity. The white man is the most deceitful, the most two-faced human being in all the world. But if he pissed in your face and told you it was raining outdoors; you damn fools would purchase umbrellas."

In another scene, he runs from his tent and shouts:

> "Gwan, Tojo! Gwan Tojo! Fly, black man! Show these white bawstards how you can fly!" He shook his fist at the planes ducking in and out of the flak and diving and laying eggs and climbing straight up again at ninety-degree angles. "Gwan, Tojo! Go on, mawn! Show these bawstards how to do it!"

There was pro-Japanese sentiment among Blacks during World War II. The historian Gerald Horne reminds us that there were more Black members of pro-

Japanese organizations than Communist ones.[2] Such a scene would not suit those who directed trends in literature. For them, World War II was a holy crusade.

Both *Youngblood* and *And Then We Heard the Thunder* show the evolution of Killens from a writer whose favorite scenes are inhabited by good, God-fearing people whom Killens portrays as "the salt of the earth." In *Youngblood*, a lengthy passage is devoted to slaughtering and dressing a chicken. But by the time of *The Minister Primarily*, written in the eighties, Killens had become a global novelist, drawing scenes from London and Africa as well as the United States.

The key to understanding both of John Oliver Killens's satirical novels, *The Cotillion* and *The Minister Primarily*, can be found in the reaction of Will Branson, a character in *The Cotillion*, to the Neo-African style of his niece, Yoruba: "You ain't no African! You're an American! Git yourself a mini skirt." Killens describes "Uncle Wild Will" as "a plain speaking unpretentious Black man . . . possessed of, and by no bourgeois affectations." For Killens, those who were continuing

---

2   Gerald Horne, *Race War: White Supremacy and the Japanese Attack on the British Empire* (New York: New York University Press, 2004).

African traditions resided in the South. Contemplating a visit to Mississippi, Jimmy muses:

> His brothers and sisters in the delta were more African than any others in the country, closer to their African culture, their African humanity. They were the honest-to-goodness diasporated Africans. With their mojo and their voodoo and their belief in "haints" and roots and their music and their churches and their shouting and their dancing.

Again, when Jimmy Johnson, who pretends to be Jaja Okwu Olivamaki of Guanaya, addresses a crowd in Lolliloppi, 'Sippi, Near-the-Gulf, he says:

> "I want all of you to know that I feel a deep sense of homecoming here in this place that reminds me so much of Mother Africa, the sun, the earth, the sky, the bright green of your rain forest, the overall fertility, all this reminds me of Africa. Your struggle, your hardships, your determination to be free, through struggle."

An Irish writer says that when the Irish left Chicago, they left Ireland. Killens is saying that when Blacks left the South, they left Africa.

Though these speeches are uttered by characters, they cohere with the views of Killens, whose targets were the impersonators, whether they be strivers like Lady Daphne of *The Cotillion,* "a pitiful imitation," or Madame Marie Antoinette Robinson, a character in *The Minister Primarily.* Lady Daphne is a striver. When learning that her Neo-African daughter Yoruba has been invited to dinner by a power couple, she says:

"This is what I wanted for you. Make friends with people like Brenda Brasswork and you'll be getting up in society. You'll go places. You'll be recognized." She threw her arms around Yoruba and kissed her roughly, clumsily—"The Brassworks is somebody, child! The Brassworks is somebody."

In *The Minister Primarily,* Madame Marie Antoinette Robinson is described as "a society lady of the middle ages growing slimmingly and inevitably toward a very slight obesity, due quite obviously to overindulgence in exotic culinary pursuits and alcoholic imbibition."

In the book, Killens describes "a gathering of the elite among Franklin Frazier's fashionable bourgeoisie of color, with a fair sprinkling of the paler people of the upper middle classes. State Department types and all. Truly high society." Commenting on the gathering is a young Black bourgeois lawyer who shares Frazier's and Killens's attitude toward this class: "The young lawyer seated too near Her Excellency said, 'That's the way it is with most of these bourgeois Negroes. You start a serious conversation and they come up with a headache. They avoid a political or intellectual dialogue as if it were a communicable disease." One member of this clique is mocked relentlessly by the author for wearing a red wig.

Killens relishes in the art of irony. Once in a while the imitators are confronted by the real thing. From *The Cotillion*:

One of the Americans with a bad bush atop said, "Dig. How come you cats don't wear Afros like us? I mean you cats are from where it's really at. Y'all from the heritage and shit. Ain't y'all got no Negritude? Don't y'all know that Black is beautiful?"

The African brother smiled deprecatingly. "Certainly, we knowing that Black is beautiful. And we in Africa are having plenty of Negritude and so on. But we don't wear our hair like you are wearing it, because in the tropical climate lice will have a feast in your head if you wear it so. There will be wild beasts romping in your rain forests."

And so, while Black Americans are ridiculed for imitating Africans, Whites are derided for imitating Black
Americans imitating Africans:

White girls with Afro wigs made some of them
bashes in the Heights, posing as light-skinned soul
sisters, spanking the plank and talking that talk,
doing varied imitations of the near-white Black
bourgeois.

A *Cotillion* character named Brassy Brenda points
them out:

"That one over there in dungarees with the ear-
rings through her nose is passing for colored," and
"That one over there grinning in my boyfriend's
face, that one with the brown powder pack on her
face and the African robe, she's passing for a
nigger!"

In *The Cotillion*, Killens could be hard on Black
Nationalists, such as the comical Harlem street orator
Bad Mouth, or

Jomo Mamadou Zero the Third, in his boss dashiki
with large black glasses covering the upper regions

of his face, [who] glared out from behind his bad black beard at the ocean of pink-white faces in the TV audience. He spat across the footlights at them. And they applauded. He growled, "I wished all of you pale-faced pigs a bad damn evening, you swinish cannibalistic motherfuckas! And after a few kind words of salutation, I'm going to say mean things to you." The audience exploded with applause.

These militant threats were entertainment for White audiences in the sixties, fully aware that the militants didn't have the military power to back up their threats.

When Killens entertains such characters, it's not just an exercise in ridicule or poking fun, or hurling barbs from the Left Bank in exile, but because these characters built no institutions. He paid dearly for his efforts. Keith Gilyard's brilliant biography, *John Oliver Killens: A Life of Black Literary Activism*, documents a life of travel, organizing Black writers' conferences, teaching engagements, and founding the Harlem Writers Guild, which helped advance the careers of Dr. John Henrik Clarke, Rosa Guy, Walter Dean Myers, Louise Meriwether, Sarah E. Wright, Audrey Lorde, Paule Marshall, Julian Mayfield, Terry McMillan, Loften Mitchell, Wesley Brown, Rosemary Bray, Alice Childress, Lonne Elder III, and Robert Hooks. Members of the guild produced more than three hundred published works of fiction, nonfiction, poetry, plays, and screenplays.

While others peddled eloquence and glittering hot air, Killens was hounded by the state. The FBI kept tabs on his travels, appearances, and residences, which included stints at Fisk and Columbia University. They tried to tie him to Communist fronts, which seems quaint nowadays given the fact that the ex-president Donald Trump, an authentic fellow traveler, took the word of Communist dictators over that of his intelligence agencies.

How many of today's writers could withstand the FBI getting into their business? The FBI spied on John Oliver Killens from November 15, 1941, when he was twenty-five years old, to September 6, 1973,[3] though a letter dated June 27, 1956, seemed to lessen the pressure. Killens and his wife, Grace, had their mail opened and were subjected to other forms of persecution.

In his introduction to *And Then We Heard the Thunder*, Mel Watkins writes about the hopes for African independence held by Black Nationalists in 1962: "Blacks

---

3   A copy of Killens's FBI file is available from the Internet Archive, https://archive.org/details/JohnO.KillensFBIFile/John %20O.%20Killens%20001/page/n1/mode/2up.

looked at Africa and other Third World countries as models for the newly emerging Afro-American nation."

In *The Minister Primarily,* Killens writes about those heady times of an Africanesque revival in the United States when Blacks were proud of their "nappy-heads," and "Black was beautiful." They "talked everywhere about their heritage, the Blacks they did, of Gao and old Ghana and Egypt and Songhai and Mali and ancient Timbuktu and Kush. Organized Yoruba Temples and Mosques and committees by the hundreds." Since many Africans do not accept Black Americans as Africans and some hold them as their inferiors, was the African revival in the United States a sad masquerade, becoming another opportunity for capitalist exploitation, like department stores co-opting some of the African customs created by Black Americans during this period? This was Amiri Baraka's criticism when he switched from Black Nationalism to Communism. He dismissed Black Nationalism as an excuse for marketing products like Afro Sheen. Both men would be appalled that the Black movement has become so safe that Black members of the "Generation Hamilton" are using the death of George Floyd to market products.

Moreover, the hopes of Black Nationalists for an independent, possibly socialist Africa were dashed. None of the Black Nationalists of the sixties who I knew would have predicted that in 2020, the French would still be practicing a policy of *Françafrique*, a term denoting the extent of France's neocolonial involvement with its former empire in Africa. Yet French and British troops are still intervening in the affairs of their former colonies, in Mali, in Kenya, and elsewhere. Both Russia and China are sponsoring infrastructure projects in Africa, for which China has the edge, since members of its political elite are engineers. Given this, a term like "postcolonial" doesn't make sense.

Black intellectuals claim that without the cooperation of corrupt Black leaders, the occupation of Africa by external powers would have ended. I interviewed the late Hugh Masekela for my book *The Complete Muhammad Ali*. He told me the Western powers learned that you could continue doing business in Africa if you just freed the president or gave an African leader a billion dollars. Though Jaja Okwu Olivamaki, for whom an American folk singer, James Jay Leander Johnson, becomes a stand-in, poses as a socialist, he's willing to do business with capitalists. Even a socialist like Stokely Carmichael accompanied his mentor Sékou Touré to the United States for the purpose of seeking investments. Masekela's comments were echoed by the Malian writer Manthia Diawara (*We Won't Budge*). He said that he had difficulty convincing a Black American that Whites still run Africa, a fact that would have astonished Black Nationalists of the sixties. To many Africans, Black Americans are Europeans. Linda Okwuchuku tells James Jay Leander Johnson, the double of Prime Minister Jaja Okwu Olivamaki, "Black or white—you Europeans are all alike. Of all the colossal arrogance!" Some Africans view Black Americans and White Americans culturally instead of racially, so thrown together abroad, Blacks and Whites bond in sometimes embarrassing ways.

> Whitey laughed happily, knowingly, ecstatically, "You're an American. I knew it as soon as I saw you. You're an American. There's something about you that gives you away."
>
> Probably my Brooks Brothers Ivy League suit, Jimmy thought. I'll do something about that also tout-damn-suite. "How many times do I have to tell you? I'm an African!" the reluctant American shouted.
>
> Whitey looked around him surreptitiously and back to Jimmy. He whispered softly into Jimmy's ear, almost nibbling it. "Come on now. I won't tell anybody. You might as well admit it. You're an—" He leaned heavily on Jimmy.

John O. Killens had already proved that his satirical pen could cut individuals and institutions to ribbons with his novel *The Cotillion*. *The Minister Primarily* is a novel replete with brilliant parodies like Killens's deconstruction of the stock Black Queen poem of the sixties:

"Dear African princess, you are the River Nile, in its passionate and compassionate journey from Lake Victoria down north past Khartoum past the ruins of ancient Thebes past Cairo all the way to the Mediterranean. You are the Niger making its way back from deep in the delta at Bonny on the Gulf of Guinea past the mangroves making its torturous way back up past Onitsha past Bamako and Segu all the way to the nearby south of Timbuktu and beyond. You are the loveless Transvaal of South Africa. You are the subtle sleepy Congo. Your deep dark sultry eyes have known the loneliness of the Bedouin in his desert tent."

These Black queens would join the seventies feminist movement and charge some of the authors of the Black Queen poems with misogyny, in a literature in which the Black Queen bards were scalded.

Like all great satirists, Killens doesn't play favorites, which is a requirement made of Black novelists by literary special interests. Feminism is the latest constituency. The writer bell hooks says that White feminists told her that in order to succeed, she had to write for them. Without consulting with Black poets or Black members of her husband's entourage or even Joy Harjo, the great Native American poet and three-term US poet laureate, Jill Biden chose her husband's inaugural poet, passing over elders like Nikki Giovanni and Sonia Sanchez. Similar demands have been made by constituencies of the past, those who have a pipeline to consumers. The people who represent my side, these interests have demanded, must appear saintly, or at least "likable," while their antagonists must look evil. Because of these restrictions, many current Black novels backed by hefty budgets and publicity harken back to Mystery Plays, where the characters who represent their values are named Virtue. Some of Killens's White characters can be pat like Carlton Carson, the Secret Service man assigned to the bogus PM, who has a face like "Porky Pig." Addressing Jimmy, he says:

"Your Excellency, Mister Prime Minister Jaja Okwu Olivamaki, please Sir, you are a great man.

You have a black skin, but you have a soul as white as newly picked cotton!"

Explaining Africans, Mayor Rufe of Lolliloppi, Mississippi, advises:

"They look like our nigrahs, but they are human beans. You will know our nigrahs from the Africans by the long white robes the Africans will be wearing. They call them 'boobies.' If they should happen to visit our restaurants, the picture show, and other places of amusement, in their long white flowing boobies, they will not be members of the Klu Klux Klan. Heh-heh-heh."

Even with these White characters, they are not as vicious and vile and even subhuman as the Black characters created by White novelists, screenwriters, and filmmakers. In *The Minister Primarily*, the Black characters come off as foolish and silly as the White ones.

With *The Minister Primarily*, Killens takes aim at the corrupt leadership of an African country, members of an entourage who accompany the double of PM Jaja Okwu Olivamaki, James Jay Leander Johnson, on his trip to the United States. The country of Guanaya has become noticed because of the discovery of precious metal.

Great inexhaustible beds of cobanium—a radioactive metallic element, five hundred times more powerful and effective than uranium—were discovered in Guanaya's Northern Province. Then—Boom! Boom! Boom! Boom! Publicity—Popularity—Prosperity—Population Explosion. The capital city of Bamakanougou got crowded very suddenly. Everybody loved Guanaya and with a bloody ruddy passion.

Other writers have written about Black middle-class Americans arriving in the homeland to find their roots, only to become disillusioned. Killens gives this cliché a twist.

After kissing the ground, "James Jay Leander Johnson, colored, Negro, Afro-American, Black man, sepia fella, tan Yank (take your choice), folk singer . . . born in Lolliloppi, Mississippi, Near-the-Gulf, Southern USA," finds himself in trouble after arriving in the Homeland. Shortly after Johnson commits his ritual kiss, he is detained and accused of being involved in a plot to assassinate the prime minister, Jaja Okwu Olivamaki.

The man wrote furiously on the pad before him and then looked up again. Smiling a broad white smile in a proud Black handsome face. "I see—I see—You never heard of our great beloved Prime Minister, His Excellency Jaja Okwu Olivamaki. Yet you're obviously here to assassinate him."

Unbeknownst to Jimmy, he is there to impersonate Jaja Okwu Olivamaki. Because the prime minister is under threat of assassination, it's decided that it's necessary to send Jimmy, from Lolliloppi, Mississippi, to the United States as the prime minister's substitute!

Tangi rose and took a phony beard out of his pocket and put it on Jimmy's face, and Jimmy was immediately transformed into the PM's spitting image. It was unbelievable. The PM stared at Jimmy like he'd seen a ghost, and the rest of the Ministers stared at the two of them open-mouthed and speechless.

Jimmy protested. He was sitting again. "Whatever it is, it's a lie, I didn't do it. I was framed. I demand to see my lawyer. I'm for Africa all the way. Uhuru! Uhuru! Uhuru!"

Tangi said quietly, "Half of us stay here with the Prime Minister," pointing to Olivamaki, "and half of us go to the United States with the Prime Minister," pointing to Jimmy Johnson.

"Oh no!" the Ministers shouted, unanimously and in unison even.

Maria Efwa, "the lovely peripatetic perambulating encyclopedia of Guanayan lore and knowledge," is assigned to tutor Johnson about Guanaya, the fictional country of which he is assigned to be the fake prime minister. This ingenious plot development, that of a naive Black American folk singer becoming the double of an African prime minister, opens up a path for the writer to engage in endless hilarity.

At first Jimmy resists the masquerade. Jimmy says, "Would somebody be good enough to tell me what this is all about? Anyhow and regardless I demand to see my lawyer first. Any lawyer! And I refuse to answer on the grounds—that—that—" He tries to back out of the deal as they approach Washington, DC, where they are about to be greeted by the president. Jimmy is afraid that he will be exposed. "Suddenly Jimmy knew that one of the gravest dangers of discovery was that one of his own people, some African American, would see through his disguise and give him away, unintentionally or otherwise." His reception is marred. After the US and Guanayanese national anthems are played, the band plays the national anthem of the slave country that though defeated still hangs around:

And then it happened. One of the bands felt real down-home good and started playing "Dixie"! And there was waving of hats and even throwing of hats up in the air this time, and boisterous rebel yells from the wonderfully responsive crowd, temporarily gone wild with their enthusiasm now.

Jimmy begins to enjoy his role as a bogus prime minister. The state dinners and the women, including the president's mistress, attempting to seduce him. She gives him a hand job in the Lincoln bedroom, pleading with him to emancipate her. Southern customs that have made life difficult for generations of traditional Black Americans are waived for visiting African VIPs whose resources might be pilfered by Western capitalists. The president, Hubert Herbert Hubert, warns the mayor of Mississippi about the bogus PM's visit to Mississippi:

"I don't give a fucking damn if he marries all of your funky steamy-tailed daughters, Olivamaki *is* coming down there and there'd better not be no fucking racial incidents, or heads will fucking roll! His Excellency is my good fucking friend, and besides, he represents the richest fucking mineral output on this fucking earth. It's more valuable than fucking gold or diamonds, or heads will surely fucking roll! Money! Rufus Rastus fucking Hardtack! Money! That's what I'm fucking talking about, or fucking heads will roll."

Johnson gets five-star treatment everywhere he goes:

Every time he came outside the Waldorf, there were thousands standing there in wait, just for a fleeting glimpse of Himself. Indeed, some actually sought and fought just to touch the hem of his garment. His immaculate boubou.

White and Black, they dearly loved His (so-called) Excellency. The uncanny aspect of it was that they seemed always to know each time he had an appointment that would require him leaving the hotel. They would begin to collect about an hour ahead of time. They would begin to gather slowly, at first, then more and more, ultimately pouring from the buses and the subway, a feverish and disgorged humanity, flooding the streets across Park Avenue, jamming the traffic. Horn blowing. Shouted oaths. You could set your watch by it.

As someone who will provide billions to Western investors, he's even allowed to hang up on the president of the United States.

A huge slice of the novel is devoted to his reception as a visiting head of state as he visits New York—where John O. Killens appears among other Black celebrities, including Harry Belafonte (Killens's benefactor in real life)—Washington, DC, and Mississippi, inviting scenes that are meticulously constructed. Readers will stay with this novel because one knows that when the trickster is set up, inevitably, he will fall.

The novel is sweeping, cinematic, epic. To write such a novel requires painstaking, backbreaking work. The fact that this novel was rejected by publishers while the genre dubbed "girlfriend books" by Elizabeth Nunez, or gangbanger books, about which Terry McMillan complains, glut the market calls for a reevaluation of the relationship between Black writers and publishers. If this kind of well-wrought novel is an endangered literary species, how are younger writers going to learn how to write? This novel is the only text that one would need in a novel-writing class to show how a pro deals with scene, dialogue, descriptions, and transitions. Though Killens derided the mechanics of fiction—he said he got all "screwed up" after taking a workshop—he is the master of angles of narration, points of view, objectivity, universality, composition, author intrusion, sentence structure, syntax, first person, second person. He excels at constructing interior scenes:

> Essentially a "country boy," Himself [Jimmy] could not help himself from staring, slyly, almost clandestinely, at the decor and the color scheme of gold and white, and beneath his feet, the deeply plushed and woven oval rug, also of gold and white and pale blue, with the emblems of the fifty states incorporated around the carpet's border. He could not help from staring openly at the panoramic mural on the wall of *Scenic America* with Boston Harbor and Blacks in slavery-time attire and at what he assumed was Plymouth Rock. And the gleaming Regency chandelier above him.

He excels at dialogue such as the hilarious conversation taking place among customers at a barbershop in a scene from *The Cotillion.* He can do exteriors as well:

> When night has fallen, it has really come down all over Mother Africa. And with a beautiful-Black awesome bloody vengeance. You can hear night

falling everywhere. On the ride back from the airport, the countryside leaped with the sounds of African night. A jam session of ad-libbing crickets
and locusts and all kinds of bugs, but the honking
frogs with their basso profundos upstaged every
living thing in this crazy African orchestra. The
fruit bats swooped down toward the headlights and
quite a few got wasted.

Killens saw this crisis for quality Black fiction coming.
In 1959, according to Gilyard's biography, Killens called
for a permanent National Black Writers Conference
and writers' union and the forming of an amalgamated
Black press, "to ensure that black myths, legends, plays,
and films were disseminated." Dr. Elizabeth Nunez
and Dr. Brenda Greene have continued his legacy and
through C-SPAN have given his mission international
exposure. We never got the amalgamated Black press,
but this novel is being published by a company founded
by one of his comrades from World War II, Charles
Harris.

While the younger generation leans toward fantasy
and science fiction and prefers graphic novels, Killens's
generation might be the last print-literate generation.

As a Killens's persona says, "Like some infants
reached for toys and lollipops, we reached for books.

We loved books. We cut our teeth on books." There are enough books cited in *The Minister Primarily* to create a Black literature syllabus. This is the rare novel by a writer's writer that could be used as a text in writing classes and appeal to the general reader as well. Norman Mailer, who, like his eurocentric contemporaries (small "e" because they don't get Europe right) favored by an equally eurocentric critical fraternity, never wrote a novel with the range of Killens's in its variety of characters and places—Africa, London, and Mississippi. Among the famous eurocentric writers, some might have written novels speckled with French, but weren't able to bring off a multilingual achievement that we find in *The Ministry Primarily* where the narrator discusses Hausa.

Using a boxing term, Mailer called Killens a "journeyman." No, Killens, John A. Williams, and William Demby were number one contenders whom the champions avoided. Demby, a World War II veteran like Killens and John A. Williams, saw his final novel, *King Comus*, rejected by publishers. His son James Demby gave me permission to publish it in 2017. Jeff Biggers in the *Huffington Post* called it the "rediscovered novel of the year."

I arrived in New York in 1962. I was in my early twenties. I soon learned that it was not enough to write pretty, but it was what you said that brought you fame or obscurity. The content. Members of the older generation were divided between those who mentored the younger writers and those who competed with them for a place in the White-controlled establishment. Like Langston Hughes, Chester Himes, Gwendolyn Brooks, and others, including Gloria Oden, who listened patiently as I read her passages from my first novel, Killens was a teacher and a mentor. He could have achieved mainstream acceptance if he'd played nice and lightened up. Offered redemption to racists, portrayed merciful slave masters, or sent up one-dimensional Black bogeymen as the source of America's social problems. Instead, from his first novel, *Youngblood*, Killens announced his mission as that of adumbrating the racist evil that dogs the American soul.

—Ishmael Reed

The Minister Primarily

Introduction

DEAR READERS:

Our name is Henry Greenleaf Emerson Longfellow Shakespeare Washington Irving the Second. Quite obviously our mother and father divined, and accurately, that we were a genius, born to the pen, destined to write incredible literature. At three we knew our ABCs, before we left our diapers for our BVDs. You have by now discerned that we have the habit of referring to ourselves in the first-person plural instead of singular; hence "we" instead of "I." It is our literary style.

In any event, like some infants reached for toys and lollipops, we reached for books. We loved books.

We cut our teeth on books. We nibbled greedily at the edges of Tom Swift and the Rover Boys and all of those Horatio Alger success stories, ad infinitum, Rags to Riches, etcetera, etcetera. We began to write our first novel at the age of seven, our second at the age of eight, our third at the age of nine. We were a beginner who never finished anything. We were frustrated. Disgusted with ourselves by the time we were eleven. "Why can we never finish anything?"

We were brought up under the prosaic adage "If at once you don't succeed, keep on sucking till you succeed." Which had us sucking our thumb through the first twelve years of our life much to our parents' profound embarrassment, "genius be damned!" And notwithstanding. We were a sickly child.

The hero of this tender missive was our first and only cousin, our direct opposite, personalitywise. Though some folk oftentimes remarked upon our striking resemblance, it was instantly clear to me, even as a child, that our similarities were entirely different. He was tall, Black, and handsome, walked always with his head tilted toward the sun, shoulders back, feet apart, unhesitantly and directly into life, unflinchingly. All through our growing-up days, if he stumbled or fell, he would get up immediately to his feet, torn breeches, stubbed toe, bruised, bleeding knees and all, and head directly into the terrible hurricane of life again. Unruffled. He'd grab the bull by the horns, or his testicles, should you prefer the earthier metaphor.

We envied him, his gregariousness, his greed for life, the women who always seemed to somehow be there near him, available. Glib our cousin always was, from birth, as if his dear tongue had been prelubricated in the womb. Even as youngsters, we assumed that he was destined to live an exciting and eventful life; that is, if he lived long enough. We knew that he would always live dangerously.

This is a true story. Sometimes truer, yes, than factual, rendered in the novelistic style, but no less true or factual for all that. Our facts were gathered, firsthand, from the original and most reliable source, from *H* in person, James Jay Leander Johnson, exaggerated now and then, as was his style, which was unique and original, the Minister Primarily, the very one and only. These things could have happened only to our irrepressible Jimmy Jay.

We have made use of tapes, recordings, TV footage, our own camera, newspaper items. We have taken the facts and attempted to deepen them into even profounder artistic and creative truths. This is the responsibility of the artist-writer as we perceive it.

For any shortcomings in this humble endeavor, we accept full blame and responsibility. Any success of literary achievement, all praises, are due to the Minister Primarily *HS*, né James Jay Leander Johnson, and to the cabinet of the Independent People's Democratic Republic of Guanaya, with especial thanks to Vice–Prime Minister Jefferson Dwight Lloyd and Foreign Minister Mamadou Benabou Tangi, with extra-special appreciation to Ms. Maria Efwa, Ministress of Information and Education, for her incredible beauty—physically, spiritually, and intellectually. She was breathtaking. We could not bear to stand too near her, for our breathing would become loud and obvious, somewhat like an exaggerated stethoscope. Hence, we always kept our distance lest we make a fool of ourselves. We worshipped from afar. Her beauty was that devastating. As you may have guessed by now, dear readers, we fell madly, hopelessly, irretrievably in love with our divine Maria, but, alas, her attention was focused elsewhere. We were invisible to her. She had eyes only for another. And what eyes!

For the few moments in this book when it exudes a little humor in the telling of this incredible tale, again I take no credit whatsoever. All praises, if you think they're due, are due entirely to *Himself,* a man who always laughed at life, especially at the Black and tragic aspect of it. He openly proclaims that Black life must be looked upon from the tragic-comic point of view, and not to do so would be to risk every single one of us Black folk going stark raving mad. Quite obviously we agree.

Sincerely,
 H. G. E. L. S. W. Irving the Second
 Lolliloppi, Mississippi (Near-the-Gulf)
 10 July, Nineteen Hundred and Eighty Seven

Prologue

When our story began, more than twenty years had passed since that glorious moment in history when—IT WAS A GREAT TIME TO BE AN AFRICAN.

A time when color was in vogue, even outside Africa. When everything was Black and beautiful. A rhapsody in ebony. The Duke of Ellington was going strong. The aristocracy of music was enthroned, it seemed, eternally. Repeat: There was the great Duke of Ellington, the Count of Basie, and the Earl of Hines. Not to forget the late, lamented Lady Day and Lester Young, the Pres-i-dent. There was of course his regal majesty, the incomparable King of Cole, who was not long to linger with us.

Young Black diplomats came with dignity to the

United Nations and gave that pallid group of Great White Fathers a desperately needed blood transfusion. Just two decades before our story began, the New England–born UN ambassador from the good ol' US of A went off into a temper tantrum–seduced coma and when he came out of it was taken in a straitjacket to an exclusive funny farm raving mad and shouting that the savages had taken over. "The savages have taken over! The savages have taken over!"

It was, moreover, a time when African-American-and-Caribbeans had become prouder of their heritage and wore their hairdos au naturel; uncooked, that is, and in the raw. Almost overnight they were proudly nappy-headed, although they were not kinky. The kinky scene was Anglo-Saxon. They *did* collect conga drums and art supposedly direct from Benin and Jos and Ife and the Dogon. Joined Freedom Rides and Sit-Ins and Stand-Ins and Kneel-Ins and Lie-Ins and Love-Ins. Organized boycotts and rent strikes and marched on City Hall and Washington. Innocent white "Freedom Fuckers" joined the Blacks in Dixieland. Talked everywhere about their heritage, the Blacks they did, of Gao and old Ghana and Egypt and Songhai and Mali and ancient Timbuktu and Kush. Organized Yoruba Temples and Mosques and committees by the hundreds. Good Lord! Thousands of them! "Identity" was a big word then. Roots, baby! Thanks to Brother Alex, which was to come a little later. Soothsayers by the dozens were saying some crazy sooth all up and down the Avenue; Lenox, that is; and Seventh too, a.k.a., these days, Adam Clayton Powell Jr. Boulevard.

Conks, processes, and bleaching creams were going out of style in Harlem. In all the Harlems of the USA. Already the great straightening comb industry was beginning to feel the pinch, as the stocking cap gave way to the fez and the handsome Touré cap. Cats were even picketing the beauty parlors.

Sir Winston Churchill notwithstanding, it was a period when more people all over the earth were free since the very beginning of man's existence. Albeit the Cold War Era and the time of so-called "Brinkmanship," and later there was "Détente" even. It was the Atomic Age. The US of A had the Star-Spangled Banner flapping up there on the moon. A Black columnist skeptic, who for obvious reasons shall be nameless, said White folks were trying to go to Heaven without paying dying dues. According to one of the soapbox-orating soothsaying Black Nationalist leaders of Harlem, all this fuss about going to the moon was simply due to the fact that: "Whitey's going back where he really came from." Notwithstanding, it was the Space Age and the Supersonic Era. It was the Age of

Independence. It was the Freedom Century. *Time* was catching up with *history* everywhere, and vice versa.

JUST TWO DECADES AFTER THE FACT, the little Independent People's Democratic Republic of Guanaya was quietly born. A bouncing Black baby, poor but proud and full of endless expectations. Actually Guanaya had a history going back thousands of years BWFDU (Before White Folks Discovered Us). All right, so neither did Columbus discover America. Weren't there people there when he arrived? The kindest thing you can do for old Chris, that great con man and world traveler, is: "He stumbled upon the place and cased the joint for Mother Isabella." It was the same the whole world over. You didn't exist until the Western Europeans discovered you. You just waited in a kind of limbo. You just stood on some "exotic" piece of real estate in that vast continuing so-called jungle that stretched from Africa to Asia to the islands of the great Pacific and the Caribbean, staring eternally out to sea looking for the boy from Europe to loom upon the horizon and discover you, you noble savage, you. You just waited to be Christianized and civilized, and shit like that. Instead of waiting for Godot or Lefty, you waited breathlessly for Whitey.

Africans in the old country used to say, "When the white man first came to Africa, he had all the Bibles, and we had all the land. But before we knew what was happening, he had all the real estate and we had all his Holy Bibles." A certain Black writer, who likewise shall be nameless, called on his people to stop celebrating Thanksgiving Day. He said it was a day of infamy in the history of First World peoples. "It was the time when the white man ran the Thanksgiving game on the so-called Indians; the 'Indians' turned out to be the turkeys. They smoked the peace pipe with Whitey. I have no idea what was in the pipe, but by the time the smoke cleared, the white man had all the realty." Surviving Indians were placed in concentration camps, euphemistically known as "*reservations.*"

Anyhow and moreover, just two months before our story began, two decades after the gloriously turbulent sixties, Little Guanaya had weaned itself away from the bountiful ivory bosom of a benevolent Great White Mother Country. And the UK was a mother, brother. Indeed, she was probably the last of the Great White Mothers. Guanaya was undoubtedly the tiniest country in giant Africa, tinier than Chad, skinnier than Togo, not much bigger than Barbados, an almost indiscernible speck on the map, a long, thin slice near the heart of that great continent. Guanaya's terra firma was an angry rage of colors. Surrounded on two sides by forest-clad mountains and on another by a long blue lake, and to the north lay a sandy wasteland where an ever-losing battle was waged with greedy, insatiable goats and the great blinding beige of the irresistible Sahara.

As far as the outside world was concerned, Guanaya was the most insignificant of nations. Unmentioned by Herodotus. Unnoticed by Thucydides. Overlooked by J. A. Rogers. Omitted by the great Du Bois. Basil Davidson didn't dig it. Marcus Garvey hadn't known about it. Ignored reluctantly by Lomax. A place John Gunther never got inside of! According to Her Majesty's Colonial Office, it was desperately poor in natural resources, almost un-African in that respect. Then it happened—early one morning as the sun came thundering out of China far away, with apologies from Rudyard, two months after independence, it happened. What happened? Great inexhaustible beds of cobanium—a radioactive metallic element, five hundred times more powerful and effective than uranium—were discovered in Guanaya's Northern Province. Then—Boom! Boom! Boom! Boom! Publicity—Popularity—Prosperity— Population Explosion. The capital city of Bamakanougou got crowded very suddenly. Everybody loved Guanaya and with a bloody ruddy passion.

Scientists, politicians, diplomats, businessmen, a motely coterie of hustlers, literally descended, since they came by jet propulsion, upon the baby country. They came mostly from those two great philanthropic powers of that historic epoch, beneficent leaders as they were, of the "Free World" and the Socialist Republics (the USA and the USSR). Came like wise men of old, wearing smiles and bearing gifts for their little Black baby brother. Newspapers, radio, television newsreels all over the world hailed and proclaimed the great discovery. Cobanium! Guanaya! The immeasurable gain for science and progress and mankind and so forth and so on, and whereas even. Brotherhood! One World! Democracy! Telephones were tied up all over the world discussing, animatedly, a country nobody had ever heard of before.

A commentator in a land that shall be nameless pointed out jubilantly that there was undisputedly enough high-grade cobanium in the bowels of the earth of the Northern Province for every country large and small to have its share. The same commentator gleefully gloated that there was enough cobanium not only to destroy the entire world, were it necessary, to maintain peace on earth goodwill toward men, but to fling destruction at every planet in the universe. Mankind could rest easier. Need not fear the flying saucers. Martians would not dare invade us.

The U.'s of N.A. either had the fastest supersonics or the most efficient telegraph. Or something. They got there firstest with the mostest and invited the young

Prime Minister to be their guest and see America first, and shit, and confer with their great and gracious President, who had the nicest, whitest smile in all the world and a face that made you know everything would be all right, somehow somewhere, and a warmth that made you feel like snuggling up. Known affectionately as "Snot Rag" in his boyhood days, he still possessed the most terrific case of hay fever, especially in the fall and springtime and most particularly in winter and the good old summertime.

Meanwhile and however, His Excellency Jaja Okwu Olivamaki, Prime Minister of the Independent People's Democratic Republic of Guanaya, was a tall, strikingly handsome Guanayan, descending nationally and tribally from a long, illustrious line of paramount chiefs, warriors, emperors, obas, timis, emirs, kings, and sultans on both sides of the family, and from several overlapping nations, tribes, and countries in that part of Africa, and also in other parts. The Prime Minister wore his black beard and his Negritude with enormous dignity. His Excellency, or H.E., as some of his colleagues referred to him affectionately, was a bachelor, writer, poet, lawyer, statesman, historian, and Pan-Africanist and a host of other things that are of no particular significance to our story. He had written several books entitled *African Unchained, Destiny of a Continent,* etc. but the Western world never heard of these books until cobanium was discovered and the Western world discovered Guanaya. Now his books suddenly found themselves on the list and shelves of Afro-American studies departments in universities throughout the USA, as well as the libraries and archives of the FBI and CIA and other federal and clandestine establishments.

Like so many men of color of his time, and even years before his time, he had done his apprenticeship. Like Nehru. Like Gandhi. Like Nkrumah. Like Malcom X. Like Kenyatta, like M. L. King, he had paid his uhuru dues. He was a member of that exclusive club of revolutionary jailbirds. He was a true soul brother. Twenty months of penal servitude for plotting and inciting against the Crown. But all was forgiven, if not forgotten. "By Jove, let bygones be bloody bygones. That's the way we do things in the You-Kay." In those days the You-Kay was the affectionate name for the United Kingdom, sometimes called the British Empire.

Jaja Okwu Olivamaki had spent five of his growing-into-manhood years in the good old USA, spending four of them at Lincoln University, where he graduated summa cum laude, and one year on the thronging streets of Harlem, where he matriculated in the University of Hard Knocks and Disillusionment. He got his master's degree in picket lines and demonstrations and race riots with a hurried doctorate in boycotts and soapbox oratory.

His father had insisted that he seek his higher education in America rather than in England or in France or in Germany as did so many of the African chosen ones. He did not wish Jaja to become a Black European or a "Bentu" (been to London, been to Paris, been to Berlin, and so on). "Go to America and to a Black school. Get to know your American brothers."

A Moscow newspaper expressed grave doubts as to the wisdom of the young PM's visit to the USA, that great capitalistic gargantuan, which would swallow him whole if he were not alert and agile. They lost much sleep over the PM's footwork. But nevertheless the great proletariat of the Soviet Union wished him Godspeed (oops!) and *bon voyage* and hoped his country still belonged to him when he returned to the land of his fathers, and likewise, of course, his mothers.

Meanwhile, back at Her Majesty's Colonial Office, the chaps in charge were a trifle miffed at the untimeliness of the Great Cobanium Discovery, which was to tip the balance of power in the world. Especially pissed off were they ("pissed off"—a quaint Western metaphor indeed, of World War II vintage, I suspect), since it had occurred in a land the old You-Kay had motherly loved and lovingly mothered for close to two hundred years, patiently training the baby colony for the ultimate adult-hood of independent nationhood. Yet two months after freedom was benevolently bestowed—just two blasted bloody ruddy months! Moreover, there were skeptics and even cynics in the colonial office who went so far as to suspect humbuggery, and even hanky-panky and skullduggery. The Queen herself was heard to comment: "Those simple naive conniving Blacks, those cunning buggers, those mother-muckers, you cannot trust them any further than you could throw Buckingham Palace! It almost makes you lose faith in human nature when honest natives cawn't be trusted. I mean, by Jove, those were *our* mother-mucking Africans!"

"Rule Britannia!" or "Hail Britannia!" in the words of Irving Burgie. "You Keeper of the flame. May they never never never!—" and so forth and so on.

1

Prime Minister Jaja Okwu Olivamaki sat at the head of the conference table in his oak-paneled study in the Executive Mansion. The chandeliered ceiling gleamed brightly overhead. He looked from face to face at the Ministers who made up his Independence Cabinet. Except for Maria Efwa Olivamaki he was the youngest of them, which was one of the reasons he wore a beard. He was thirty-nine and she was twenty-nine. A few years ago when he first began to cultivate his beard they used to jest with him about it, but now it was his trademark. Short cropped it was and much much neater than Fidel's ever was, or ever even hoped to be. All day long they had been discussing the great trip to America.

Jefferson Lloyd, the Vice-PM, was holding forth with his falsetto and staccato voice. He went on and on and on, a compulsive talker, the fastest gabber in Guanaya, the words gushed out so swiftly from his thin lips sometimes, they stumbled over one another, but usually they bounded gaily out of his mouth, or cascaded like the rapids of Niagara. He was the original babbling brook of Bamakanougou. Though he was almost humorless and pompous and devoid of comedic bent, he was known throughout his country for the faux pass he had committed two years earlier at a Commonwealth conference banquet held in London attended by all of Her Majesty's colonial leadership. In a wave of euphoria and under alcoholic influence, he had risen from his table and said, clearly, precisely, pompously, and prissily, "In the name of the people of Guanaya, we wish to thank our gracious Queen for her hospitality at this great Commonwealth banquet and conference from the bottom of our hearts and also from our wives' bottoms."

There had been a suddenly deafening silence in the brightly chandeliered ballroom, then some uncouth one from another member country of the Commonwealth perversely giggled and the place broke up with laughter.

The story traveled back home to Guanaya and followed him wherever he went. He became known, affectionately, as "His Wife's Bottom."

"America is the home of the free and the land of

the brave and we have nothing at all to worry about and nothing to fear but fear itself and they welcome us into the world of free men and independent nations—and—"

His Wife's Bottom (or HWB) was seated at the PM's right hand, and the PM stared at him and nibbled at his beard with his long and slender fingers. His Wife's Bottom went on and on like he was reciting something he had memorized or was reading from an idiot sheet. "It is the land of George Washington and Thomas Jefferson and Abraham Lincoln and where their pilgrims died and also of their father's pride." He paused a hundredth of a second to catch his breath and clear his throat. "And furthermore it's the richest country in the world and Americans are known everywhere for their generosity, which is proverbial and universal. If we are able to forge a friendship with them, we wouldn't need another friend in all the world." He cleared his scratchy throat again. "Financially I mean, of course." He owned the most nervous throat in all Guanaya. "They would put money and technicians at our disposal with no strings attached out of the bountifulness of their hearts and also out of their love for freedom and fair play, which is hysterical, I mean, of course, historical . . . And the only thing we would have to assure them is that we're not communistically inclined, and you cawn't blame them for that, you know, what with the New Cold War and the untimely demise of détente . . ."

Mamadou Tangi, Minister of Foreign Affairs, quickly, sharply interjected. Actually it was more of a swift thrust than an interjection. Albeit he spoke much more slowly. "Those are precisely the tactics we must not pursue. First sign that there's no danger of us drifting toward communism, and we wouldn't get a tuppence from them. Keep them guessing is the proper tactic. As they say in the vernacular of the American cinema, we must play difficult to acquire. Like I always say: 'Long Live the Cold Ruddy War.' We must juxtapose both termini contra to the medium, or is it play both ends against the middle?"

Jaja Olivamaki looked from his Vice-PM to his FM. They were his right hand and his left hand respectively and politically. Always seated nearest to him on opposite sides of the table. Lloyd and Tangi were diametrical opposites in looks and outlooks in personalities. Lloyd was thin and nervously underweight and overanxious and liberal minded and optimistic and conservative and worried-looking and a bloody chatterbox. As for Tangi, most Europeans considered him unbearably and insufferably arrogant. He was of medium height and thickly constructed and sour faced and distrustful

and sarcastic, and fanatically nationalistic, thoroughly
Pan-Africanistic, some thought. Especially Europeans
thought, possibly with justification. It might serve the
purpose of enlightenment here to state categorically: in
those days, even liberal-minded, humanitarian-type
Europeans, Americans included, frowned upon indigenous nationalism. Oh yes, indeed—even socialistic
radicals. I mean, Right and Left and from the middle.
Many thought it not good at all for the proper "native"
to be nationalistic. It simply was not healthy for him. It
developed in the Blacks negative characteristics such as
bitterness and dissatisfaction and arrogance and inso-
lence and even self-importance. In a word, it made the
Black man dreadfully unhappy. And moreover it did
considerable damage to his natural disposition toward
humbleness and profound humility, which after all
were the saving-grace qualities in any "noble savage."
Look at Gunga Din! Witness Uncle Thomas! Not to
mention "Moses and Mosetta," in the inimitable words
of Professor William Mackey Junior.

Even William Faulkner himself, that shining ex-
ponent of noblesse oblige, that great unreconstructed
libertarian and plantation owner, during the onset of
the sixties gave to American persons of color the following revolutionary slogans: "Patience! Cleanliness!
Politeness!" Or words to that effect. Which in one

word means "humility," that rare quality that was almost unknown and nonexistent amongst the play-boys of the Western world. Let Western man wallow in the strength and courage of his convictions, but let the Black man have humility, that greatest of all virtues residing in the soul and bosom of every single Black man, and let him not deny it. They wanted to save the Black man from himself and keep him happy.

Well be that as it may, at the other end of the table sat a Black man who completed the Big Four in the ten-men-one-woman Cabinet of Ministers. He was Joseph Oladeli Babalumbi, Minister of Defense. At forty-eight, he was the oldest in the cabinet. He had a hard brilliance, a tough rugged intelligence, bred in revolution and British prisons and nurtured in European schools of learning from London all the way to Moscow. He was Olivamaki's Great Black Father Image. A large handsome Robesonian head, a deep-black-brown face framed by a great unruly head of hair that was integrated black and white, as the saying went in those days. "Integration" was a great word in the folk myth of America back in those European-dominated days. It became a world-word. No one knew precisely what it meant but everybody used it. Again, be that as it may, and apropos of nothing, Babalumbi's nickname was "the Lion." And where he walked the earth did tremble.

He roared softly from the other end of the table. "We will make no political commitments at this juncture. We are committed only to African freedom and independence. We have the largest, richest bed of the best bloody cobanium in the entire world. It may be the only one for all we know. This is our bargaining point north, south, east, and west. This is our position of strength. We have something the world wants and needs, or thinks it needs. We do not go forth as beggars."

Maria Efwa was the Minister of Education. She was the prettiest member of the cabinet. She was the only woman member. Five feet four of burnished ebony, and seemingly five or six inches taller than her actual height, and roundishly slim, and as fiercely proud of her womanliness as she was of her African comeliness, and she had plenty of both, and some to spare, especially around the edges. Her hair was au naturel and beautifully cropped, and her eyes were large and warm and black as the blackest warmest nights of Africa and slantingly shaped like almonds. A full curvaceous mouth; when she spoke in her small voice, reminding you of Miriam Makeba, the others listened. They had learned from experience that she would not be quashed by loud and masculine vocal cords.

Maria Efwa said, "Next to financial aid, we need an educated citizenry. Trained people. We need schools and teachers, and while we're over there, we must make arrangements for sending hundreds of Guanayans to American schools and colleges. They have some of the best in the world."

Mamadou Tangi said, irritably, "We would be wasting valuable time and energy. They do not allow Black people in their colleges. Why do you think those African American students were sitting in all over the place during the decade of the sixties? And now they're starting up again."

His Wife's Bottom could not restrain his indignation. "You are entirely misinformed, and, it had nothing to do with education and those students were concerned with the right to eat warm canines seated, because it seems that Americans had some eccentric superstitions regarding Black people eating warm canines in horizontal or vertical positions and while some Americans were for vertical, some were unequivocally for horizontal, and that was the basis of the Big Debate that is raging again over there, especially in Southern America."

James Osburn, Minister of Health, pulled at his ear and stated calmly, "The one thing we must remember is that Americans are a wonderful people but they're incredibly schizophrenic. They mean no harm at all. It's a national characteristic, but they will smile on one side of their faces and simultaneously growl at you from the other side. They will turn down one of their own people of African descent and in the same breath take one of us to their bosom. And even so and furthermore they will welcome you at the North and kick you at the South. They have strange personality problems. But they're wonderful when you get to know them. They are the epitome of Western Man."

"They are the epitome of Western Man," Mamadou Tangi agreed, sarcastically.

Olivamaki stood, and as his long body unfolded, all eyes looked toward the head of the table. He was an incredibly handsome Black man of remarkable bearing and tremendous presence, a presence that he evoked and exuded effortlessly, and indeed seemed to be unaware of. No matter, the presence was real, almost tangible and tactile. He reminded one of a young Robeson of Rutgers. He leaned toward his eager colleagues. He stared down the length of the mahogany table into the fierce eyes of the Lion, and then his eyes went from face to face on each side of the table, holding momentarily on his first cousin, Maria Efwa, the most beautiful woman in Guanaya, perhaps in all of Africa. He felt warmly toward his colleagues. Three days from that very moment they would be thousands of feet in the atmosphere winging their way to the USA, every one of them, excepting the

Lion, Babalumbi, who would be left behind to guard the nation and to mind the richest store in the world. So much had happened to them and their country in the last months, crisis after crisis, climax after climax. If he could only show them wisdom, if he could share with them his deepest feelings.

"We stand here today," Jaja Olivamaki said in a resonant and quiet voice, "in the center of gravity of history. Our deliberations, our actions, our strategy, our tactics, affect the very universe and the earth as it turns on its axis. We are a young independent nation and we are young leaders and will make many blunders and this is our inalienable right. But it is a right we cannot afford to indulge in very often. Our people are free and independent, but they are also poor and ignorant. What we do within the next few days will affect them for generations yet unborn. The discovery of cobanium within our borders has changed our economic outlook. Everything is possible now, and not tomorrow but today. Suddenly our horizon is vast and endless. But as we go forth to meet the entire world, East and West, North and South, we must remember, our greatest natural resource is not our rich beds of cobanium, not our timber or our gold. Our greatest resource is our people."

His Wife's Bottom said absently and pompously,

"Hyah-hyah. Hyah-hyah." American translation: "Hear! Hear! Hear! Hear!" or "Amen! Amen! Amen!"

Afro-American-Caribbean version: "Right on!" and "Let it all hang out!"

"Our people's independence and their dignity we must never ever barter."

His Wife's Bottom said, "Hyah-hyah!"

"Our purpose is to reconstruct a nation oriented more to people than to things."

At this moment a sub-cabinet member tiptoed into the room and whispered excitedly into the Lion's ear and when he finished, left as quietly as he came. The Lion said, "Pardon me, Jaja, but this discussion may have suddenly become academic."

The PM stared at his Defense Minister as did the others. "You obviously have a reason for this observation."

"I have just received word that leaves no doubt, there is a plot to overthrow the government while His Excellency is in absentia."

Suddenly there was a deafening roar of silence in the room. Then they talked all at once, excitedly, till finally the PM got them quiet, and they listened to the Lion tell them of the plot, which he had suspected but had never had positive proof until the present moment.

Tangi said impatiently, "Round them up, arrest

them, and throw the key to the jail out on the desert into a harmattan" (sandstorm). "What does this have to do with the trip to America?"

"We don't know exactly who the leaders are as yet," Babalumbi said.

The PM said quietly, "Obviously we have to postpone the trip."

"Exactly so." From the pompous Mr. Lloyd, His Wife's inevitable Bottom.

"On the other hand, if we do postpone the trip," the PM thought aloud, "the world will know we're having difficulties and will think we are unstable. Great nations do not lend their money or technicians on this basis. And furthermore, it will encourage outside interference in our affairs. We have enough spies and intriguers here already. It's difficult to say what steps we should take."

Mr. Lloyd's contribution was again, "Exactly so."

They kicked it back and forth for another hour and finally decided that, despite the damage it would undoubtedly do to their international image and their bargaining power, despite the threat of outside intrigue inside their beloved country, they would have to postpone the trip. They had no alternatives. At this point Tangi got to his feet and announced that he had a solution to the dilemma. They all stared at the Foreign Minister.

"We could let half of the cabinet stay behind with the Prime Minister, and let the other half go to America with the Prime Minister."

They stared wordlessly at Tangi. Obviously the tensions of the last months had been too much for the fiery Foreign Minister. First freedom and independence, then unimagined prosperity, not to mention notoriety.

"Kindly tell us how H.E. can be two places at the same time?" Slight intolerance in the Lion's voice. He was usually rather patient with his younger colleagues.

"Just give me two hours, my brothers, and I will bring the answer back to you."

All of them began to speak at once, but the Lion roared, almost sarcastically, "The people of Guanaya will be in your eternal debt, my brother."

"Hyah! Hyah!"

Tangi stood unshakable. "Will His Excellency give me two hours?"

Jaja Okwu stared at his watch and looked at the members of his cabinet. He rose to his full length in his long white flowing boubou (robe). "We gather here again at ten o'clock."

"Two more requests," Mamadou Tangi said. "I should like two internal security men assigned to me immediately, and a few bottles of champagne here at the conference room by the time we reassemble, so we can drink to our successful journey out there into the other world."

One of the ministers got to his feet and gave the Guanaya freedom salute and softly shouted, "Uhuru!"

They all stood up and gave the salute, and—"Uhuru! Uhuru! Uhuru! Freedom! Freedom!"

His Wife's Bottom said, "Exactly so."

2

James Jay Leander Johnson, colored, Negro, Afro-American, Black man, sepia fella, tan Yank (take your choice), folk singer, was born in Lolliloppi, Mississippi, Near-the-Gulf, Southern USA, where he lived as a boy but could never grow up to be a man, Black manhood and womanhood (for that matter) being highly hazardous pursuits anywhere in Mississippi back in those days when European Americans dominated the great southern territory. Also anywhere in Alabama and Georgia, South Carolina and Louisiana, a fact every Freedom Rider would attest to, North Carolina, Tennessee, and every sit-in student would have been witness to, and every Black man, woman, and child understood instinctively, even two decades after the fact. Life insurance policies were astronomical on

Black manhood and womanhood everywhere in dear old Dixie. The era of NeoReconstruction was caught up in the ebb tide. History was in repetition. The prophecy of Sam Yette's *The Choice* was entering its fulfillment as were Lerone Bennett's pronouncements on the New Reconstruction.

Exactly three months to a ticktock before our story began, the same James Jay Leander Johnson (colored) fell from London via BOAC over Europe, his heart pounding like the four engines in the jet airliner, over the Mediterranean over Libya over the Great Sahara to the northern reaches of Guanaya. He was on his way to Lagos in Nigeria. The plane stopped over in Bamakanougou for only a half an hour, but Jimmy was so elated, so filled up all inside him with four hundred years of homecoming, he got off the plane just to put his feet on African soil and he could not help himself, he got down on his knees and kissed the soft sweet dark earth of Mother Africa. "I salute you, long lost Mother!" He wet the warm dark earth with his tears, which he could not keep from spilling down his cheeks onto his Africa.

"Your wayward son salutes you!" He started singing: "Where is my wandering boy tonight. The boy of my tenderest care?" He thought, Your boy is home, Mama. Your wayward son is finally home! Thrill after chill after thrill raced across his back from shoulder to shoulder. His eyes shamelessly overflowing. You're in Africa! His happy heart cried out to him. It was like he'd been on a long long journey all the lonesome days of his life and finally he was home again. Now he knew how the prodigal son must have felt. Great God from Ancient Timbuctoo! Behold your errant son returneth! Kill that fatted calf!—Jimmy has made the scene at last!—and Lordy Claudy!

Fortunately or unfortunately, depending on your retrospective point of view, it was a time when the Guanaya gendarmerie was alerted against infiltration of colonial agents and provocateurs and saboteurs of foreign powers who came in varying disguises. A vigilant officer of the law who was always on his toes saw Jimmy on his knees, and, thinking the chap had either lost something, possibly his marbles, or was up to something, signaled to another member of the constabulary and they dashed quickly out toward Jimmy with whistles whistling and torchlights flashing in the early African darkness that was falling all around them. It was not exactly the kind of African welcome Jimmy had envisioned.

They pulled him roughly to his feet and demanded to know what he was looking for. He told them with a face full of the warmest feeling (fighting fiercely back his tears), told them with the greatest gravest dignity, "Brothers," choking up, "I am here to find my heritage. I'm looking for my roots." (Don't let them see you cry, you fool!) They were the most wonderful-looking cops his glad eyes had ever witnessed. And he hoped like hell he could restrain himself. In Lolliloppi, Mississippi, Near-the-Gulf, as a boy, he'd never been overly fond of the blue-suited men who made up Lolliloppi's finest. But it was just that these cops were so damn black and beautiful. These were—

"Are you Guanayan?" the tall Black Cop inquired.

"No," he answered. "I—"

"Are you Hausa?" from the short one.

"No— I—"

"Are you Bambara? Kikuyu?"

"Are you Tuareg or Watusi?" They threw the questions at our bewildered hero. "Are you Zulu or Mandingo?"

"That is just the trouble," he told them. "It's hard to say what I am or where I'm from. Maybe Nigeria, maybe Zaire, maybe Togo or Dahomey. Maybe Guinea. Maybe Mali. Maybe Zimbabwe or Kenya. It's been so damn long." Suddenly he felt profoundly sorry for himself. "Between one and two hundred years ago, maybe three or four hundred, perhaps even five. I don't know when, I don't know where. That's why I'm here

to find my roots and learn the folk songs of my people."
He sounded pretty corny, even to himself. Good Lord!
Suppose they didn't believe him!

The cops looked at each other as if to say, "What is
he? Some kind of a nut?" And Jimmy felt precisely like
some kind of a nut, although he could not identify the
species.

"What people?" the big cop asked him cagily.

"I don't know what people," Jimmy helplessly admitted. And he looked from one to the other, as if he
thought they should have recognized him by now. He
thought, They're pulling my leg. They must be. They'll
throw their arms around me any minute. What a sense
of humor my African brothers have. What jokers!
Practical, that is. He laughed briefly, very feebly.

The short cop said to the big one, "There's something familiar about this chap. I have seen his face
before somewhere."

And Jimmy thought, Maybe on the jacket of my one
and only record album!

The big one glared at Jimmy and nodded his head
in agreement, and said, "Aanh-aanh." Jimmy's heart
filled up and overflowed with the desperate hope of
recognition and acceptance. He had traveled years and
years and thousands of miles from Rejection to this
place, and he could not take rejection here.

"I'm also somewhat of a Calypsonian," he volunteered, meekly, in all modesty. "By profession and adoption." He struggled desperately for some faint sign of recognition. Anything at all!

But seemingly neither of the members of the constabulary had heard of the Republic of Calypsonia, because, after giving him the third degree they threw their arms around him, but with very little affection, and dragged him away to the immigration authorities, young Black men who also made his face fill up with dignity and pride, and who also agreed he looked familiar, as they searched their files to see if they had a picture of him, or if he was wanted for a prior offense, since he was obviously an agent of some foreign power. This was just too much for Jimmy.

"I am not a spy!" he shouted.

"Of course you're not." The immigration chap agreed, pleasantly, sarcastically. "You're His Excellency Jaja Okwu Olivamaki, incognito. Come now, you might as well admit it. Modesty will get you nowhere or everywhere, as the case might be."

"I never heard of him!" Jimmy shouted with indignation. "Whoever he is! I'm innocent! I deny the allegation and defy the alligator!" He tried to calm himself. It was simply a case of mistaken identity. "Most of all

I am insulted. Highly," he added. His timing was off, slightly. And his timing was rarely ever off.

The immigration officials smiled knowingly at each other. The one doing the questioning scribbled furiously on a pad before him on his desk. He wrote, mumbling to himself, in monotone. "This one is an unusual specimen. Honest face—without a tuppence of integrity. Boldly proclaims his innocence as if he has been accused of something specific. Guilty conscience or persecution complex. Paranoid definitely!"

He looked up at Jimmy again. "Are you sure you're not Jomo Kenyatta come back from the dead? Sékou Touré, perhaps? Kwame Nkrumah reincarnated?"

Jimmy thought he must be having a nightmare in the daytime, wide awake.

"What is the matter with you people?" he demanded hoarsely. "Everybody knows Kenyatta and Nkrumah are dead!" he added as an afterthought. "And so is Sékou Touré."

"Oh I see. Something is the matter with us now, is it?" the interrogator said to Jimmy, smiling patronizingly. "That's an interesting approach—remarkable psychology."

He wrote, as he mumbled to himself now, more audibly. "Intelligent-looking without a treppence of intellect. Very shrewd though. Claims he never heard of our beloved Prime Minister. His tactic is obviously to put the interrogator on the defensive. An experienced malefactor. A hardened criminal of dangerous proportions. Undoubtedly a professional assassin."

"Do you have a gun, sir?"

"A gun! What in the devil would I want with a gun?"

"Do you have a dagger hidden on your person?"

Jimmy thought he was out of his mind. His heart was pounding now way up in his forehead. His brain was on fire with anger and frustration. Perspiration pouring from all over him.

He said, "What would I be doing with a dagger on my person?"

The interrogator wrote on his pad, and muttered aloud, "Very clever the way he parries every question with another question of his own."

Jimmy said, "You people must be kidding!" But he looked around at the rest of the serious-faced Africans, and he knew they were not kidding. One of them was even gleefully not kidding.

"What the devil is the matter with you people?" Jimmy asked.

"What the devil is the matter with *you people*—" the interrogator repeated Jimmy's question aloud, and immediately Jimmy wished he hadn't asked it.

"We'll find out what the matter is and very shortly," the interrogator assured our hapless hero.

"Search his bags," one of them suggested. "He probably has an arsenal in them."

"My bag's on the plane!" Jimmy shouted. This couldn't possibly be happening to him—*in Africa!* he told himself—without conviction.

The interrogator smiled at Jimmy patronizingly and asked politely, "May I see your visa, sir?"

"I don't have one," Jimmy admitted helplessly. "I don't want to spend any time here. I just want to leave—"

The man wrote furiously on the pad before him and then looked up again. Smiling a broad white smile in a proud Black handsome face. "I see—I see—You never heard of our great beloved Prime Minister, His Excellency Jaja Okwu Olivamaki. Yet you're obviously here to assassinate him. You don't have a visa, because of course, you don't want to stop here. Oh—not at all. Yet you're the only one who got off the plane. You're a very clever saboteur, sir, but it won't work in Guanaya. You're the worst kin of all, sir, because you come disguised as a brother." The interrogator's voice hardened and he was no longer smiling. "Take him away," he said to the delighted policemen. It was their most exciting moment in an otherwise dull day. They grabbed him roughly by the shoulders. He pulled away from them.

"I'm an Afro-American Negro!" he shouted to the men of Immigration. "I got some rights in Africa!"

In unison they shouted, "Aanh—aanh! Oh-ho!"

The interrogator turned to the policemen. "What the devil is this?"

The big cop turned to Jimmy. "Why did you not tell us in the first place?"

"I'm an Afro-American. A serious folk singer, and I'm here to find my roots." He showed them his American passport.

They all jumped to their feet. "Welcome home, American brother!" They shook his hands, they embraced him. They kissed him on each cheek. They said "Uhuru!" Relief flowed through his body like hot coffee in the cold wintertime. He could not help from weeping, shyly, slyly. The short cop said, "Excuse me, please. We thought you were a Black European, a bloody Bentu." Jimmy stared through bleary eyes at the little Black man. What the hell was a Black European? A Bentu? Then the fog-of-London lifted, and he began to laugh and laugh and laugh some more, the tears spilling down his cheeks, unrestrained, into his mouth. He couldn't help it. It bubbled up and overflowed and finally they joined him in the laughter.

They had thought him a Black European saboteur assassin. Or something maybe even worse. An Uncle Tom! A Gunga Din! Oh wonderful African brothers! How could you? How damn ever could you? But he forgave them instantly.

There was a rumbling of thunder overhead. "My guitar is on that plane," he said weakly, as he heard it winging noisily and southwestwardly over the building toward Lagos in Nigeria almost a thousand miles away. With his guitar and his luggage, all his clothing. The cops and the Immigration people couldn't care less. But they did dig Jimmy Johnson. One of them was a folk singer himself in his spare time. It was mutual admiration all the way and at first sight, almost. Ernest Bamaku, Jaja Segu, and the two friendly cops and Jimmy Johnson. It was knocking-off time for the Immigration chaps, and the next plane for Lagos was not due for several hours. They gave Jimmy a twenty-four-hour visa, and Jimmy went with them and had a natural ball with them at Bamaku's house. Others gathered for the party. Eating groundnut stew and singing and drinking Scotch and Schnapps and Palm Wine, with the women seated shyly on one side of the room and the men on the other. (He gibed them gently on the Woman Question.) They drank and sang and talked about Martin King and Malcolm X and Ben Chavis and the Wilmington Ten and the riots in Miami and in Harlem and the District of Columbia and Watergate and democracy and socialism and capitalism and Stokely and Gil Noble. And Robeson and Du Bois. Their mutual ethnicity.

Jimmy had never felt better about anything in all his life, not since the day he made his great escape from way down yonder on the delta, where his people were so interminably happy. His head was reeling with the spirit of belonging, and much much palm wine, when Jaja said quietly, "We had better be getting back to the airport. It's fifteen minutes before eleven."

Jimmy shook hands all around with the men and the pretty shy-faced women, who took his hand in both of theirs in a kind of ritual of farewell. They wished him "safe journey" and each gave him a gift of kola nuts and beads and amulets; one elderly woman gave him a live and cackling chicken, and then they went up the middle of the narrowest of tarmac highways to the airport in a cloud of dust and gravel, slowing down cautiously to eighty-nine kilometers an hour as they went around the many curves, carefully avoiding by the matter of the length of the hair of a short-haired camel's shortest hair only about fifteen or twenty head-on collisions. When they reached the airport they ran Jimmy through Immigration with no formalities at all, and out onto the airfield they dashed with him, Jimmy with the cack-ling, frightened, shitting chicken dangling at his side, just in time to see the airplane at the other end of the strip leaving the ground and going off into the black black African night. Jimmy was tempted to say, "Muck it!" as the blokes all used to say in the old You-Kay. "Muck it all!"

When night has fallen, it has really come down all over Mother Africa. And with a beautiful-Black awe-some bloody vengeance. You can hear night falling everywhere. On the ride back from the airport, the countryside leaped with the sounds of African night. A jam session of ad-libbing crickets and locusts and all kinds of bugs, but the honking frogs with their basso profundos upstaged every living thing in this crazy Af-rican orchestra. The fruit bats swooped down toward the headlights and quite a few got wasted. The smell of wood smoke from the villages along the countryside and into the forest assaulted Jimmy's nostrils and his throat and reminded him of a thousand early washday Monday mornings in Lolliloppi when he was a little boy, before washing machines and detergents were available to the "cullud" people of his hometown, in the days of octagon soap and scrub boards, with the fire crackling and spitting underneath the black washpots. A funny but familiar taste in Jimmy's mouth now and a quiver in his stomach, as a wave of pure nostalgia almost overwhelmed him. "Don't kid yourself, Buster. You ain't homesick for dear old 'Sippi. That's for cotton-picking sure." He laughed as he remembered it was cotton-picking time in dear old 'Sippi, where mechanized cotton picking had come into vogue.

When they reached the capital city again they stopped at Club Lido and had more drinks and watched the people do the highlife.

Jimmy was drunk, or else he would not have insisted that highlife derived from calypso. What the hell did he know about it? "Like, I'm some kind of a Calypsonian my own self," he said, in all modesty. "That is, in my spare time. I'm really working at it." In all humility.

Ernest Bamaku said, "It's a question of what comes first, the mother or the chick. This music went to America and West Indies from Africa and you make it into calypso, and now it has come back to us and we make it into highlife."

Jaja said, "Actually, mawn, actually!"

Ernest Bamaku said, "That is the thing. For example, you have an African heritage. No?"

Jimmy said, "Yes!"

Ernest said, "That doesn't mean I have an American or West Indian heritage. Yes?"

Jimmy said, "No—"

Ernest said, "That is the thing. Mother Africa comes first. Always and forever."

Jimmy said, "Actually, mawn, actually!" Quite drunkenly.

Jaja threw his arms around Jimmy's shoulders and said joyously, "You speak with our accent already."

And they all cracked up with laughter. Palm wine could make you say almost anything.

Jimmy's head was swimming and the women at the Lido were getting prettier and svelter and prettier and svelter. They were pretty enough to begin with. One particular long-legged swivel-hipped lady was dancing with a huge Guanayan who looked like he might have made it big with the New York Knicks. This couple was cool cool cool and could really do the highlife, and had danced everybody off the floor, excepting a Euro-American struggling valiantly with another lovely Guanayan woman, as if he thought the highlife was a prizefight or a wrestling match. He looked like a former college fullback long out of condition, as he went through the paces, his fists balled up, his face screwed up, and the perspiration raining from all over him, his pretty soft-eyed partner smiling patiently and indulgently through it all.

Jimmy said, "Somebody should tell Whitey this *is not* Madison Square Garden."

"Can you do better?" Jaja asked him, mischievously.

Jimmy was his own shy retiring self. (If you didn't believe he was modest and even bashful, you could ask him.) "I don't know, maybe, perhaps. I think I might be able to, if . . ." His voice drifted off somewhere.

Ernest egged him on. "Come on, American brother. Give it ruddy go. In the name of Calypsonia."

Jimmy shook his head. "I don't have a lady to dance with. And besides and furthermore—and whatnot—and after all—"

When the music stopped Jaja went over and sounded out the tall shapely one who had been dancing with the six-foot-five Guanayan. He brought her back to the table and introduced her to Jimmy. And she was Linda Okwuchuku, and she was all woman, and all African unadulterated, unmiscegenated, and he could not keep his eyes off her, even as he also kept one eye on her scowling escort seated at a nearby table. The music started and she asked him if he cared to dance. And what could he say? He was chivalrous, he thought, always had been. He was like the reluctant African American, when they started, but after a while the music got to him, Africa called him as she always calls her own, and when the young Black and comely woman beckoned him to relax and open up, relax he did, and began to move, baby, move, and it was definitely first cousin to calypso, the music and the dance was. And Jimmy Johnson answered the call of Great Black Mother Africa. Linda smiled at him encouragingly. The Africans are so polite, he thought. They have "couth" to squander. But he wanted to believe her when she said, "You dance the highlife very excellently. Like a proper African." And when he looked around him, everybody else was off the floor and he became self-conscious again. Everybody smiling at him. Perhaps they were laughing at him.

The music stopped and the gracious lady stepped back from him and bowed slightly, and Jimmy had a feeling of behindedness, and turned quickly in time to see her partner coming toward him in a hurry. When the powerful Guanayan reached Jimmy, he drew back as if to knock our hero out into the middle of the Sahara. Jimmy ducked. Actually, he almost fell over backward, but not in time. The Guanayan's aim was on target, and he smacked the now-reluctant African open-handedly and left a shilling sticking to Jimmy's forehead, and also left Jimmy with a headache and a crick in the small of his neck.

"Welcome, American brother! How did you learn to dance our dance so good?"

Jimmy quickly regained his cool and drew himself up to the full length of his dignity. "Thank you, my brother. It must be my African heritage!"

He heard the laughter all around him. They were laughing with him and not at him, he insisted to himself. It was the laughter of approval—Love—Acceptance—Admiration. Brotherhood and all that jazz.

Many drinks and hours later, his brothers took him floatingly to the fabulous (expensive) Ambassador Palace Hotel and got him a room and poured him into bed and left him to die a plush and posh and proper European's death.

3

He was awakened early that next morning by a telephone ringing somewhere in the buried recess of someone else's mind, he thought. His head felt like it weighed a ton. He thought this could not possibly be his head that lay just beyond his neck upon the pillow. Somebody must have taken advantage of him when he was drunk and like a thief in the night made off with his head and left another in its place that was fifty times as heavy. How long had the phone been ringing? He reached out blindly from his bed and knocked the telephone off its cradle and the whole contraption to the floor. He stumbled from the bed and reached down for the damn thing, almost fell face-forward to the floor. Ultimately now, the receiver was in his hand. "Hullo," he uttered vaguely, wondering where he was in time and space, who he was, and did it really matter anyhow?

A strange-to-him accented voice came through from the other end. "Hello, Brother, Jaja hyah."

"Who?"

"Jaja Segu, mawn. Not Olivamaki, Sah. Did you make it through the night successfully?"

"Where am I?" Jimmy asked, stupidly.

"Where are you? You're home, mawn, in Africa, the land of your ancestry. You're in Bamakanougou. Don't you remember? You disembarked here."

"Vaguely," he mumbled. He had thought briefly he had dreamed the whole damn beautiful thing. *Paradise Regained.*

"We are coming for you, shortly, today or tomorrow, and take you out of that European den of iniquity."

He said, "Thank you much and very very." And tried to lift the phone contraption from the floor and got disconnected, just as someone rapped upon the door.

A young Guanayan came into his room with a tray of tea and crumpets and placed them on a table near his bed.

"Good morning, Sah. I trust you slept not too badly. I am Cecil Oladela, Sah."

Jimmy said, "Yeah."

"I'll come back, Massa, and fix your room after you get dressed and make the little chop on the table there."

"Don't call me 'Massa,'" Jimmy said firmly. "I am nobody's master. I am your American brother." The young Guanayan said, "Exactly, Massa." And he bowed and left the room.

Less than a half an hour later he was back before Jimmy had a chance to get into his trousers. He made up the bed all round his American brother, as if he were in fact invisible, picking up here and hanging up there. Jimmy's Mississippi Grandma would've called it "a lick and promise." Now that he was finished he stood before Jimmy Johnson stiffly. "How long do you plan to be with us here, my brother?"

He learns quickly, Jimmy thought. "I will probably be here no longer than tomorrow." He wondered at the sad expression that suddenly encompassed the young Guanayan's handsome face.

"That is really too bad, Sah, my brother, since tomorrow will be my day off from this place. That is really too too bad. We will probably never see each other again."

Jimmy thought to himself, Then there really is

something to this thing of blood between men and women of African descent. We've known each other for less than a couple of hours, we've been together a few minutes only, and he's so sentimental about the thing. He was ashamed of his own cynicism, his lack of sentimentality, of African fellowshipness. No matter, Jimmy said sadly, "That's life, my brother, like *c'est la vie.*"

The young man said, "Then perhaps you dash me now, since I will not be here to see you off tomorrow."

"Dash you?" Jimmy asked, inquiringly, and puzzled. There were images in his mind now of hundred-yard dashes and sprints and two-hundred-yard dashes, with the brothers always finishing first, second, and third, but what about the mile and the two-mile and the marathon?

Cecil Oladela brought him back to the real world. "Dash me with—" Then Cecil hesitated. Then he said, "The currency is in pounds here in Guanaya, Sah. Did you get your dollars changed? If you only have dollars, Massa, there are places of exchange that I know about."

Jimmy hated him for the moment for destroying his romantic illusions, for he was, at heart, hopelessly romantic. Sentimental to a fault. Ask him. Then he began to laugh good-naturedly. He went to his trousers and gave the lad a couple of dollars.

Cecil was ready to split now, and he did leave after wishing Mister Jimmy Johnson a "safe journey." Wherever it was that his American brother was journeying to. The last thing Cecil mumbled as he went out of the door sounded like "Get some good protection." But from whom and what? Jimmy wondered.

Jimmy stood there for a moment staring at the closed door. Then he began to laugh and he could not stop laughing. He laughed until the tears spilled down his cheeks. These days he cried so easily. He fell upon the bed and went immediately to sleep and awoke less than an hour later. His head seemed twice as heavy as it had been before.

Somehow he made his way down to the Ambassador Palace Hotel lounge. He was afraid to look into the mirror behind the bar. Scared he would verify his suspicion that he really wasn't who he thought he was. Ooh! Oooh! His head felt like a jet prop airliner coming in for a landing and using the top of his poor head for an airstrip. The African sun already coming into the softly lit room in thick hot heavy yellow slices. Sweet and musty was the smell of last night's great indulgences. Jimmy looked around him, but there was not one solitary recognizable bona fide soul-brother African club member in the lounge that time of morning, not even behind the bar. Not one club member.

He made up his mind. He was going to move from this place tout-damn-suite into less fabulous less expensive and more indigenous living quarters. Yeah! He hoped his African comrades came for him today. He would not wait until tomorrow.

The riotous living of the night before roared in his head and through his nostrils and seemed to have taken up permanent housekeeping in his mouth and throat. He could taste the smell of his breath like a host of 'Sippi bedbugs, dead from bloody inebriety. He breathed a deep sigh and turned to leave, realizing, shrewdly, he would never find his roots in this place. But alas, his great white American brother lunged from the bar across the lounge and high-tackled Jimmy around his neck, and they both went down into the very very plushness of the carpet, almost sinking out of sight. Jimmy panicked, thinking he was back in 'Sippi, where he was born and where his President spent so much of His time. When he and his Great White Brother came up for air, he wrestled himself loose from the big blond handsome crew-cut plug-ugly, and he drew back and started to throw a punch, but even way over in Guanaya, just several hundred miles from Timbuktu, as the vultures fly, he remembered the late Reverend Doctor Martin Luther King, and he drew himself up in all his dignity, and *humility*, and he eschewed violence, piously.

The big blond slob draped his heavy arms around Jimmy's shoulders and slobbered happily and proudly. "You're an American! A real honest-to-good-ness red-blooded full-blooded cotton-picking American! And you're good for these poor sore eyes of mine!"

Jimmy thought he'd like to make both of this cat's eyes poorer and sorer than they'd ever been. But he drew himself up to even greater heights of dignity, and lost his great innate humility, but only momentarily. "I'm not an American! I am an African!" he asserted firmly without shouting.

The big blond laughed in Jimmy's face. His baby-blue eyes were bleary now. His heart overflowed with joy, or something. He wagged a pinky-white index finger at Jimmy. "You can't fool me—you're an American I know—I know—I'm an American myself."

Jimmy said sourly, "I never would have guessed it. Like, baby, I thought you were a great big Housa-man from Kano."

Whitey roared with laughter, almost crying, he was so happy. Jimmy wondered: How can I insult this cat? White folks wouldn't believe you were insulting them, even when you intended them to believe you were insulting them. He threw his heavy arms around Jimmy again. "My name is Bill Barnsfield—William Clarence Barnsfield the Fifth, and I'm pleased to meet you, my fellow American." His breath smelled like a concoction made up of the funk around the Calvert's whiskey factory when you're coming out of Baltimore together with a great big whiff of Chicago when the wind changed out at the stockyard, before they moved further westwardly. Meanwhile, he showered Jimmy's face with his succulent dialogue.

Two chaps from the UK sat at the bar watching the two Americans (one hysterically happy, one rabidly reluctant), watched them absently, while they themselves religiously downed their beer-and-cognac highballs. One of them turned to the bartender and said, "Four more orders of proper scrambled eggs." Which meant beer-and-cognac all over again. The Lebanese bartender smiled patronizingly and poured up more beer and cognac and shook it all together. It was like a hydrogen bomb explosion before the historic treaty was signed and the optimistic ban was consummated.

Jimmy spoke a little louder to his Great White Brother, and this time more emphatically. He was weary of being manhandled. He was damn tired of it. "I am an African! My father is Watusi! My mother is Ibo! One of my grandfathers was a great Hausa emir. The other was a Tuareg chief! The most notorious pirate ever to roam the great Sahara. He killed two hundred peckerwoods per annum!" In those days, dear reader, "peckerwood" was an affectionate name for European Americans, very similar to "cracker" and "Whitey" and "Charlie" and "bastard," and so forth and so on.

Whitey laughed happily, knowingly, ecstatically, "You're an American. I knew it as soon as I saw you. You're an American. There's something about you that gives you away."

Probably my Brooks Brothers Ivy League suit, Jimmy thought. I'll do something about that also tout-damn-suite. "How many times do I have to tell you? I'm an African!" the reluctant American shouted.

Whitey looked around him surreptitiously and back to Jimmy. He whispered softly into Jimmy's ear, almost nibbling it. "Come on now. I won't tell anybody. You might as well admit it. You're an—" He leaned heavily on Jimmy.

"Will you get off my back, motherfucker!" Jimmy was slowly but surely losing touch with his Black non-violent temperament. He pulled violently away from his Great White Brother and began to amble out of the cocktail lounge with fireworks exploding in his head like it was celebrating the Fourth of July. William Clarence Barnsfield the Fifth lunged for him like he was gang-tackling a quarterback for the LA Rams, his arms around Jimmy's neck, as they went down to the floor again. Jimmy got up swinging. And his Great

White Brother's undernourished mouth got in the way. He felt the bite of Barnsfield's teeth on the knuckles of his fist, as a tooth leaped gaily from his Great White Brother's mouth. Barnsfield's smile was bleeding, as still he stumbled toward Jimmy mumbling, blindly, sublimely, ecstatically, "You're an American—You're an American—I know it—I know it!"

Jimmy breathing deeply. "All right. So I'm an American. So what, mother—dear?"

The big blond smiling now, sweetly and triumphantly. "Know something?" he said seriously, his mouth still dripping blood, "I'd have never guessed it in a million years. Like you had me fooled completely."

Jimmy stared at Whitey, angrily at first, incredulous. Then he started to laugh and moved with Whitey toward the bar to join the British chaps for breakfast. Whitey introduced him. "Trying to deny his true heritage, just because he thinks all white Americans are mothersfuckers," Whitey explained to them triumphantly.

"Don't worry about it, boopy," Jimmy said offhandedly. "Some of my best damn friends are motherfuckas."

The Lebanese bartender creased with laughter and winked his eye at Jimmy and proceeded to mix up another portion of the hydrogen bomb concoction.

Three or four atomic breakfasts and a couple of hours later, his Guanayan brothers rescued him and took him away in their great Land Rover. The Ambassador Palace Hotel was located on the outskirts of town, away from the teeming hustle-and-bustle humanity of the Capital city, out where the pretty white government buildings were, which originally had been constructed "for the British, of the British, and by the African," in the words of Jaja Segu. Jimmy thought grimly, some of his African brothers were bitter too, even some of the friendly lighthearted ones. As they moved closer to the heart of town, the traffic got more and more frenetic and chaotic, like Broadway before curtain time. Like moving toward the Meadowlands at the time of Super Bowl. The World Series at Yankee Stadium. A traffic moving irresistibly to and away from the hub of the city. Automobiles, trucks, buses, goats, men, women, children on foot. Some people on bikes with their raincoats on backward and ballooning in the wind and rain. It had begun to drizzle. Misty California dew. Now and then an ugly distrustful Tuareg-ridden antihuman camel clogging up the traffic. People walking, thousands of them, women with babies on their backs and the marketplace atop their heads. *C'est ça!* These Guanayan women could walk that walk. They made the products of the New York charm schools look like skinny pimply-faced unsophisticated and ungainly adolescents.

They were well into the city now, and the traffic got slower and slower, actually crawling. People everywhere. The long and short and the tall, all ages and denominations, a caravan of Black humanity in perpetual motion, and a sprinkling here and there of Americans and British and all types of combinations. Sartorially speaking, the average Guanayan wore anything that came to mind. Or to hand. The most noncommitted, nonconformist, unconventional dressers Jimmy Johnson ever witnessed. He grinned from ear to ear and kept telling himself, sometimes aloud, "You're in Africa! You're at long damn last in Africa!" His eyes his ears his nose his mouth his throat his heart his mind his spirit saturated with his long-lost Africa. He had fifty dollars in his pocket, and change. Other than that, he was as broke as a New Year's Resolution of the Ten Commandments. His only clothes were on his back, but he felt no pain or apprehension. He felt at home for the first time in his life.

They took him to the Hotel Lido, not one-tenth as fabulous as the Ambassador Palace, or nearly as expensive, but it was inhabited by proper Africans with Club Lido on its first floor. And he dug in for the duration however long it lasted. He meant to get to the heart of being African and all at once and in a hurry.

First thing on his agenda: learn the language of the

people! He bought book after book written by enterprising Englishmen out to make an honest quid. Language books with such titles as *How to Learn Conversational Hausa the Proper Painless Way.* The first book was written by the very pious Reverend Michael Bodley Richardson, benign benevolent missionary from Yorkshire in the old You-Kay. On Page 1, the first translation into English was a deeply profound question calculated to make it easy for a greenhorn like Jimmy to win friends and influence people. It was: "How much sodomy is there in this town?" The second translation was "This one will do as our housekeeper. She is nice and strong and plump."

"I know where that missionary was at," Jimmy said aloud to himself, and tossed the book into his wastebasket. "I know what his mind was on." The second primer was equally provocative, written as it was by a British Army captain. Translation I, Page 1: "Whose donkey is kicking my daughter?" It quickly joined the other primer in the basket, as did others and others and countless others.

Nevertheless our dauntless hero learned the language of the people by talking to them, endlessly, incessantly, ad infinitum, ad nauseum. Sometimes he talked too blooming much. Sometimes his foot found its inevitable way into his irresistible mouth—always and forever with the very best of intentions. Par exemplar. Or, to give you a for instance:

That first week he went everywhere and all at once, all over town all over the suburbs and out into the fervid, ecstatic countryside. Talking talking talking touching tasting loving everything and everybody. He loved the touch and taste and sound of things and life and love and things. It was like he really thought he was at long last *home*.

He stood with beautiful womanful Linda Okwuchuku one evening way out on the northwestern edge of town and stared westwardly and watched the sun sit down out on the rim of the endless desert. He knew a sweet full choking sensation, as he thought he saw the sunset dripping with unbelievable greenness and splashing the whole horizon with varying shades from soft pastels to the deep green of the ocean's edge. He'd never heard or even dreamed of green sunsets before. He closed his eyes. He squeezed Linda's hand unknowingly. Keep your big mouth shut, he thought to himself. You are overwhelmed by the reality that is Africa and the romance that is Africa and the fact of your actually being here, so if you happen to see one little old green sunset, who the hell's business is it? I mean, everybody has optical illusions under certain circumstances. The conversation with himself kept his mouth shut for a moment only. He opened his eyes and beheld again the glory of the dying day. Aquamarine! He could contain himself no longer. He turned toward Linda and heard his foolish self say ecstatically, maybe even argumentatively, "That's a green sunset. My eyes don't fool me. It's really green. I mean, don't tell me it isn't."

"Exactly!" she answered him with great and righteous indignation. "Did you expect the sunsets of 'exotic' Guanaya to be different from the ones in Europe or America? Black or white—you Europeans are all alike. Of all the colossal arrogance!"

That kept him quiet for a terrible moment.

And when the moon rose it was a deep deep dark blue, but Jimmy did not mention it. He learned later that the whole thing had something to do with the desert haze due to the winds and sand and so forth and so on. But he never learned to keep his big mouth shut.

His Guanayan brothers helped him to get a permanent visa and a job at the Club Lido. And so, Jimmy Johnson like had it made. Not only was he happy, he was joyous even, maybe even just a little slap-happy. He loved *Afrique* unreservedly. And his great love did not go unrequited.

This is where he was in time and space just after Guanaya caught up with Independence. This is where he was shortly after cobanium was discovered and the whole world caught up with Guanaya. Jimmy Johnson never had it so good. The way he figured, he was the luckiest Negro ever to escape from that state of colored happiness by the name of Mississippi, known affectionately as "'Sippi."

Then suddenly his luck ran out.

4

In Bamakanougou, intrigue was as ubiquitous as London fog. Rumors were a shilling a dozen, plotting was as frequent as the scampering playful monkeys and the thornbushes and the greedy goats out on the nearby blinding-beiged Sahara. You could not tell who was who or what was what or where you were going or whence you came, or what you were going to do when you got where you were going. Sometimes it was a proper mess. Sometimes it even got confusing. Take our venerable Foreign Minister, Mamadou Tangi, for example.

It was an hour and fifteen minutes since the Foreign Minister left his colleagues at the Executive Mansion. He had exactly forty-five minutes to deliver the coup. He was as serious as a midair collision and a massive heart attack, combined. As sincere a man as was ever a Foreign Minister in any country on this earth. Why in the name of all the gods and devils, and Europeans, had he wandered into Club Lido? Of all places! This night of all nights? True, almost every Friday night you could see him at the Lido, ordinarily. True, Tangi was a real-gone devotee of highlife and calypso and modern jazz and Black folk songs, which were the club's chief staples. It was the sole diversion from his work that he allowed himself, except that he was an avid reader. Sometimes he would be at the Lido with his wife, but more often than not he would sit alone at the table near the back. Sometimes he would dance, but more often, he would just sit and look and drink his palm wine and dig the sounds and nod his head and pat his feet. True, Jimmy Johnson had become his favorite performer, but this was no ordinary night. But force of habit is a powerful factor. And so the Foreign Minister had come to the Lido this night of nights when he should have been concerning himself with the most important matters of state. With the fate of Guanaya hanging in the proverbial balance (where else?), here he was sitting alone listening to an African American singing highlife. A six-piece orchestra was wailing a tune the lyrics of which were written by the fabulous Jimmy Johnson himself—come lately. The Lido was low ceilinged and dimly lit and filled to capacity with Guanayans and a sprinkling of Europeans (American and British). Jimmy Johnson was swinging his hips in that inimitable style that African Americans used when imitating Africans and singing his song with a very very British accent.

"Now why don't the natives love us anymore?"
Sir Winston did inquire.
I ask you, why don't the natives love us anymore?

The Guanayans laughed, the Europeans smiled good-naturedly, uneasily, but good-sportedly. That's the way they were, you know. Tangi hated to take Jimmy Johnson away from this life he had carved out for himself in his beloved Africa. But precisely because Mother Africa came first and last with Tangi, Jimmy Johnson had to go. The first time he had seen Jimmy, there had been something strongly familiar about him, something he could not put his finger on. He had been strangely fascinated, Tangi had come again and again and again but Jimmy had always remained just out of reach. Then, a week ago, suddenly everything had come together, and Tangi had had Jimmy placed in time and space. He was sure he had his man now. There could be no doubt about it.

Why aren't they like they used to be?
So simple and naive, so gloriously primitive?
Noble savage, what has happened?
You're too sophisticated and much too complicated
Oh the natives just don't act like natives anymore.

Guanayans laughed and shouted and applauded. Naturally the Europeans were jolly good sports about it. Mamadou Tangi stared unsmilingly and blank-faced at the African American. He regretted what he had to do, even as he nodded at the internal security men at a table near the front. They got up and moved with a vengeance toward blissful, unsuspecting Jimmy, who was bowing and smiling to his applauding public. They loved him dearly, even as he loved them. The two big Savoy Ballroom bouncer-type men seized him and took him protesting to a big car outside the Lido where Tangi was waiting.

"I didn't do anything!" Jimmy shouted. "It's a lie! I didn't do it! I know my rights! I'm a loyal African!" It did him no good. He didn't fool anybody. They had their man and knew it. They shoved him quietly into the back of the car. He was still resisting arrest when they dragged him into the conference room where the rest of the Ministers had already gathered and were waiting, but impatiently.

"I haven't done a thing! This is a free country. Jaja Segu will vouch for me. You can't do this to me. I'm not a spy! I'm a true friend of Africa! Uhuru!" he shouted, waving his arms frantically, "Uhuru-Uhuru-Uhuru! Freedom! Freedom!"

The Ministers, excepting Tangi, were even more puzzled than Jimmy Johnson.

"Be calm, brother," Tangi told him. "You're not under arrest. Not yet." He introduced the perspiring Jimmy to the Ministers generally and to the Prime Minister primarily. He told them what Jimmy was doing in Guanaya and how the people loved him and how he loved the people. Some of the Ministers already knew Jimmy, and particularly his reputation. And that was all very well, but what the devil was Tangi driving at? The Foreign Minister asked them to be seated again, including Jimmy, and for God's sake (and Africa's) have a little patience.

"Now let's drink to Jimmy Johnson. He's our man without a shadow of a doubt." Jimmy protested his innocence again and name-dropped Ernest Bamaku. A steward poured up the champagne for all of them excepting Olivamaki, who was a teetotaler. He drank ginger ale instead. Tangi stood again. "To Jimmy Johnson, African American, folk singer par excellence, expert on European psychology, and a dedicated and loyal friend of

Pan-Africanism and African independence." They all stood up, excepting the PM, who sat there staring from Tangi to Johnson and back again.

"I'll drink to that," Jimmy said humbly, in all humility, and downed the champagne with one swallow. They sat again and Tangi poured Jimmy another drink and turned to his colleagues. "Mr. Jimmy Johnson can warn us of the pitfalls as we go out into the Western world. He's invaluable to our historic journey."

Jimmy gulped another glass of champagne. "You ain't just whistling Dixie, comrades. I can give it to you straight from the horse's hindparts. I know the white man backward, forward, and sideways. Better than he knows himself. I had to know him to survive. I really should be going with you distinguished people as your adviser. One thing you'd better do when you go out into that other world, you'd better look those gift horses in the mouth, down the throat, and up their royal pink posteriors. Say, I even made up a tender little lyric about the rear view of a white gift horse. You want to hear it, gentlemen—I mean, Your Highnesses?"

The Ministers were delighted with Jimmy. But what point was Tangi making? Jimmy rambled on in high gear. "You know what happened to the Indians, don't you? And they weren't even Indians yet. So when an American shakes your hand, count your fingers afterward in his presence. It's the custom. It's expected." He took another swig of champagne. "And be mistrustful, even as you pretend not to be. They'll respect you for it, even as they pretend to be indignant. And don't ever act straightforward, however else you act. Never ever act straightforward or altruistic. They don't trust an altruistic or straightforward chap at all. They'll think you are either a damn fool or that you have something up your sleeve, even though you're shirtless. Always pretend you're sly and cunning and not to be trusted, and they'll welcome you with open arms and believe that they can trust you. Honest-to-goodness con men and hustlers are the most respected and trusted men in the good old USA, and the richest and the most successful. All you remember Ronald Reagan—"

He was running off at the mouth and downhill all the way with a good wind at his tail. And the Guanayan Ministers stared at him open-mouthed and could not believe their ears, but they believed that he was serious, even if he was not sincere.

His Wife's Bottom, Mr. Lloyd, said, awestruck, "But surely, Mister Jimmy Johnson, you are not serious. You are, how do you Americans say it? You are jerking our legs?"

Jimmy took another drink. "You'd better believe

I'm serious, Your Excellencies. And another thing, whatever an American tells you, believe the exact opposite. Listen, take politics, for example. An honest politician doesn't stand a ghost of a chance in the USA. Nobody'd believe anything he had to say. That rarest of birds, an honest politician would have to pretend he's dishonest before anybody would believe in him or trust him."

"By Jove!" Mr. Lloyd (or His Wife's Bottom, or HWB, if it pleases you) said. "The chap is serious."

Jimmy was more than serious, he was actually sincere.

Jimmy went on and on and on. "The *raison d'être* for government in the US of A simply stated, the entire hullabaloo of an election campaign is to determine who will be in charge of equitably distributing the graft and keeping the Black man in his place. It is rumored that an elected official takes two separate oaths of office, one publicly and the other one in private. In the latter oath, he or she swears on a stack of Bibles, that he or she will be completely racist and as corrupt and as cynical as he can possibly be. That he will honestly and deliberately steal everything and anything that is not nailed down. But don't get me wrong, Your Excellencies, I love the beloved country, the good old USA."

Mr. Lloyd, His Wife's Bottom, said, "We understand your bitterness as a Black man in a white land,
and we sympathize, we empathize, indeed, but surely,
sir, I can't believe, I mean—you are exaggerating!"

Jimmy stared at Mr. Lloyd and decided not to say
what he started to decide to say. He cleared his throat.
"Now," Jimmy continued, "on the racial crisis in
America, the longest crisis known to man. You will
be told"—he mimics—"'You're not like our nigrahs
at all, you know. You have industry, you have am-
bition. You are not lazy. You're different, but we're
making progress.' And that is supposed to explain
away lynching, bombings, slavery, Hiroshima, the Ku
Klux Klan, Birmingham, James Crow, discrimina-
tion, Watergate—everything. Nicaragua, Grenada.
And remember, all colored folks are nigrahs to them,
despite the fact that the Negro is a totally American
invention."

He paused again to catch up with his rapid breath
and take another swig of champagne.

"This is very valuable information, I'm sure,
Mr. Jimmy Johnson," the Prime Minister interjected.
And then the PM turned to Tangi. "This is all very
well, but need I remind you, we have a grave situation
on our hands? Kindly get to the point, if there is one."

Tangi rose and took a phony beard out of his pocket

and put it on Jimmy's face, and Jimmy was immediately transformed into the PM's spitting image. It was unbelievable. The PM stared at Jimmy like he'd seen a ghost, and the rest of the Ministers stared at the two of them open-mouthed and speechless.

Jimmy protested. He was sitting again. "Whatever it is, it's a lie, I didn't do it. I was framed. I demand to see my lawyer. I'm for Africa all the way. Uhuru! Uhuru! Uhuru!"

Tangi said quietly, "Half of us stay here with the Prime Minister," pointing to Olivamaki, "and half of us go to the United States with the Prime Minister," pointing to Jimmy Johnson.

"Oh no!" the Ministers shouted, unanimously and in unison even.

Jimmy said, "Would somebody be good enough to tell me what this is all about? Anyhow and regardless I demand to see my lawyer first. Any lawyer! And I refuse to answer on the grounds—that—that—"

Tangi took a mirror out of his attaché case and gave it to Jimmy, who stared into it and then at His Excellency and shook his head in disbelief. "My old man sure did get around," he muttered, "or maybe vice versa, perhaps. Most likely," he conceded.

It took a lot of talking but Tangi talked the PM and

his Ministers into the idea, with the help of Jimmy Johnson. "Why not?" Jimmy demanded with self-righteous indignation. "Have you so little faith in your Afro-American brother? Does our mutual Negritude mean nothing after all?"

After hours of wrangling they agreed reluctantly with Tangi. But when they turned their eyes upon the smiling triumphant Jimmy, he seemed for the first time to grasp the enormity of the undertaking, and that, he, Jimmy Jay Leander Johnson, himself, in person, col-ored, Black, Negro, Afro, of Lolliloppi, 'Sippi, Near-the-Goddamn Gulf, in the United States of Dixiefied America, was to be the masquerader. The grandiose impersonator. And he said, "Oh, no!" He backed away from the table. He shouted, "Hell no! I haven't had that much to drink. Excuse me, lady, please ma'am and please sirs!"

They cajoled the poor downtrodden colored Black Negro Afro-American fellow from Lolliloppi; they threatened him, played upon his suddenly flagging race pride, his Negritude, his colortude, his loyalty to Pan-Africanism, and to African independence, to the New World, to the Third World, to the First World, and the Really New Frontier, and on and on ad infinitum. "Here is your chance, comrade, to strike a blow for African freedom"—"You are a man of destiny"—"History has chosen you"—"You must rise to the occasion."

"But they'll be asking me all kind of questions. I don't know enough African history. Especially Guanayan. I'll be honest with you cats. I had never heard of you dudes before I landed here. And I'll never get away with it. Somebody's bound to recognize me. What? I mean—please!—I mean, I'm with you, but you must be kidding! Come on already!"

Tangi said calmly, "Her Excellency Miss Maria Efwa here is our Minister of Education and Culture and iInformation, our National Historian and Folklorist. Our national anthropologist. She'll be making the trip with us and will fill you in en route, and she'll be by your side while you're there, as will the rest of us who go." The Minister of Education's full name actually was Maria Efwa Olivamaki Mamadou, but she had shortened it to Maria Efwa, professionally, in affirmation of her female independence, though she took great pride in her family name, which was revered throughout Guanaya and the entire continent.

All the while Jimmy shook his head as if he wished it would drop off.

"No-no!" He stared at Maria Efwa, she smiled benignly at him, and his stomach flip-flopped. He shook his head again. "No-no—Hell no! The American white man may be crazy but he damn sure ain't no fool."

Tangi said, "Besides you know your white folk better than they know themselves, don't you, Mr. Jimmy Johnson? You have just given us an outstanding dissertation on them."

Jimmy looked at Maria Efwa again. The beautiful, smiling one said quietly, "And furthermore all colored folks look alike to Europeans don't they? I've heard you sing about it at the Lido."

"Yes," he answered weakly. "Yes, but—No—no—no! Hell no!"

"How can you be discovered then?" Her voice was like sweet string music. Violins playing mellifluously.

The Lion said, "Our Afro-American brothers are great rhetoricians, wonderful singers, and excellent tap dancers, but when it comes to action—the European Americans have them quaking in their boots."

Jimmy said, "Just a minute, Buster—I mean, of course, Your Excellency—Just a damn minute—"

"So it would appear." From Maria Efwa and her silken voice.

Tangi smiled at him sarcastically. "Are you for Pan-Africanism or aren't you? Do you not want to build a better world?"

Jimmy looked at the beautiful Maria Efwa again. He

took another swig of champagne. "Yes," he answered thickly, weakly. "Yes, but—"

Maria Efwa said, "What is the problem then? Do you stand in such awe of your great white father that you would spit into the face of history? Here is your chance to make history, Mister, and for history to make you. Will you turn your back on a great chance to get back at your great white father?"

Another glass of champagne another look at Maria Efwa and he hardly knew what he was saying. "Yes—I mean, hell no. Excuse me, I mean—let's get the show on the road. I mean—what's the holdup? Let's drink to our magnificent venture."

They all drank, excepting the PM, who kept staring doubtfully at his double, as if he didn't believe what his eyes beheld.

The last drink gave Jimmy brand-new courage. The drink and Maria Efwa's smile. "So what can they do to me anyhow, even if I *am* discovered?"

You could hear the quiet in the room. Then His Wife's Bottom, Mr. Lloyd, the Vice–Prime Minister of the Independent People's Democratic Republic of Guanaya, answered cheerfully, maybe even hopefully, "They could drum you out of your country, or hang you for conspiracy, shoot you as the sun comes up. Or is it electrocution in your country?"

5

As he rode in the jeep through the Bamakanoug-
ouan night with its symphony of sounds of giggling crickets and honking frogs, the fireflies blinking
off and on, the sweeping fruit bats, thoughts of what
had just transpired collided in his mixed-up mind with
visions of what might lie ahead. He looked sideways
at the little soft-faced Guanayan soldier who was his
driver. They were moving him into the Executive Mansion suite. The new fake beard on his face had already
begun to itch. Perhaps he should discuss the pros and
cons with his driver, he thought desperately. At once
he recognized the unwisdom of such a move, since, as
far as the driver was concerned, he was, in fact, His
Excellency Jaja Okwu Olivamaki himself. He laughed
quietly at the irony of it.

Jimmy tried to laugh but it didn't come off, as the champagne went down the wrong way and came back through his eyes and nose and throat, as if his plumbing were in disrepair. He almost died of strangulation. It might have been more merciful for him if he had.

He had made his pilgrimage to the Motherland to find himself, and now he found himself on his way back to the USA as somebody else. Life was an expert knuckleballer, a curve, a changeup, a fastball, and a slider.

"A truly lovely night, Sah," the quiet-faced little driver said softly.

Before he could reply, Jimmy Johnson's consciousness suddenly knew a heavy premonition. His heart began to pound away. He was lathered with his perspiration.

There was always a kind of prescience that traveled alongside Jimmy Johnson as far back as he remembered, a premonition that he had learned the hard way, through experience, to pay strict attention to. Sometimes the prescience came to him slowly, almost imperceptively. Sometimes it came as a growing uneasiness, sometimes as a vaguely remembered sound, sometimes magnolia scented, sometimes honeysuckled. There were times when he had pushed it aside as an absurd superstition unworthy of a man of his intelligence and sophistication.

A long long time ago in 'Sippi, when he was a boy about eleven years of age, he had gone swimming with some of his buddies in an old swimming hole in the forested outskirts of Lolliloppi. Old Man Johnson's place.

NO TRESPASSING. THIS MEANS YOU! the sign read. It was a hot day in July, blazing hot, the hottest day on record at the Lolliloppi weather bureau.

"Damn!" Bruh Jamison said. "It's so damn hot, our chickens laid some hard-boiled eggs this morning."

They roared with laughter even as they undressed, leisurely. It was too hot to hurry.

Zeke Jefferson said, "It's hot as hell out here today."

Bruh Jamison said, "Where in the hell did you think hell was except in Mississippi?"

Bubber Broaders said, "Damn that! The last one in, I had they Mama last night, and it wasn't too hot for her." By the time he finished speaking he was running naked toward the swimming hole.

At which point Jimmy Johnson had a premonition, a heavy and funereal-scented premonition. "Hold it! Hold it!" he screamed. "Don't jump in, Bubba! Don't jump! Don't jump!"

Bubber was at the very edge. He halted, momentarily, swiveling about. Jimmy picked up a big heavy rock and heaved it into the water hole. It made a loud splash as it struck the water, and the boys stood dumbfounded as they watched a den of water moccasins scooting here and there across the surface.

Bubber stood there chilled with fear, and shivering in blinding heat, urinating uncontrollably. It was common knowledge that if a water moccasin bit you, you had less than half an hour to prepare to meet your maker.

These premonitions came periodically, sometimes in tandem, once a decade, sometimes monthly, sometimes weekly. Even now, as he rode through the darkness toward the Lido in a jeep seated beside the little Guanayan driver, he recalled an episode in Vietnam. He'd had a buddy from his hometown with whom he played checkers every Wednesday night in his buddy's company mess hall. G Company was fifteen miles up the road from his own Company H. It was one of those interregnums between actual combat. As he had driven that evening toward G Company in a Weapons Carrier, he had become suddenly aware of the nighttime sounds of giggling crickets, bullfrogs croaking, honking. Lightning bugs were blinking. A smell of forest wetness in the air, the imagined smell of Mississippi cypress swamps. And with all this his entire being knew a strange discomfort, an uneasiness he could not explain, as he drove into the night; he knew an awful sense of déjà vu.

He had been there more than an hour now, but the unease would not leave him, still persisted ominously.

Finally he gave into it and he said, "Hey, Bubber, why don't you come down to my company sometimes? Why do I always have to make the trip up here?"

Bubber said, "Man! It's so far down to your place."

Jimmy said, "It isn't any farther from here to H Company than it is from H to G."

Bubber said, "Yeah, but you travel in a Weapons Carrier. I ain't got nothing but my two number tens."

The evening blew cool breezes through the mess hall, but Jimmy was perspiring suddenly. He said, "Let's get the hell out of here and go to my place."

"Come on, man. We're already here now. That don't make no sense at all."

There was a desperation in his voice now. The negative vibes he felt were overwhelming. "Let's get the hell out of here and be quick about it!"

"Come on, soldier. What's wrong with you?"

Jimmy said, "Something here just doesn't feel right. I don't know what it is."

Bubber said, "Something don't feel right—what're you talking about? What's the matter with you?"

Jimmy said, "Bubber, you remember that time we went swimming at Johnson's hole in Lolliloppi?"

Bubber stared at Jimmy. "Swimming hole in Lolliloppi?"

"You remember the water moccasins?"

And then Bubber began to freely perspire. He said, quietly, "I remember." And began to prepare to leave. He gathered the game up and looked around him. "Any of you soldiers want a ride down to Company H? They got a big happening down there tonight." He went around desperately from table to table. Only three other soldiers were interested. They piled into the Weapons Carrier. They had been driving for about five or ten minutes when the night lit up with sirens blasting out an alert. Searchlights scoured the night from earth to sky. Hunt and destroy. Then there was the drone of motors coming in beneath the searching beams. A few minutes later they heard a deafening explosion. They learned later one of the planes from the North had laid a death egg in the middle of the mess hall. None were wounded, all were killed.

Suddenly now he was back in Bamakanougou, and the vibes became too much for Jimmy. He was overwhelmed with premonition. A prickling feeling at the nape of his neck. A frothing perspiration lathering his entire body. Breathing now was difficult. He suddenly yelled, "Jump!" And jammed the brakes, and pushed the little Guanayan driver out of the right side of the jeep, as he jumped from his side, all in one motion. The jeep went unattended for no more than fifteen yards and detonated. As if to blow the night apart, even as it blew the jeep apart.

He came back from death in a strange place in an unfamiliar room. He knew not where he was or why he was or even who or when he was. Perhaps he was in Heaven. Perhaps he heard an angel's voice.

"How do you feel, Your Excellency? You had, how you say in your country, a much close call."

Hers was the first face he saw as he came back from death. It made him glad to be alive. Then he saw the other cabinet members as they stood around the bed. His handsome bearded double told him, "The African gods were watching over you. As Maria Efwa said, you had a very close call. The only way we can explain what happened is that God saved you for the mission you are destined to perform for Africa."

"You must have had some powerful protection," a voice asserted. He was not sure who spoke the words. He was not sure who said what.

"Perhaps the gods were warning me of the danger of this mission." This crazy madcap escapade, he thought.

As if he had not heard Jimmy, His Excellency said, "Of course we had to postpone the trip for several days. Meanwhile get yourself some rest and strength, and if you want for something you have only to let us know. Anything at all." The Prime Minister was beardless now.

Jimmy thought, I want to get the hell out of here as soon as possible. His Excellency said, "We'll be looking in on you from time to time. The doctors have assured us you will be all right and fully recovered within a week or two. A slight concussion. Sleep well, and Her Excellency Miss Maria Efwa will be in to see you tomorrow morning and begin to work with you on Guanayan history and folklore."

They were gone now and an overburdening sense of foreboding descended heavily upon him. His mind was filled with images of escape and flight away from Paradise suddenly lost never to be regained, he thought. It had been his custom since his arrival in Bamakanougou to go to the window of his hotel room every morning and stare out at the breathless beige and green and feral-flowered beauty of the landscape and marvel all anew at his incredible good fortune. He would stretch and sigh and thank whatever gods there be and softly shout, "Peace! It's truly wonderful!" He knew by now that he had been brought back to the Executive Mansion, since obviously he belonged there as the Head of State. The Prime Minister had ordered him to get some rest. But rest would not come easily, that night. He had slept less than fitfully. He lay, at first, on his back, and could not fall asleep. He crossed his legs at the ankles and then remembered the nurse who tended to him in the hospital during his brief stay in the Nam. It was one time he had ignored his prescience, and he had paid the penalty. The big blond nurse had warned him that crossing his leg would cause him premature problems with his blood circulation. Whenever she caught him with his ankles crossed underneath the sheet, she would squeeze his feet. At first he'd thought she was getting fresh with him, which was before he found out definitely she was getting fresh with him, else why would she come and put the screen around them and when she bathed him, would fondle his member and giggle at it when it hardened, oftentimes against his will. Then one night long after midnight she came and got into his bed.

He uncrossed his ankles and lay on his left side and felt a tension in the calf of his left leg. He turned over on his right side with no better results. When he did finally fall asleep for ten or fifteen minutes, he would dream of water holes and moccasins and Vietnam mess halls and bombings and blood and disconnected legs and arms and heads and feet. When daylight finally came he lay exhausted and frustrated.

He lay there debating with himself and scheming as to how he would get himself out of this holy mess he'd gotten into. He felt like an extraordinary jackass with the phony beard hanging from his chin, which they insisted that he wear at all times so that he would become accustomed to it. He would just tell her that he'd changed his mind, especially after his "much close call," as she herself had termed it. He'd tell her he was no hero and had never pretended to be one. He'd tell her and she could tell the rest of them. And that would be the end of it. He had a terribly ominous premonition and this time he would not disregard it.

But then she would come and all his uneasiness would be forgotten. Each morning he would be mesmerized by her unearthly beauty, which was physical and intellectual and especially was it spiritual. She was indeed a triple threat. He put up all kind of defenses against her, and to no avail. He was too experienced and sophisticated to be taken in by a pretty face, he told himself. He'd known faces just as pretty, perhaps not as beautiful as Her Excellency. There was the exquisitely lovely brown one back in the nation's capital. There was his high school sweetheart down in Lolliloppi, the high-hipped one with sweet construction. Her facial features eluded him, maliciously, but he remembered she was beautiful. There was devastating

Debby Bostick. There was Daphne Jack-Armstrong of his recent London days, the coloratura soprano, and there were the crazy ones in Hollywood. None of these defenses helped him, because he knew that there was no woman on this earth as beautiful as Her Excellency Miss Maria Efwa of the slimly rounded structure, the eyes so wide and brownly dark, now dark brown and now entirely deeply ebony and slanting, *them there eyes!*, the high cheekbones, the ample and curvaceous mouth. All that beauty plus a quiet dignity eloquent in its manifestation. Perhaps it was the slight concussion they said he'd suffered from the explosion that made him so susceptible and vulnerable to a lovely woman.

He knew only that when she spent the day with him, teaching him Guanaya's lore and history, all his forebodings were entirely swept away. But then at the end of the day, when she was leaving him, she would take his hand in a sisterly gesture of farewell-till-morning, but when he wished to make the much much more than that, and he would squeeze her hand too warmly, she would gently and firmly take her hand away from him and leave him in a mild despair, which would deepen as the darkness of the night came on, and especially the loneliness. And then would come the doubts and fears and sleepless nights.

But finally a combination of the enchantment of Her Excellency's beauty (a triple-threat woman she), his sense of challenge and adventure, his deepening sense of his Africanness and his racial pride, his almost irresponsible uncontrollable sense of humor, the exciting idea of putting one over on his Uncle Sam; all of this put to flight his persistently deepening and ominous premonitions.

He was ready for the grand impersonation and to hell with premonitions.

Actually, he had always been a wild one, a taker of outrageous chances. Even as a young lad back in 'Sippi, he was never one to take a dare. Six and seven and eight years old, he'd loved to hang head-downward from limbs of trees with nothing to keep him from falling on his noggin except his barefooted toes wrapped around the limbs. When he was ten and eleven and twelve years old, he and one of his buddies would go into a neighborhood grocery store (white-owned and managed), and while one of his buddies engaged the clerk in argument or conversation, he would be lifting cookies and other goodies from the bins and filling up his pockets. Sometimes he wouldn't even eat the goodies. It was the doing it that counted. The name of the game was escapade and *daring*. He'd always been the kind of boy who took shortcuts through 'Sippi graveyards at midnight, because he would not take a dare. Before he ever learned to swim, he jumped into a ten-feet-deep swimming hole and splashed his way to the other side.

Nevertheless, you might have thought that his experiences with prescience would have taught him greater caution, but as they say in Paris, "*C'est la vie*," or perhaps more appropriately, "*Cherchez la femme*."

For fairly obvious reasons, the trip across the ocean had to be postponed for several weeks. Even after Jimmy Jay Leander Johnson was released from the hospital, he remained in comparative seclusion in the Executive Mansion at Robeson House for a couple of weeks before takeoff time. He was attended daily by a steady flow of executive physicians, staring down his throat and through his ears and up his nose and up more embarrassing and unpleasant places. And he was attended each day by his teacher, Maria Efwa, and by another brother, Special Assistant to the Prime Minister Barra Abingiba, who, like the Prime Minister, had spent several years in the States getting a college education at Howard University in the District of Columbia, then to Harvard and to Yale. "Whatever Maria omits, perhaps Barra can fill the gap for you. You've had mutual experiences," the PM counseled him.

At Jimmy Jay's insistence, Jaja Okwu also spent at least an hour a day with the phony-bearded Jimmy Jay. "If I'm going to impersonate you, then I must get to know all about you, your ways, your traits, your characteristics, your reading habits, your family background, your beliefs, so that I'm able to speak with some authority and with your voice and with your nuances and especially your intelligence."

Jimmy learned that the PM had been a flaming radical in his younger days, had spent a year in London, and another year in Moscow at Friendship University, a.k.a. Lumumba University, went to the States for four years at Lincoln University in Pennsylvania near the Mason-Dixon Line, walked the thronging streets of Harlem for another year, soapboxed and demonstrated. He'd read *Das Kapital* and the *Manifesto*. He'd read Du Bois, Richard Wright, and Langston Hughes, John Maynard Keynes and Bernard Shaw. "I'm a Pan-Africanist Black Nationalist," he told Jimmy, "with a socialist perspective."

"What the hell is that?" Jimmy asked the learned PM.

"With all due respect to Professor Marx," the PM quietly explained. "We, in Guanaya, are admiring this Karl Marx man very much indeed for his important contribution to universal thinking, but we were living in a very sophisticated society of communal being long before Professor Marx was a being in this universe."

All Jimmy Jay could say was "Come again? Run that one back by me one more time." He felt like the biggest ignoramus he himself had ever heard of.

"Come again?" the PM queried. "Run it back? Oh I see." Then Jaja Okwu complied patiently almost word for word. Jimmy thought it sounded like a tape recording.

Conscientious Jimmy Johnson tackled his homework scrupulously. Tried to make up for lost time, relentlessly. He had them bring him all kinds of books. He almost read two books a day. Erudition was coming out of his ears. Between the books and Maria Efwa's information and Barra Abingiba and Jaja Okwu, the dear fellow almost lost his bearings. Most nights he finally went to bed with a headache of the migraine denomination. Where in the hell had he been when all this was going on? Being written, spoken, happening?

Jimmy Jay and Barra Abingiba hit it off immediately, from the "get-go," a term Barra loved to use, and frequently.

One evening they sat together in the PM's study sipping mucho palm wine and laughing and joking, rhapsodizing in the hip idiom of Afro-American-ese.

Barra seemed bent on proving to one and all that Whitey's hifalutin Ivy League education had not cut him loose from his Black roots. Some nights Barra sounded so "down with it," Jimmy Jay suspected him of actually being an Afro-American posing as an authentic African. Perhaps that was why the PM had put the two of them together. They were "birds of a feather."

"You're going to be going out there in that other world," Barra told him in his hipper-than-hip Afro cadence. "Sometimes you're liable to find yourself between a rock and frigging hard place. Somewhere out there by your lonesome between the devil and the deep blue great big drink. You'd better get yourself some protection. Hey, and I'm the cat that can get it for you wholesale." Barra Abingiba was so hip he couldn't stand himself.

"Protection?" Jimmy Jay questioned, uneasily, as the skin began to crawl across the middle of his back. He hadn't heard "protection" since that first morning in the hotel with Cecil Oladela, the hundred-yard-dash man. Then he remembered the unidentifiable voice at the hospital.

"What do you mean, 'protection'?"

"*Protection*, baby. Hey, that's some heavy shit you going to be into. Believe me when I say so."

Jimmy sobered up immediately, completely even. "I haven't the slightest idea what the hell you're talking about. What in the hell is this 'protection'?"

"You need some help to carry out there with you from a heap bad Juju man, the motherfuckering witch damn doctor. And your boon buddy, Barra Abingiba, knows the baddest motherfuckerer in all Guanaya."

"But you, I mean, you're too intelligent," Jimmy Jay protested. "You're too educated. I mean, you got your PhD from Harvard and another one from Yale. I mean, you can't actually believe in Juju and-and-and in witch doctors, I mean, you don't, do you? You're a clinical psychologist."

"What's intelligence got to do with it? And education? I mean, you show me an African that doesn't believe in Juju, or witchcraft, or whatever you want to call it, and I'll show you an African who is off his cotton-picking rocker." Sometimes Barra got his idiomatic metaphors all screwed up and bass backward.

Barra was laughing now, hysterically, as he stared at Jimmy's quizzical face. And Jimmy felt a sudden dizziness. He said, "Surely you don't really—"

Barra stopped laughing, momentarily. "Is the fuckering Pope Catholic? Was the Messenger Islamic? That's like asking an African is the sun going to rise tomorrow morning anywhere on this earth, or is there sand in the Sahara."

Jimmy mumbled, "But surely, I mean, somebody like Jaja and Maria Efwa don't actually believe in that kind of shit."

"That's because you haven't been here long enough to be Africanized. You're still an African American." He stared at Jimmy Jay. "You're a white man with a black skin." And he erupted with laughter again, the American kind of "colored" laughter. Jimmy Jay felt like a fool.

"Yeah," Barra went on, laughingly. "Like Hugh Masekela said, 'The Americanization of Oooga Booga,' right? I was sure as hell Americanized, when I first got back, but it didn't take long to get that shit out of my system. I mean Juju, I mean witchcraft. A rose by any other name. I mean that shit is pervasive throughout the Mother Continent. Every living ass is a solid true believer. It's some shit that you can't live without. It's in your blood."

The lovely image of Maria Efwa came, against his will, before Jimmy Jay, and he felt a sudden nausea, and he didn't want to think about it—Maria Efwa and witchcraft! He didn't want to believe it. He wouldn't ever believe it. So he steered the conversation into other more familiar waters, where the sea was calmer, because he didn't like seasickness.

For a couple days afterward he thought of little else. Perhaps his friend Barra was pulling his leg, he hoped fervently. Having a joke at Jimmy Jay's expense. Sometimes these Guanayans showed the weirdest sense of humor. But then what if his good buddy wasn't joking? Every day and all day long, when he was with Maria Efwa, he was usually distracted. Trying desperately to figure out how to broach the subject to her. He knew he was bewitched, by her. He was charmed by her unearthly beauty. He was surely mesmerized. Undoubtedly she had cast a spell on him. Perhaps she was in fact the Juju Queen, High Priestess of the Guanayas.

Ultimately he couldn't live with it any longer. He could not bear the strain of wondering, not knowing. The agonizing doubts and fears. He bolstered up his courage, and he asked her. "Do you think I need a little protection before I go out into that other world?" He laughed, to make her think he was only kidding—just in case—

She stared at him, seriously, out of those deep and large and dark and mesmerizing eyes. Wide and mysterious and knowing and almond shaped, diagonal. Jimmy Jay felt immediately Jujued and witchcrafted.

She stared intently at him, through him. "You believe in it already?"

He laughed weakly, then uproariously. "No indeed. Of course not. Heh-he-he. Like I was only kidding. I mean—"

She said only, though emphatically, "Stay away from it. Do not get involved in it. God will give you adequate protection." He'd figured already that she was a Christian. She had told him she'd attended a Catholic secondary school, before she went to the University at London.

The next time he was with his palm wine drinking buddy, he brought the subject up again. "You *were* kidding, weren't you, with that Juju and that witchcraft stuff. I mean—"

Barra laughed his funny laugh again. "Did or not old bad Denmark Vesey believe in Gullah Jack?" Barra was a heavy dude in Afro-American history and folklore. He was perfectly at home with Vesey and Nat Turner, Gabriel Prosser and David Walker. And he loved to show off his Afro-American erudition.

Jimmy Jay countered with "All that Juju Gullah Jack possessed didn't save his and Denmark's asses from getting strung up."

"Perhaps his Juju wasn't powerful enough." He went off into his demonic laughing jag again. When he stopped he said, "I told you, that Juju shit is pervasive, I mean, all over Africa. Some of these ordinary everyday motherfuckers can put a natural hurting on your ass. One of the most revolutionary presidents of an African country is reputed to be the baddest Juju man on this earth. He can put you on a plane headed for Accra in Ghana, and then he'll get into his Land Rover, and by the time you get there by air, he'll be out there at the Accra airport waiting for you when you arrive. I know a couple of dudes he did that to."

Jimmy Jay was almost out of breath. "What's his name? Who is this revolutionary Juju president?"

Barra said, "No way. No way you're going to get me to even whisper the cat's name. My man is not a small boy. He's listening to our conversation at this very moment. He doesn't need any kind of spy equipment. He doesn't need any mechanical bugs or any other electronic devices. He's got the biggest eyes and ears in Africa." Barra began to sing, burlesquing,

> He sees all you do ooh ooh,
> He hears all you say—aye.
> My man is watching all the time.

He stopped singing and he laughed at Jimmy Jay. "My man is so bad; he scares the hell out of himself sometimes. He's no small boy, you'd better believe me."

"Oh come on already." Jimmy Jay was sweating freely now. He knew the term "small boy" was the "baddest" put-down in Guanaya. You call a man a "small boy" and you have relegated him to total insignificance. He is underneath beneath contempt. Likewise if you said, "He's no small boy," you have accorded him elevation to Mount Everest and beyond way up there to that big place in the sky.

"Baby, they got families here in high places who trust one another about as far as you could throw the motherfuckering Empire State Building. Go around all day watching one another, suspiciously. Everybody in the family suspecting one another of hexing them, casting a spell, their fathers mistrusting their mothers, sisters do not trust their brothers, and vice-fuckering-versa."

Jimmy Jay said, "Now I know you're joking. Be serious." He laughed weakly. "Heh heh heh."

Barra got up and went to the telephone. He picked it up and turned toward Jimmy. "Is there anything you want that you left back in the States?"

Jimmy mumbled, almost inaudibly, "I left my manuscripts for some lyrics back in New York with my landlady. Some calypso stuff. West Indian music."

Barra said, "Say the word, and I can have it here into your hands in fifteen fuckering minutes." Jimmy Jay felt that sudden giddiness again, severely now, like falling from the steepest cliff. He was vertiginous. He could hear Maria's voice again. *Stay away from it.* His flesh began to crawl again. He shouted softly, "Hell naw! Forget it! Leave it alone! Leave it alone!"

Barra insisted, "You want it, or don't you? All you have to do is say the word. We'll see how tough Guanayan Juju is. Get you some of that mamba Juju. With them bad snakes all around you, and no evil can ever harm you."

"Mamba snake Juju? Naw naw, hell naw! I'm deathly scared of snakes."

Barra said, "But they'll be there to surround you and protect you. You won't be able to see them."

Jimmy Jay envisioned invisible snakes. He could see them by the thousands all around him, even though they were invisible. He thought again that Barra must be kidding him.

Then his macho and his natural daring rose up in him. Jimmy said courageously, "What the hell—what can I lose? Get my manuscript. Let me see you do your stuff." His heart began to leap about.

Barra answered, "You can't lose a thing. It's free of charge. However, once you're into it, you're into it indefinitely, from here unto eternity, and one of these days you'll be called upon to pay your dues. Okay, what's the landlady's number?"

Jimmy Jay felt faint. He shouted in a froggy voice, "I told you to forget it. I don't want anything to do with it."

Barra said, "In the words of Purlie Victorious, 'You the boss, boss.'" He burlesqued. "You is the natural massa, Massa."

Jimmy Johnson felt a great relief, as the perspiration poured from him, as if his body had sprung leaks, suddenly.

6

Before he went to bed that last night before they flew away, he made up a poop sheet for the PM's party. And he was dead serious the next morning when he distributed it to each of the ministers who would be traveling with him to the good old US of A. And so, the poop sheet—

JIMMY JOHNSON'S POOP SHEET FOR JUNGLE TRAVEL

Now you are going on a hazardous journey into the wilds of North America, where so-called *Homo sapiens* live in a vast jungle of steel and stone and concrete and run around like crazy in mechanical monsters on terra firma and way up in the atmosphere and pretend to each other and the world that they are highly civilized supermen, but that is hardly the case.

While in the land of the free and home of the brave, the venerable Dr. Du Bois called it "The Land of the Thief and the home of the home of the slave," always wear your Guanayan attire and thereby avoid unnecessary unpleasantries. Remember! It is a peculiar land that treats any foreigner in the world better than it does its own Black citizens. However, if for any reason any one of you are caught alone, God and/or Allah, Buddha, honorable ancestors, etc., should forbid, on one of their asphalt footpaths, and you are not wearing your Guanayan robes, but wearing instead the skimpy costumes of the drab American natives, you are accosted by one of the pale-faced natives, you are to immediately forget you ever knew English and move swiftly in Swahili, Hausa, Yoruba, Pig Latin, patois, Chinese, whatever, gesturing violently to make your point. Take my word for it. They will not know a word of Swahili or whatever, but they will understand what's happening. If you spoke to them in Americanese it would cause a great misunderstanding. The subtlety here is: All they need to know is that you are not an American citizen. Dig? Understood? Secondly: Wherever you go out into the jungle, North, South, East, West, beware of masked men-like figures, sometimes even child-like figures, wearing white costumes, with tent-shaped heads and carrying lighted torches and illumined crosses. They will not be of your own kind. Neither will the torches represent the torch of freedom, nor will the illumine crosses represent the cross of Jesus. These torch-bearing, white-sheeted, cross-bearing pyramidal-headed natives are an unfriendly lot, to say the very least. The torches and the sheets and crosses are all a part of their savage ritual. Cannibalistic at the core, except for the fact that they do not eat their victims, usually. Notwithstanding, these natives are absolutely hostile.

Finally, here is a glossary of American terms you might run into from time to time. This is just so you will understand their peculiar nuances. I will add to this list from time to time during our sojourn in the Western jungle. The important thing to remember is white is white and black is black regardless of the pigmentation.

GLOSSARY

WHITE	BLACK
White American Citizens	Black American Subjects
White man—Courageous, with strength of his convictions	Black man—loud-mouthed, arrogant, downright sassy
American Revolution—Glorious, patriotic	Black Revolt—Irresponsible, hate-inspiring, racist
White man—Militant, courageous, honorable	Black man—"Crazy nigger"
Hungarians—Freedom fighters	Black demonstrators—Extremists, radicals, troublemakers, "Communists," N.A.A.C.P.ers even
White man who drives a Cadillac is affluent	Black man who drives Cadillac is a conspicuous consumer, uncouth, stupid, loud, etc. etc.

NOTE: My own attitude is: Black man driving Caddy is symbol of rebellion. White man's Caddy is a monument to his insecurity. We call them "hang-ups" in the USA.

7

MEANWHILE BACK AT THE GREAT GOLF COURSE, in Lolliloppi, 'Sippi, Near-the-Gulf, that region of the USA where the living was easy and the colored folks were always happy with plenty of nothing, and forever weeping when 'Ol Mass'r got the cold cold ground that was coming to him. 'Twas indeed an idyllic picture of romantic degradation—difficult to imagine these days (in any context), two of America's most famous golf pros were engaged in the annual "Battle of the Century." Once a year, and aside from any of the national or international tournaments, they always got together in Lolliloppi, Mississippi, Near-the-Gulf (deep deep in the 'Sippi bush, whose only claim to fame was its great golf course where professional golfers played and Presidents and other big shots. Had it not been for the golf course, Lolliloppi would have suffered the terrible fate of absolute oblivion and total invisibility.).

Notwithstanding, these two old cronies played eighteen rounds of their greatest most competitive cut-throat golf at a thousand bucks a hole. It was not the money they won from each other that counted. That wasn't the reason they went for each other like it was the last golf game on earth. They did it mainly for kicks and out of deep and lasting friendship, they would tell you, Bobby Snide and Johnny Higginsby. All year long they looked forward to the "Struggle of the Titans," as a certain newspaper columnist gained immortality by describing it so originally. It was winner-take-every-damn-thing.

It had been nip and tuck all the way, and sometimes even tuck and nip, ever since they had teed off from the first hole. They always took a little nip along with them (two fifths of bourbon) and had it tucked away in their golf cart. If the slightest breeze blew they would cuss aloud and storm and rage. It was dog-eat-dog, rat-eat-rat (choose your own metaphor), every step of the way. And now they were "nipping and tucking," as they called it, laughingly, at the thirteenth hole and

Snide had just nipped and passed it on to Higgy, who likewise tuck another nip. He was on the green about twelve feet from the fourteenth hole and one shot down, standing there in his tweedy knickers. (Both men were old-fashioned and imagined they were the Second Coming of Bobby Jones. Therefore they were always tweedily knickered.) Higgy's sun-cooked leathery skin pulled tightly over the bony frame of his cunning face (He almost looked *colored* sometimes), and his face was red-nosed and leaking perspiration and sweat was draining, ungentrifiedly, from his armpits. His light brown eyes narrowed into slits. He took another short nip and tucked it back into the golf cart, and again he sighted long and carefully from ball to hole. He stared up at the merciless sun of the Southland and swore underneath his bourboned breath as was his habit lately as he moved through the middle ages of his sojourn on this earth. Now he was ready with his putter with a thousand dollars riding on each shot, not that money mattered, *BUT*, and notwithstanding even. He had just assumed that pose, that concentration, that inimitable form, for which he was world famous, and which had won him numerous international loving cups and other stuff, including that filthy currency of the realm. It was that moment of dramatic rectitude, when a group of extra-duty caddies went around the edge of the crowd of spectators shushing them for absolute quietude, one of the most tranquil moments on this earth. Then at that split-hundredth-of-a-second before the club made contact with the ball, when the whole world held its breath, on television even, he was interrupted. Well, sir! I mean, that is, well sir! His language we will censor here, dear patient readers. Because, as you must have gathered by now, we are a high-class author. Though sometimes we have felt compelled, for the sake of verisimilitude, to tell it like it is and let it all hang out, obscene linguistics notwithstanding. Pray forgive us for these earthy lapses.

Old Higgy turned violently toward the interrupter and swung his golf club like he was driving down the fairway. The serious-faced young pale-faced gentleman jumped from 'neath his panama hat like Willie Mays running bases, and just in time to avoid his head being substituted for a golf ball and a possible decapitation. He shouted softly, dignifiedly, "Secret Service! Secret Service, Mr. Higgingsby!" He and his colleague quickly produced identification.

But this could not pacify old Higgy, when you interrupted his kicks. It was against his way of life and it was unconstitutional and surely did upset his constitution. He was so irate his voice was trembling. "What the hell do you want with me? And I know damn well it can wait!"

The other panama-hatted gentleman said politely. "The President wants to—"

Old Higgy growled, "The President can wait too. This is a free—The President!?"

"Yes, sir. We're very sorry, but we have to ask you to kindly step aside for a moment and let the President's party through. It is of international importance that he gets to the eighteenth hole just as rapidly as he possibly can. A national emergency!"

Higgy and Snide stared past the two serious-faced young men at the party standing patiently on the edge of the green near a golf cart, a classy glassy Fairway VI fiberglass job with the dignified inscription on the front: OUR BELOVED PREXY, FRIEND AND BENEFACTOR OF ALL MANKIND. There were panama-hatted gentlemen all over the place interspersed among the crowd. There were almost as many SS men as there were spectators.

It was then that their eyes filled as they saw that famous smiling chubby-wubby face that always made the "Free World" know everything would be all right in those weary nervous Cold War days of "Brinkmanship." The two old crotchety middle-aged tweedily knickered golf pros pulled off their tweedy caps respectfully, and then a frightened look came into Higgy's craggy face. You could see him aging.

"What happened?" he asked the two young men, and he was deathly scared of the answer. "Has World War Three been declared? Good Lord! Have they dropped the bomb?"

The first young man said indignantly in his accent which was a curious mixture of Georgia cane syrup and Harvard Yard, "Certainly now! Everybody knows His Excellency Olivamaki Okwu is arriving in the nation's capital on tomorrow!"

Higgy and Snide were profoundly impressed, yes, and greatly relieved. "In that case we would be honored to make way for our beloved President," Old Higgy said respectfully.

Meanwhile on the front pages of the nation's press was nothing but news of the PM's visit and his arrival on the morrow. His face had been plastered on the front page of every newspaper in the USA, on every TV station. There was not a single red-blooded American, red, white, yellow, black, or brown, or otherwise, who would not know the briefly bearded young PM on sight. His face was as familiar as Muhammad Ali's had once been. An Emergency Presidential Order declared the day of his arrival a holiday for government workers in the nation's capital. Even the filibuster, which was already six or seven years

old, stopped filibustering for a time. Washington exuded an air of festivity as if it was Inauguration Day.
Like the time the last of the Great White Mothers and
her consort made their visit from the You-Kay, and it
rained forty days and forty-five nights, and Charlton
Heston grew a beard and declared that he was the Second Coming of Noah and began to construct an ark,
with approval of adequate appropriations from the
Congress and the President. Like the time the hostages had come back from Iran.

In downtown New York City and along Seventh
Avenue they were also getting ready. Stands were
being constructed along the line of march or the line of
ride, whichever, and a platform had been constructed
where His Honor would give to Olivamaki the keys to
the greatest city in the world. Buttons with the PM's
handsome picture were being sold down in Times
Square, on Broadway, and even on sleazy Forty-Second
Street. East side, west side, all around the town. They
sold sweatshirts with the PM's picture.

Take the A train up to Harlem, USA, where the
people are preparing to welcome their very own. On
the corner of 125th Street and Seventh Avenue diago-
nally across the intersection from the Hotel Theresa,
the house that Fidel had made even more famous than

it already was, on the sidewalk in front of where the famous Michaux bookstore with its "HOUSE OF PROPER PROPAGANDA" and its "HUNDRED THOUSAND FACTS ABOUT THE NEGRO" used to be, a leader of one of the countless Black Nationalist organizations is holding forth on a stepladder to a gathering of black and brown, and light-brown brethren; women, men, and children too. He is just finishing his speech with: "And Ethiopia shall stretch forth her arms, in the words of our own Langston Hughes, but dig, she damn sure ain't gon draw back no nub. Not in the year of this nineteen hunnert and eighty whatsoever!"

The people laughed and shouted and applauded and waved their brand-new flags of young Guanaya.

Somebody yelled, "Talk that talk!"

The speaker said, *"Am I right or wrong?"*

The crowd shouted back, "You're right!" "You're right!" "Right on! Right on!"

The speaker waved his fists and shouted, *"Uhuru! Uhuru! Uhuru!"*

And they shouted back, *"Uhuru! Uhuru! Uhuru!"* *"Freedom! Freedom!"*

All over Harlem Town the top-drawer leadership-of-the-colored, as Ossie Davis's Reverend Purlie would have called them (all those colored deputies), were vying with each other for spokesmanship in their welcome to the great African leader whom a couple of months ago they'd never heard of. At least a dozen Black Nationalist organizations, including the Sepia Moslems, the National Improvement Committee for the Colored, the Suburban Guild, and Mamadou Allah from Birmingham and Bambidido Mamadou from Mississippi. Each of them claimed seniority and priority and statesmanship superiority. It was a power struggle pure and simple among the Negro "power structure," another phrase somewhat like the "Black Establishment" that had been overused and underdefined back in those days, until Lerone Bennett clarified it in the *Negro Digest* almost two decades ago.

One fine-as-wine slightly overfed brown-skinned lady got up at one of the welcome-planning meetings in her gorgeous mink. (It should be stated here, categorically: This was not a meeting of radical Black Nationalists or even Militant Integrationists. This was E. F. Frazier's fabulously classic, unbelievable "Bourgeoisie." Brother Nathan Hare designated them "Black Anglo-Saxons.") Remember *The Cotillion*?

"Let me tell you Negroes something." She had her hands on her high-placed hips.

A very high soprano voice came from the back of the hall. "You starting off on the wrong foot, Sister."

"I ain't your sister, Sister, and it ain't nothing wrong with neither one of my feet. No corns and no bunions, no nothing. What I mean to say, and Mother is beautifully shod. These are three-hundred-dollar shoes from Gucci's and I got the sale slip here to prove it."

Somebody yelled, "You're out of order."

The thin shrieking voice from the lady in the back pitched higher and higher. "Don't make no never mind if you bought your shoes from Hoochie Koochie's, you listen to Mother McCree. You ain't talking to no Negroes here tonight."

Lady Debby turned toward the back of the brightly lit hall, adjusted her lorgnette to stare at the owner of the high-pitched voice, a light-skinned freckle-faced elderly woman, five by five, very heavily gotten together.

"Well, I know my pretty light-brown eyes haven't got that bad, and these people here do not appear to be of Caucasian ethnicity."

"You ladies are out of order."

Mother McCree said, "That's all right about that, we still ain't no Negroes. That's what the white folks call you, but we ain't that. Let me break it down for all of y'all." She pronounced the word lingeringly, contemptuously. "Nee—gro—Nee'gro! 'Nee' means never and 'gro' means grow, and 'Negro' means we ain't never gon grow."

Some of the brothers and sisters didn't have any better sense than to laugh out loud.

Lady Debby retaliated. "Well, I must say, you don't seem to have had any trouble in growing. The trouble is, you grew frontwise and sideways. You didn't ever grow straight up." She turned around and looked up at the chairman. "Now as I was about to rhetorize, when I was so crudely interrupted."

Some brother shouted from the Amen Corner, "'Rhetorize!' Go ahead with your bad self. Talk pretty for the people!"

Lady Debby continued, smilingly. "Who married to the white man?" She paused. "Me!"

"Who got the Cadillac car?—Me!"

"You're out of order, madame." The chairman rapped his knuckles on the table. With dignity. Judge Rivers Jordan of the New York County Criminal Division was the chairman and had dignity he had not used yet. A lot of colored people had, and had not.

"She is very much in order!" a Black man shouted. "Rhetorize your ass off, Sister!"

"Who got the Cadillac car!" from another bourgeois brother.

"The question is, madame, who is going to be in charge of the Welcoming Committee—and who's going to plan what program. These are the knotty problems." The judge was patient with the lady. Give him credit.

"Who got the sable coats and the diamond rings?" As if the good judge had not spoken. "Me!" She smiled patronizingly. "So you know who the white folks going to be listening to. And that's how come you nee-grows better listen to mother."

The judge rapped again for order. "We are not discussing white folks, madame."

The lady stared at the chairman with deep indignation and incredulity. "Are you for real, buster? Who invited that African to our country? White folks! Who's he coming particularly to see? White folks!" And then the deluge.

Well? All right—they worked it out ultimately. With enormous dignity. But now—on to Washington. The following day. Out at the airport in good old Virginia, which State was known as the Mother of Presidents (this was not meant in a derogatory sense), the then-beloved President, whose mother was not from Virginia, by the way, the then-Secretary of State, whose mother also was not from Virginia, and the Secretary of Commerce, whose mother was, and of Treasury and of Defense and some Underecretaries and some big-businessmen and labor leaders, and last and very very least and way in the back at the end of the line were some happy nervous Negro leaders. They had status this day, and, By God, they knew it. And thousands of roped-off government workers waving flags and banners, welcoming the young Prime Minister and his entourage. From the many and different national flags being waved, a cynical mind might conclude that there was a bit of confusion on the part of the happy wavers as to which African country was being welcomed. Flapping gaily in the breeze was not one flag from Guanaya, but there were flags a gracious plenty from Guinea, Ghana, Niger, Egypt, Togo, Chad, Kenya, Ireland—and never mind. The wavers all had good intentions. We must not be hypersensitive. Colored folks' flags do look so much alike. And yet one does wonder just how Ireland got into the act. Black Irish? Oh, never mind.

The President's cherubic face was glowing with expectancy. He loved to meet new friends and particularly at airports. It gave him a feeling of faraway exotic places. He was probably the friendliest most openhearted President the USA had ever produced up to that time. He was shy and at the same time terribly gregarious, bashful and outgoing, an introverted-extrovert or an extroverted-introvert; he could never figure out what was what and which was which. He never was much good at that kind of semantic introspection.

He was an ambivert but didn't know it. Many Western newspapers insisted that it had been the sheer warmth and magnetism of the President's personality that had made the difference between whether Olivamaki paid his first respects to Washington or to bighearted heavy-handed Moscow, which had also put out the welcome mat, the Red Carpet, so to speak.

Hubert Herbert Hubert had not sought the presidency of the United States. He did not *run* for office. He "stood" for it like they do in jolly England. A modest man of simple taste and mind and even simpler beginnings, he had been caught up in the jet stream of a national fervor. Left to his own devices he would have probably been much happier as a chicken farmer (he said jokingly to a news commentator one day), or president of the Willing Workers Club of Friendship Baptist Tabernacle (his own dear mother's church), or a private eye or head coach of the local football team, semipro, he said jokingly one day.

Albeit he was a man at one with his times, for he had double vision and always saw two sides to every question, and always walked unerringly down the middle of the road, which might not have made much sense in heavy traffic, but politics was different. Everything about him of importance was symbolic of his great ambivalence, always had been. He was a southpaw pitcher and a right-handed batter. He was born in a state of great unrest that was neither North nor South, East nor West, but right smack dab in the middle of his country. A state that made a liar out of honest Abe, *for days*, since it existed half free and half slave, for days—and years. White folks free and Black folks, well, but I'm sure you get the point, darling readers. His father's folks had been slaveholders, his mother's folks had been rabid raving abolitionists. His mother was a hard-shell feet-patting bench-beating Baptist, his father a proper Presbyterian. As a boy he joined both churches. His parents called him a "Nothinerian," affectionately. He was a joiner as a little lad, joined both the Baptist and the Catholic church. In his lisping years, he called himself a "Bafflic." His mother's folks were staunch Republicans, his father's were not so staunchly Democrats, and Hubert Herbert Hubert was a member of a party in his state known fondly as Republicrats. He looked like a combination of Herbert Hoover and Harry Truman rolled into one, and was often mistaken, even as a boy, for both and either, and sometimes neither, and therein was the rub.

It was a time of great ambivalence; politically, socially, economically, sexually. Western man could not make up his mind whether he was going to hell or Heaven, and whether he was on AC or DC current. But now it must be stated here categorically: The President had definite ideas about sex. He was old-fashioned. He knew the difference between a boy and a girl, and he liked his whiskey straight, *neat*! No martinis or Manhattans for him. He was strictly heterosexual, an oddball in the Space Age, no two ways about it, as far as many Western men were concerned. Two damn many! the old-fashioned President opined. Some Western men didn't dig the Africans with all those wives. It wasn't civilized, they thought. Even one wife was getting unpopular out here where the West began. Notwithstanding, the President staunchly refused to appoint any of those type of ambiguous undecided fellows to his cabinet, if he had the slightest suspicion. Hubert Herbert Hubert was a man from head to toe. You would have thought him *macho* had he not be so tenderhearted.

If he indulged himself in one obsession it was fornicating. He wearied of playing with himself very early in his uneventful life and sought other means of satisfaction and gratifications. Fortunately or unfortunately, there was a twelve-year-old and older cousin who spent a vacation with his family in the tenth summer of his youth, and sensing his profound frustration, caught him several times playing with himself behind the barn. Feeling sorry for him, she took his matters in her capable hands and taught him all the facts of life he needed to know at that terrifying moment. But summer came to an end and Sue Ida went away and left him more frustrated than before. He was crazy for it, dreamed about it, wet and sticky dreams he dreamed. He would shine his black shoes to a sparkle. He could see his homely face in them like a mirror. He could also look up the little girl's dresses. His schoolmates called him "pussy happy." They said he had "it" on the brain. It began to pervade his conversation, every sentence. Every other word was "fucking" this and "fucking" that. As a congressman he had a reputation of chasing his secretaries around desks and even up and down the corridors. Red faced, chubby, out of breath. "What d'ya mean, you ain't gon give me none? I'm the fucking junior congressman." He didn't really want to be President and the only way they got him to run was to tell him that, if elected, he could get all the pussy there was on this earth. "Look at Jack Kennedy," the fun-loving national chairman of the Republican Party cajoled him. "Look at all the pussy he got. And he had a bad damn back!" That clinched the matter, as far as the junior congressman from Mid-Americana was concerned. The only problem was he had to learn to keep the "fucking" adjective out of his vocabulary every time he made a "fucking" speech. It was never easy. In his inaugural, he almost pledged to uphold the "fucking" Constitution of the United States. He began to substitute the word "fabulous," just to be on the safe side.

When the White House got the news that the PM of Guanaya was coming to Washington first, it was considered to be the grand coup of the Twentieth Century, and they celebrated all night long. Tippling, sniffing, toasting, dancing, dipping snuff, and fornicating. Ms. Bessie Sue Zadilia Hubert, Our Beloved First Lady, was off for a visit with her ailing mama in Yamacraw, Arkansas, which was just as well, because when Hubert Herbert Hubert got happy, he invariably got horny. And Ms. Bessie Sue would have none of it.

Some said it was due to her Christian fundamentalist upbringing, that she believed devoutly and even fundamentally that fornication was for the Divine purpose of procreation only. Others said, maliciously, it was due to the fact that in his latter days, the Prexy had become afflicted with a very flaccid member (of the wedding). Apparently Miss Bessie Sue had a big mouth, or something. In any event, the word got around, and he became known in elite circles as "the President with the limber member." For whatever reason, soon after she decided her productive days had ended, she insisted on separate bedrooms. Whereas Hubert Herbert Hubert was much *macho* and Him personified. Our Prexy liked them young. He was known in inner circles as the "cradle snatcher." He craved his snatches infantile, he'd tell you jokingly. But he was serious.

He had been known to boast that "every now and then I have to have my battery charged for heavy duty, and only young boosters can assume the awesome task."

Since he never knew precisely when the happy mood would hit him, he took his dildo in his private briefcase everywhere he took himself. It was guarded as "Top Secret," and it was marked as such. A few of his cabinet members were playful pranksters and would spirit away his dildo and hide it from their President "with the limber member" whenever they were in a devilish mood. For old Hubert to be without his dildo was like being up a stormy creek without a paddle, or like being on the stool with diarrhea without a single sheet of toilet paper.

Which was what happened to our President, the evening he received the happy news. The drinking, sniffing, snuffing, singing, dancing had subsided, and all of his buddies had gone home or wherever it was they customarily went to sleep it off, or to do whatever. It was nobody's business but their own. Meanwhile there was this Miss American Starlet in the Lincoln White House bedroom wearing nothing but a happy smile. She was almost as pretty as her counterpart, Vanessa Williams, who would certainly go down in history. Honey Bunch was rosy-cheeked and plumpish and nubile, the way he liked them, with scarlet ribbons in her hair.

"Come on, Honey Bunch. Let's play mommy-poppy." Miss American Starlet lay there purring. He burst into joyous song.

I peeked in to say goodnight.

He went now toward the four-poster with his avoirdupois in much evidence around the middle of him. He made sucking noises with his lips as if he were playing with a lovely kitten. His eyelids blinking, he went, "Pussy! Pussy! Pussy!"

And I saw my child in prayer—

When he suddenly remembered, as he stood limply above her near the bed. The song was gone from his heart and soul. He stumbled drunkenly in his birthday suit around the room, cursing to himself, looking first one place and then the other. He pulled out drawers, crawled underneath the bed (which was quite an athletic feat) and looked. "God-fucking-dammit to hell!" the Prexy mumbled. He began to sneeze outrageously. He wiped his dripping sharply pointed nose, which resembled somewhat a horizontal obelisk.

"What is daddy looking for, baby doll? Maybe Honey Bunch can help you find it." She was purring like a kitty cat. Kitty cats could get impatient. "Your briefcase is right here on the foot of the bed, sugar pie."

"God-fucking-dammit!" he said. "I fucking fabulously found it!" He grabbed it up and opened it, threw all its contents onto the floor, but his precious dildo could not be found. "God-dammit-to-fabulous-fucking hell! God-fucking-dammit to hell!" He fell on the bed and telephoned his personal secretary.

"Round up all the fu-fuh-fabulous members of my fucking cabinet and get them here within the fucking hour," the Prexy ordered drunkenly. "Have the fucking bastards here by four o'clock."

"But, Sir, you realize what time it is?"

"Of course I do. Now you get your fucking ass out of a fucking sling and get them here within the fucking hour." He slurred his words. "Issa snatchernal smergency—"

"But, Sir, what's happened? Have they pushed the Doomsday button?"

"It's worse than that. One of them fucking bastards stole my fucking dildo!"

The personal secretary fell onto the floor and dropped the phone and began to roar with raucous laughter. He could not contain himself. What the President heard on his end sounded like Donald Duck in hysterics. When he could finally contain himself, he picked up the phone again. "But, Sir, it's impossible. They're all over the place all over the globe. Besides, we can buy another one."

"This time of night?" the President was fuming. He was no longer happy. He was left with nothing but his limber member and his horniness and his scarlet-ribboned Pussy Pie.

"We could get one in the morning, Sir."

"I want it now! I need it now! What's the fucking good of being President if I can't get it when I want it? Jack fucking Kennedy got it, didn't he? You want to keep your fucking position, don't you?"

"Very well, Sir," his personal secretary mumbled, resignedly. And got dressed and went out into the night in a desperate search of dildos.

But despite the Prexy's indecision in the country, it had been a time when more Americans voted in the

National Presidential Elections than any other time in history before or after. Hubert Herbert Hubert came out of the Middle Belt like a Middle Belt tornado sweeping all before him. In a climate of good feeling, the country landslid him into office, because nobody knew anything against him, because nobody hardly even knew him. But he was accused by many far and wide of being absolutely incorruptible, and that therefore he could not be trusted. To repeat Jimmy Johnson: In those days nobody trusted an honest politician. But back to our story.

Out over the wide Atlantic in a great jet airliner, the lights had flashed to "fasten your belts" and the announcement had been made that "we are approaching our destination, the capital of the United States."

The bogus Prime Minister fastened his belt with trembling hands and looked around him and out of the window at the great white clouds rushing by in the other direction, and as the jet lost altitude he wished vaguely that he was out there with that white fleecy stuff shagging it back toward Bamakanougou. And maybe not so vaguely after all. On the way over they had filled his head with Guanayan lore and history till it was coming out of his ears and other places less mentionable. They ganged up on him. They took turns. They worked in shifts, pounding knowledge into his weary brain. Now he knew what it meant to be brainwashed. It was more like being brain cluttered.

Guanaya is a country bounded on the south by such and such and on the north by so and so. It goes all the way back to the magnificent empire of Emperor What-not the Great, the illustrious second cousin to the king of Timbuktu, which built tremendous city-states and had highly developed civilizations when white head-hunters were chasing each other all over the face of Europeland. Guanaya's natural resources consist of such and such, etc., etc., and on and on and on and on, they had no mercy on the fake PM. A couple of times he fell asleep in self-defense, went to the toilet, but they still kept after him, not even knowing that he slept, or caring. He felt they had washed his poor exhausted brain and hung it out to dry. Sometimes he would try to absorb everything about Guanaya and all at once, so much so that he thought he heard his brain scream out in protest. Sometimes, he'd take frantic notes until his fingers ached and tingled. And other times, he would shut it out of the ears of his mind and take quick trips to his days of recent yesteryears. And relive all the millions of little white lies that he had heard and lived in London Town, where he had thought that he was finally free, just as he'd thought he was finally free in California and New York, and even thought it in the

Nam. But it was in London that he'd found the ultimate truth; the Western Truth; the European Truth; the Anglo-goddamn-Saxon Truth, that every Black man must know ultimately, or else remain a noble savage; or in other words, a slave.

Yet at this moment he somehow longed for London. He never thought that in this life he would regret leaving jolly England.

8

London Bridge is falling down
Falling down, falling down

London Bridge is falling down,
His fair lady—

Jimmy Johnson simply had had to find himself. From 'Sippi to the army and to Vietnam, to Los Angeles, he'd sought himself, and desperately. From LA to the Apple. New York, New York, a city so nice, they named it twice. He fled so damn fast from himself, and from New York, he ended up in London Town. To find himself all over again.

On a thick and misty London evening he'd landed at Heathrow airport in a jet airliner via beautiful, soft-faced, dark-eyed-stewardessed Air India, and when the soupy fog had lifted, he'd found the living much much easier. And far less frenetic. Now at long damn last, he would surely find himself, Jimmy Johnson told himself.

London City was old and firmly established, and yet it had a certain youthfulness about it. Vast gray limestone edifices stood their ground with the dignity of elderly statesmen among the modern streamlined whippersnapper buildings and the erstwhile Beatles and the Teddy Boys of yesteryears and the revival of the more than many miniskirts. It was a country where people stood for election rather than *ran* for it, as they did in the good old USA. That was London as Jimmy saw it. Changing even as it remained the same. And he could really get to like this place, he decided with unseemly haste. No one seemed to push him here, racially or otherwise, he thought, at first. Not even his homely Welsh landlady, who bugged him only when she talked too much, which was every time he didn't see her coming and get the hell out of her way. Her cooking was atrocious, but be that as it may.

He had saved enough money on his last singing gig in New York and the only album he'd recorded to tide him over for a time. And time was the only thing he'd ever needed. That's how he always conned himself. Only time and breathing space. The thing he liked especially about London was it was a city that didn't need to work overtime at being a city. It was a great city, Jimmy thought, and it knew it was, and that settled the matter, *period*. You didn't even need an exclamation point! The difference between London and New York, Jimmy thought, was the difference between a truly gifted artist who knew he was truly gifted and one whose profoundest gift was his artistic temperament, Jimmy Johnson thought. The difference, if you please, between self-confidence and desperate kind of egotism. London did not have to throw fits or temper tantrums or things at people. In a word, London was "cool," as far as Jimmy was concerned. "Cool!"—that is—most of the time.

For the first couple of weeks Jimmy Johnson took it easy. Checking out everything and everybody. He walked the streets, goggle-eyed, like a country boy he was, essentially, haunted the restaurants in Soho, African and Indian cuisine and otherwise. He frequented the bawdy burlesque houses. Despite the superabundance of weather, which was always there, prodigiously there, he breathed the free and easy air of London. And evenings, dark and large of eye, tall, profiling, assuming postures, brownish-black with reddish hue and knowing of his macho handsomeness, he got caught up in the mad labyrinth of Piccadilly Circus, rubbing elbows, seeing shows, drinking Scotch and shouting Bravos!

Piccadilly Circus was Times Square with a vengeance, almost. This was where miniskirts must have been invented, he thought, and reinvented in the eighties. He got a crook in his neck from staring fore and aft at perambulating skirts that reached up beyond the navel. It was disconcerting. Moreover it was embarrassing even, since he seemed the only member of the male species that took notice of the sparsely decorated scenery.

Two bully boys followed him one day for half a block huckstering their wares. "Two quid for an unblemished white woman, myte. Only two quid and she's yours for the awsking."

"An honest-to-goodness virgin, myte." From the other bully boy. "Pure and white as the driven snow. She's yours for only two quid."

While our hero was fascinated with the scenery and its feminine backsideness, he was not that interested in the sampling of the merchandise. He did not believe in "lay for pay" or "pay for lay," whichever. He got bored with the bully boys very quickly. "Come on myte—a lousy two quid for a pure white virgin. She'll do anything your heart desires." One of them tapped him on the shoulder. Jimmy turned and squared off at them. "Get lost, motherfuckers!"

He walked out on Birdcage Walk one balmy day, exceptionally balmy for old London, to the west end of Saint James Park, and he could not believe his eyes, as he jolly well witnessed the pomp and circumstance of the changing of the guard before that great symbolic fortress of a castle known as Buckingham Palace. Grown men on their pretty horses in their brilliant-red jackets and their brightly colored hats and plumage, playing "soldier" like little boys at Christmas with their toys Santa had left them. This was not "cool," not "laid back" as he imagined London. He window-shopped in Mayfair, he rode the marvelous underground with its upholstered seats and noiseless wheels; stared open-mouthed like a proper rustic at one of the most re-nowned addresses in the whole wide world, a simple red-bricked building on a narrow unpretentious street by the name of Downing, with the famous number "10" above its entrance. This was "cool," again as he imagined London.

After a few weeks, his money suddenly grew shorter than his close-cropped Afro, à la Stokely, but he was lucky as he somehow knew he would be in jolly England. He got a job singing in a restaurant in Soho, and he sort of had it made, despite the fact that he had to fight off a few obnoxious selfish ones from time to time. Likewise from time to time, he passed the early

before-day morning hours away with a few innocu-
ous Anglo-Saxon women. (Not all at the same time,
of course, but singly, since Jimmy Jay did not believe
in orgiastic happenings—he was not that sophisticated.) He hardly knew their names, these women,
nor did he care to know them, really. Lest there be a
horrible misunderstanding here, let us set the record
straight. These women *were not courtesans*! Categorically. They just loved to make the scene every now
and then, and they never passed up a morsel, large
or small, that came into their POV, within their pur-
view, so to speak. They hung around the place where
Jimmy worked, and they worked their desperation out
on him, with him, quietly, matter-of-factly, therapeu-
tically, in the spirit of international togetherness, as
quietly they became more desperate. He told himself,
these affairs would have more meaning if only there
were more "sisters" in this place. But foxes were still
in short supply, relatively, though the numbers were
increasing. Jimmy figured it had to have something
to do with the fact that the fox hunt had been, anciently and historically, a national pastime. Perhaps,
he thought, mi lords and mi ladies had tallyhoed them
almost into extinction. Then again, perhaps they'd
always been a rare commodity in the homeland of the
old You-Kay. It was a vicious circle, which often found

our man Jimmy in the middle of it, a backbreaking thankless bit, but he smiled and suffered quietly, heroically, and bore the Black man's burden like the stoic that he was. Then the mood hit him again.

He got fiercely lonesome for the real thing, whatever the real thing was wherever it was. He wearied of the hurried sounds of clipped accents. He tired of the one-night stands with the nameless faceless women, with the silken locks, some harsh and dry as hay in haystacks, he told himself, and halfly he believed himself. Especially did he tire terribly of fighting off the constant pixies, who, seeing him with no women in particular, figured him for a great long tall piece of beautiful Black ambivalence up for grabs to the highest bidder, and the mother-muckers bidded like proper mother-muckers.

He had made half-hearted guilt-ridden gestures toward clusters, here and there, of his kind of people, darkly hued, West Indian–West African–and East Africanly accented. Sometimes East Indians and Pakistani. He'd hung out briefly in volcanic Brixton. But he had not come to jolly England looking for a fight. He'd done his share of fighting in his homeland of the brave and free. That was in the young days of his raging angry innocence. He could have stayed at home for that. Oh! the great days of his embattled youth! It was common knowledge back home where he came from that the Black man was an endangered species. Sometimes at the "colored" gatherings in London he'd encounter East Indian and Pakistani accents, black-straight-haired, dark-eyed and dark-to-light-skinned men (fewer of the so-called weaker sex) who talked bouncingly as if their mouths were filled with agate marbles. Their tongues seemed to him to dwell on roller coasters.

He attended all the "colored" meetings and cheered them as they damned the damnable British. He went to several of their parties, and they welcomed him, at first. But when the few women always present (very very few they were, usually) gravitated toward the handsome "rich" American, he began to feel their dark and masculine hostility. Back home in the States the situation was entirely different. Directly opposite. Women always were in such great abundance at the parties and the get-togethers. So that men would just stand around profiling, assuming much macho postures. You didn't even need a rap to get over with the ladies. Black men were in such short supply.

Most Black men back home were lying neath the earth in Nam, or wearing out their welcome and the vaunted hospitality of the American prison system, or nodding in their endless sleep on the pretty white and deadly poppy.

He met one pretty dark-eyed sister in London from the Island of the Barbados in hot pursuit of the legal profession. He was lonesome and he wanted to get close to her in an other-than-brotherly relationship. But her lovely head was full of legalisms, and quid pro quo and vis-à-vis and sine qua non and a whole lot of legalistic gobbledygook (to him) with which he had not even an ephemeral acquaintance. It was difficult for him to break down her automatic resistance vis-à-vis his rhapsodizing in which he prided himself an expert. Charisma yeah! He had a hard enough time following her swiftly clipped accents when she was speaking ordinary English. The good Queen's version.

But our man persevered, and ultimately they found themselves in her flat all alone together. But every time he hinted, delicately, at beddy bye, she waxed matrimonial, invariably, a situation from which he had recently escaped back in the States, an institution that he had no current enthusiasm for enrolling in. She seemed to think all Americans, Black and white, were as rich as Belafonte and Poitier, especially if they were athletes or performing artists. "We could work together," she fantasized. "I could be your business manager. I could handle all of your legal transactions," she heatedly proposed to him, excitedly.

There was the other one he took out several times,

dear sweet lovely Sandra with rich and full and sweet and curving lips, Black Beauty in the natural flesh all the way from Trinidad. She had known Claudia Jones. Proclaimed Claudia her patron saint. She was as militant as Angela Davis, and equally aggressive, perhaps more so. They would be sitting in a restaurant, and she'd point and say loudly, "Look at that red-legged buckra making eyes at me, getting fresh with me. Go over there and hit him in the mouth."

Like the man said, Jimmy Jay had not come to jolly London looking for a showdown with the Anglo-Saxon race. So, Jimmy would say, "Hunh?" Hesitatingly. And if he hesitated more than thirty seconds, she'd rise from the table. "If you're not man enough, I'll do it myself. I'll slap him in his goddamn mouth." And she'd always choose the biggest bastard in the house, King Kong with a permashave, hairless, at a table inhabited at the moment with his big plug-ugly buddies. Our hero was not that heroic. Though he could pass for twenty-five, he was, in fact, thirty-five. His barricade-storming days were over. He was at the moment a staunch believer in nonviolence. He'd already done his stints with Malcolm X and SNCC and those wonderful Black Panthers all up and down the wild and wooly western coast of North America. He figured he'd paid his Liberation dues. He'd sung his Liberation Blues.

Just as he thought he'd finished with the "liberation" bit, the Brixton riots caused in him a reaction that was reflex conditioned. He found himself manufacturing, scientifically, cocktails à la Molotov (he preferred the kinds you sipped, complacently), speaking at rallies, running up dark streets with comrades he hardly knew, ducking and dodging, out of breath, ultimately the unwilling guest of Her Britannic Majesty's constabulary. He felt old before his aging time. One or two or three or four or five or even six or seven ASPs (Anglo-Saxon Protestants. Who needs the "W"? Why be redundant in this case? Did you ever hear of Black Anglos? ASPs they were, and equally as venomous and deadly.) coalesced with them and helped rescue them from Her Majesty's institution or incarceration. ASPY Jack-Armstrong was one of them. Missionaries, don't you know. No matter, London to him was no longer jolly.

Just as Jimmy had reached the conclusion that London Town was not his city after all, decidedly not his cup of tea, kept him eternally at sea; that London was even more of a fairyland than Hollywood, that picture-pixie paradixie, funky, fake, and phony all the way, he met a raven-haired, green-eyed, vivacious English woman by the improbable name of Daphne Jack-Armstrong. And suddenly he told himself he liked London all over again. And everything was cool again. Okay, she wore no Afro crown upon her head, she was undoubtedly an Asp, but who was he to pick and choose? He was lonesome among strangers. A lad who'd always loved to live dangerously, liked to play with sticks of dynamite, though he was utterly afraid of snakes. And repeat: Jack-Armstrong *was* an Asp. Let's say, our hero was confused.

Daffy had a flat in a fashionable section of the city, and he asked her no questions and she told him no lies. She was the intellectual type, a real book bug. She had a passion for them. Her commodious living room was in truth a library, with bookshelves everywhere and stacked they were and with books even. Jimmy loved books. He loved people who loved books, he suddenly discovered, especially when they were as handsome and as womanful as Daphne (can you believe it?) Jack-Armstrong. And far into the night of early morning, after they had driven to her place from the club, she would talk to him about her books and about the world and peace and Lord Russell and Freedom-Marches-in-the-States and GBS and O'Casey and Jim Baldwin and Lebanon and Palestine and Israel and Jesse Jackson and the schism between the Chinese and the Russians (she leaned like Pisa toward the East and China) and about socialism and the Labour Party. And love and sex and the awful awful prevalence of British leprechauns who were mushrooming all over the British Isles and were flamboyantly in season even out of season.

Moreover Daff was possessed with a voluptuous body as well as a brain, and vice versa. And was full of life and wanted to live it to the brimming overflow and here and now. Hurry up, please, let us live this life before it bids us Cheery bye, she seemed to always be shouting, softly though excitedly. Daff was all woman, 125 percent. She could not possibly weigh more than a hundred and fifteen pounds soaking wet. Five feet, five inches of Anglo-Saxon womanhood and in her natural state of birthday garments. She was gentle, she was generous. She was greedy but not miserly. This university professor born wealthy of the middle class.

They had known each other a week when one night she showed up down in Soho where he was doing a gig, and he drove her home in her Volvo, early before day one misty dew-dripped Saturday morning. And when they reached her flat they had more to drink and had breakfast, and talked and talked and talked about the problems of the world, till there was nothing else to say. And then she lay her head in his lap on her long brownish-beige goose-feathered couch, too close to the Him of him for comfort and she said, "I bloody well do like you, Jimmy. You know I really do." She didn't beat around the bush. She came right to the point. She knew where the point was situated.

He said offhandedly, "Likewise, I'm sure." Feeling deeply now her aspishness. Resenting now her self-assurance.

"I mean," she said, complacently, "I'm truly rawther fond of you." Daphne stretched and yawned, and he hoped she wouldn't fall asleep, because she had awakened the himness of him. What was he doing in this aspish place? his conscience asked, rhetorically.

"That is precisely what I thought you meant," he said, still offhandedly.

She shook her silken dark head in his nervous lap. "No—I don't mean that. I mean I like you because you're you. Well, you certainly are the handsomest of lads, in any context. You know that. But I mean, I know that some white women in London are in hot pursuit of colored boys because they believe in this myth of their sexual powers and that sort of bloody poppycock. But that is not what attracted me to you at all."

"Of course it isn't," Jimmy said sarcastically. "You were not attracted to me because of bloody poppycock."

"I would fancy you, my dear, even if you were not colored at all. I fancy you for yourself, the inner you, which has no color. I like you of course because you are terribly outrageously attractive, I mean even if we never went to bed together and we probably never will, because I'm not that facile. All the same I should still like you very very much. You must believe that about me. I am not facile or promiscuous. I'll have to know you a dreadfully long time before I go to bed with you, and yet I feel I've known you for a dreadfully long time."

"An entire week exactly is how long we've known each other," our hero added thickly. "That's how long it's been since I was incarcerated. I'm deeply grateful for the part you played in securing my release from prison. It was truly very white of you." Jimmy relished his sarcasm.

"Do you feel that you've known me a terribly long time, dahling?" she asked him. She caressed his sober face with her tender fingertips.

He weighed his words before he answered, trying them out for size and heavy duty and endurance. Finally he said, "Yes—a long long time." And he wanted to feel as if he had known this woman for a long time. He wanted so very much to feel at home in this place with her head in his lap. But she was making him nervous now.

She laughed like she was truly happy, like a pretty little spoiled bourgeois girl with a delightful plaything she was playing with. She pulled his head down, his mouth to meet her eager misty mouth. When they came up for air, she said, "Nevertheless, it's actually been only a week, and we must know each other much much longer before we go to bed."

Jimmy feigned an unfelt boredom. "We're going to be two mighty sleepy people if we wait that long to go to bed." With her head again upon his lap, and her cheek in careless contact with his member (of the wedding), he felt a thumping in the middle of him. There was this tug-of-war raging now between his lively member (of the wedding) and his racial consciousness. His member vis-à-vis his intellect.

She laughed nervously. Her voice was getting froggy now. "You're teasing me, dahling. But we really haven't known each other long enough, you know, and I'm bloody well not like those women chasing the colored boys all over London because they believe the sexual myths. I don't believe the myths at all."

He wanted to like her, desperately wanted to like this comely woman-child of the American Mother Country, and he wanted to like London. Where else would he go to find himself? One of these days he was going to Africa.

He had read every book he could lay hands on about the Mother Continent, his Africa. In the eyes of his imagination he'd seen it all, had traveled from north to south, from east to west, had followed the fertile and sensuous Nile from Lake Victoria down north past Khartoum all the way to the sea. He'd seen Cairo, Lagos, and Johannesburg, Dar es Salaam and Zanzibar. He had traversed the great Sahara all the way to ancient Timbuktu. He'd drunk from a thousand oases, sat with Bedouins at their campfires, in their lonely tents along the way. He knew the old "countree" like he knew the back of his hand.

That he would really go there in person was a dream he knew one day he would actually fulfill. It was a dream he'd dreamed for years. But when he went, he wanted to go in style. He didn't want to go simply because there was nowhere else to go, he told himself. He did not want to *escape* to Africa. So now, this moment, he wanted to like Daphne Jack-Armstrong, and he did like her, goddammit, but every time she talked like she was talking now, he heard the little pale-faced aspish innuendoes in what she said, and in what she left unsaid, and felt the danger signals flashing somewhere deep inside the darkness of him. He closed his eyes and shut tight the ears of his mind, and he cast out of him all the Afro-oriented suspicions that he wanted to be unfounded.

She said, too contentedly, "We could have a platonic relationship. Don't you think so, Dahling? Intellectual and spiritual and so on. We could be like brothers and sisters. You do believe in platonic relationships, don't you, duck? That's what I should like for us to have—a platonic relationship, pure and simple and uncomplicated."

"Yeah," he said drily. "Me and old faggoty Plato." And suddenly he was terribly bored.

"But—but what is 'faggoty,' dahling?"

"'Faggoty' is the adjectival form of 'faggot,'" he said sarcastically and with a very very British accent.

"But—but what is 'faggot'?"

He said, "A faggot is a queer fellow, a chap of very profound Oedipus complexity, and ambivalence. And you'd better get yourself another boy. I am not frantically looking for a girl just like the girl that married dear old dad."

She said, "There are faggots in England in great abundance dahling."

"I'm hip," Jimmy said drily, in Afro-Americanese.

"The public schools turn them out by the thousands. The 'public' schools are 'private' here."

"So what else is new?" Jimmy asked his platonic lover, in sarcastic Brooklynese.

Then he said, "It's getting kind of late, old dear." And he moved her tousled head from his lap and stood up to go, and she stood up and went into his arms *very* unplatonically.

He cracked, "I never knew brothers and sisters to be so ever-loving amorous. It's like bloody well incestuous."

A fine perspiration had broken out above her peachy slightly mustached lips.

"Don't leave me, Jimmy. I'm so terribly lonesome, dahling."

"Plato would definitely disapprove," Jimmy Jay reminded her.

She said, "I have no desire to sleep with Plato."

In bed, she lost all her inhibitions, even those she never had. She forgot they had known each other for only a week. Forgotten entirely was old faggoty Plato. She busily undressed him first. She turned the lights off and she undressed herself quickly and got shyly into bed beside him. She was soft and quiescent at the beginning of their journey. Jimmy felt her swollen softness all up against his hard manhoodness. He was not unresponsive as she nibbled at the nipples of his manly chest, which had now become tumescent. She touched him here and there and everywhere and finally took the growing hardness of *Himself* in her soft hands and fondled it. She squealed, "Oh, ducky! You do fancy me!" And a warm chill shook her body as she felt Himself vibrating. She guided Himself gently to the secret humid treasure of Herself, even as her body trembled, and he smelled her fragrant perspiration.

Then she purred and simpered, as she began to get the message from her African camel rider all across the vast Sahara. Pure, hot, arid, endless. Then they left the desert and she went absolutely wild when she reached the outskirts of the city that was high above Mount Everest, and now she glimpsed the peak and sought to scale it. How on this crazy earth could the heat be so severe at Everest?

"Baby! Baby! Baby! Ducky! Lover!"

She shouted, "Yes! Yes! Yes!"

She was the frenzy of a jet airliner, after it has cavorted out to the other end of the strip and has turned and faced the runway, and now it has warmed up and throbbed and panted and has finally reached the moment when it is ready to take off for the wild blue yonder, because it just can't wait a second longer. "Jimmy! Jimmy! Jimmy!" It seems to almost shake apart from sheer excitement and the greatest expectations. And just like jet propulsion, Daphne literally took off.

"Yes! Yes! Yes!"

Emphatically yes! Forever yes! Indubitably! Up and down, from side to side, her thighs, her gleaming buttocks, she lunged, she bucked, she climbed the air. She rode bicycle upside down. She almost threw our hero from the saddle, but he held on for dear life; he dug in for the duration and drove her home. She bit him, her rough-and-ready easy camel rider, who got rougher as the going went; she dug her nails into his flesh and drew his blood. She screamed many many muffled screams, bit her own lips, her face lost color, then regained it. She shouted like she had religion. She exhorted.

"Oh! I knew it would be like this! I knew it would be good and big and black like this! Give it to me! Give it to me! Oh! I'm dying! Give it to me!"

Then the dear one realized she had completely lost her cool, as her Jimmy would have termed it in his quaint Afro-American idiom; she'd lost her nonchalance, her legendary British poise. To show that she was ever in control, she suddenly began to sing.

Oh! sweet mystery of life at last I've found you—
Oh! at last I know the secret of it all—

She startled him at first, and he didn't want to hear her singing or her exhortation, so he smothered her dear voice with kisses. He tongued her tongue and she whimpered pitifully. And when they scaled the peak together, and it was together that they scaled it, almost, she shook like a palm tree in a typhoon; then she simmered and slowed down to a small gale, then to the quiver of soft summer breezes on some blessed and "discovered" island where the sun would never set, till eventide, then complete tranquility, they rode out the storm together, *almost*. She began again to sing in coloratura soprano.

For it is love alone—

lyric, florid and high-ranged—

That rules the world—!

Almost goddammit, because the storm still raged inside our calisthenic hero, gymnastic lord and master of the bedchamber heroics. Because, as he was coming with her from the desert to the city, gathering all before them for the final joyous celebration, he experienced a visitation from a long-forgotten buddy, old Charley Horse, himself, in person. It started grabbing, gripping, griping in the calf of his right leg and moved up through his thigh and would not let go. The pain hit him so suddenly, he could not restrain a muffled scream, which she, of course, interpreted as a primitive expression of ecstatic unabashment. He had not known a charley horse since his college football days. It was like he remembered growing pains, like a cramp he had once when he went swimming in old 'Sippi.

"Goddamn! Goddamn! Goddamn!" he shouted softly to her. And tried to straighten out his leg, but she wrapped her long legs about him more tightly than ever. She started to giggle at his happiness, which caused him to shout again, "Goddamn! Goddamn!" He was so natural and uncomplicated when he made his love, she thought, and she loved his wild abandon, as her giggling went to laughter. She could sing to him no longer. He was hurting, she was laughing. She envisioned him in "savage" loincloth somewhere south of Timbuktu. East and West the twain had met. He was her black and wild Arabian knight. She was his oasis on the blazing-hot Sahara. He was the great avenger, she the human sacrifice.

The pain subsiding now, he said sarcastically, "If this is what is meant by platonic love, then I say to hell with Plato." He slapped her not too gently on her comely arse.

Then she wanted to rationalize it. She must put it in perspective, as she lay there beside him, surfeited and complacent, like she was basking in the sunlight at the seashore. He must not think she was promiscuous.

"Shit!" he thought, and, "Double shit!"

Never think she was promiscuous. Truly he must never ever.

She said, half serious, "Dahling, this is one way to solve the racial problem—through love. If everybody could feel like we do this precious moment, there could be no more antagonisms, no hostilities, socially or otherwise. No wars in Vietnam or Beirut, no sit-ins, no demonstrations or racial upheavals, no nothing." She vibrated like a vacuum cleaner.

He was annoyed with her for feeling the need to create a whole ideology around a fairly good orgasm.

Jimmy explicated, sarcastically, as he rubbed his calf and the back of his thigh, "A good orgasm may very well be a thing of beauty, but it is not a joy forever, sixty seconds at the very most, and it is not why Jason sought the Golden Fleece. It is not what really makes the world go around. Power and money, baby, is why Whitey went to Africa and Asia to 'civilize' the 'natives.' Not to have a great orgasm." He grew angrier as he verbalized, and the color drained from her lips and cheeks, as she paled before his anger.

She said, "Dahling, I didn't mean—"

He said, "If all the human race got together for one great worldwide therapeutic orgy of a couple of billion people, we might all have one helluva good time, but the white problem would still be here after the funk had cleared away."

Her eyes were filled with awe now. "I didn't mean it like that, Dahling. You bloody well know I didn't."

He continued as if she hadn't spoken. "Of course, and on the other hand, if this international orgy were without the benefit of diaphragms or any other birth-control devices, nine months later there wouldn't be any white problem, because there wouldn't be any more white folks. We would have fucked y'all out of existence. After all, we are a powerful people. One drop of Black blood and you have been joined up to the human race." He laughed harshly to himself. "Maybe that's another thing that's scaring Whitey." He laughed till the tears rolled down his cheeks. "Mayhaps that's the deeper fuller meaning of this interracial fucking. A long-range program of nonviolently screwing the white race into extinction." He laughed now without restraint and she laughed, but she was horrified.

He said, "Substitute the phallus for the gun. My English lit teacher at the university said the gun was a phallic symbol anyhow."

And Sundays they went everywhere together.

"There's the Cadogan Hotel," she told him, "where Oscar Wilde was arrested for buggery." And he laughed and squeezed her hand more tightly.

"And here's the pub that Sherlock Holmes frequented." And they went into the pub and drank much ale and stared at 'authentic' Holmes memorabilia and antiquities including a taxidermic job of the famous hound of the Baskervilles himself in person. Jimmy imagined he could hear him bark. "And this is where Sir Conan used to sit," the publican assured them. "And Watson over there—" And so forth and so on and especially etcetera.

One Sunday they went to Saint Paul's Cathedral and Westminster Abbey and to a pub where people stood outside queuing up for opening time, which was twelve thirty p.m. on the Sabbath. They drank many gins and tonics, and they went to Hyde Park and the fabulous Speakers' Corner. Hyde Park's Speakers' Corner made his 125th Street and Seventh Avenue in Harlem and Washington Park in the Windy City look like an American Legion Loyalty Day celebration. His first time at the Corner there must have been at least twenty-five different meetings going on simultaneously. And thousands of people drifting awfully and aimlessly from one harangue to another. The "Authentic Anarchists" were there and holding forth, the Worker's Workless Party, the Black Nationalists, and the inevitable "Irish Revolutionaries," damning the British everlastingly. And scores of other groups and causes. You name them, they were represented.

With the green flag flapping angrily now beside him on his soapbox, a black-haired Irishman is giving England her comeuppance, and a redheaded freckle-faced Irish heckler shouts at him. "If you don't like it here, you can bloody well go back to that ruddy place where you came from!"

At the anarchist meeting, the speaker looks like he has slept in his clothes, for days, and some joker is giving the ungroomed uncombed one a very bad time. "Who is the president of your organization, sir?" the heckler asks politely. The speaker replies, with patient indignation, Cockney-accented, "Comrade, we don't believe in presidents. We are true anarchists. We do not fancy any kind of organizations. Any kind of organization equals tyranny."

"Where's your office? I mean—where's headquarters? I mean, how do I get in touch with you?"

"No offices—no headquarters, myte. Now, if you don't mind—"

"What's your address? How can I get your newspaper?"

"We're the only true authentic genuine anarchists,

myte. Not like those bourgeois bawstards who believe in political organization and planning. Hence no address, no office, no nothing. Now bugger off, will you, myte, and hire your own bloody hall." The crowd loves this and laughs its approval, as Daff and Jimmy move on to greener pastures, or redder?

The bloke from the Worker's Workless Party with his red flag flapping is giving the imperialistic United States and United Kingdom hell and giving the Labour Party hell for selling out the working classes. Jimmy is in the spirit of things by now, what with several ales and gin and tonics under his belt and the intoxications of Speakers' Corner gone to his head. He heckles the short and squatty speaker.

"What did your blawsted working class do about colonialism in Africa and Asia? What about the Nigerians? The South Africans? The Chinese? The West Indians? You and your bloody working class—the greatest sellout artists of them all. You sold out your own damn class of people everywhere on earth. China, India, Africa, the Caribbean—"

And now they move toward the largest crowd in the park that Sunday, mostly white Englishpersons, a little Black middle-aged man on a soapbox, staring down at their pale British faces, contemptuously. He has a Du Bois-like goatee and his tiny eyes are smiling down at

them sarcastically. He is Deighton Johnson from Trinidad, and he has been in London twenty years but he
sounds as if he just got off the boat, the one that hasn't
yet arrived. He taunts the upturned faces. "You worried 'bout what's happening in Zimbabwe? In Johannesburg? In Angola? You worried about the virtue of
them precious nuns in Tanzania?"

There is worry in their pallid faces.

"You ain't seen no miscegenating!"

The British have a sense of humor, and they laugh
back at their Black tormentor. Give them credit. They
are a very sophisticated people, this special breed, descendants of the original Anglo-Saxons.

The little Black Trinidadian shouts at them. "Just
wait till we take over this here little undernourished
island. The president of Pan-Africa, His Excellency
himself, has put me in charge of this minor operation,
when the word is given. Then you will see some fornicating, mawn. And we're bloody well going to fornicate
Her Britannic Majesty, the dear queen herself, first of
all! I shall see to that miserable chore myself, personally. And you know something? She's going to enjoy
every blawsted minute of it! She is bloody well starving
for it! You tink the Ponce of Middlesex is consorting to
her satisfaction?"

When the laughter subsides Deighton Johnson from

Port of Spain starts to give them a serious lecture on the nature of colonialism. One of the awestruck Britishers interrupts him with a question. "Sir, where do you get all of your information?"

"From books, mawn. Where you tink? Doesn't you Englishmen know how to read?"

The Englishman asks politely, "Will you give me a list of books on the subject, sir. I should appreciate it greatly."

"Certainly," Mr. Deighton Johnson answers cordially. "Now take pencil and paper in hand all of you and listen carefully, cause like Shakespeare I doesn't ever repeat meself." Several of them take pencil and paper in hand and await his pronouncements eagerly.

"Are you ready?"

"Yes," they answer anxiously. "Yes," "Yes—"

"If you want to understand any t'ing atall about colonialism, the very first book to read is—"

"Yes?" "Quiet!" . . . "Yes?"

He has them hooked now and he says with the gravest of dignity. "The first book to read is—'Lady Shatterly's Lover' and the second book is 'Jonathan and Lady Jane'!" He pronounces it *Joe-Nathan.*

There is one split second of deafening silence, and then the park explodes with the laughter of the white sophisticated Englishpersons. And Jimmy Johnson laughs, thinking to himself, as Daff and he walk away to still another, What would happen if a Black man in the USA spoke of the American First Lady in terms such as Deighton Johnson spoke of Her Britannic Majesty? He squeezed Daphne Armstrong's hand and she responded squeeze for squeeze, as if they were Indian wrestling. Was London really the place he had been looking for? Would he at long last find himself in this place? He wanted desperately to believe it. He wanted to believe that Daphne Jack-Armstrong could help him find himself. Oh! the deviousness of self-deception!

That night in bed she would change into another woman as she always did, especially when the city atop the mountain came into view. "Give me all of it! Every bit of it! Give me all of the beautiful black thing! I love it!" And then she shocked the hell out of him with—

Dear one, the world is waiting for the sun—rise—

Higher, higher, higher, higher. He fought hard to keep from cracking up with angry laughter.

Every rose is covered with dew—

And when they had ultimately reached the highest peak together, *almost,* because Charley Horse had made his presence felt at the very last moment, paining, griping, cramping, she lay there quiescent for a moment, purring and quivering, luxuriating in the sweet and salty taste and smell of the love already made, and then back to the wars again. She smothered him with kisses all over his "sweet and salty" body, and fondled him, till she saw that things were no longer crestfallen but on the up and up again, and she coaxed him back into the saddle, at which point she watched the action for a moment as if she were a Peeping Tom. Daphne Jack-Armstrong was definitely voyeuristic.

"I love your big black penis in the soft pink tunnel of my sex," she murmured. "And I love your black curly grass at the roots of your big black thing and I adore your black grass intertwined together with my own black silken threads." He lay there pissed off, for eternity, he and his fucking charley horse and she and her divine contentment. He figured the Man Up There was saying something to him. Perhaps He was opposed to interracial fornication.

But after it was over, he lay there beside her, rubbing the pain from the calf of his leg, listening to her quietly snoring, inhaling all the sweet and pungent sea-like love smells, and wondering about her always shouting of his blackness every time they made their love. Was this blackness of his a big thing with her? And did it matter if it were? And he finally put it out of his mind, not really out, just set it aside in some far-off corner of his consciousness where it rested, but uneasily.

He got out of bed and walked the floor, shook the painful tension from his leg. Then he stopped at the bed and stood there staring down at her with the help of the moonlight that came in through the window. She was snoring loudly with her mouth loose-jointed, hanging open, and her wide dark eyes unshut, opaque, and full of vacancy. There was no beauty in her face now. Asleep like this, relaxed, she wore an idiotic expression. He felt guilty, as if he actually spied upon her. At the same time he was glad he'd seen her like this. Ugly almost, unintelligent-looking, vastly unsuperior, her great eyes openly vacant, all her defenses gone cherry-bye in the great depths of her snoring slumber. He told himself that he was glad. He stared so hard he must have stared right through her guileless sleep, and he awakened her.

When her eyes first became aware of him, there was that brief moment of panic in them. But then the comeliness of the woman came back with her wakefulness. It was miraculous. She smiled complacently at him, as if he actually belonged to her. "I'm truly fond of you, dahling, but I just cawn't help this very very slight contempt for you. After all, you are enchanted by my alabaster body. I mean, certainly, you know I'm not prejudiced, but you are a Black man, duck, and I am a white woman. Aren't you? Aren't I?"

"Yes," he agreed sarcastically, as he dressed. "And you just can't resist my fine Black frame and my prodigious Black penis. Right? My legendary big Black dick!" He had put on his shirt, but he was naked from the waist down. He walked toward her with the awesome Blackness of Him dangling. "This is what it's all about, isn't it Daphne dawling? Well, what's the verdict? Myth or reality?"

"Oh, no-no-no-no!" Daphne Jack-Armstrong protested. "I told you already, duckie. I am not that way at all."

"Lying wench! I could tell you it's not your white virginal body, it's your great intellectual capacity. That's some Black dude's lame excuse for fucking pale-faced women. That the sisters are intellectually incompatible. Bullshit!"

"But, duckie! You're being positively vulgar. Please!"

"I could say Black women are the great male castrators. That's another bullshit rationale. Or I could tell you that I'm getting even with the hunkie for taking advantage of our Black women during slavery when they could not defend themselves and neither could we." He laughed. "Historic fucking retribution."

"But, duck—"

"But why don't we just blame it on the lack of Black women on this island? Or just say you're easier and far less complicated and a fair-de-middling pretty good fuck, and let it go at that? I mean, we don't have to deal with the questions of marriage and other long-range complexities." He was enraged by now. "It's like wham, bam, thank-you ma'am. And that means I don't give a damn."

She said, "Oh dear me! I have hurt the big boy's feelings. Come here, duckie, and let me make it up to you." He was fully dressed now.

She sat up in bed and the covers fell away, and she was naked to her waist, her gleaming breast tumescent and exposed to him, and her pale arms reached out to him, as he went out and slammed the door. She called for him, left messages and telephoned, but he did not return again until three or four weeks later when she gave a party in his honor.

9

Wine, women, song, men, and leprechauns. Sometimes you couldn't tell the difference without a scorecard. He got there late. The flat was already crowded. Most of the women came escorted, which didn't seem to make a bit of difference. Most of them were openly curious about the guest of honor, James Jay Leander Johnson, colored. Some of their male escorts were equally curious. Everybody got high very quickly. The watchword was ambivalence.

When he arrived, a wasp-waisted, pretty faced, curly-haired, blonde and blue-eyed lad, when introduced to Jimmy, took him off guard, in his arms and kissed him loudly on each cheek, much much too close to his lips. "Like, man, you know, man, like welcome to the mother-mucking club. I'm hip, you know, man. Understand? I dig you the mother-mucking most. Dig it, baby."

His voice was an unlikely mixture of Harlem slang and Southern drawl with an unequal portion of Brooklynese and Number 10 Downing Street thrown in for good measure, or bad, depending on your point of view. A New York hippie with an Oxford cadence.

"They called me Old Blue Eyes where I come from. Can you dig me where I'm coming from?" Old Blue Eyes stepped back from astonished Jimmy Johnson. "Gimme some skin, my friend, I mean on the Black hand side!"

Before Jimmy knew what was happening, he'd held his hand out toward Old Blue Eyes, whose hand was already extended toward him. Blue Eyes slapped Jimmy's palm and went into his greeting by the numbers, with audibles. "Left! Right! Left! Right! One! Two! Three! Four!" He ended his performance by bumping his sparse arse up against Jimmy Johnson's.

Jimmy looked around him in an act of desperation to see if any men in white from the funny farm were there with nets. He looked for Daffy Jack-Armstrong, or for someone, anybody to come to his rescue. *Throw me a life belt, somebody quick!* But no life belt was forthcoming, as if Old Blue Eyes' conduct was common practice, nothing out of the ordinary.

Old Blue Eyes stayed, smilingly, up in Jimmy Johnson's face much of the night. If Jimmy sat on the brownish-beige goose-downed couch, he somehow found Old Blue Eyes seated next to him, coincidentally. When he moved to one of Daffy's chaise lounges, Pretty Boy seated himself on the floor beneath him, and back to the goose-downed couch again and on and on. Whenever Jimmy's glass became empty, Blue Eyes would leap to his feet and disappear and soon return with a whiskey and soda in hand and exchange it for Jimmy's empty glass. The first time it happened, Jimmy said, "Thank you very much."

Blue Eyes said, "Think nothing of it, my main man. After all, baby, you are the guest of honor, and like somebody has to look out for you, and I have appointed me, myself, and I to be your humble servant. Do you dig where I'm coming from, sweet daddio?"

Blue Eyes made the strangest vocal noises Jimmy Johnson ever heard. A living human anachronism, linguistically speaking. Fifties, sixties, seventies, eighties in a cataclysmic collision with one another, idiomatically. An apocalypse, linguistically. Slang, brogue, dialect, Cockney accent, the whole shebang. Jimmy thought of *My Fair Lady*.

Jimmy said, "Booby, with those weird funny noises coming out of your mouth, you'd give Professor Higgins a migraine he would never rid himself of in this life, or the next."

Blue Eyes broke up with laughter, slapping Jimmy on his knees and shouting, "I love it! I love it! I love it! You're the mother-mucking most!"

He patted Jimmy briefly on his knee again. Jimmy stared very hard at Old Blue Eyes and drew his knees away. Each time a funny cigarette was passed around, Blue Eyes inhaled it long and deeply like he was in the throes of orgiastic ecstasy. "Ooooh—aaaah!" and passed it on to Jimmy, who passed it to the next man, or woman. Our hero was a natural square.

"Dull! Dull! Dull! Dull!" Old Blue Eyes murmured to Jimmy, patting a soft hand gently on Jimmy's knee this time, for emphasis. "The English truly do not know how to party, dig it? Check it, you should come to *my* pad for a party. You should be *my* guest of honor."

When Pretty Boy's hand lingered, tentatively, Jimmy deliberately took the hand away from his knees. Jimmy did not dig playing kneesy with another man. Like the man said, Jimmy was square, perhaps rectangular even.

Jimmy said, "But you *are* English. I mean, aren't you?"

"My little old mama birthed me here on this little old island," Blue Eyes grudgingly admitted. "But I grew up in the Big damn mother-mucking Apple, baby, actually just a few blocks from your Harlem. I mean, like man, I bit some great big hunks out of that apple, baby, believe me when I tell you. Like I did my stretch at Columbia U. I mean I even graduated. The West End was my natural habitat."

Blue Eyes closed his eyes and nodded, then opened them again like he was coming out of a daydream in the nighttime. "Far out!" Blue Eyes leaned close to Jimmy's face and whispered, almost nibbling Jimmy's ears. "I was so far out I never did get back in, man, baby or baby man, whichever, what's the difference?"

Jimmy agreed. "You never did get back in is right. And hey, my ears may be big, but I hope you're not mistaking them for apples."

Old Blue Eyes cracked up again with laughter. "I love it! I love it!" He put his hand on Jimmy's knee and squeezed it, gently, perhaps even boldly this time. Testing-testing. He said, "One of the biggest problems facing the world is—people are afraid of touching one another. Man, you dig where I'm coming from?"

Jimmy thought, If this cat squeezes my knee one more time, I'm going to really have to touch him up and hang him out to dry. Jimmy took Blue Eyes' hand away from his knee. "Touch somebody else for a change. Why should I have all the fun, even if I am the guest of honor."

Pretty Boy shouted, "I love it! I love it!" Roaring with laughter.

What was he doing in this goddamn madhouse? What was he doing on these British Isles? Among the crazy people, who thought they were the most civilized throughout this earth?

Meanwhile and furthermore, there was a certain super-mini-skirted, blond-haired, gray-eyed hyperactive distraction seated on the floor across from him on the couch engaged energetically in myriad variations of exhaustive calisthenics. She was perpetual motion and seemed proudly and desperately determined to show off her pink-and-blue-and-flowered panties. She executed push-ups. She sat primly before bashful Jimmy Johnson with her skirt up to her elbows. Then she sat Buddha-like with her rubescent ankles plumply crossed. He averted his embarrassed eyes. Immediately she moved once more into Jimmy Johnson's POV and shyly smoothed her mucho-miniskirt down to cover her gleaming thighs, only to seconds later rearrange her skirt in such a way as to give him a fleeting glimpse of her skimpily-bikinied arse. He would have blushed had the Good Lord previously endowed him with a pigmentation equal to the execution.

Old Blue Eyes began to mumble. "The brazen bitch! The shameless harlot! Bitch! Whore! Slut! Trollop!" As the saying goes in 'Sippi, our hero, Jimmy Johnson, didn't know "whether to shit or go blithely blind"!

Jimmy leaned toward Old Blue Eyes and whispered, "Do you imagine she's attempting to attract our attention?"

Miss Shameless Harlot got to her feet and began to dance back and forth in front of them, belly dancing to begin with, then jumping up and down as if her dainty drawers had been suddenly invaded by a host of ants and grasshoppers. Now she danced around in circles, pirouetting, her whirling skirt flung up so high it was difficult to see her eyes, even as Jimmy did his damndest to pretend that the lady was invisible, with apologies to Ellison. But she would not despair or be discouraged. Suddenly she fell upon the floor and did a split that was perfection, and upside down already. So perfect was her upside-down execution of the split, you could see edges of the curlish down of her pubescence extending shyly around the perimeter of her flowered-pink-crotched panties. At

which point she made a foul and unpardonably anti-
social noise that would have made a camel blush with
shame. And did not even say "excuse me." Again, at
which point Jimmy split the scene.

Daffy's flat was beginning to smell all over like a
pothouse. Her living room was like the Mississippi,
long, deep, and very wide. There were little gatherings
of pot smokers here and there around the room, small
wigwams of people sending up smoke signals, prayer-
fully, to the holy Gods of Grass. Jimmy was getting
high from inhaling other people's smoke.

Old Blue Eyes followed Jimmy across the room. He
was getting loud and wrong. "Let's have a mother-
mucking party! Like, man, I mean a party party!
Come on 'round to my crib, baby. Ain't nobody home
but me! Like have a party party! Jimmy'll be the guest
of honor! Like whooo—weeee!"

Jimmy's football experience came in handy at the
moment, as he executed, niftily, a combination of
double-reverse-and-flanker maneuver together with a
bad flea-flicker. He could still hear Old Blue Eyes on
the other side of the room. "Where is Jimmy? What
happened to the guest of honor?"

Which is when he ran smack into another honest-
to-goodness soul brother, a cinnamon-colored, powerfully constructed angry cat very obviously from

home. In this endless sea of whiteness, he was so visible and pretty, he brought tears to Jimmy's eyes. Jimmy was so glad to see the brother, he wanted to take him in his arms and kiss him. Perhaps Old Blue Eyes was contagious. The brother pulled away from Jimmy.

"Ain't no hiding place down here, baby," he told Jimmy, apropos of God knows what. "It's the same damn thing all over Europe and I've been all damn over, baby. I've been the Black playboy of the Western world. You better believe me when I say so. I'm from the Windy City."

The cat from Chi Town was as high as a Georgia pine and as loud as a public address system. Jimmy looked around him nervously and back to his soul brother from Chicago. "Believe what, man?" Every party produced at least one loudmouthed one. You could make book on it. Jimmy felt like a dude who had leaped happily from the fire onto the brimstone, never mind the frying pan.

The cat got even louder. "You can get all the pussy you want, but you can't get no jobs, unless you can sing nigger folk songs, or calypso, or buck dance, which is the same bloody thing, only different." He laughed at the expression on Jimmy's face and with an angry vengeance.

Jimmy said, "Aw come off it, with that colored propaganda be-ess. You're not in Mississippi now."

By now they had attracted a crowd, and Jimmy laughed at his soul brother. He wanted to pretend that his brother was joking, even though he had a feeling he was dead serious. Correct that, deathly serious.

His brother went on and on. "A spook is a spook is a spook all over the Western world. Ain't but two roles he can play. He got to be a stud or a eunuch, which is the same damn thing only different. Black manhood is against the law here, just like it is any-goddamn-where else in the whole damn Western world. And that also goes for Black womanhood. You don't see no foxes at this party."

Jimmy tried to move away from his newfound brother. "Lay off the booze and grass, buddy boy. I mean, you've had it."

"Go home!" the soul brother philosopher from Chicago was shouting at him now. "That's what I'm talking about! Go home before it's too damn late! Go home or go to Africa!"

Jimmy stared back into the soul brother's eyes, and the pure and righteous madness he saw scared him half to death. He turned away, but the brother grabbed hold of him as if to throw him off the British Isles. "Look at me! It's already too late for me! I've been in this shit for nine damn years, France! Spain, Sweden, Denmark. You name it. I've been there. I'm a pimp or a stud or a eunuch. Take your mammy-fucking choice!" Then suddenly, without warning, the brother from Chicago broke into tears and sobbing. His shoulders shook as if his insides were erupting. "Go home, baby! Go home, brother!"

Jimmy went out into the hall where some of the party had spread to, by then. Near the end, he wandered into the kitchen, and there was Old Blue Eyes with a bottle of Scotch down inside the front of his trousers with the neck of the bottle protruding from his fly. Another dude was on his knees drinking neatly from the bottle, making gurgling noises.

Old Blue Eyes shouted at Jimmy. "He's taking the Fifth! Like man, he's taking the mother-mucking Fifth." He gestured to Jimmy. "You want to take the Fifth too, Jimmy baby? You want to take the Fifth?"

Jimmy said, "You got to be out of your fucking mind."

Jimmy turned to leave the kitchen. The last glimpse he had of Old Blue Eyes, the pretty blue-eyed lad was moving toward him with a hurtful expression, the white boy on the floor following him on his knees still gurgling, Blue Eyes calling after him, "Where's your sense of humor, baby? Like an Afro-American spook without a sense of humor. An unheard-of phenomenon. A contradiction in terms. I love it!"

Jimmy responded, "Your pale-asses mammy is a contradiction and an unheard-of phenomenon!"

Blue Eyes shouted, "I love it! I love it! I love it!"

Later that night, just before the Western world was about to see a new day dawning, Jimmy went to bed with Daphne, and as they reached the outskirts of the city and she began to get the message, and he was sending her the message as he never had before, she rose to meet the postman. She went into a spiraling motion, and Jimmy went into an action, as if he would grind this thing that they said made the World go around, this sweet mystery of life, right down to the nitty-gritty, as she sang "We Shall Overcome." Laid back. And with feeling yet. Both of them had to make the great scene this night, desperately had to, like combatants in the combat zone. Jimmy was Jody-the-Grinder for mama-mucking real. As they came into the home stretch this sweet girl went singingly for bloody broke, and she wrapped her long legs around him, like she would never ever let him go, and she almost broke our hero's back. He thought he heard something snap—*Pow!* And thought he felt it. But he did not desert the saddle. Our hero was too gallant.

"Fuck me!" sweet darling gentle proper Daphne shouted. "Fuck me! Fuck me, my big black stud! My big black stud—*My big—black—stud!*" He told himself he imagined the "big black stud" part of it. It was the cat from Chi Town's fault.

Even as she sang, "DEEP IN MY HEART, I DO BELIEVE."

Her backside left the bed again. "Big black stud!" she shouted. "Big black stud—Big—black— motherfuckering stud!"

His love muscle knew he hadn't imagined it. He went limp inside her, but she hardly noticed the difference, as she scaled the heights one more time. And fell asleep immediately afterward.

He got up and stared down at her sleeping with no pain or apprehension but with a smile of sweet contentment on her face as if she were an angel resting on the bosom of Jesus.

He had been "had" one more time.

But he had also done himself some "*having,*" he told himself, without conviction.

He swore softly now, as he dressed quietly and took a walk across dark and foggy London as day came slowly out of China. And by the time he reached his flat the mist had cleared completely.

And he saw London clearly for the first time.
And eight days later he took flight to Mother Africa.
To find himself.
Which was his everlasting mission.
Right?
Wrong!
Per-damn-haps.

10

The plane was descending now, and his heart descended into his stomach and God knows where his stomach went, but he felt queasy in his buttocks, and the doubts began to rise in him and multiply. In a few minutes he would be face-to-face with the President of the United States, the greatest of all the Great White Fathers, and the Grand Deception would be on, and there would be no turning off or turning back, and how in the hell had he let these slick-talking Africans talk him into this helluvamess? And without "protection" even! He hadn't brought his Juju with him. Stupidly he'd refused it. He'd let his big mouth and his sense of humor and adventure get him into trouble again, and his rabid nationalism and his love of Mother Africa and his goddamn swaggering bravado. And the champagne. And Maria Efwa's smile. He was no hero. He was no fighter, or he would not have run from 'Sippi to California to New York City and across the sea to London Town. All the way to Africa. That's why he hadn't made it with sweet Sandra of his London days. He'd always believed in the pious proverb "A good nun is a whole heap better than a bad damn stand." The universal motto of guerilla fighters, he rationalized. And what the hell made him think he could get away with hoodwinking the whole great powerful United States of Caucasian America? They would probably get wise to him pronto and exile him forever, and two or three years longer just for good measure, and he would be a fool without a country, and jolly England wouldn't let him in again. Guanaya would disown him even. He was the Great Goof of the nineteen eighties. They would slap him in jail and throw the key away, or tie it to a rabbit's tail and shoot at Brer Rabbit out on the wide Sahara, and charge Jimmy with espionage and sabotage and put him in the electric chair and sentence his dead body to life imprisonment—and—and—

The plane dropped a couple hundred yards straight down. Now that he was arriving, he had not only gotten cold feet, his entire body was freezing and covered with a damp cold sweat. He felt faint and nauseated like a pregnant woman's morning sickness—perhaps? The tip of his arse (as they would say in London) nibbled angrily at the airplane seat. His ass sucked wind (as they'd say in dear old 'Sippi). Could bite a ten-penny nail in two, his scared ass could have. If he'd had a parachute, he would've busted the damn window open and trusted his miserable luck. In any event he could not go through with this unpatriotic masquerade, this unconscionable treasonable sabotage. He felt his deeply loyal, often-flagging, red-blooded, Boy Scout American Legion–type born-again Christian Americans fiercely and profoundly now all inside him and choking him. He wanted to join up with Billy Graham, saintly singing in his choir. He wanted to wave the dear star-spangled banner so badly, he could hardly breathe. He looked sideways at Foreign Minister Mamadou Tangi's adamant face lost in his own deep thoughts, and the sarcastic smile that always seemed to lurk just beneath the surface of his polished ebony skin. Jimmy shook his head and shouted softly, without knowing, "No! No! I can't do it! Hell naw! I can't do it!"

Tangi stared out of his daydream at the bogus and fainthearted PM. "What is the problem, Your Excellency?"

"I can't go through with it! I can't go through with it! I must've been completely out of my cotton-picking mind to—!"

Mamadou Tangi said, without raising his voice, "You are out of your mind, if you think you can turn back at this late date, unless you leap out of that window."

Jimmy stared pleadfully almost tearfully at Tangi. Then the bogus PM looked out of the window. The city was below them now. White on white. Looming larger every second. Dollhouses becoming doghouses, becoming human dwelling places. Ants becoming cockroaches, becoming automobiles. But it was still too high for Jimmy Jay to jump.

The President of the USA stood there bravely in the cool breeze with the rest of his contingent, smiling with all his great benevolence. As the plane came in to land at the airport across the bridge in Virginia, Jimmy thought ironically about the colored poem. He could not remember the poet's name. "Carry me back to ol' Virginny. That's the only way you'll get me there." He grinned courageously.

On the ground a band started playing the people started cheering, but instead of sitting down and standing still, the plane sashayed way out on one of the landing strips and sat out there indifferently, snorting and puffing and blowing off steam, dust, and gravel, and then, and finally, it turned around and headed toward the place where all the thousands of people had gathered. The motor off, the steps put up, the red velvet carpet rolled out, and the President and his party stood there smiling and expectant. A couple of bands began to play "For He's a Jolly Good Fellow." The stage was set.

The door to the airplane opened and cheers went up from the wonderful American crowd of happily contented government workers, who had sacrificed an entire day from governmenting, but the first face at the door was a white one, and likewise was the second face (what tribe of African were these?) and then came the bewildered face of the Soviet ambassador. (He never got such a stateside welcome before in all his diplomatic life; he never had it so good, before or after.) But the fellows were good sports about it and continued to play "For He's a Jolly Good Fellow," which he obviously was. Some were puzzled by the strange lettering on the side of the monstrous airliner, which looked like Greek to them, and the hammer-and-sickled insignia, but what the hell— In any event he stood there living it up while he could, and smiling gaily and waving his big hat, which reminded you of Texas. Suddenly the welcome party of VIPs, including the especially beloved President, started moving swiftly toward another plane taxiing in from another landing strip. The crowds broke through the ropes and almost trampled the Soviet jolly-good fellow. Adulation is a many-fleeting-fickle-minded-thing, or something or other, as the saying used to go. And so be it.

The second plane turned out to be the one bearing the honest-to-goodness Africans and Jimmy Johnson, expatriate, Mississippi Negro, colored man, African American, bogus prime minister. Traitor? Assassin? Saboteur? Jimmy Johnson stood in the door of the cabin scared to death but smiling and hamming it up for the army of photographers and newsreel and television. Then he came jauntily down the steps flanked on one side by Lloyd and on the other by Tangi, as if they thought he might try to make a break and run for it, which was not a far-fetched possibility, but also which went to show you just how much they really trusted their dedicated Afro-American brother. He was highly indignant over that aspect of it. Insulted even. The rest of the party was a few inches behind him, alert and ever at the ready. The red carpet, which was literally pulled out from under the jolly good Soviet ambassador fellow's feet, was hurriedly rolled out again. And all the bands were playing "Jolly Good Fellow" again and this time they were sincere. But Jimmy felt neither good nor jolly. He felt scared.

The American government workers were cheering and waving again, the women oohing and the girls ahing, because the bogus PM, like the real McCoy, was dignifiedly handsome in any language in any culture. He was a cool kitty from the city, down with it and couldn't quit it, even though he would have loved to split it (the scene, that is). Anyhow, the policemen and SS persons had their hands full keeping the screaming shrieking crowd in line, especially the younger women and particularly the older women and the middle-aged ones, and the girls. They were beside themselves was what they were. It was worse than when the Beatles landed. Michael Jackson couldn't have topped it.

A group of African students from the colleges in Washington began to beat out a message of welcome on their ethnic drums, and Jimmy forgot where he was or who he was supposed to be. It got very confusing sometimes. The drums reached him, and he started to go into his sexy swivel-hipped Afro American version of the highlife, à la Belafonte, at which point he felt the point of a hard jab in his ribs from Tangi, and he suddenly remembered time and place and circumstance. But just as he was striking a posture of profound excellency-type African dignity, the twenty-one-gun salute began and almost made him put a puddle in his trousers a split second before he jumped out of them. But generally speaking, he was cool. Laid way back. Because that's the way he always was. Sangfroid every step of the way.

Jimmy and the President stood there shaking hands like they were priming a pump, as they worked desperately to upstage each other before newsreel and photographers and television. But the fake PM was much younger and slimmer and far more athletic and agile and had much cleverer footwork than the jolly obese President. Jimmy was an ex-athlete, a singer, which also meant he'd always been a frustrated actor, and this moment was his finest hour. He introduced his party to the Last of the Great White Fathers, with the aplomb and urbanity of one used to introducing ministers of African states to presidents of the United States. In the midst of it all, he thought to himself, here he was, a black cat who had just a few years ago managed an escape from the carefree life of dear ol' 'Sippi, where it was always easy-living summertime. Here he was matching wits and witticism with the Man Himself in person. If his poor dead Mama could see him now! Not to mention his poor lynched Papa. But why not mention his poor lynched Papa?

The President posing with him again and cameras grinding and popping all over the place, and the shortsighted thick-lensed Great White Man began to read his speech of welcome, holding the paper so close to his face he seemed to be rubbing his bulbously pointed nose with it. Welcoming the distinguished Prime Minister and "your official fu-fu-fu-fabulous party who have come from the grateful respectful, I mean greatly respected nation inspiring freedom-loving people everywhere. Come all the way to the very fu-fu-fu-fu fabulous rock-bound shores of liberty as represented by that fu-fu-fu-fabulous government of the people by the people and for the people which shall now perish from the fu-fu-fu-fu-fabulous earth." He held the paper away from his face, so that the photographers could shoot him. "I mean shall not fu-fu fu-fabulously perish, not now perish—"

As he stared at the amiable President and listened to his simple peasant-like sincerity, Jimmy's unpredictable sense of humor almost did him irreparable dirt. He had a way with him of looking you dead in the eye and mouth when you were talking to him, as if he saw every word as it left your brain and followed its course till it finally emerged from your lips. When you talked to him you were sure that you were being listened to. But he found it almost impossible to keep his eyes on the President's sincere face. Jimmy kept thinking, You're the President of the most powerful nation on earth and you don't know the difference between an African Prime Minister and a hungry Negro from Lolliloppi, Mississippi. All of us colored look alike. He struggled desperately to keep a straight face as he watched *his own* beloved President struggling desperately with the printed word. Paper up against his pimply nose one moment and away from his face the next. Any moment Jimmy would howl with laughter and fall down on the ground and kick up his heel and laugh and laugh till the tears flowed like the River 'Sippi. Don't let me laugh! Great God almighty from Lolliloppi, Near-the-Gulf! Don't let me laugh! He was scared to death that he would break up there and then, and the great Black hoax would be over before it ever really started.

"In the name of the freedom-loving fu-fu-fu-fabulous people of the United States—I—" The PRESIDENT PAUSED. He had lost his place again on the piece of paper in his trembling hand. Doesn't the poor chap know his own name? the bogus PM wondered. The Prexy found his name: "I, Hubert Herbert Hubert"—he glanced down at the paper again—"as President of the fu-fu-fu-fu-fabulous United States, welcome you to the community of the Free World and independent nations. I welcome you in the name of self-determination and brotherhood and the God in whom we trust." Poor fellow, he lost his place on the intelligence sheet again. Up against his obeliscal nose one more time. "And may your stay in our great country be a joyful and fruitful—one—bringing our two countries closer together in a bond of fellowship against totillitary—I mean totallytiri—I mean totalitarianism." The President took a handkerchief from his pocket and wiped the cold sweat from his brow.

The laughter at the irony of the situation, which Jimmy had fought to keep inside him, had moved from his aching stomach up through his chest and shoulders into his face and was spilling from his eyes. Jimmy's body began to shake, and he could not keep a smile from creasing his face, or the tears from spilling from his eyes. But he needn't have worried, because it was impossible for the president to believe he was being laughed at by an African. The President never entertained evil thoughts about his fellow man, especially if he was an African. He thought the young PM was crying because he had been so deeply moved by his speech's great sincerity and profundity. The President himself almost burst into tears. He thought: The Africans are such wonderful simple naive childish people. And so profoundly perceptive. Meanwhile Jimmy was getting himself together, and now he was alert and sharp as a double-edged blue-bladed safety razor (stainless steel), and he remembered that his great mission and his responsibility were much more important than his audacious sense of humor. He also remembered, belatedly, that when he was a boy a-way back yonder in good old Lolliloppi, he had been this great man's caddy, years before folks had known he was a great man. The President had called him "Hot Shot." And "Hot Shot" he had been until he left Lolliloppi. They'd spent a few weekends on the golf course together on successive summers. The wind was biting now as it swept across the airport, and the President wondered at the PM's perspiration-covered face. What was an African doing sweating in chilly weather? He also was trying to place the young Prime Minister's familiar face. Where had they met before? If ever? The voice—the face—the manner—in Europe maybe? Paris? During the Great War? In London?

Jimmy was tongue-tied for another moment as the whole world held its breath on radio and television. Finally, he said in accents more British than Guanayan (perhaps West Indian?), "I cannot find words to express how profoundly I was moved by the sincerity of your welcome to us, Mr. President." And the President believed him with all his heart. (Bless his heart.) The Prexy's problem was he was essentially a bashful

man, shy and reticent, and full of that innate modesty
that always characterized truly great men, like Julius
Caesar and Napoleon and Stalin and Eisenhower and
Churchill and Adam Clayton and, and never mind. He
did not realize the power of his own words, his ability
to move people deeply. He thought himself (and accurately) to be a horrible speaker, a terrible reader even,
and did not like to speechify. But it was obvious even
to this humble soul that he had reached a new plateau
of depth this time. Let his cabinet members snicker in
their hankies if it suited them. (Hide his dildo, would
they?) Let Burt Lancaster lose his patience. (Lancaster
was his speaking coach.) He thought, Let's face it,
Mr. President. You're so modest you're actually twice
as good as you think you are.

The fake PM continued, "To us the representatives
of a great and proud people who realize, along with you,
that the most impelling force on earth is human dignity. We come from a nation old in tradition but young
in independence. The sky is the limit for our potentials, and though the road to progress will be rocky, we
will inevitably find our way. With the help of Almighty
God and the fellowship of nations, especially yours,
and particularly all the others, and peace on earth, we
shall ultimately triumph. And we shall triumph swiftly.
We shall over—"

The President mumbled, "Yes-yes," like he was shouting softly from deep in the Amen Corner of Friendship Baptist Tabernacle. The President was a down-home boy from the Middle Belt, a natural rustic to the core. His religion was of the old-time variety. Always had been. Although oftentimes he tended to the Modern View.

"Our people," the fake PM continued, "have suffered long, but now we are free, and just as your country has never ever done, we likewise will never follow the dictates of a foreign power—no matter how big that country might be—no matter how powerful—no matter how rich—" He felt his Vice-PM tugging anxiously at his boubou. "No matter how—no matter how—" A vicious jab in the ribs from Tangi this time, and his voice trailed off into nothingness. There was a great clamor of silence for a moment and Jimmy thought humbly of the Gettysburg Address, with all humility, naturally. Frederick Douglass's Fourth of July speech was his favorite. Then came the wild thundering applause and the photographers taking more pictures and the perspiration of relief raining from all over him.

He needed a drink. Where was the palm wine?

And now the rest of the nation's leaders were passing in review to be introduced to the PM and his entourage, the colored leaders last in line. Naturally? The pale-faced icy-eyed Undersecretary of State made Jimmy's stomach turn head over heels (heels over head?), as he stood there shaking Jimmy's hand and staring at the bogus PM and through him like he was looking for his chauffeur who had previously flown the coop. The last Negro leader also made him nervous. Gazing at him long and hard, as if to say, "Are you for real?" Suddenly Jimmy knew that one of the gravest dangers of discovery was that one of his own people, some African American, would see through his disguise and give him away, unintentionally or otherwise.

After the last colored leader came a chubby jovial round-faced man who extended his hand and spoke to Jimmy with a Russian accent. He was the jolly good Soviet ambassador, recently and fleetingly the object of the great crowd's adulation, albeit short lived. And Jimmy thought to himself: Everybody's getting into the act. I am an *important* colored man. Why fight it any longer? A Secret Service man almost knocked the friendly-faced Russian's arm off, and two of them tried to hustle him away. But Jimmy's fast footwork put him in good stead again, or bad stead, depending on your point of view. He moved quickly and pushed the panama-hatted serious-faced young SS gentleman gently but firmly away, and he took the Ambassador's hand, took the red-faced President's hand, and he put all three of their right hands together and raised them in an unmistakable sign of solidarity and fellowship and friendship and peace on earth and all the other platitudes. The cameras and the newsreels and the TV snapped and ground away again, the wonderful crowd applauded, knowing and mostly not knowing who the third party was. And caring less—what the hell—"A man ain't nothing but a man—" Somebody said, sometimes some place. John Henry was a steel-driving man. Or was it Harry Belafonte? Paul Robeson perhaps?

Be that as it may, the next day the opposition party in the US Congress accused the guiltless President of open-faced appeasement. This infamous photo went out all over the world and caused a mild panic among the nations of NATO and SEATO, of the Warsaw Pact, and of the long-since forgotten Bandung Conference even. And the rumor ran wild that the USA and the USSR had concluded a unilateral treaty with Guanaya, which obviously created an ominous threat to the peace of the world. Wall Street went up and down and sideways. And the world went to the brink again.

Notwithstanding, after the infamous clench was over, the bands all played Yankee Doodle dandily, and the great crowd shouted and waved and jumped up and down and cheered, they were just tremendous; the President uncovered his wispy head and waved that famous hat of his and his party followed suit, and Jimmy wondered when in the hell he was going to get off this spot at the chilly sweaty airport (he needed a good stiff drink), but then the bands played "The Star-Spangled Banner," which was for some weird reason the American anthem (He preferred "My Country, 'Tis of Thee"), and the hats off again and over the heart, this time, and then the national anthem of Guanaya and hats off and over the heart *one more time*. And then it happened. One of the bands felt real down-home good and started playing *DIXIE*! And there was waving of hats and even throwing of hats up in the air this time, and boisterous rebel yells from the wonderfully responsive crowd, temporarily gone wild with their enthusiasm now. What love they had for dear old Dixie! One Caucasian lady threw her brand-new baby in the air like it was up for grabs. Everybody singing, excepting most of the colored people, who acted as if they'd never heard the song.

Den I wish I was in Dixie
Away away
In Dixieland I took my stand
To live and die in Dixie—

Confused now, the members of the Prime Minister's party uncovered their heads again, as did the American President and all of his party excepting one embarrassed Negro leader. But the bogus PM's fez remained stubbornly on his own head. *His Wife's Bottom*, Mr. Lloyd, the very nervous Vice-PM, tried slyly to remove the PM's elegant fez and got his hand slapped hard for his trouble. This far Jimmy Johnson would not go, not for all of Africa's Uhuru. The embarrassed Negro leader of the American President's party cased the situation and trotted nervously from the back of the contingent toward his beloved Prexy. Jimmy Johnson leaned toward the President and said, "What nation's anthem is that, Your Highness? What and who and where is Dixie? And why does everybody want to go there? And why don't they if they really do?"

Before his red-faced majesty could answer Jimmy, the un-uncovered colored leader reached him. But the ever-vigilant SS men intercepted him and might have roughed him up a bit, had not the President interceded.

"Let him through," the President ordered. "That's Mr. Percy."

Mr. Percy finally bared his head and whispered to the great man, suggesting politely that maybe and perhaps this was possibly not quite the kind of song the PM of Guanaya would most probably appreciate, didn't he think or didn't he? Witness the circumstantial evidence of the PM's head remaining covered. The President thanked Mr. Percy and turned and witnessed. Then he put his hat back on his head and sent one of his SS men a-running toward the "Dixie"-playing bands. After that, Dixie'd had it, and the bands jumped lively into the BATTLE HYMN OF THE REPUBLIC. At which time Jimmy forgot again who he was supposed to be and started singing in his very best voice a powerfully robust JOHN BROWN'S BODY. The President was startled for a moment. Who wouldn't be? But then the PM leaned toward him and said smilingly, "One of our favorite freedom songs in Guanaya. Yes indeed, we really like your 'John Brown's Body.'" And the President joined in, to the best of his ability, which wasn't much, but sincerity he certainly had his portion of it, and the rest of his party sang nervously and tentatively about old John Brown, their faces carrot colored with embarrassment, excepting of course, the colored contingent, whose faces did not could not turn the color of overripened carrots at the singing of JOHN BROWN'S BODY, for various and diverse reasons, most of them rather obvious. The PM's party also sang, which feat was miraculous, since they'd never heard the song before.

And now they were in the long limousines, Secret Service men in the first car, the PM and the Prexy in the second car, which was an open convertible, SS, men alongside on custom-made running boards, driving a cross the bridge toward Washington, where the great cheering waving crowds of jubilant Americans lined both sides of the broad boulevard. Particularly the girls and women folk.

"There he is—Mr. Maki!"

"Ooh!—Looka there—ain't he pretty!"

"Just as cute as a speckled puppy!"

"Can I have him for Christmas, Daddy?" a little lady of the middle ages screamed to no one in particular.

"Handsome as a moom pitcha star!"

One colored lady waved her hand and shouted proudly, "He is Black and sure is comely, oh you pale-faced Jezebels! Hands off that pretty colored man!"

"Your eyes may shine. Your teeth may grit. But none of that pretty man will you git!"

The PM and the Prexy smiling and waving back at the crowd as they rode down Fourteenth Street past the Bureau of Engraving buildings, where they made those little pieces of paper coated with chlorophyll each with a pretty picture of a past American President.

Jimmy forgot who he was again and said to the great man sotto voce, "Like where're we going now, old baby?" He really needed a drink now. And bad!

The great man stared at Jimmy with a shocked expression. Jimmy laughed and poked the Prexy in the ribs, playfully, with his elbow. "I'm only kidding, Your Majesty, Your Grace. We see a lot of your Hollywood movies, old chap, and read too many of your beatnik novels, I suspect. That is the thing."

The great man was still speechless. And Jimmy thought, Mr. Charlie is trying to remember where he saw my face before. If he calls me "Hot Shot" I'm going to jump out of this car and catch the plane back to Guanaya, I mean *the one that just left!* Jimmy said, "What I mean, Your Majesty, is I should jolly well like very much to get to my hotel as quickly as possible. Fright fully bushed, don't you know? The trip, and the emotional stress of just being here in your great country and the welcome at the airport and all that sort of thing. It's something I would never have dreamed of three months ago in all my wildest nightmares." The fake PM did not know what made him say to the President, "By the way, Mr. President, if there are any bugs in our lodgings, please have them removed *tout suite,* before we arrive. Fumigate exterminate the place for bugs. We get very very bugged with bugs. We go wild with anger. It's a national superstition. If there's a bug within a mile of the place, we will know it. Our nostrils are naturally radared for insects, man-made or otherwise."

The simple-hearted president said, "But, Your Excellency, we wouldn't think of bugging your fuh-fun-fun-fabulous lodgings. I can assure you. I mean—"

He was cut short by the expression on the PM's face. He was gone. His eyes were glazed and yet opaque. As if he had suddenly left the presence of the President. Perhaps he was back in Africa. Listening absorbedly to a different drummer. The PM seemed possessed. Like "coming through" in the Friendship Baptist Tabernacle. Suddenly his eyes lit up. The President tried to continue. "Your fuck-fu-fu-fabulous Excellency, how could you think that—"

The PM shouted to the President, "Hold it! Shh! Quiet!" Then he said to the Invisible One, "You're coming in loud and clear. Loud and clear! Like a Sunday church bell deep in the bush. You don't mean! Just as I suspected. Well I declare! Ciao! Signing off. Uhuru."

He turned to the befuddled President. "With all due respect, Mr. President. I just made contact with my Juju man back in Bamakanougou. The doctor tells me the suite is definitely bugged. You may be totally innocent and ignorant, of the fact, that is. But the suite is crawling with bugs, so much so that they may fly away with the place. It's happened many times before."

The President mopped his feverish brow. "Surely you don't expect me to believe you were really in fu-fu-fu-fabulous communication with Africa?"

"You don't believe me, Mr. President? You want me to put you on the phone with Him or Her, because it has no special gender? The 'phone' of course is an idiomatic euphemism for the direct connection. You want to speak to the baddest meanest one in Africa?"

The President was leaking perspiration. "No-no—Of course not. I do not doubt you for a single moment."

The totally bewildered President reached for the telephone. "Carson, this is the President."

"I'd be happy to connect you with the doctor, Mr. President. It wouldn't take more than five minutes at the outside even through a harmattan. Just say the word."

Sweat was foaming the President's forehead. Obviously, he was frightened shitless. The President was screaming now. "See that His Excellency's lodging accommodations are cleanly swept of any intelligence apparatus whatsoever. See to it immediately." Not that a President of the United States would ever believe in Juju or Black magic or whatever, but just in case—

"But Mr. President!"

"No goddamn fucking bugs, Carson. Dammit! Get it done immediately!" The President turned to the fake PM and patted him on the knee assuringly.

"We also have our communication system." Jimmy remembered Old Blue Eyes of his London days.

"Everybody to his own Juju, we always say back home."

The President sat back partially relaxed. "Yes—yes, of course, of course." Perspiration of relief was pouring from him. "You remind me so much of somebody I knew somewhere some fu-fu-fu-fabulous place sometime—" His voice trailed off. And Jimmy remembered the moment three-and-one-half months before, when he first set foot on African soil. He was forever reminding somebody of somebody else. It would one day be his great undoing. And maybe that day was not far off. He settled back in the limousine and closed his eyes. To hell with it.

In the car behind him Carlton Carson of the Secret Service shook his head and said to the Secretary of State, "I can't put my finger on it but there's something definitely fishy about that boy."

The Secretary turned to him smilingly. "What boy?" he asked absentmindedly.

"That Prime Minister Olivamaki feller. There's something about him not quite right. Something downright un-American."

The Secretary said absently, "Un-American?"

Carson said, "He's up there right now working some kind of voodoo or Black magic on our beloved President."

11

JIMMY JOHNSON NEVER HAD IT SO GOOD. At the tough and tender age of twelve, to be an orphan without pot or window, chicken or child. (But enough of the pathos bit.) He would have none of it. He was made of the heroic stuff of the epic and the tragique, despite his latent chicken-heartedness, which would flare up, occasionally. He would have been an inspiration to Willy Shakespeare. Footballed and scholarshiped and sang and caddied and glibly bee-essed his way through high school and all the seats of higher learning. (He did time in three or four of them.) A long stretch here and a short stretch there. A touchdown here—a field goal there. A bases-loaded home run over there somewhere. Then he finally put those kinds of gigs down and did his doctoral work at the University of the Real World and often it was cold outside, from Mississippi to the Golden State of Hollywood to New York City to London Town. In between was Vietnam. Operation Boot Strap and Jockstrap too. Shamelessly, he jocked himself through quite a mess of lassies from the foggy smog of LA to the smoggy fog of London Town, as he looked for himself in all these far-flung widespread places. His machismo was more bluff than tough. But then, and ultimately, and maybe even inevitably, suddenly, all roads led to Africa. And Bam! Wham! Damn! Thank-you Mama! There was Bamakanougou all the while! And Club Lido! And, baby, baby, look at you now.

A suite that ran the length of the fifth floor in the posh and plush of the gaudiest most expensive hotel in Washington, Das Capital. There was no doubt about it, he was the most sought-after man in the USA. He thought, They're soughting after you all right, Buster, and if and when they find you, you'll be up six creeks without a paddle. Coming up on the hotel elevator he thought how easy it would be to give his everlasting uhuru-loving African brothers the everlasting slip. The show had just been put on the road and already he was beginning to feel the strain. He could feel his brothers and sister staring at him as they listened to the endless chatter of Carlton Carson of the Secret Service and

Jack Parkington of the State Department, who would be their escorts everywhere they went during their sojourn in the USA. After the show out at the airport and the ride into the city, Jimmy had suddenly crawled into his shell and clammed up. But he was thinking. He was thinking. He could shed his disguise (dark glasses and phony beard) and his African brothers in the same breath and catch himself a whole heap of train ride and make it to the City, his city, favored tenderly by him above all other cities, with the possible exception of Bamakanougou. Despite the pain and disappointments he had known there, New York Town was still his city, and he could lose himself all over the place. The first chance he got, he would split the scene completely is what, and let these frantic ethnic cabinet ministers face these brass bands by themselves. He owed nothing to Guanaya. Repeat: He was no hero. He never ever claimed to be.

When they reached the suite, Carson and Parkington of the US government entered with them, bowing, and scraping like proper Uncle Toms or Hollywood yes-men (they were the same breed, only different colors), sycophants, all. Armed guards stood on each side of the entrance to the suite. Jimmy knew sycophancy in all colors and disguises. Having Uncle-Tommed once or twice himself in this life (show him a Black American who hadn't), he had witnessed the white counterparts in the movie capital, where they were a couple hundred grand a dozen, the best arse-kissers that money could buy.

When they were inside the suite, the fake PM came back to life even as he witnessed the carryings-on of Carlton Carson, grinning and obsequious, unadulterated Southern drawl and "Anything we can do for y'all Excellencies. Just anything at all. We are entirely at y'all's disposal."

Jimmy spoke to Lloyd in some very rapid and raggedy-assed-makeshift Hausa. "Tell him he can order us some whiskey and soda on his way out. That's what he can do for us. *On his way out.*" He always sprinkled his Hausa with a heavy portion of Americanese and Negritude. Afro-Americanese, Mr. Lloyd broke down a rough translation of some very rough Hausa and relayed it politely to Parkington and Carson. Always Mr. Lloyd was the epitome of courtesy. His Wife's-Inevitable-Bottom.

Carson bowed and Frenchly replied, "*Certainement!*" for some peculiar reason, and with Southern accent yet, since Guanaya had never been a French colony. Carson sank into one of the club chairs with a sweet smile on his alcoholic face.

Jimmy spoke in his potluck Hausa again, and

Mr. Lloyd timidly explained to the two American gentlemen that when His Excellency the Prime Minister got very tired, he spoke in Hausa only. So please excuse him. And also, please excuse him until later this evening, at the White House reception, because they all were very tired. Whereupon Lloyd and Tangi very politely ushered the bewildered Americans out of their suite and into the hall and closed the door in their flabbergasted faces.

They stood for a moment outside the door among the armed sentry and could not believe that it had happened to them. In those quaint days white people found it impossible to believe that people of color would under any circumstances not be honored by their company. White folks were paranoid in that respect. They took Black rejection very hard. Carson was fuming, livid even. He said, "Well if that don't beat Bob-tail and Bob-tail beat the devil! Of all the black and uncouth arrogance!"

Parkington said, "I don't know about that. I assume they were really tired. They've had a hard day. Didn't you ever suffer from jet lag?"

Carlton Carson said, "I sure would like to see them when they think nobody's looking. Trying to pretend like they're not colored."

Parkington told him patiently but firmly,

"Mr. Carson, you're in charge of this security operation. It must go off without incident, or heads will roll, I warn you, Carson. The Secret Service must at all times be on hand, but unobtrusive. This is your most important assignment so far. Don't goof it."

"There's something fishy about them, especially that Olivamaki fellow. My nose don't never lead me up no dark alleys. Some thing's rotten in Guanaya. There's a nigrah in the woodpile just as sure as old Rob Lee sitting up there in Heaven. We ought to wire the place again for sound, don't care what the President say."

"No wiretapping," Parkington said firmly. "The President just gave specific orders, that it be swept clean and kept that way. Africans have a loathing for wiretapping. They are plagued by so many varieties of bugs at home, they are terribly bugged if ever they find out they're being bugged. So, forget your infernal nostrils this time. And another thing, in dealing with Africans you must overlook their color. You must never regard them as Negroes. You must deal with them as people. Dignitaries."

Carson said, "Oh—" As if he had just learned something of tremendous value and profundity. Something that would go with him and stand by him forevermore. One of these days he would be as smart as Parkington and join the State Department. Meanwhile something was fishy in the woodpile in Guanaya. He didn't care what nobody said. He didn't even care if he got his metaphors fucked up.

Inside the suite Jimmy collapsed on a deeply softened silk-covered couch and almost submerged out of sight. A great nervous exhaustion moved through every limb of his body. Suddenly he leaped from the couch and looked under cushions, behind pictures, looked under toilet seats, flushed the toilet, and watched the flow. He put Mr. Lloyd's hat over the telephone.

Turned on the stereo, turned it up loud. Then he took off his beard and flung it without looking across the room and it landed in a wastebasket. He fell into an easy chair. He heaved sigh after sigh after sigh. He looked around him at his eager-faced cabinet ministers and he started to laugh loud and boisterously, and he couldn't stop laughing. They laughed with him, at first, tentatively, but when he didn't stop, they got worried. Mr. Harold Tobey, his personal secretary, brought him a glass of water. He shook his head. "I need something stronger than that." And he continued to laugh with the tears spilling down his cheeks, as he lay full length on the sofa now.

His secretary called room service and the anxious Mr. Lloyd retrieved the PM's phony whiskers and stood over Jimmy shush-shushing him. Foreign Minister Tangi, the impatient one, came over to the laughing fake PM and shook him roughly and actually drew back to slap him. Whereupon Jimmy stopped laughing, abruptly, and sat up on the sofa. There would be no slapping of His Excellency. It was not that kind of a party, masquerade or otherwise. And Jimmy was all right as long as he kept his mouth shut, but when he tried to talk, to explain, he started to laugh again and then he was laughing and talking at the same time, mostly laughing. When the whiskey came, he took a drink, which seemed to help. Then he tried to talk again but instead went off immediately into peals and peals of laughter. He stretched out on the couch and held his stomach, as the members of His Excellency's Cabinet gathered around him and above him and stared down at him and looked anxiously at each other. Maria Efwa took his hand and patted it and rubbed it, and finally he stopped laughing.

Jimmy said, "I got a Great White Father and you people got a Great White Mother, and they don't know us one from the other." He started to laugh again and this time they all joined in the laughter. As the laughter slowly died away, he was still holding Maria Efwa's hand. But when his grip began to tighten a warmth crept into Maria's face and she firmly took her hand from his.

His eyes had been closed but he opened them when

he felt her withdrawal. He felt it sharply and he stared up into her lovely face. "How did I do today, my colleagues? My brothers and my sisters? How was my performance?" He knew the question was for her especially. She also understood. He wanted her approval.

Mamadou Tangi said, "You did a bloody good job, Your Excellency, especially considering the few days you have been in office."

"Thank you very much indeed," Jimmy said to Tangi.

His Wife's Bottom agreed. "An excellent job, except that you overdid it with your 'Brown John's Body' and the Soviet ambassador." And Lloyd would have been off on one of his inevitable talkathons, had not Jimmy held up the palm of his hand like a traffic cop and turned from him and addressed himself directly to Maria Efwa. "And what did you think, my illustrious teacher?"

"You did rawther well," she answered, "except that your accent was more British than Guanayan. You talked as if your nostrils were clogged. Do you have an allergy?"

He made a face and said, "By Jove! It was those blawsted ruddy months I spent in England being Londonized. Everybody knows the British speak the way they do because they stuff English peas up their bloody nostrils to keep out all that horrendous weather."

Her lovely face creased in a dimpled smile against her will.

"Whose fault is it if I talk Britishly? You and you alone have the patriotic duty to make me over, and moreover, make me more Guanayan than any other Guanayan including His-one-and-only-Excellency, Jaja Olivamaki himself. And you must teach me all at once and everything about your country. No?"

The lovely dimpled one said, "Yes."

He rose from the couch with an obvious effort that was just as obviously exaggerated, and he took her hands in his again.

"Your success with me," he told her, "is crucial to the success of our venture, which is crucial to the success of Guanaya, which is crucial to the success of Pan-Africanism, which is—"

"Yes," she said. "Yes-Yes-Yes!" He could not tell whether she was angry or pleased with him. He would not believe she was indifferent.

"I know you don't approve of me, your-lovely-ladyship. I don't blame you. I don't approve of myself, but I'm the best that you can do until the real thing comes along. So, you must spend every minute of your pretty precious time with your bogus Prime Minister. No?"

She said, "Yes. But I'm not your-lovely-ladyship. I am the Minister of Education."

He laid it on with a heavy trowel. "I have never in all my life undertaken a venture fraught with such great danger and at the same time such magnificence. No?"

She agreed. "For the magnificent cause of African freedom."

Jimmy countered with, "For you and Africa. For beauty and magnificence." He was half bee-essing and half serious. He himself did not know where one stopped and the other began. Nor did he want to know. Maria Efwa, like Africa, was beautiful and magnificent. Their eyes held each other's momentarily.

She liberated her hands from the pressure of his warm hands, getting hotter every second. "For Africa," she said firmly. "We must not lose our perspective. We must not confuse our mission."

"There's no confusion on my part, Your Ladyship. You and Africa are one and the same." He was suddenly sharply aware of the others watching them now, watching anxiously. He turned to them and said cavalierly, "Come on already. Let us drink to our noble venture in this Western jungle."

"I am neither your ladyship or my ladyship, or his, hers, or its ladyship," Her Ladyship insisted, as Mr. Tobey poured up the booze. Jimmy held his glass toward them, particularly toward Her-Lovely-Ladyship, Maria Efwa. "To Her Excellency Maria Efwa and to African freedom. To the symbol and the reality!" And before there could be protest, if any, he added the magic word, "Uhuru!"

And they all joined in and said, "Uhuru!" This time with feeling.

He took another drink and said, "Up the Republic of Pan-Africa!"

They said, "Uhuru!" And once again with feeling.

He took another drink and shouted, "Up the Pan-Africanists—Up the PAs!"

And he reached for another drink, but Tangi moved the booze from out of his reach.

Tangi said unsmilingly, "It's time for you to get some rest, Your Excellency. We have a reception tonight at the Executive Mansion, or do you chaps call it the White House?"

Jimmy smiled at Tangi arrogantly. "What do you mean—you chaps? Don't you recognize your leader? I am His Excellency Prime Minister Jaja Okwu Olivamaki of the Independent People's Democratic Republic of Guanaya. And don't you ever forget it, buster."

12

1 600 Pennsylvania was the address of the White House, which was no military secret. The White House was white, of course, and large and vast and pretentious, in a kind of modest context.

The White House was also brilliantly lighted—that's for sure—and most of the people were lit inside the White House in that fabulous East Room with its dazzling Bohemian cut glass chandeliers overhead and its oaken floor of Fontainebleau parquetry gleaming underfoot. Everybody was there that memorable night. They had eaten with the special chosen few in the State Dining Room, exactly one hundred of Washington's elite, a room that sparkled in gold and white with the portrait of a brooding Lincoln staring at them from above the fireplace. Then into the East Room, where hundreds gathered and drank and talked and drank and talked. And *Ebony* and *Jet* took pictures. Along with *Time* and the *New York Times* and *Look* and *Life* and *Newsweek*, and so forth and so on.

Earlier that evening when he'd arrived, with the admiring mob outside the gates, and as he went toward the big white mansion, he'd thought to himself that this was really *the* Big House, constructed, specifically and intentionally, in the antebellum tradition of the old plantation Big Houses, in all of its elegant and plantation splendor, with tall Georgian columns done in gleaming pinkish white, as was all the exterior. He remembered them as a boy, he'd seen them still there, relics of another time, deep in among the stately oaks deep into the 'Sippi bayous. It was an awe-compelling structure. The President was lord and mass'r. Even as a boy, he would imagine soft honeysuckled summer evenings in the "good old days" of slavery, with music floating on the air. Wrought by Black slave music makers, and field hands gathered in the front yards singing glad songs to old mass'r and his gentlemen and lady friends. He had never lived comfortably with these optical illusions of the days of sweet nostalgia, the good ol' times of honeysuckled happy and contented slaves, gone with the wind in the Uncle Thomas's cabin, him and little Eva, and sensitive Willie Faulkner and Hattie McDaniel. It had always seemed unreal to him.

Jimmy Johnson, the Fake, as he thought of himself of late, quite bitterly and introspectively, ate and drank and talked at length with the pleasant-faced President, Hubert Herbert Hubert, who was a living doll, plump and jolly and serious minded, and nearsighted and who could hold his whiskey with the best of them, and Jimmy Johnson (colored) was the best of them, when it came to holding his whiskey, or anybody else's, for that matter. Lloyd and Tangi were ever by his side, especially when he was talking with the President. You might have thought they didn't trust him; that is, if you didn't know they didn't trust him. The other cabinet members floated. Circulated?

Later in the evening the President's tongue got heavy, as he told Jimmy Johnson for the umpteenth time, "This is a social evening, Mr. Prime Meneceter, but I want you to know, we think of your fuh-fuh-fuh-fabulous country as the bulwark of democracy against godless communism, even though I loathe the renewal of the Cold War situation."

The more whiskey the President drank, Jimmy thought, the thicker his tongue became. His jolly red-nosed chubby face reminded Jimmy Jay of the friendly-faced Premier Nikita Khrushchev.

Notwithstanding, Hubert Herbert Hubert continued unabated. "And with certain democratic provisional provisos and assurances and Free World commitments, but with no strings attached, we are ready, willing, and able to give all kinds of assistance, financial, educational, technical"—he cleared his throat—"and especially we are willing to help you get that cobanium out of the ground just as quick as we possibly can. But again, I want to rest assure you, I mean you to rest assured, this is a social party kind of party."

His Wife's Bottom, Mr. Lloyd, was about to put his tuppence in, at this point, but Jimmy was faster on the draw, particularly due to the fact that His Wife's Bottom usually cleared his throat before beginning, which put him at a disadvantage with a cat like Jimmy who had a faster draw than Sammy Davis Jr. Jimmy leaped into the throat-clearing vacuum feetfirst. "In the name of the great Guanayan people I want to thank you, Mr. President for your generous offer and your warm assurances, especially with no strings attached. This is the way nations must conduct themselves with one another in the spirit of equality and true democracy."

George Jefferson Davis Huey Jr. was the senior senator from Alabama and he stood close by the President, even though he was short in stature. At fully extended height he was like a catcher squatting behind home plate. He always walked around in an attitude of bowel movement. He had a great red mop of hair atop his head so red it seemed to be afire. When he was a little boy other little mischievous devils used to ring fire alarms to put his hair out. His nose was as red and as incandescent as the beloved Prexy's. He said pleasantly, "I believe in putting my cards on the table faceup, Your Highness. Are there any Commonists in your government?"

Except for the clearing of nervous throats and coughs of embarrassment and shuffling of fidgety feet, it became suddenly so quiet you could have heard Mickey Mouse urinating on new-fallen snow in the Rockies just outside Denver. But the suave PM was unperturbed. He smiled charmingly down at the jovial senior senator. They also used to call the senator Shed-House Shorty that year he went to college. "Senator Hooey," Jimmy answered, mispronouncing the Senator's name accidentally on purpose, "in the name of the great Guanayan people I plead the First and Fifth Amendments and with no strings attached." He threw back his head and roared with laughter, which was the signal for everybody within earshot to laugh, for after all he was His Excellency, the guest of honor. They were standing beneath a full-length portrait of the father of the great country. Old George stood there, his right hand extended, in frock coat and black knickers.

The senator's red face turned as white as a Ku Klux Klansman's sheet.

"The name is Huey, Your Highness. Senator George Jefferson Davis Huey Jr."

"Pleased to meet you Senator Hoo-ey." The PM deliberately murdered the senior senator's name again.

His Wife's Bottom, Mr. Lloyd, cleared his throat and said that he agreed wholeheartedly with Their Respective Excellencies. This was not the time or place to discuss business or politics. This was a social reception. "And now that the air has been cleared so notably and profoundly by you, Mr. President and you, Mr. Prime Minister, the exploration of details may be left to your subordinates."

The Prime Minister turned to Mr. Lloyd and bowed slightly. "I couldn't agree with you more, Mister Lloyd." He almost called the Vice-PM "His Wife's Bottom." Then with an aristocratic flourish, that did honor and great dignity to a man of his apparent station, the PM shook the President's hand and the hands of a few others and excused himself and turned and moved toward greener pastures. He became bored very quickly with people like Senator Hoo-ey.

He had always had a quick getaway in football, in track, in trouble with the police or with some woman's misunderstanding husband. He moved so quickly this time he left Tangi and His Wife's Bottom stranded with President Hubert Herbert Hubert and company, as he drifted through the vast unpretentious brilliantly lighted ballroom. Sparkling chandeliers and equally sparkling people of all colors and nationalities, even including Negro leaders. Jimmy's eyes took in everything and every living human as he moved with grace and majesty in his long white flowing boubou. He moved past the raised platform where an orchestra was playing genteel music, softly, sweetly. He was aware of the tall stately windows with the white lace curtains and the golden damask draperies. In a way though his eyes saw nothing, because he was looking frantically for Maria Efwa, who, herself, was in the powder room. He stopped momentarily to take a drink from a tray of one of the African American waiters who were dressed in white coats and black trousers and were circulating among the guests.

As soon as he stopped, he was surrounded by a group of admiring people, especially women, who shook his hand and talked with him about this and that and mostly nothing, and he was equally as eloquent. He remembered some of their faces because he had shaken some of their hands already when he stood in line with the President and the First Lady and his own entourage during the first hour of the reception. He stood there now, smiling charmingly, his mind wandering even as he stared at those worshipful ones around him, as if he were totally absorbed by them and with them, his adoring public. He was thinking about the thousands of people especially young ones and the middle-aged ones and the elderly ones, who had stood outside the Big House, pinkish white, for hours just for one glimpse of him, and had said, "Ooooooh!" in unison, as he had driven up in an open long black limousine. Some had even swooned, and he had waved for the briefest second, nonchalantly, three fingers turned down briefly, like the Queen does, and then there was another *Ooooooooh* even longer than the other one, and he had turned from them as he had been driven swiftly up the driveway to the Big White House. The same thing had happened when he'd left the hotel that evening. It was worse than Frank Sinatra or Harry Belafonte. It was ridiculous! It was simply terrible! He hated it. And he loved the hell out of it.

Actually, he was human, so he loved adoration, especially when it was aimed at him. He hated it, he told himself, but he suffered quietly. He ate it up, actually. He'd always wanted to be a "moving pitcher" star like

Belafonte or Poitier or Sammy or Ossie Davis, and he didn't believe in segregated thinking (crow jim) jim crow in reverse, so he'd always wanted to be a movie star like Marlon Brando and Robert Redford and Burt Reynolds. And why not? He'd, since memory, been a handsome bloke, and since he obviously had this latent sex appeal, why in holy hell not? Where had modesty gotten him? If any?

Just as he came out of his daydream visit to Holly-wood back to the brilliant reality of the dazzling East Room of the White House, one fair lady, blond and placid faced, said to him graciously, "Of course you are undoubtedly from one of those African tribes, Your Excellency? I mean, with all your *savoir faire*, your suavity and urbanity, I mean you're incredibly handsome and you're debonair and you're terribly sophisticated. Yet and still—" She laughed ecstatically. "I mean—" "Tittered" would have been a more precise description of what she did so elegantly. "Does your tribe practice cannibalism?"

He looked up and beyond the tittering lady, at the full-length portrait of Martha Washington in a long white gown. He thought, amusingly, she might be eavesdropping. He smiled back at the excited lady and at the group around them with equal portions of suavity and urbanity and a slight dash of sardonic bitters.

"*Mais certainement, madame. Vous avez raison.*" Why was he always speaking his half-assed French? Perhaps Martha was a ghostly spy. "I am descendent historically from a long illustrious line of distinguished missionary eaters. Our special tribal *pièce de résistance* is missionary stew *au gratin.*" He stared at her and licked his lips. "Cannibalism is one of the principal qualifications for prime ministership."

The little lady paled, as the powder on her face vanished suddenly and her tiny eyes grew large and wide, and she panicked momentarily, as did others in the group around them. As a matter of fact, the lady swooned.

Meanwhile the group around the President had dispersed and over in a corner of this proud but unpretentious salon, this brightly lit gymnasium, Senator Huey of Alabama and Carlton Carson of the Secret Service and Parkington of the State Department had their heads together.

Senator Huey was holding forth. "I still say something didn't smell right out at that there airport today. And when my nose leads me to a tree there's bound to be a possum up it every time. Three things prove it. One: he didn't like our Southern National Anthem."

Parkington said belligerently, "I don't like your

Southern National Anthem either. What does that make me?"

Huey said, losing color, "Two: he was singing over 'John Brown's Body.' And Three: he had the President and the Russian ambassador shaking hands, and that's an ominous threat to the peace of the Free World. Suppose all of a sudden, every American and every Russian started shaking hands unilaterally? Can't you see the dire consequences of the kind of avanty-gardie symbolism Olivamake was perpetrating out yonder at the airport this afternoon? It could get outa hand and run hog wild."

Even liberal-minded Parkington was stunned by such an overpowering image. Carlton Carson, himself, was speechless—temporarily.

Senator Huey held forth. "This here symbolism is more subversive that that damn white dove Picasso painted." He worked himself into a fury. "It's—it's—it's—it's downright un-American! It—it could lead to almost any damn thing! Think of it! Everybody all over the world shaking hands unilaterally!" He was ashen and unnerved by the flights of his own fancy.

"The whole damn performance looked like Commonist infiltration to me," Carlton Carson of SS growled after he recuperated.

Parkington of the State Department also recuperated and still insisted vigorously, "Forget your stupid nose, Senator, and your symbolisms, you're barking up the wrong damn tree, as usual."

Huey's eyes were wide with fear. He wiped the sweat from his narrow forehead. "If everybody on earth shook hands with each other, what would happen to the Commonist threat? That's the greatest danger of it all. Enough to drive a man to drink!"

Parkington stared at Huey as if he could not believe his eyes and ears.

"Don't pay Parkington no mind," Carson said truculently to the senator. "I'm gon keep my eye on that witch doctor. He don't act like they supposed to act. I know nigrahs and he don't act like one."

"He is not a Negro," Parkington of the State Department said, losing patience with his colleagues by the second. "He's His Excellency Jaja Okwu Olivamaki." The three of them might have gotten into a fistfight, had not Daniel Throckmorton entered at that moment and saved the day.

Daniel Throckmorton had been an ex-ambassador-at-large assigned to Africa and spent many months in Guanaya when it was a colony of Her Majesty's United Kingdom. He considered himself an old friend of the new Prime Minister Olivamaki. He was fiftyish, a tall strikingly handsome dark-haired blue-eyed important-looking gentleman, of Irish extraction, who would not have missed the reception for Olivamaki for all the world and was sorry as hell that he was late. Another gentleman came into the glittering drawing room along with Daniel Throckmorton. He was Wilfred Ellington Vaughan-Johnson, very lately of West Africa, but originally of Wales in the Queen's United Kingdom. Short legged and a bit on the roundish side, he had difficulty keeping pace with his long-legged colleague, the ex-ambassador-at-large. Vaughan-Johnson was an "Old Coaster," one of the very last of that dying breed that had gone to Africa as a buggerish lad as a part of some glorious You-Kay civilizing scheme of commercial benevolence and economic liberation and Christian deliverance and had stayed for thirty or forty years, and sat in the shade in Accra and Lagos and Ouagadougou and Port Harcourt and Calabar and Khartoum and Bamakanougou, and sipped their gin and tonics and pined for jolly London Town and talked with each other about the bloody "lazy natives," and became experts on colonialism. They were legendary. There were as many stories about them as there were about the American traveling salesman and the farmer's daughter.

When Senator Huey saw Throckmorton enter, his

red face beamed, as glowingly as the Bohemian cut-glass chandeliers above them. "That's just the man we need to talk to. He was all over that colored continent. He's bound to know this Olivamaki fellah." He moved through the elegant mob toward Throckmorton with Carlton Carson breathing heavy on his heels.

In another corner two distinguished-looking elderly white-haired gentlemen of Caucasian descendency were bending their elbows with Kentucky bourbon and profoundly discussing the weighty problems of a troubled world. One could tell at a glance that these were men of great substance and tremendous erudition. One of them smacked his lips and stared past the other one and sighed long and longingly.

"Oh me-me-me-me-me!" he said wistfully. "I sure could use me a nice young piece of virgin poonytang this evening of our Lord and Savior Jesus Christ—nice and plump and maiden-headed—with grand new feral uncombed heavenly pubescences—!" He smacked his lips again and shook his grizzly head.

Tears of nostalgia came to the eyes of the other white-haired gentleman and his quivering mouth ran water, even as he gently admonished his tried-and-trusted friend of yore. "Congressman, you ought to be ashamed of yourself, you lecherous bastard, taking the name of the Lord thy God in vain."

In still another corner a group of distinguished-looking colored gentlemen (African Americans) were also elbow-bending. There were about seven of them, all ages, college professors, doctors, lawyers, and one sepia performer, who was a big-time celebrity, which makes it obvious why he shall be nameless. The big-time celebrity, who shall be nameless, had just left his white admirers and walked over to them and chided them good-naturedly.

"That's what I say about you colored folkses," he mimicked. "Always segregating yourselves. Even all you saddity Black boogwuggies! Frazier had you dead to rights."

They laughed appreciatively. He was so famous and so celebrated not one of them individually could take obvious umbrage, or else the great one might not give that one of them his address when the others weren't looking so that he might one day dare to invite the Famous One to one of his more intimate parties—intimate to the extent of being exclusive, that is.

The Great One put his arms around the shoulders of a couple of them and they all came together gratefully into a football huddle. "This big Black dude from the Big damn Apple was driving through Georgia in a big white Cadillac two blocks long," the celebrated one began in his famous resonant voice. "He was doing seventy-five down the middle of the highway when he passed a speed cop in a police car sitting in ambush off the road. He knew the speed limit was sixty and he glimpsed the white cop in his black Ford, but he did not slow down, because how can a little black Ford catch up with a big white Cadillac?"

They laughed anticipatingly and out of tremendous expectations. The Famous One continued. "The Ford car started to give chase and gain on our man in the Caddy, and he promptly put his foot further into the gas tank and the speedometer went to eighty, but when he looked into the rearview mirror he saw that the black Ford was still gaining, whereupon our hero's dark face lit up to face the challenge and he shoved it in and let the drivers roll. His great white hog was doing a hundred now and the little black Ford was still gaining. He shoved it in from a hundred to a hundred and twenty, and the little black Ford whizzed by him like he was standing still and pulled in front of him and made a roadblock across the narrow highway. Our black hero got out of his long white defeated Cadillac believing in that great White Magic or something or other that was always defeating colored people. 'I'll willingly pay my fine double, Mister Charlie,' he said, 'if you'll just show me what you got underneath that hood that makes your little old black Ford outrun my big long white Cadillac!' . . . 'Fair enough,' the officer said, and he lifted the hood and there, to our disgusted hero's great chagrin, were four panting Negroes wearing sneakers. Our hero shouted, 'Wawa!' and paid Cap'n Charley a hundred dollars."

The colored gentlemen roared with laughter, but roared gently, and with moderation, because to roar boisterously would be to contribute to the stereotype white folks had diligently constructed about them, and they were all dedicated "race" men. They were the kind of men who would never join a march or a picket line or order watermelon in a public restaurant, or pork chops, or—but you get my point, dear credulous readers. Meanwhile, during their aborted outburst, the Famous One had slipped away from them in search of greener pastures. (In explanation of the word "Wawa!" which in those troubled times was always spelled with an exclamation point: It was an expression that simply meant "White America Wins Again!" Hence the acronym, WAWA!)

Meanwhile, back to the ersatz Prime Minister. He was surrounded by another group and engaging them in conversation, but had for the last half hour a feeling of being under sharp and heavy surveillance, but he had not been able to locate the owner of the eyes that watched his every move and motion. The Secret

Service? The FBI? His host of long-lost creditors? The CIA? He was smiling charmingly at a lovely lady, when he heard a voice behind him, a friendly strangely familiar voice that struck terror in his buttocks. Instinctively he moved swiftly away from the group to a vantage point where he could survey the multitude and spot his friendly tormentor. That voice-that-voice-that-friendly-terrifying-voice! Who the hell belonged to it? His tormentor had disappeared completely. What he did see was His Wife's Bottom and Tangi looking for him desperately, and he outfoxed them once again with his great footwork and moved to the other side of the drawing room.

Halfway across the room he saw it coming out of the rightmost corner of his right eye, he glimpsed the blond one leaping for him, but alas too late for his fast footwork to put him in good stead this time. Just as he turned, the blond long-haired one landed around his neck, and it was embarrassingly undignified for His Excellency and also undignifiedly embarrassing for His Excellency as he tried to extricate himself. In one terrifying moment he had placed the unseen voice of a few months ago, as that of the blond plug-ugly from the Ambassador Palace Hotel in Bamakanougou who had caught up with him at the White House. "You're an American! You're an American!" he imagined he heard the blond apparition saying as it lunged toward him. But when he saw and felt that this one was soft and roundish and bumpy and swollen, in special places, he was relieved but immediately embarrassed again.

This luscious, lushed, eloquently equipped, blond young woman, bountifully chested, admirably hind-parted, shouted, "Darling! It's been so long, you beautiful manful hunk of brown-black sugar lump! I have not seen hide nor hair of you since I can not even remember when I ever did see hide nor hair of you—It's been so—"

The poor lad finally and valiantly fought himself firmly out of her clutches and rose to ever greater heights of dignity, even as he wondered whether she was some Hollywood escapade, some chickadee of his long-lost innocence come home to roost. He said very gravely, "Madame, I assure you, we have never met before. And for that discrepancy on my part, I am indeed regretful." She was double-breasted and had the kind that were displayed in such obvious abundance and well below the cleavage point, you could never look her straight in the eyes. Hers had been known to drive men permanently cross-eyed.

Her knees buckled slightly, and she straightened up again all up against our chagrined hero. "I'm sorry too," she assured him. "I'm sorry that I've never been to Guanaya, or to Africa for that matter, so how could we possibly have met before? But it would have been such great fun meeting you for the first time somewhere out there in the bush."

Well?

Also meanwhile, His Wife's Bottom was waylaid by the umpteenth white guest who asked Vice–Prime Minister Lloyd to fetch him a Scotch and soda, which was due to the fact that His Wife's Bottom was the only member of the PM's party who had dressed in Western style in an American tuxedo. The rest of them had worn their long white flowing glowing ethnic boubous like they had some sense and according to the Jimmy Johnson poop sheet. Obviously, His Wife's Bottom was being mistaken for an American, which in those days was a disastrous thing to happen to you if you were a man of color. Even during the most heated days of the great Cold War, no Russian wearing a tuxedo was ever mistaken for an American Negro waiter at the White House. Mr. Lloyd learned his lesson thoroughly. From that evening on, during the rest of his entire visit in the USA, he would not even go to the bathroom back at the hotel without putting on his long white flowing boubou.

Also, and again meanwhile, Senator Huey and Carlton Carson finally waylaid the ex-ambassador, Throckmorton, and his improbable colleague, the Old

Coaster. After a series of hearty handshakes, the senior Senator from Alabama bubbled over, yea, percolated with enthusiasm. "You're just the man we wanted to see, Mister Ambassador," he dribbled obsequiously. "You must've known this Olivamaki feller."

"Know him?" the red-nosed Old Coaster said pompously, like a British-type W. C. Fields. "I knew them all. Yes indeed. Three whacks on the bu-ttee takes care of them every time. They love it—they can't live without it—and it's jolly good for the bloody buggers. By Jove, in my day they didn't blather about independence. They tipped their hats to quality. They knew their place, by Jove."

Carson and Huey were taken aback momentarily and looked askance at the Old Coaster. Then they returned their attention to the ex-ambassador.

"Certainly, I knew the Prime Minister. We were fr—"

Huey interrupted enthusiastically. "You knew him before these African uprisings, didn't you? What kind of feller is he? He's a Commie, ain't he?"

The ex-ambassador told him bluntly he was out of his mind. He had communism on the brain, taking for granted, of course, that the senator was in possession of a brain. Then the ex-ambassador moved quickly and deliberately away from them, leaving the Old Coaster in their grimy kindly clutches. One might say the three of them deserved each other, admirably. "I was in Accra in the Gold Coast," Vaughan-Johnson told them continuing in his kind of W. C. Fields–type singsong, but with very British accents, "when we gave them their independence. Just as the sun was setting over the wide Atlantic, the Union Jack was being lowered for the last time. My colleague of thirty years man and boy on the Western Coast and I—we and people like us—we who built the bloody place with our hands and sweat and brains, and there we sat, sipping our gin and tonics and weeping for the tragedy of it all, and the bloody Blacks were cheering like mad, the ungrateful buggers. My colleague turned to me and said, 'By Jove, from now on we'll have to brush our own teeth.'"

Huey and Carson stared at him, incredulously, not sure whether Vaughan-Johnson wanted them to regard him seriously or humorously. Finally, Carson decided to play it serious. "You knew the Prime Minister of Guanaya?"

"Knew him?" the Old Coaster said indignantly. "Knew them all, lads, every last bugger of them, from Calabar to Ouagadougou. They were our children, we natured and we nurtured them. I know the Niger River all the way to Timbuktu. I know Gao—I know Kano—I know Jos—I know Enugu—"

"Is the Prime Minister pink?" Carlton egged him on.

"Pink, sir? Hardly, lad. Bamako, Niamey, Accra, and Porto-Novo—" He sounded like a train announcer. "I stood on the spot at Segu where Mungo Park first saw the Niger, sir—"

"He's straight-out red! Isn't he, Mr. Johnson?" the senior senator from Alabama asserted with enthusiasm.

"The name is Vaughan-Johnson, sir. And he's a bloody Black from head to toe. We didn't bugger around with them like you people did in America. We kept them pure and Black and unadulterated."

His Lovely Ladyship was surrounded by admirers, most of them of the male species, when the bogus PM saw her finally. And still she seemed oceans away from him in time and space, as he himself stood near the middle of the salon hemmed in by a group of diplomats and an assortment of other miscellaneous people, including a chap from high up in the State Department echelon. They asked him what he thought of the legacy of Malcolm X and nonviolence and Martin King and affirmative action, Black unemployment, and voting rights. Busing, Jesse Jackson. Segregation, integration and South African liberation? He parried each thrust with a fine dexterity.

What did he think of Malcolm X? "A great American indeed. Red-blooded, hard-hitting, courage of his convictions—and that sort of stuff—In the American tradition—a frontiersman of the New Frontier. A shame to lose him."

Nonviolence? "I believe in the kind of nonviolence your American government believes in—"

"Our government, sir?" From a bewildered gentleman from the Pentagon.

"Yes indeed! Preventive nonviolence. I believe we should keep everybody nonviolent, even if we have to blow them off the face of the earth, in the American tradition."

"But surely you are jesting, sir."

"Yes, I am surely jesting, sir."

Reverend King? "He was a truly great man. I wish even now that I had been able to meet and speak with and have dinner with and ask him some questions. When I learned I was visiting your country, I said to myself, if only that great man were still alive, what a difference it would make throughout the world. The greatest man your country has produced in the Twentieth Century."

"Jesse Jackson? A quantum leap, sires, in the evolution of the *Homo sapiens*. Greatest American presidential candidate the world has ever known."

The man from the higher echelon of the State Department changed the subject. He said importantly, "We are prepared to give your people substantial financial assistance, with no strings, so long as we know that your national budget is reasonable and proper." He cleared his throat. "And not based on such anarchistic hogwash as governmental planning, which always creates a hopeless situation of economic chaos."

"Our government is always reasonable and proper with its planning for its national budget," Jimmy Johnson replied vaguely. He was distracted now by the sight of Maria Efwa surrounded by so many dignified wolfish dignitaries and especially by the fact that she seemed to be enjoying every damn minute of it. He felt a sense of deep and ethnic betrayal. How could she turn her back on her Black brothers and sisters all over the world? How could she sell out the cause of Pan-Africanism so lightheartedly, so laughingly? How could she forget the struggle for uhuru so offhandedly? To put it bluntly, he was jealous. It was an emotion rarely felt by him, almost unremembered. When he saw her surrounded by all those pale-faced drooling goggle-eyed male hyenas, he forgot about all the women who had been grinning in his face the entire evening. That was different anyhow, somehow, he told himself, when it was brought to his attention by his damn kibitzing never-sleeping conscience.

"I don't mean," the high-echeloned man from the State Department hastened to assure the distracted

Prime Minister, "that we expect you to have a national budget that's always in the black."

"Black?" the phony preoccupied PM repeated.

"Oh no," the bogus PM answered with great urbanity. "We are all for Pan-Africanism, but we are not that nationalistic. We would never keep our budget in the black." When he heard his own words he had to laugh, which saved the day because the people around him, including the State Department man, knew then that he was making fun with his special African sense of humor, which was completely over their heads. Whereupon they naturally laughed uproariously.

The State Department man assured him further, "A government whose national budget doesn't annually run in the red consistently is untrustworthy and not worth a tinker's damn."

Jimmy believed he had not heard the State Department man properly. Nevertheless, he heartily agreed with him. And when he looked away this time, he spied a face staring at him from about fifty feet away, and his throat grew hot and his knees gave in and he almost fainted. It was the face that belonged to the voice he'd heard earlier that evening. It was the American who had wrestled with him in the lounge of the Ambassador Palace Hotel back in Bamakanougou, when he was Jimmy Leander Johnson from Lolliloppi, 'Sippi,

Near-the-Gulf. The friendly face was smiling at him.
Jimmy panicked. His own face broke out in cold perspiration. He turned and walked away in the opposite
direction. He had to struggle hard to keep from running. Nevertheless, in his great hurry, he ran smack
into Daniel Throckmorton Esq., the ex-ambassador,
the good friend of Prime Minister Olivamaki.

There was a brief and painful moment when the
two tall strikingly handsome men stood staring at each
other, the ambassador's smile ultimately beginning to
fade when he saw that there was not the slightest sign
of recognition on the young Prime Minister's face. The
ex-ambassador extended his hand and they shared a
warm handshake.

"You remember me, Mr. Prime Minister. I was a
good friend of your father's." And of course, the pan-
icky bogus PM said, "Of course I remember you.
How could I ever forget? You were a good friend of
my father's." As he looked around desperately for
someone to throw him a life jacket, but his dedicated
ethnic brothers were nowhere in evidence, excepting
his lovely dedicated ethnic sister, whose eyes he caught,
but briefly. In that split second, he sent an SOS to her
and he fiercely hoped she got the message.

Throckmorton began to ask about this person and
the other, venerable citizens of Guanaya, about whom

the ersatz PM knew absolutely nothing. He then waxed reminiscently and nostalgic about old times before the PM was the PM, about which the ersatz PM knew less than absolutely nothing.

"Remember the time, Jaja—may I still call you Jaja? We used to know each other by our first names, but you're a Prime Minister now. We used to call each other by nicknames."

Jimmy said, "Call me Jaja, by all means," and wondered what the hell he used to call this tall distinguished pink-faced drink of gin and tonic who used to call him Jaja before he was Prime Minister, and so forth and so on.

Throckmorton picked up the threads of his African nostalgia.

"Remember, Jaja, the time you and I got lost out on the desert in a Land Rover? And we went around in circles for hours and might have ended up in Libya or Algeria or Chad or God knows where?"

Jimmy said, "Yes—as if it happened yesterday." He felt a headache coming on, a thing that almost never happened to him. His head was leaping, thumping.

"You remember who it was that rescued us?"

Jimmy could feel his forehead throbbing now. *Bomp! Bomp! Bomp! Bomp!* He thought perhaps his erstwhile nameless-at-the-moment friend could hear and see the thumping in the temples of his forehead. He said, "Yes indeed." And Throckmorton began to laugh at the memory of their rescue, which must have been hilariously funny. So, Jimmy joined in the laughter. Suddenly Throckmorton stopped laughing and stared at Jimmy with a funny expression (funny-queer, not funny-ha-ha).

"Do you really remember, Jaja?"

His Excellency stared absently past Throckmorton at the gleamingly polished mantelpiece above a fireplace enclosed in the west wall with glowing candelabra of golden bronze atop the mantel.

Jaja said, "Of course I remember. What do you mean?" He needed six aspirins in a shot of Cutty Sark and White Label mixed with OLD GRANDAD and a jigger of Jack Daniel's.

Throckmorton said, "I had a funny feeling that you didn't even remember me. Perhaps the new responsibili—"

Jaja said, "Of course I remember you. You were not only my friend; you were my father's friend before me."

Throckmorton's eyes lit up in joyous reaction to this conclusive evidence that his good friend still remembered him. "We were rescued on the desert by two Tuaregs!" he reminded Jaja.

Jimmy decided to live dangerously with his throbbing

headache. "And we thought they were going to sell us into slavery," he reminded his good friend whatever-his-name-was.

"Yes!" his good friend agreed. "Yes! You do remember!" And he started to laugh and could not stop laughing and the tears stood in his eyes and Jimmy laughed, genuinely this time, at his unknown friend's infectious laughter, and also at the episode, which at this point he could almost relive himself, and vividly. He even thought that he remembered it.

His old friend, newly found, stopped laughing. "Our Land Rover broke down and they brought us back all the way to Bamakanougou on their camels. We couldn't sit down for a week."

"Not even for a fortnight," Jimmy insisted, and they both began to laugh and relive that day out on the desert all over again. Even as he laughed, Jimmy thought, How many people will I meet who knew me before I knew myself?

After they stopped laughing, Throckmorton threw him a combination curve-knuckler-and-illegal-spitball. "Whatever happened to Abraham Malabuvu? I thought surely he would have been a member of your Independence Cabinet?"

At this moment Jimmy hated his newly found old friend profoundly, murderously. He felt like taking the golden-bronze candelabra on the mantel and beating him till his head was bloody. He hadn't the foggiest notion about Malabuvu. Maybe he had been arrested for un-Guanayan activities, maybe—but—perhaps he was one of the treacherous conspirators responsible for getting him in this horrendous mess.

"Oh, you mean our old friend Abraham Malabuvu—" Obviously stalling.

"Yes," Throckmorton agreed. "Abraham Solomon Mamaiumbi Malabuvu—Whatever happened to him?"

With a smile still on Jimmy's face he broke out into a cool damn sweat. All the jive is gone, he thought. This is the ever-loving nitty-gritty. He saw the gates of Alcatraz closing behind him, where they would keep him till they burned him. And all because he couldn't answer a stupid question like, Whatever happened to Abraham Malabuvu? "He was a pillar of strength and dependability—" The fake PM kept up the stall. "He—"

"Abraham Malabuvu died suddenly with a heart attack, six months ago," he heard her say in a silken voice that was like violins playing in a celestial orchestra.

Throckmorton's puzzled face broke into a thousand smiles. "Maria Efwa! How delightful!"

"Ambassador Daniel Throckmorton!"

Jimmy watched these two reaffirm an old friend, as

perspiration of relief poured from him even more pro-fusely than the sweat of fear had poured. He had never been relieved to learn of another human being's death before, excepting possibly Hitler or Bilbo or Talmadge or Eastland or McCarthy or—or—His possible excep-tions were mounting, so he decided to drop the morbid list of wish fulfillments, fulfilled already. He needed a drink. He turned to the ex-ambassador. "I should like nothing better than to spend the rest of the evening reminiscing over old times, Danny Boy, but because of my position I must talk with many others before the evening is over. You do understand, don't you, Danny Boy."

"Yes—quite," the puzzled ex-ambassador replied.

Jimmy turned to his Minister of Education and took her hand and squeezed it warmly, very very warmly, even perhaps heatedly. "I leave you in the company of the most charming most intelligent most beautiful of all Guanayans."

"Yes—quite," the ex-ambassador repeated, bewil-deredly.

Jimmy turned away and headed for the bar, wherever it was. Just before he got out of earshot, he heard Danny Boy say to Maria Efwa, "Jaja acted very strangely. He never used to call me Danny Boy. He used to call me Throckyboubou, ever since he was a little one." Jimmy did not hear her answer, because he quickened his pace away from them because he did not want to hear her answer.

He didn't have to find the bar. He came across one of the floating colored waiters and took four fast Scotch-and-soda highballs from his tray, drinking one right after the other. He was quickly getting cockeyed.

After Throckyboubou and Maria Efwa separated, Carson and Huey moved in again on Danny Boy, at which point the ex-ambassador admitted there was something strange about the Prime Minister's behavior, now that Carson and Huey mentioned it. "He seemed changed and somehow different."

Carson literally jumped up and down in ecstatic jubilation. "I knew it! I knew it! He's sold out to the Commies. He's un-American!"

They say all good things come to an end, and bad things linger on forever. In any event, when the amiable President said good night to the estimable PM, he assured him for the umpteenth time, "Anything you want, Mr. Prime Minister. Anywhere you want to go in our great country, anything you want to do, just let me know. Your every wish is my command and all that fuh-fuh-fuh-fabulous sort of thing."

At that cockeyed moment Jimmy had a sudden perverse inspiration, possibly due to excessive imbibition.

"I'd like more than anything in the world to visit Lol-liloppi, Mississippi, Mister President, after my visit to New York," the bogus PM said, malevolently.

"It shall be done," the President responded graciously—and thoughtlessly.

Another vast crowd of young and middle-aged and elderly diddy-boppers of varying ethnicities and colors and denominations stood waiting outside the White House and ooohed and aahed as Jaja's party left in two long black limousines with long black SS cars front and back. The city of the snow-white buildings was lit up like daytime outside as they proceeded down Pennsylvania Avenue to the hotel. Carlton Carson was in the limousine with Jaja.

He engaged the PM in a friendly kind of conversation. Did His Majesty know Mr. Throckmorton very well? And of course, the PM knew the ex-ambassador very well. They were old friends, and even the PM's father knew Throckyboubou very very well. Then Carson wanted to know did His Majesty know that the ambassador was suspected of being kind of pink.

"But of course," the PM answered. "He probably always has been."

Carson got excited. His ruse was working quicker than he dared to hope or even dream. These damn Africans were not so damn smart after all. Vaughan-

Johnson was right! They were naive children. From now on he would listen to the Old Coaster.

"And you, Your Majesty, you admit you are a friend of his?"

"What difference does it make?" the PM asked. "Look at your own President. He's as red as they make them."

This was too much for Carson. He wiped his forehead and sank down into the seat almost out of sight.

The PM stared down at him smilingly. "I don't hold it against a man that he is pink or red or whatever, I'm democratic."

Carson pulled himself together out of sheer patriotism and determination, and he told the chauffeur to stop the car immediately. He had to make a telephone call. He could have used the telephone in the car, but he did not want His Excellency to overhear his conversation. The chauffeur pulled up to the curb near a phone booth and Carson opened the door. Jimmy reached out and took the telephone and handed it to old Carlton Carson. "Here you are, Mr. Carson. No need to waste your precious coins, inflation being what it is these days. Eh? All the comforts of home are at your beck and call."

Carlton Carson paled and stammered. Finally, Carson said, "It's . . . it's . . . it's kind of personal, Your

Hi-hi-highness. Please excuse me." And he started out of the car again.

Jimmy detained him again, momentarily. "Look," he said, "you're red in the face right now. Believe me, there's no such thing as a white man. You're either red or pink, and some of you are even tan. When you're white, old chap, believe me, you are no longer among the living."

As the car door had opened, the lights inside the car had come on. The Black chauffeur produced a comic book from beneath him and he began to explode with laughter. He began to beat the steering wheel as he roared with laughter. "You got him, Pogo! By God, you got the rascal! Whooo—a quad-gua-gua qua! Woo-woo-woo! That Pogo is a funny Mary Francis! Woo! Woo! Gi-gi-gi-Whoowee!" Banging on the steering wheel, he accidentally banged the horn, and it blasted the after-midnight silence of Pennsylvania Avenue.

Carson finally got the drift, and he closed the door again, and quietly told the guffawing chauffeur to continue to the hotel. He said not another word until they reached the door to the ambassadorial suite, at which time he said a subdued good night.

Once the PM's party was safely inside, he took off his bogus beard and took Maria Efwa, without giving her fair warning, into his arms and kissed her fully on her luscious mouth, and she slapped the bogus PM's sassy face.

His head rang like the sweet bells of Saint Mary. He said, "I'm sorry, I just wanted to express my appreciation to you for saving my life with Ambassador Throckyboubou."

As angry as she was, she had to smile a wee sweet smile at "Throckyboubou." She said, "I'm sorry too, Your Excellency." And she meant it. And she bade him good night and went down the corridor to her room and went in and locked the door, and put an armchair up against it, which was not very trustful of her. *Mais— c'est la vie.*

Her Excellency's face still flushed warmly, as she deliberately disrobed, her rich lips still aflame. There was nothing between the two of them, she told herself, emphatically, and there could never ever be. *Period.*

Beneath the shower now, she reenacted the scene of a few moments' past. She was making (how did they say it) "a mountain out of a molehill." It meant absolutely nothing. And yet there was that briefest of moments when she'd responded to those sensual and devilish lips, one-hundredth of a second when she kissed him back and then suddenly withdrew as if she'd been bitten by a deadly mamba. It meant absolutely nothing. He had taken her by complete surprise was all. He could never mean anything to her, except that he was just a person, a human being, asexual actually, part of a plan to liberate the Mother Continent. A mere fortuitous convenience. Fate had chosen him to play a role in this charade for liberation. Nothing more. He was a typical American womanizer. African or European, they were all the same. She'd met many of his kind in London when she'd studied at the university. She would never take the ersatz PM seriously. He was extraordinarily macho, vain, egomaniacal in that regard, lacking in depth of feeling, or even intellectuality. Too handsome for his own good.

She came out of the bathroom wrapped in a terry cloth towel. She took the towel from around her as she stood before the floor-to-ceiling mirror in her bedroom. Her reflection stared back, critically, at a medium-height statuesque woman, five-feet-fourish, slimly constructed and curvaceous (she seemed taller than her actual height), tiny waisted, with a wee bit of lingering baby fat here and there about the midriff. Her taut breasts were not overly large; neither were they undersized particularly, but firm and very darkly nippled and forever pointed heavenward somewhat like a nubile maiden. Ever graceful, she seemed always on the move, her body never static, effortlessly evanescent.

She would work closely with him and at the same

time keep him at a distance. It would not be difficult. It might be (if she were emotionally involved, and she definitely was not); it was simply because of his striking resemblance to her extremely handsome cousin, Jaja, whom she loved and admired as if he were her own brother. Though he appeared to be her cousin's identical twin, facially and physically (she would not have been surprised to find that they were the same height, same weight, and likewise in the waist and shoulders, even the same shoe size), she knew there was a fundamental difference in them, the way they handled themselves, the way they moved about. Whereas Jaja exuded solid strength, feet firmly planted in the earth, Jimmy Johnson's strength was tiger-quick with a tiger's gracefulness, ready to spring at a moment's notice. Jaja was intractable with the totally awesome strength of his convictions. Durable. The marathon man. Jimmy Johnson was the incorrigible romantic. Jaja had always waged a total all-consuming, no-holds-barred romance with change and revolution, with little or no time for the frivolities of flirtation or chitchat. Whereas Jimmy Johnson carried on an unrelenting romance with himself and with dare-deviltry. Like Robeson, whom she'd seen in London as a child, Jaja walked this earth with a dignity that came naturally. Whereas Jimmy Johnson strutted. Perhaps his strutting also came naturally.

She stretched her entire slender body. She moaned and sighed pleasurably. She donned her nightdress and she eased herself into the canopied four-poster. Again, she stretched her long slim body, as the exhaustion of the frenetic day came down suddenly upon her in every nook and cranny of her being from her head down to her tingling toes. Albeit a sweet exhaustion that she somehow reveled in. She felt her sensuality now, and joyously. She recognized it as a feeling entirely rare to her, a feeling she would not bother to investigate, or analyze, except to tell herself it had nothing to do with Jimmy Johnson.

She felt her womanness more than ever now and felt a weary welcomed smile move over her body from her face down to her tingling-more-than-ever toes, sensuous and sensual, as her mind recaptured the last few days. The feverish preparations for the trip, the discovery of the plot; enter Mr. Jimmy Johnson, the superb impersonator, the tutoring of Jimmy Johnson, the proximity of Jimmy Johnson, the scene out at the airport, Jimmy Johnson at the White House party. This man meant not a thing to her.

She thought fondly of the elderly distinguished man back in Bamakanougou who was her husband. She had married him at the age of seventeen, a man who had been more than twice her age. It had been much more than a marriage of political expediency, though political expediency had certainly been a factor. Ever since she could remember, she had regarded John Segu Mamadou, worshipfully, as the legendary leader of her country in its struggle for independence. Even as a little one she had loved him from a distance as vast as the Atlantic, loved him, respectfully, before she had fully awakened to her dormant sexuality just coming into being, not fully realized yet. Their marriage had been an occasion for joyous celebration through the nation's capital and the villages nearby. It was a marriage sanctioned and arranged from above by African gods with assistance here and there by the families in question, as was the tradition in Guanaya.

A marriage consummated more out of respect than romance or sexuality, but no less sacred, no less holy matrimony. Perhaps the lack of sexual passion made it even holier. As the years passed, he grew aged and sickly, but no less regarded as a legend. Mamadou had had several wives, all of whom had demised, before he took Maria Efwa to his lone connubial couch, and suddenly adopted monogamy as a way of life. She had never violated her marriage vows, nor had she been tempted to.

And she certainly wouldn't begin now with this egotistic macho man of African Americano.

She got nimbly out of bed and went to the bedroom door and took the chair away from beneath the knob. She tested the lock. It was secure. She glided blithesomely back across the room and took herself again to bed.

And smilingly she fell asleep.

About three o'clock in the morning the President of the United States talked in his sleep for the first time in a very long time. And he said, "Lolliloppi, Mississippi!" And he spoke so loudly he woke himself up, and he called the Prime Minister of Guanaya on the extra-special private telephone.

The lady at the hotel switchboard said, "I'm sorry, sir, but they're all asleep up there and we have orders not to awaken them till nine thirty in the morning."

Hubert Herbert Hubert said, "I don't give a damn how asleep they are, ring them. This is the fucking President of the United States."

When he finally convinced her, and when he finally got the sleepy-headed Prime Minister on the phone, the President said, "Did I understand you to say, Your Fuh-fuh-fuh-fabulous Excellency, you wanted to visit Lolliloppi, Mississippi?"

The bogus PM said, still half asleep, "Yeah—but I don't feel like going this time of the morning." And unquietly he banged the phone back on the hook and went immediately to sleep again.

About three quarters of an hour later he awoke again with a start. He thought he'd heard a telephone ringing somewhere in the Western world. He reached for it sleepily and suddenly realized that it wasn't really ringing. He lay down and then jumped straight up in bed again. He was fully awake now, as he realized what had happened. He had banged the telephone down on the President of the United States! Unceremoniously! Good Lord! He felt pimples of perspiration breaking out all over his body. He must apologize immediately. He reached for the telephone and when he got the operator, he said, "Operator, this is Jimmy Johnson. Get me the President of the United States tout-damn-suite!"

She said, "Jimmy who? What is this, some kind of big joke at this time of the morning? What are you? Some kind of a stay-up-latenik nut or something? And what are you doing in the African quarters?"

He heard a clock somewhere in the sleeping city striking four o'clock in the morning, as he replaced the receiver slowly back in place, softly and tenderly, even though his hand was trembling. He had called himself "Jimmy Johnson" to the operator, despite the fact that he was really His Excellency Prime Minister Jaja

Okwu Olivamaki. He had to always remember who he was. He must remember, sleep or wake.

He stumbled to the bathroom and stared at himself in the mirror, and was relieved to find that he was still the same person he always was, but was at the same time somehow different, and that was the thing he must always remember and yet somehow forget. It was damn confusing. He wouldn't take any chances. He left the bathroom and looked frantically for his phony beard. And when he found it, he put it on his face again with a sigh of profound relief and went back to bed and closed his eyes with a soft smile on his face. And he was scared, even as he drifted sweetly into that strangely familiar land of nervous nod and nap, that turf that was the sandman's territorial prerogative.

No matter, he was nonchalant, even as he slumbered.

13

The next day Jimmy and his entourage had a conference with the President at the White House,
which lasted several hours in the Cabinet Room. The
Cabinet Room was chosen instead of the Oval Office,
because of the convenience of its long conference table,
with Lincoln staring at them from above the fireplace.
The Cabinet Room instead of the Oval Office was a
presidential preference, almost a superstition with this
President. It was common knowledge that Lincoln was
his patron saint.

It was a friendly chat that Tangi seemed very
pleased with, but which kept the nervous His Wife's
Bottom, Mr. Lloyd, clearing his scratchy ministerial
throat every minute. And Maria Efwa was proud of the
way Jimmy handled the situation. He could tell from

the rays of warmth that were beginning to beam from her to him, or were they beaming from him to her? And he, himself, was beginning to enjoy the role of His Excellency the Prime Minister of the Independent People's Democratic Republic of Guanaya, even though he could never completely dispel the fear of sudden discovery, imprisonment, disgrace, and disgrace not only to him, but also to the proud little Independent People's Democratic Republic of Guanaya. Sometimes he made-believe even to himself that he was the real thing. He was, in fact, His Excellency Prime Minister Jaja Okwu Olivamaki of the Independent People's Democratic Republic of Guanaya, in person! And it felt damn good, even though he knew that therein lay potential madness and great danger. He nevertheless indulged himself in self-deception. While in a corner of his mind lurking always the smiling face of William Clarence Barnsfield the Fifth of the Ambassador Palace Hotel lounge in Bamakanougou and more recently, of the presidential reception at the White House, Washington, DC. He expected the handsome friendly faced American plug-ugly to show up, anywhere and everywhere and at any moment, shouting for all the world to hear: "You're an American! You're an American! I know it—I know it! I know it!" He looked and listened for Bill Barnsfield the Fifth with all his senses in every gathering large or small. He was always on his everlasting guard. It was a nerve-racking business.

Meanwhile the Cabinet Room was like Grand Central Station and the United Nations Delegates Lounge and Union Square subway station at five o'clock all rolled into Bellevue. Diplomats, military aides, and intelligence experts who didn't look very intelligent (maybe the stupid look was a disguise, Jimmy thought), and protocol officers, moving to and from, tiptoeing in and out of the Cabinet Room smiling politely, standing nearby, making comments, keeping their mouths shut, asking questions. Being obviously and boisterously unobtrusive. They were as subtle as the hydrogen bomb. And Jimmy thought that all of them were nervous wrecks. In the words of Jesse B. Simple, "It were a proper mess."

Also, meanwhile, during the frenetic moving back and forth, the constant whispered chatter, Jimmy Jay's mind wandered capriciously back to Bamakanougou and to all of Africa. Even as he stared out of the lordly french doors of the Cabinet Room past the famous Rose Garden to a vague imagined impression of the Jefferson Memorial in the far-off distance, he vividly remembered the many trips he'd made outside Guanaya. He had Mondays off at the club. And every weekend he would take off to a different place, to fulfill a different dream he'd dreamed, by air flight or in an old secondhand Land Rover he had purchased. He'd take off for Lagos, for Ibadan and eastward to Enugu. He flew to Khartoum and to Cairo. One Monday on a whimsy, he drove from Gao along the southern edge of the desert all the way to Timbuktu, got lost on the way. He was gone an entire week. No one knew what had happened to him. A veritable APB was put out for him. His missing was announced every day every hour on the radio. His missing became a national incident. They were overjoyed at his return. Guanaya loved their Jimmy Johnson and the love affair did not go unrequited.

President Hubert Herbert Hubert had earlier that morning called his cabinet and White House staff and his subcabinet, whatever that was, and a few select congressmen and senators together in the Oval Office, and he read to them the riot act. He'd walked back and forth in front of them. He had large hands that made him look as if he were always wearing boxing gloves. He seemed never to know what to do with them. He'd try to hide them in his pockets, which made such unseemly bulges, as if he were doubly endowed on each side instead of in the middle of him. He sometimes waved his hands above his head, as if he had just won the world heavyweight championship. He sometimes tried to hide them behind his big head, behind his back sometimes. To paraphrase the great Joe Louis, his hands could run but they could not hide. He would put the knuckles of both fists in his mouth sometimes, nibbling at them nervously, as if he thought that, through attrition, he would wear them down to normal proportions. They had never seen him work up such a sweat before. He pounded his great fat fist into his fat other hand.

"There must not be a single slipup," the gentle Prexy badgered them. "There must be no incident at all. This is the most important African nation in the Western hemisphere—I mean—anywhere in the entire world! And another thing—we must not be overly pushy at the conference table. We must be very subtle. Africans are very sensitive, especially the new breed. While they're in our country we must protect them from any isolated incidents of racial strife." He stopped and banged his desk and shouted. "They must not, under any circumstances, be treated as if they are Black Americans, or fuh-fuh-fucking heads will roll! Do I make myself clear?"

Parkington spoke up in a trembly voice. He'd never seen his chief of state in such a state. "I was telling Carlton Carson yesterday; we must make our Guanayan guests feel at home. We must make them know that we don't see the color of their skins at all, and that we don't look upon them as Negroes, but as ordinary people." He was considered an expert on the African scene, had spent six months as cultural attaché to the American embassy in Bamakanougou.

Carlton Carson countered with, "But they *are* Negroes. They sure don't look like Eskimos."

The President said angrily, "*They are not Negroes! They are not people! They are dignitaries!* Or fucking heads will roll!"

The conference between the Guanayan delegation and the President included, among others, Jeffry Hillman, great American scientist and engineer, chairman of the Atomic Energy Bureau. He was a beetle-browed personable chap in the all-American tradition, with a Harvard-type Southern accent or maybe a Yale type or a Princeton type. It didn't make that much difference. He looked like an improbable combination of Steve Allen and Scotland Yard or John L. Lewis and Caspar Milquetoast. And maybe even Frank Sinatra. Sometimes he lapsed into a German accent, unconsciously or otherwise, possibly because in those days, the popular view of the American atomic scientists was that they were all of German descent and spoke in guttural accents. It seems that many of them had been Nazis and/or had cooperated with the Nazi regime, not out of any love for

Der Führer. Heavens forbid! Actually, they were anti-Hitlerites one and all. Their theory was that the more atrocities they committed in the name of Herr Schickelgruber, the more insufferable they would make life for the freedom-loving German people, and the quicker the people would rise up and say "No more!" And throw off the Nazi yoke. The only thing that prevented this from happening was the treachery of the Russian army, which would not wait until the regime fell of its own weight and calumny, which surely would have happened, eventually (nobody seriously believed Der Führer's boast that the Third Reich would last a thousand years). The whole thing was one mendacious Communist plot to prevent the natural evolution of the democratic process. Anyhow, Dr. Hillman was not really German anyhow. Even though there was a strong resemblance between him and Henry Kissinger.

The great scientist thought to disarm the Prime Minister with a charming smile, but his teeth were bad yellowish and tobacco stained, and the bogus PM had a bias against bad-teethed people. Dr. Hillman said, "Do you have any idea at all, Your Excellency, how much cobanium there is in Northern Province?"

The PM stared at the smiling scientist with the decadent teeth and cleared his throat. With dignity. This seemed to be a signal for Mr. Tobey, his personal secretary, to clear his own throat, significantly, and stare at Mr. Langford, who was the American chief of protocol officer, which seemed to be a signal for Mr. Langford to clear his own throat, cautiously. "I think we'd better leave the technical questions to the technical people, Dr. Hillman," Mr. Langford said.

Dr. Hillman looked at the amiable President, who cleared his throat wholeheartedly and smiled his agreement, at which point Dr. Hillman turned to Mr. Langford and smiled and said, "Yes—" who turned to Mr. Tobey and on down the line till they got back to the Prime Minister, who looked at Maria Efwa and then turned to Dr. Hillman and said, "I don't mind the question at all. There are inexhaustible beds of cobanium in the Northern Province. Not to mention the other provinces." He threw the last sentence in for good measure, or out of pure cussedness.

Not only did Dr. Hillman nibble at the line, he took the whole bait in his teeth and started for the open sea. He was like a dog who'd just caught scent of the rabbit. He asked excitedly, "You mean to say, Sir, that cobanium has been discovered in the other provinces?"

The fake PM stared up at the chandelier above the darkly polished conference table and deliberately assumed a crafty expression. Always with dignity. "No, sir. I meant to say just what I said. Nothing more."

Whereupon Dr. Hillman immediately assumed that His Excellency meant the direct opposite of what he said he meant, because it was the way diplomats talked to one another. They very honestly never told each other the truth about anything, no matter on how friendly terms the governments involved might be. It was tradition in Western diplomacy. Only scoundrels were completely honest. Honesty was the last resort of diplomats. A resort they never resorted to. Dr. Hillman tried another tack. "Your Excellency, may I ask you? Has cobanium been discovered in any of the other provinces?"

"Yes and no," the PM answered emphatically and with deliberate ambiguity.

Dr. Hillman was not sure whether the PM's "Yes and no" was in answer to "May I ask?" or to the second part of the question he had asked. The smiling scientist stared at the suave Prime Minister and then he looked from face to smiling face of the people seated around the long mahogany table, excepting that Tangi was not smiling. He never smiled for Europeans. It was against his personal religion.

Men and women were still dancing in and out of the cabinet office on their tiptoes, some of them even waltzing, bringing papers to be stared at and whispering excitedly to one or more of the conferees.

Dr. Hillman changed the subject. "Of course, Your Excellency, we want to put our technical experts at your disposal, to extract the high-grade ore as efficiently and as expeditiously as possible. We would hope that our expedition would be the only one and would have full charge *carte blanche* without outside interference from anyone, responsible only to the American government."

His Wife's Bottom said, "Exactly so." And pompously.

Tangi gave his colleague a mean white look and then turned to Dr. Hillman and said, matter-of-factly, "The first responsibility of anybody working on any project in Guanaya will be to the Guanayan people represented by His Excellency and the Guanayan government."

Jimmy Johnson said emphatically, "Exactly so."

President Hubert Herbert Hubert gave the scientist a black look and then turned to His Excellency and said, "Yes, of course, Your Excellency, indeed. I'm sure Dr. Hillman did not mean to imply anything at all." If his legs had been long enough, he would have kicked the doctor on his shin. He tried so hard that the muscles in the calf of his legs began to contract, severely, miserably.

Dr. Hillman's face broke into a cool damp sweat. He lapsed into a peculiar combination of Dixie drawl and

German guttural. "Of course, Mr. President, I meant nothing at all, indeed, Your Excellency."

"He meant nothing at all," Mr. Langford repeated.

"I understand English," His Excellency assured Mr. Langford.

Metaphorically speaking, Dr. Hillman's head was bloody but unbowed. He was a man of derring-do. He was the kind of scientific genius whom nobody had ever accused of being intelligent. An *idiot savant*, so to speak. Though there was none who dared to doubt his scientific genius. "What I really meant was, we would certainly insist that we would be the only outside experts working on the project inside."

"Insist?" His Excellency inquired, with an aggrieved and puzzled look on his face. Then he turned to his Foreign Minister and rattled off a rapid ragged ad-libbed Hausa.

Tangi spoke back to him in Hausa. They engaged back and forth in a brief though animated dialogue. Then ignoring Dr. Hillman, Tangi turned to the President of the United States. "His Excellency says that you had given him your honorable assurances that in our two countries' dealings with each other, there would be no strings attached. But, His Excellency says, the word 'insist' sounded to him more like the rattle of colonial chains."

His Wife's Bottom, Mr. Lloyd, cleared his throat and explained, "Please to understand that whenever His Excellency the Prime Minister of the Independent People's Democratic Republic of Guanaya gets excited or exhausted, he always speaks in Hausa. Thank you very much."

The President colored slightly but did not lose his poise. He tried again to reach Hillman underneath the table, but alas his legs had not grown any longer. "Yes, of course," he said, "'*insist*' is a very strong word. Very aggressive word indeed, Dr. Hillman. Possibly the word 'suggest' might suggest a sentiment a little more or less suggestive."

Tangi stared at the President long and hard, as if to make sure he had heard him clearly. Finally, he said, "Exactly so," as did His Excellency, and finally the great scientist, who had somehow lapsed suspiciously into a Guanayan accent, agreed. "Exactly so." Jimmy thought that Hillman was probably a better dialect man than he was a diplomat.

But in fairness to the doctor, it must be said, he did not give up easily. "What I really meant to say was: We would certainly hope that we would not have to work with any other outside forces inside the project. For example: If there were an American expedition, there would hardly be any need for a Russian one, although, don't misunderstand me, I hate to bring up the question of Russia into this discussion. I mean, this amiable discussion—because certainly as a scientist, I am loathed to bring the Cold War into this great expedition of the Twentieth Century. Nevertheless—"

The fake PM seemed to hear only one phrase in Dr. Hillman's speech, and that phrase was "Cold War." He stared at Dr. Hillman with all his pearly white showing in his dark face, but they all knew he was not smiling pleasantly. Then he turned to Tangi and his face turned into one of righteous indignation, and he said, "Coldwar!" making one word of the two words. And then he launched into a tirade of potluck Hausa at Tangi as if his Foreign Minister were a white devil in a black disguise. Now and for good measure, or to make sure Tangi perfectly understood the context, he threw in a few words of Afro-Americanese.

Tangi stared understandingly (tongue-in-cheek) at His-Angry-Excellency and accepted his scolding like a man. When H.E. finally ran out of steam (most probably because he ran freshly out of his Hausa vocabulary), Tangi said quietly, "Exactly so, Your Excellency."

Then he turned to the perplexed cherubic Prexy of the USA, and said, "His Excellency says, he is loath to bring the Coldwar into this, the great expedition of the twentieth century."

And they all agreed, "Exactly so."

The President gave Dr. Hillman a dark dark look, and the great scientist got the message this time and kept quiet for the remainder of the conference. But Dr. Hillman notwithstanding, the PM and the Prexy got along, but famously. It was like love at first sight. And they made good ballroom partners, adroit as they both were in dancing nimbly around the burning issues of the day. When they had finished not-discussing communism and profoundly not-discussing Peking and not-discussing Cuba with such tremendous insight and perception and not discussing South Africa and Angola, and Zimbabwe and Namibia and Grenada, they discussed generally the question of cultural exchange and teachers and trade and finances. Then drinks were brought in and the President suggested that they drink to peace on earth.

The PM said, "Peace and *freedom*, Mr. President. We cannot have one without the other. A slave is never at peace with his master." How could the President not agree?

By the time they finished this session, Jimmy had worked his short-ranged Juju on the President and had him drinking out of the PM's calabash, so to speak, and drinking to uhuru, to Pan-Africanism and to an end to colonialism and everything else. Somewhere near the end of it the fake PM held out his glass toward the President and shouted softly, "Up the PAs! Up the Pan-Africanists!"

The kindly President immediately upped the PAs and the Pan-Africanists, and with vigor. He was determined to keep the PM in a jovial mood. He would *up* almost anything to keep the "noble savage" happy.

But this time "Jaja the Magnificent," as he thought of himself modestly, sometimes, this time he lunged his glass toward that of the President's, and his aim was off target, and all his highball ended up on the bosom and in the lap of the chief executive.

Presidential flunkies rushed forward and wiped the front of the President hastily and put another drink in the dark hand of His Excellency.

The red-faced President said, "It was all my fault, Your Excellency. How can you ever forgive me for such impropriety?"

His Excellency said, "Exactly so."

Perhaps there was a breakdown in communication?

The PM stared at the Prexy long and hard, as again he struck his glass (with better aim this time) loudly against the Prexy's. "Up the Black folk in South Africa!"

And the Prexy immediately upped the Black folk in South Africa. It did not cost him a red cent. Upping after all was an inexpensive exercise.

The bogus PM shouted, loudly this time, "Up His Excellency, Olivamaki!" Forgetting that he himself was His Excellency Olivamaki. The rest of the party stared at Jimmy; the Guanayans because they thought he had exposed himself, either as an egomaniac or as the great fraud of the twentieth century; the Americans because they thought him drunk never before having ever heard of a man offering a toast to himself. Fortunately, the President thought that the PM was following a good old native African custom. He looked around at the rest of them and held his glass toward the PM and shouted, "Up the President of the United States!"

And everybody followed suit, even the bogus PM, who thought it very strange for an American President to be toasting himself, but he went along with the gag, if any.

They upped quite a few other things, including the Black folks of the USA, and downed quite a bit of the White House liquor. But the PM was not drinking as much as he pretended to be, and neither was the jolly cunning President. And both the President and the PM finally got wise to each other. And yet they kept the pretenses up; each pretending that he was getting drunk and that he was not wise to the other pretending that he was getting drunk. They each knew that the other was wise to him, but it did not stop them from

pretending, but it did get very confusing, and furthermore it was the easiest way in the world for both
of them to get completely stoned, which is what was
happening and almost happened and would have happened, had not Tangi reminded the PM of a previous
commitment that they did not have.

The PM asked the President again about Lolliloppi,
Mississippi, which had a sobering effect on Hubert
Herbert Hubert as if a bucket of ice-cold water had
been thrown onto the front of his trousers. He jumped,
and in a second, he was as sober as judges are supposed
to be but rarely ever are.

Then he got himself together and stared shrewdly
at the PM. "Why would you want to go to a place like
that, Your Excellency? Wouldn't you rather see America first? How about Chicago?"

"Isn't Lolliloppi in America, Mister President?
I mean, it did not secede from the union yet, did it,
Mr. President?"

The PM laughed and everybody followed suit—
naturally.

"Wouldn't you rather go to a place like the golden
shores of California, the home of the moving picture
stars, and Sammy Davis Jr. and the Brooklyn Dodgers?"

"Lolliloppi, Mister President," the PM said with
malice aforethought. "Lolliloppi, Mississippi."

"How about Florida?" the President persuaded desperately. "The land of sunshine and ocean breezes? That's further south than Mississippi."

"A promise is a promise, Mr. President, and Lolliloppi is Lolliloppi."

"Yes indeed—a promise certainly is a promise, and Lolliloppi is Lolliloppi," the President agreed bewilderedly, as under his breath he swore off whiskey. How could he have made such a promise to this innocent-youth-of-noble-savage-and-Black Prime Minister? He took the pledge forthwith, and it was the water wagon for him. For the duration. Or certainly as long as the PM and his party were around to make naive requests like "May we visit Lolliloppi, Mississippi?" How much native naivete can a naive native have? he asked himself rhetorically but not aloud.

14

Now the newsmen and TV and photographers were let loose into the room, and they were the wildest bunch of American natives the Guanayans had ever witnessed, even in the moving pictures. Flash-bulbs were exploding all over the place, and TV cameras grinding, and the PM posing now with the beloved Prexy.

And Maria Efwa posing with this one, that one, and the other.

"What do you think of our country?" one of the newsmen asked Jimmy Johnson, on television. Live TV.

He glimpsed Maria Efwa getting her picture taken with Mister Parkington of the State Department.

"Yes indeed," the PM answered cagily.

Now they had her posing with the bad-teeth scientist.

Jimmy imagined that Hillman had a sensational case of halitosis. He felt like galloping to her rescue on his great Black horse.

"What do you think of the Cold War climate, Mr. Prime Minister?"

Now she was posing smilingly with the Secretary of State, Jimmy Johnson observed.

"Too much weather," the PM cagily answered, even though he was distracted.

"How does it feel to be in the Free World, Mr. Prime Minister?"

"Oh, it's very nice indeed, and I bring you greetings from it. You should visit us sometimes." He smiled whitely, Black and pretty for the people of the press, and Lloyd jabbed him in the ribs. His ribs were getting tenderized from the constant elbow jabbing by His Wife's Nervous Bottom and Foreign Minister Mamadou Tangi.

"You are a bachelor, aren't you, Mr. Prime Minister?" a newsman from a liberal American paper which shall be nameless asked. "What do you think of our American women?"

The other newsmen laughed and giggled.

His Excellency was unperturbed. "I have not seen much of them, but from what I have seen there're plenty of them."

He let them figure that one out.

"Where are you going from Washington, Mr. Prime Minister?"

"I am going to your fabulous New York City, of the extraordinary monstrous Apples of which I intend to bite into extensively, and where the buildings scrape the sky and people wash their faces in the clouds."

He could hear some of the newsmen snickering politely, and then he politely lowered the boom.

"From New York I am going down to sample some of your good old Southern hospitality in Lolliloppi, Mississippi."

Suddenly it got very quiet. One of the Southern newsmen fainted. It was quiet hot in the Cabinet Room, despite the air conditioning, what with the klieg lights on, and everything.

Now they were moving, PM and Prexy, shoulder to shoulder, like old buddies, down the red-carpeted hall toward the northern entrance to the White House, flanked by distinguished conferees from both countries, and G-men and SS-men and newsmen and photographers. When they were about fifty feet from the northern portico, a door opened suddenly, and two young SS men ran breathlessly toward them. Had he had the proper pigmentation or lack of it, whichever, Jimmy Johnson would have paled visibly. As it was, he settled for other clichéd manifestations. He perspired profusely. His stomach doubled into knots; crabs staged an orgy in his entrails. And he knew somehow the jig was up; the masquerade was over. He felt a sudden wave of claustrophobia, saw visions of the Rock of Alcatraz. Everything closed in on now. He looked around him for some place to run and hide, but there was no place. He thought about the great Joe Louis. He could run but he could not hide. He almost lost his cool completely.

When the two excited young men reached them, they spoke rapidly to Carlton Carson, who whispered nervously to the President. The President paled visibly.

He said, "Dammit to fu-fu-fucking hell!"

Carlton Carson whispered further.

The President's second contribution was, "Dammit to fuh-fuh-fucking hell!"

The party had stopped about ten or fifteen feet from the northern entrance and Jimmy (he was Jimmy now, from head to toe, no more no less) could hear a commotion outside that sounded like a lynch mob. He almost paled visibly despite his pigmentation. But even at this dire moment, our hero never lost his sense of humor. The jig is up, he thought, and I will be the jig that's up.

Finally, the nervous President turned to His Most

Distinguished Excellency from the Independent People's Democratic Republic of Guanaya. "Mr. Prime Minister, I wonder if I might show you one of the other entrances to the White House. You would be surprised at how many entrances there are."

But abruptly he was the PM again and the wave of claustrophobia all mixed up with paranoia suddenly subsided, and he thought he smelled another kind of rat. He almost said, "Ah-ha!" Furthermore, in his role as a Black man of the American diaspora, which he had almost but not entirely forgotten at the moment, he automatically took umbrage toward back door and side door entrances.

He threw it on the President, his great disarming smile. "We have an ancient belief in my country, Mr. President, that a man should leave by the same door he entered, unless there are compelling reasons or circumstances that dictate to the contrary."

He heard the noise outside clearly now, and he was both Jimmy Johnson (colored) and His Excellency Jaja Okwu Olivamaki, and nothing could have kept him, short of gunpoint, from going out of the northern entrance. At the moment his role as prime minister was overshadowed by his American-Negritude or vice versa. He thought he heard chanting outside and he giggled deeply in his abdomen.

"We could ride the White House elevator," the President suggested. "Or we could leave by the East Gate. Or even better, go through the Oval Office through the french doors and we could see the famous beautiful Rose Garden. They didn't even show the Rose Garden to Premier Krookshelf."

"Are there compelling reasons why we should not leave by the same door through which we entered?"

"Certainly not," the President admitted.

"Well then, there you are," the PM said decidedly.

The poor President did not know what to do. Whether "to shit or to go blithely blind" as they say in 'Sippi in educated company. "But surely, you're not superstitious, Your Excellency. You're a modern man in every respect, and from this side entrance there is such a magnificent view. The famous Rose—Gar—I mean, every morning I—"

He felt very sorry for his brand-new buddy the President; at the same time, he relished the Great White Father's keen discomfort. It was his duality acting up again. Du Bois had written of it in *The Souls of Black Folk*. He smiled sweetly at the Prexy, and underneath the smile, he sneered at his Great White Father. "We all have our indigenous Juju, Mr. President. Believe me, we marvel at some of the naive superstitions of the natives in America. You believe that black is bad, and white is good. For example, you never have elected a Black man president, have you old chap, not even Jesse Jackson."

"No, we haven't," the President admitted, smiling weakly and wondering what cul-de-sac this crafty naive "noble savage" was leading him up, and wishing he'd never brought up the question of superstition.

The PM had developed a mannerism of laughing quietly before he delivered his punch lines. "It couldn't be because you're not in favor of Black people, yes?"

"No, it definitely couldn't." The President's voice got progressively weaker.

"Americans have a tradition of always being for the underdog, no?"

"Yes," the President answered very weakly.

"Well then you see it must be just a silly superstition, no?"

"Yes," the President admitted, grudgingly.

The PM gave his funny laugh again. "By Jove, that is a bizarre superstition. And you also believe that quantity is quality, the bigger the better, whatever. And you people actually believe that in order to preserve the peace you must prepare for war." He laughed his quick short laugh again. "That's a jolly good idiocy, eh? But we don't hold your culture against you, old boy. Every man to his own Juju, we democratic Guanayans always say." He laughed and slapped the Prexy's back and almost knocked the breath and false teeth out of the by-now bewildered gentleman.

"WE SHALL OVERCOME SOME DAY," Jimmy heard the voices outside singing now, and he was almost overcome himself with pride and sorrow, even as he wondered when that "some day" *they* would overcome was coming. *They* might be the very last folk on earth to overcome, he thought, whatever overcoming meant. At the moment *they* were his Black and distant brothers in the American diaspora (a term of recent Afro vintage, co-opted from the Jewish people for whatever reason), where he was visiting, and he, himself, was His Excellency, Prime Minister of the Independent People's Democratic Republic of Guanaya, and he was their Great Black Brother image from across the ocean in Mother Africa. "I'm the Messiah they have waited for," he told himself, almost aloud. He felt his face filling up and tears were in his eyes now, almost, but just in time it came to him exactly who he really was. He was one of them outside the White House. And he'd better never ever forget it. He managed a straight face for the President, as he turned and started for the northern portico again.

The President was up a tree without a shotgun. Clearly, he could not force the PM to go out of a side

door against his will. It certainly would not be the diplomatic thing to do, and furthermore, these Africans
were hypersensitive. That was quite clear to him now,
so he went along with the PM, who had quickened his
pace. Needless to say, the others followed suit.

Outside Jimmy saw a mammoth picket line, mostly
Afro, with picket signs and slogans. From where he
was, he could not make out the wording on the signs.
He didn't need to, because he knew somehow it had to
do with why he'd left America. He knew the picket line
bit by heart. He had paid his dues in so many of them
from California to Manhattan Island. He got a brief
glimpse only, because they hustled him into a big black
Cadillac limousine and took off swiftly down the driveway from the White House and before they reached the
avenue, instead of continuing straight ahead and turning rightward, which would have taken them in the
direction of the hotel, but which would have also taken
him within spitting range of the picket line, the chauffeur did a totally impossible rear-maneuvered U-turn
and went around the side of the White House and departed through the East Gate across from the Treasury
Department. Looking back at the picket line through
the back of the car, Jimmy could barely make out the
large letters at the top of most of the picket signs. He
rubbed his eyes. Surely his eyes were deceiving him.

The word on the top of the signs was, or at least it seemed to be

CRAP

and in big bold letters.

CRAP

That evening all the papers carried variation of the same headline:

NEW YORK CRAP
IN FRONT OF THE WHITE HOUSE

It was a real peculiar country, Jimmy Johnson thought to himself. But later that evening the mystery was solved. CRAP was the acronym of a newly formed civil rights organization that called itself the Committee for the Rights of All the People.

Hence *CRAP.*

15

In the late late of that same afternoon, one of the President's secretaries called Lolliloppi, Mississippi, with great trepidations and posed the question. And the mayor said, "How come you people pickin on us? We ain't done nothing. We got the happiest colored folks anywhere in Dixie, in the whole wide world. We support the Supreme Coat one hunnert percent, when we got to it, when it catches up with us, when our nigrahs find out about it. We got a human relations committee making a survey on the problem. Our folks in Lolliloppi have learned to live together separately, even though we are desegregated."

"Good!" the president's third secretary said. "Glad to hear it. They'll be arriving there on the twenty-second."

"GreatGodA'mighty!" Mayor Hardtack said. "You can't do that to me. It's unconstitutional!" He jumped up and down. "It's un-American!" His false teeth fell out and bounced on the desk. "It's against all the rules of Southern hospitality. I mean hostility. It's even outrageous!" He lost his voice and found it again. "And besides, I'm running for reelection in a couple of months. And the nigrahs deep down here in the delta don't know they got a right to vote. The news ain't reached um yet."

Lolliloppi was proudly famous for being the only "city" in the Southland that was more segregated than it had been before that infamous day in May 1954. The Supreme Court be damned! They were "anti-Commonist patriotic American born-again Christian of the first magnitude. Let George Wallace betray the sacred cause of Southern Womanhood. Let him meet his God on Judgment Day."

"They'll only be down there for two or three days," the presidential secretary said patiently. "What's the matter, Mister Mayor? Do you hate colored people so much?"

"No, sir!" Mayor Hardtack answered with righteous indignation. "Some of my best friends and so forth and so on, including my dear old colored mammy by which I was successfully suckled." He smacked his lips, nostalgically. "I can almost taste them brown-skinned tit-ties even now. It's just that we got such a big powerful White Citizens Council here in town. It's the biggest one in Mississippi. It's the only one in Mississippi, I reckon." His specs had fallen from his face, and he was feeling frantically over the desk for them—and for his almost brand-new choppers.

"You'll have to sit down and talk with the president of the council and tell him the facts of life, Mister Mayor. The Supreme Court outlawed segregation more than twenty years ago."

"It won't do a bitter good," Mayor Hardtack said bitterly.

"Who is he, Mayor Hardtack? What's his name?"

"Who is who?" the Mayor asked, stalling, reddening everywhere. "What's who's name?" Losing color now. He could not locate his choppers since he couldn't see without his glasses and he could not locate his glasses because he could not see without his glasses.

Now the secretary was losing patience and perspective. "You know what whose I'm whoozing!" the president's third secretary shouted.

"I can't make heads or tails of what you talking about," the mayor said. "And I don't believe anybody as confused as you could possibly be third secretary to the President of the Uniney States."

By now the third secretary to the president was hopelessly confused. "Who's the President of the United States?" he screamed. "That's who's whose I'm whoozing!"

"If you don't know, son, you must not be his third secretary," Mayor Hardtack said almost with sympathy, certainly with tolerance. Cagily. He had his glasses now.

The secretary said, "Just a minute, Mr. Mayor."

"That's all right with me, son," the mayor said. "Long as you didn't make this call collect." Now he put his teeth back into place.

The third secretary got himself a drink of Scotch and water, sniffed a little white powder, put a dip of snuff in his lower lip, in order to get himself together for one more go at it. Now he was ready. "You have a big White Citizens Council down there in Lolliloppi?"

"All day long and halfway through the night," Mayor Hardtack answered patiently. "I told you that when you first drove up. You got a bad memory, Mister Third Secretary-to-the-President, if you really is who you say you is."

"Never mind," the secretary said, "What is the name of the president of the White Citizens Council?"

"Which White Citizens Council you talking about,

Mister Third Secretary to the President of the Uniney States?" Richard Rufus Rastus inquired, drawlingly.

The third secretary responded, "What is the name of the president of the White Citizens Council of Lolliloppi, Mississippi?"

"Oh, you meant that outstanding upstanding, and understanding gentleman?"

"The very same. What's his name?"

The mayor said clearly and distinctly, "Richard Rufus Rastus Hardtack Jr. is his name."

The third secretary repeated wearily, "Richard Rufus Rastus Hardtack Jr.—why—why that's your name, isn't it, Mister Mayor?"

"You sure do catch on mighty quick, son," the mayor said proudly with a nervous giggle. Then he went off into gales of laughter, then subsided to his nervous giggle again. Then soberly he said, "At your service."

"Well, they're coming down there, Mister Mayor or Mister President, whichever you are, and they are to get the full VIP treatment."

"No! No! Naw! Naw! Hell naw!" the mayor shouted. He almost lost his teeth again. They did the cha-cha-cha in his tender mouth. You could hear them clattering all the way to the nation's capital.

"They *are* coming down there, Mister Mayor, because our nation is the leader of the Free World and Mississippi *is* a part of our nation."

"What's that got to do with it?" the mayor asked, in all sincerity. "We ain't done nothing. We support the Supreme Coat every day in the week and twice on Sunday."

"And Guanaya has one of the greatest potentials for being a democracy of any of the new nations in Africa and being friendly with the Free World and the West."

"What's that got to do with Lolliloppi?" Mayor Hardtack seriously wanted to know. "We're down deep here in the South. Lolliloppi ain't even in Western Mississippi."

"And besides it's one of the richest countries in Africa—maybe in the whole world. Cobanium is money, Mr. Mayor. Money-power-money-power-money! Loads and loads and loads of it. In a fundamental sense, Guanaya could well be the last frontier. Money, Mister Mayor!"

"Now you're talking!" Mayor Hardtack said with unreserved enthusiasm. When he heard the word "money," his response was like a conditioned reflex. "And you tell them Ethiopes the Southland is the friendliest place on God's little old green earth. Since when did the wild west get so goddamn hospitalitary?"

The mayor's question threw the third secretary off his horse for a moment, as he tried to figure out how the wild west had galloped into the picture. By the time he relocated the mayor in time and space, Mayor Hardtack had had time to look at visions of "Ethiopes" descending upon the peaceful town of Lolliloppi from every angle, and it damn near scared his brand-new choppers out of his quivering mouth again. And to hell with money! He was a man of high and Southern principles.

He shouted, "No! No! No! It's still no-go!"

"Oh yes," the secretary answered. "We'll get back to you on this tomorrow."

And he hung up on Mayor Richard Rufus Rastus Hardtack Jr. And he went and reported his conversation to the President.

The mayor called an emergency session of the city council and/or the White Citizens Council of Lolliloppi. Without a scorecard you could not tell the difference, since the membership was almost entirely the same, and the chairman of both was Richard Rufus Rastus Hardtack Jr. They jumped up and down. They ranted and raved. They picketed themselves. They demonstrated. They all sent telegrams to their congressman and to the President of the United States telling them that those African nigrahs were not welcome to Lolliloppi and if they came, the citizens council, oops, the city council could not be held responsible for what would happen. A more spirited group of loyal Lolliloppians you just could never have imagined.

The President made much palava with his cabinet and some leaders of the House and Senate. After heated debate, the decision was to let the question ride for a couple of days. Maybe in the excitement of being in America and especially in a place like New York City, the Africans would forget all about their very twisted obsession with Lolliloppi, Mississippi.

One senator suggested that if the Africans mentioned Lolliloppi again, "Maybe they could be persuaded instead to take a trip to Disneyland in California. Tell them, that way, they could steal a march on the Great White Father from the Kremlin." A couple of the dignified gentlemen laughed, and everything got quiet and they let it go at that. For the time being, that is— hopefully.

Meanwhile there were the embassy parties and receptions and drinking drinking everywhere. The bogus PM learned that the diplomatic circle was one great protracted drinking bout that went on and on and on and never ended. Hangoverville, everlastingly.

And as much as this wearied him, he liked more and more the image of being prime minister, even as it scared the hell out of him, and he liked the *oohs* and *ahs* that grew larger louder longer every time out, as the crowds outside everywhere he went grew vaster and much wilder. And every moment inside their suite was spent with Maria Efwa, the lovely peripatetic perambulating encyclopedia of Guanayan lore and knowledge. They spent more time together than the rest of the PM's party thought was necessary. But the fake PM insisted that every moment with her was essential to their noble mission, as in his eyes she became more beautiful by the moment. He was hooked, lined, and sunken. And she never gave him one title of encouragement. She was always business. She was the private tutor, the *uchitel* of His-Phony-Excellency Jimmy Johnson; she was the Minister of Education, Information, and Culture, a fact she did not hesitate to call to his attention whenever things got out of hand, or whenever he held her hands too long. Female rejection was not the kind of rejection he had been used to suffering. And he suffered painfully. He agonized. He sulked. He pouted. He actually lost his appetite.

About six one evening they were having one of their

private tutoring sessions in the midst of a bedlam of telephones ringing and Mr. Tobey banging away on a noiseless typewriter that made enough noise to wake up the dead, even a dead drunk, and Tangi and His Wife's Bottom arguing a question of the New Cold War diplomacy. Détente, it seemed, was dead and buried, despite dear Hubert Herbert Hubert's feeble efforts at resurrection. Maria Efwa was telling Jimmy the story of how the British conquered their great land with firepower against the proud but pitifully armed might of the Guanayans' Spear-and-Arrow Regiments, at which point many Guanayans of long ago had been convinced that the white man had some powerful Juju working for him. Jimmy sat there near her across from her, their knees almost touching. He stared at her in open-mouthed fascination like a little boy listening to a fairy story before beddy-bye time. A black satin burnished doll face. Her lips were full and obvious and curvaceous and even more so when she talked that talk, and her eyes were large warm black shiny almond-shaped African midnights, in which he almost always lost his way. But not unwillingly. Sometimes he wandered aimlessly in the endless midnight of her lookers. She didn't really ever look, she stared at people, from great depths and dimensions. Her lovely amply plenished mouth did sweet dimpled tricks when she talked that talk, whatever talk she talked.

The telephone rang, and Mr. Tobey answered it and called to His Excellency, but he was gone, long gone, hopelessly lost in the lovely darkness again of the breathtaking African midnight of Maria Efwa's eyes. Finally, Mr. Tobey came over and tapped him on the shoulder and brought him back among the living, and wide awake. And also brought Maria Efwa back to the here-and-now. Jimmy looked up at Mr. Tobey as if the PM's secretary had committed some outrageous sacrilege like peeing in the Amen Corner during Lent.

"Well?"

"The United States Information Agency is on the phone, Your Excellency." Mr. Tobey was always formal with him, as if he really believed in the reality of the fake PM. "They want you to speak on the Voice of America. Shall I make the arrangements?"

Jimmy's eyes lit up. The Voice of America! "I'll take the call myself, Mr. Tobey." He'd give the whole damn world the true voice of America. The Black man's voice. Here was his great opportunity!

Mr. Tobey brought the phone to him. The woman on the other end of the conversation cooed and purred as she explained to him that the Voice of America wanted him to do a program with them for overseas consumption. He said he'd be delighted. She cooed and purred and giggled. He was suddenly aware that Maria Efwa was watching him, as he spoke to the cooing-purring-giggler, sight unseen, and he grew warm under Maria's midnight moonlit stare, warm all over, but when he looked toward her, he could never catch her watching him, which was awfully disconcerting.

The lady giggler said, "I'll let you speak to one of our program directors so that he can arrange an appointment directly with-with-with you." She was making like an outboard motor.

Jimmy stared deliberately at the live and breathing African carving that was Maria Efwa's profile set in a burnished ebony, as he waited for the program director's voice, and he knew Maria knew that he was staring at her, and brazenly. Her breathing, a little different somehow, told him she was not entirely unaware of him. He sighed a deep protracted sigh and noted that her face flushed warmly. He was lost again in the darkness of her beauty and the beauty of her darkness, and only half heard the male voice talking on the other end, at first. The familiar sound of the voice only partly reached into the buttocks of his great uneasiness. The man had talked for two or three minutes and the danger signals had flashed like crazy in the far comers of Jimmy's consciousness, but he paid no heed at all, as he gave the USIA man a real short measure, mostly. "Yes—" . . . "Good." "*C'est ça, monsieur.*" Why was he speaking his jive-ass French? Absent-mindedly, until the man repeated his name for the third or fourth time. "William Clarence Barnsfield the Fifth, Your Excellency. I believe I met you once while in your country—at the Ambassador Palace Hotel—I—"

Jimmy was suddenly wide awake, and a fine perspiration broke out all over him and the disturbance in his stomach was a bubbling-over coffee percolator. He could still hear Barnsfield-Fifth's voice like the quickened pace of a tape recorder, as he took the receiver from his ear and held it at arm's length out from him and placed it quietly back in place. Jimmy wiped his face and took a drink. The phone rang again, and the lady explained to Mr. Tobey that they had been cut off, and would he please put Prime Minister Jaja Okwu Olivamaki back on the phone again? But when Mr. Tobey called to him, Jimmy told him to make the arrangements for the broadcast himself. "You're my secretary," he said shakily. "You work out the details for the third Friday in next month."

"But, Your Excellency," Mr. Tobey protested, "we'll be back in Guanaya by then."

"You sure do catch on quickly," the PM told him. "Like you sure got swift perception, Mr. Tobey, Secretary to the Prime Minister of the Independent People's Democratic Republic of Guanaya."

16

Each morning as he got out of bed and went through his ablutions, he wondered if this would be the day when the whole charade would explode in their faces. The entire mansion of treasonous pretensions would come crashing down around them as if wrought by an earthquake of cosmic-like proportions. How would it happen? What should he be on the lookout for? Old Ambassador Palace Hotel Barnsfield from the USIA? A cover for the CIA? Would they come at him in the disguise of a soul brother? A foxy sister? A lady friend from out of his dissolute and wanton past? Was he becoming paranoid? Was it paranoia to be apprehensive while walking through a rattlesnake farm? Hell naw! The snakes are real, and they will bite, and they are venomous! The most powerfully malignant ASPs in all this earth. He had figured it out. Like he once said, "Why be redundant? Why call them WASPS? White Anglo-Saxon Protestants?" He'd never heard of Black Anglos, except in Nathan Hare's satirical title. ASP was more accurate in description of their venom. "They'll take your ass right out of this world!" He worked himself into an angry sweat. He sometimes felt uneasy all through the day, especially when he was out there in that world away from the hotel, felt that he was walking stupidly through a field that had been booby-trapped and mined especially for boobs and boobies such as he. ASPs! The fear would stay with him through much of the morning. Seated on the commode, under the shower, shaving, getting dressed, then gradually wear away as morning moved toward afternoon and got involved with early evening. By then, he was ready to make war against the whole world, if it came to that. There was a Don Quixote romanticism in him that always fought for hegemony. And then there was Maria Efwa, the bewitching beauty of her strength and the strength of her bewitching beauty. Overpowering, to one like him, so susceptible to beauty.

Apprehensions be damned! Let the ASPy rattlesnakes come. He'd deal deadly with the mother-muckers! He'd been an expert on the rifle range. He'd detonated the booby traps. Then a slightly calmer inner voice would caution him. "Go forth militantly, but dammit keep your guard up, *ALWAYS!*" It was an ASP that caused the early demise of the fabulous Cleopatra.

They had been invited to attend an "intimate" reception the next evening, given in their honor by a very very colored lady who was reputed to be the Elsa Maxwell of the Black elite of the nation's capital. If you were not invited to her little old make-do domicile to be the center of attraction, you could not possibly be *that* important. She was the colored social indicator. The fake PM knew of her reputation, had met her casually during his brief sojourn at Howard University in Washington, when he was Jimmy Jay Leander Johnson, fox trapper *nonpareil*, before he'd made his sacred pilgrimage to the Mother Continent and his life had changed forever. He smiled when they received the invitation, actually he laughed aloud with excited expectations. These were Franklin Frazier's Black and beautiful bourgeoisie, he thought, and he intended to enjoy them to the fullest in his fake role of the Minister Primarily. He forgot about his apprehension.

All night long the night before he had found sleep elusive. And when finally sleep did come, it dealt with him fitfully, he dreamed nightmarishly. Replete, his nightmares were with premonitions of danger, attempts at assassinations on the next evening along the line of convoy to the palatial mansion of the Black (change that) *colored* Elsa Maxwell. Snipers perched on rooftops with telescopic rifles. In his mad dream, they even let him take dead aim at himself. That one was the first nightmare, from which he awakened with a sweet relief. And glad he was to be awake and still among the living. The second dream had him running smack into one of his sweethearts at the party of his former Washington days, a lovely colored Mata Hari working for the CIA. The third dream had him back in Bamakanougou riding through the dark in the same Land Rover as before, and this time he did not jump before it detonated. He awakened in a drench of sweat and shaking as if he suffered badly for Saint Vitus.

What did it mean? Were his nightmares trying to tell him something? Were his dreams a forewarning? Did his prescience come in nightmares now? Perhaps he should forgo this reception. Beg off this time for the reason of sheer exhaustion, which would not be far from the truth of the way things were. Again, his sense of adventure took precedence over his fear of premonition. Preposterous! Yet an ominous foreboding lingered with him the whole day through.

It was mid-September, a time of autumnal equinox, and a tender breeze blew gently its soothing breath among the golden brown-leaved trees that lined the avenue on Sixteenth Street; the tall trees were afire with autumn, as they rode in long black limousines, led by a convoy of the capital city's motorcycled finest. This time all of them were dressed in their national attire. The bogus PM stared from the open limo, as they moved up the boulevard past Malcolm X Park (formerly named Meridian), past the Howard University extension of dormitories, where the students stood outside, it seemed thousands of them, and threw flowers at the entourage. He thought that quite easily a bouquet of flowers could conceal a hand grenade. Each time one was thrown he fought hard to keep from ducking. And also kisses from the women; they waved Guanayan flags at the famous PM's entourage past the churches at Columbia Road and Harvard Street, the Universal Church to the left, past the proud baroque establishments once known as "EMBASSY ROW" before the coming of the great Black horde, which laid waste everything and everyone in its path, past the great apartment houses, with armed men on rooftops as if his dream were being reenacted, complete with his own perspiration. Now past the fabulous and fashionable Black bourgeois–owned mansions ultimately past the District line into the Maryland suburbs. Several blocks more and then a turn to the left, another sharper turn to the right, and shortly they were in front of the humble abode of Madame Marie Antoinette Robinson (known to her intimate bourgeois friends as "Toni" and to less intimate ones as "Madame Guillotine").

A three-storied edifice constructed of stone and mortar, a realistic replica of a castle out of Tuscany in the Middle Ages, turreted and towered. Replete with sentinel and security agents of all denominations, plainclothed and uniformed. The bogus PM thought, amusingly, all that was needed was for the house to have been encircled by a moat with drawbridge even and some idiot in the tower walking back and forth and shouting, "Seven o'clock and all is well!" The medieval illusion would have been complete.

Uniformed policemen were all over the place, every entrance to the castle, trampling on Madame's mani- cured lawn, a lawn that resembled a college campus in its breadth and vastness, uniformed parking attendants always at the ready. Proud Black SS men stepped anx- iously forward and opened the doors of the long black limos and surrounded the fake PM and his entourage and hurried them into the front entrance. Armed SS men on the roofs of all the nearby elegant edifices, rifles pointed. They had the PM and his retinue covered.

Our man of 'Sippi and lately of the Guanayas made an entrance to end all entrances. In his long white flowing silk brocaded boubou, he made a theatrical ingress like the Prime Minister he was not, as if he had been trained since he was a babe in the cradle for His Excellency's Ministership, primarily. With his exquisitely bouboued coterie he glided into the hallway and henceforth into the vast living room with its wall-to-wall carpeting and its wall-to-wall Black boogwuggies. The *haute monde* Africaine for sure. Doctors and their spouses, lawyers and their spouses, dentists, university professors, here and there a congressperson, a couple of recognizable movie actors, and one or two real live labor leaders. He could not help hearing a concert of murmurs of admiration as Madame Marie Antoinette moved gracefully toward him and offered up her glowing cheek to be kissed. She was a sensually faced woman elegantly gowned and sequined in a long black silken caftan garment that hugged the contours of her body, passionately, lasciviously, *sans bra, sans girdle.* There was apparently nothing 'neath that finely clothed caftan but her fine brown-framed sensuous self. Madame Marie Antoinette Robinson was a society lady of the middle ages growing slimmingly and inevitably toward a very slight obesity, due quite obviously to overindulgence in exotic culinary pursuits and alcoholic imbibition. Notwithstanding Madame Guillotine was not slack of face. Her flowing light-brown skin pulled tightly over her high oriental cheekbones *à la* Sophia Loren (many of her friends had remarked admiringly of the resemblance), brown walnut-shaped eyes, a full-lipped rich-red avaricious mouth. It was a gathering of the elite among Franklin Frazier's fashionable bourgeoisie of color, with a fair sprinkling of the paler people of the upper middle classes. State Department types and all. Truly high society. Through it all he looked apprehensively for a recognizable face. He was threading through a minefield that might detonate at any moment. He told himself, heroically, that he would do the detonating.

"Well," she said flamboyantly in a breathless voice. "We have ultimately arrived."

The fake PM wondered which or what "we" the elegant lady referred to. He looked behind him and around him. And apparently Madame seemed to have forgotten that the other members of his retinue existed, as she took him in tow and led him to the bar in an oak-paneled room across the hall from the drawing room.

Jimmy Johnson said, "But the others— I mean, my cabinet—"

"What others?" Madame inquired cavalierly, mischievously. "Dearest of all excellencies, there are no others when His Excellency makes an ingress."

He started to say, "But—"

When she interrupted him with, "First of all we will refresh ourselves in the Tavern Room. Then we will conduct you on a tour of Madame's humble abode escorted personally by yours sincerely."

He looked behind him and saw that he was being followed by the others of his entourage.

They refreshed themselves in the Tavern Room, as Madame kept up a constant soliloquy. They all drank to Madame's health and her continuing prosperity. And, as always, to African liberation. It was one of the few moments since the fake PM had known His Wife's Bottom that Mr. Lloyd had opened his mouth and even cleared his throat, and yet had remained speechless. Even Foreign Minister Tangi with his perpetual sarcastic smile was suddenly and ominously without the powers of articulation. The Minister of Education, Her Excellency Mamselle Maria Efwa, looked on with amusement, silently. Already she had been taken in tow by a tall dark brown-skinned young man, thirtyish and handsome, one of the up-and-coming legal lights of the nation's capital. They had met before at another gathering. There had been so many in the last few days it was impossible to keep up with them. Whites and Blacks vied viciously for His Excellency's appearances. All of Washington society went to parties expecting to see His Excellency Jaja Okwu Olivamaki of the Independent People's Democratic Republic of Guanaya.

From the Tavern Room up the spiral staircase to the five bedrooms on the second floor. By now the tour contingent had multiplied.

The fake PM said, "Aah, the master bedroom."

Madame said, "Yes, but there no longer is a master to occupy it with its lonely mistress. The poor dear passed away three years ago." She wiped her eyes with a silken handkerchief. He feared she would be overcome with grief, but then she mustered strength from some unknown source. Who said women were the weaker sex? Then: "This canopied four-poster is of course French Renaissance Louis Quatorze seventeenth-century rococo (she pronounced it *row-cock-co*, with emphasis on the middle initial, lingeringly), as is the damask drapes and the dresser and the bidet in the bathroom there. All baroque and row-cock-co."

All the fake PM could say was "Very very nice."

"They were shipped directly from Paree to me."

He heard a feminine and what he thought to be a familiar voice behind him say, "His Excellency is a combination of Sidney Poitier and Robert Redford and Harry Belafonte all put together and combinated." He broke into a sweat. He knew that voice from days gone by, he thought. She giggled. "You see I am an integrationist all the way. I do not even segregate my fantasies."

He had become aware since he started up the circular staircase of someone tugging gently at the bottom hem of his flowing boubou. He didn't dare look around to see who the guilty party was, but the constant gentle tugging was getting on his tender nerves. At the entrance to every bedroom there was a tuxedoed waiter standing stiffly at attention with a tray of alcoholic beverages and hors d'oeuvres. In the second bedroom it was, according to the Mistress of the house, "Italian Renaissance all the way. It cost us fifty-five thousand dollars and eighty-seven cents, tax included."

"Did you get some hors d'oeuvres, honey?" Madame inquired. "All drink and no chop-chop will get sugar pie drunk as a cooter in the bayous." She pronounced it *horses douvreys*. "The main course will be served around about midnight."

Jimmy Johnson reached back for a handful of "horses douvreys."

Then on to the next bedroom, which was "thirty thousand dollars twentieth-century modern" as the master (or is it mistress?) bathroom with the sunken bathtub and its aquamarine bidet and telephone and bookshelves with tapes and albums and stereo equipment. And so forth ad infinitum, even ad nauseum. Up to the third floor and the rec room replete with swimming pool and pool and Ping-Pong tables. Back down the spiral stairway, where pictures adorned the wall, copies of Gaugin and Van Gogh and Toulouse-Lautrec, but no evidence of books in this mansion, with now the feeling of the hem of the back of his boubou being constantly lifted higher and higher, as if the holder thought she or he held the train of a wedding dress and that she or he was a flower girl.

When he reached the first floor at the bottom of the stairway, he turned toward the little tuxedoed mouse-faced gentleman with the black bow tie so large it hid his face. His beady eyes seemed to be peeking frightfully through a great black bush. The thick lens of his glasses made him look like a frog staring blankly from and through a lake of frozen ice. He apparently tried to conceal himself beneath the PM's boubou, since he almost disappeared from view, momentarily.

The PM said, "What on earth do you think you're doing, sire?"

Perhaps it would be inaccurate to describe the frightened little wide-eyed small-faced thick-spectacled gentleman as being tongue-tied, as the clichéd metaphor goes, since his mouth did open and his red white-coated tongue worked frenziedly, up and down, twisting turning, pirouetting, though no sounds intelligible to human issued forth. Perhaps he thinks he's speaking Hausa, the bogus PM thought, sarcastically.

Madame Guillotine said, contemptuously, "The stupid little mousey limp-wristed bitch is trying to find out what you're wearing underneath your magnificent boubou, if any."

The fake PM said, "Oh—in that case, sire, why did you not inquire of me?" And he lifted the bottom hem of his silken boubou, dramatically, theatrically, inch by inch, as the gentleman stood there owl-eyed, past his ankles past the calves of his legs now past his knee-caps up the very dark brown hairless thighs, now to the final excruciating moment of rectitude, all eyes trained on him breathtakingly, when he reached his purple jogging trunks. The little man gasped as his eyes grew larger, wider, larger; they seemed finally to outgrow the sockets that contained them. His poor little mouth worked out feverishly, but again no intelligible sounds came forth, as the floor came up and claimed him, or, in other words, he swooned. Two good-hearted Samaritans dressed as hospital attendants, and present there for such exigencies of overindulgences, took the dear gentleman in hand, gasping now for breath. They stretched him forthwith on the floor and one of them lay astride him, mouth to mouth and belly to belly. The PM wondered if this wasn't carrying things a bit too far. He was that puritanical, according to Himself. Now the white-coated ones took the upset one up the stairs, waving fans in front of his perspiring face. The party'd ended early for him. Curiosity had damn near killed the cat.

The mild commotion having subsided, Madame Marie Antoinette had him and his cabinet members stand in a long reception line as the ladies and gentlemen of the reception also lined up and passed before them to meet him and his cabinet, formally. Some giggling ladies bucked the line, including several who were obviously of the masculine gender, tuxedoed and trousered, as it were. Any moment he feared a familiar face would materialize before him and find his face familiar and call him by the name his mama and papa had given him. It was not the most enjoyable part of the reception for him.

It was shortly after nine o'clock and the bogus PM found himself seated in a den-of-an-oak-paneled tavern room in front of a marble cocktail table shaped like a map of Africa. A busy bar was at the other end of the room. Seated next to him and swilling mucho vodka was Ms. Virginia Oregonia Washington, a middle-aged woman of some forty years, give or take, mostly take, underneath a wig as red as ripe strawberries. She was consuming Bloody Marys like they had just become of vogue. To his left was Judge Herman Startling Thatcher, salt-and-pepperedly bearded, dignifiedly, discussing a case he had decided that very same afternoon. "I gave that nigger so much time, when he gets out of jail, we'll all be well into the twenty-first century. He'll be worse off than Rip Van Winkle."

His wife piped up, "Oh Judge baby, must we always discuss shop?"

A young lawyer who sat on the thickly carpeted floor in front of Jimmy Johnson and too near Her Excellency for comfort, for the fake PM's comfort, that is, asked the venerable judge, "Judge Thatcher, are you empowered to pass judgment and mete out sentences to white felons of the District as well as Black ones?"

Herman Startling Thatcher answered indignantly, "Why of course. What the hell did you think? I'm judge of all the people of the District of Columbia."

"Judge, why have the DC prisons always been overcrowded with Negroes and very few white inmates? Are white folks in DC so goody-goody and law abiding?"

"Hell naw," another young Black lawyer interjected. "You answered the question your own damn self, when you asked it. It's because they are Black. It's because they're Negroes. That's why they drove

Judge Livingston from the bench, because he stood up for Black folks, Rich Livingston was my main man. I know what I'm talking about."

Red-wigged Virginia Oregonia Washington seated next to the bogus PM interpolated, apropos of who knows what, "My first and only husband was a doctor, but he was also a revolutionary. Poor thing. I'm glad he died when he did, because they surely would've killed him just like they did poor Malcolm X." The red-wigged one had pulled off her expensive pumps and had begun to play footsie underneath the cocktail table with the phony PM's ankle.

Under her breath she whispered froggily to the ersatz Prime Minister, *"Don't try anything funny, buster. I know you Africans, especially you good-looking ones, but I tell you in front, I don't go for no hankum-pankum."*

The PM did not believe his ears. His imagination was playing tricks on him. Perhaps it was the first cocktail. It had been a very potent one.

The good judge said, "Not true at all. True at all. Richard Livingston was removed from the bench because he was a heavy drinker and committed acts unbecoming the dignity of a gentleman of the bench."

The young Black lawyer said, "Bullshit! Judge Thatcher. Nobody swallows more booze and chases more whores than Harry Jackstone, and he's going to be on the bench until the day he kicks the bucket."

The young lawyer seated "too close" to Her Excellency asked Judge Thatcher, "Are you for home rule here in the nation's capital, Judge? I mean real home rule, not this jive representation we have now."

A voice from near the bar piped up with, "The only reason the District doesn't have authentic home rule, there're too many people of color here. That's common knowledge. Right, Judge Thatcher?"

"I've got a terrible headache," the venerable judge replied. "Let me see if I can find a couple of aspirins." The good judge got up and departed.

The young lawyer seated too near Her Excellency said, "That's the way it is with most of these bourgeois Negroes. You start a serious conversation and they come up with a headache. They avoid a political or intellectual dialogue as if it were a communicable disease."

The red-wigged one said, "My husband was the most famous nigger doctor in all of Washington. I'm glad he died of a heart attack. They would have killed him sure as he was born to die, like they did poor Malcolm X. He was a militant revolutionary, don't you know?"

Out of the side of her mouth, she muttered, "*You just watch it, buster. I'm a lady of distinction.*"

The PM pretended it was not happening. He would just ignore her this time. Then he thought perhaps she was a CIA agent.

"The most famous 'nigger' doctor?" His Excellency heard himself inquire, rhetorically.

"He was the richest nigger doctor in the District of Columbia, and I'm glad he died before they killed him."

In an altogether different voice, she mumbled. "*I know you Africans upside down and sideways, especially you, pretty one. All you want is one thing from a genteel lady.*"

Perhaps this was a case, he thought, of paranoiac schizophrenia. The film *The Exorcist* came to mind. Her froggy voice sounded as if it came from a different person altogether.

"Nigger doctor?" the bogus PM questioned further. "A specialist, was he? Is nigger some kind of dread disease we have not heard of in Guanaya?"

Now the red-haired lady's left foot had begun to play some desperate dynamite footsie higher up on the PM's leg.

"*You can't fool me,*" she whispered hissingly. "*I know every trick in the book. You're trying to lull me into a sense of false security.*"

The PM thought, Perhaps this one is unsafe. He began to feel a premonition coming on. He remembered the Rev. King at the autograph party up in Harlem. Perhaps he should change his seat.

The young lawyer too close to Her Excellency Maria Efwa said, "Niggers is that rarest of devastating diseases found mostly in the Western world, Your Excellency. But if you stay here long enough, you will not get by unscathed. It is the most contagious disease ever known to man or beast, especially Black folks. And most of the time it's terminal."

His Wife's Bottom sighed. "Oh dear!" And wiped the perspiration from his forehead.

The bogus PM glanced at His Wife's Bottom. "*Oh dear* is an understatement!" And he took a silken handkerchief from a pocket of his boubou and tied it around his face from nose to chin. He looked just like a stickup man. "No offense intended, sisters, brothers," the fake PM assured them apologetically. "Nothing personal, but we wouldn't want to transport such a virulent disease back to the old country." He stared at the amused expression on Maria Efwa's lovely face. "Is there any successful inoculation against *niggers*?"

A dark-brown young man in a carefully coiffured Afro à la Stokely Carmichael and a kente-clothed dashiki, seated too close to Her Excellency for Jimmy Johnson's comfort, said, "The only cure for *niggers* is Pan-Africanism."

"Niggerism is a state of mind," Maria Efwa explained, patiently, to His Excellency the Minister Primarily. "A psychological disease. We have a few niggers in Guanaya already. So, you may take the handkerchief from your face, Your Excellency. One does not breathe it through the mouth or nostrils."

The dark-brown young lawyer in the carefully coiffured Afro à la Stokely Carmichael seated too near Her Excellency said, "It is a disease of the brain, Your Excellency. It is contracted through a process known as brainwashing."

The red-wigged lady with the hyperactive left foot whose late husband had been a revolutionary "nigger" doctor, untied the handkerchief from around the PM's face and began to mop his perspiring brow. "Poor poor dear!" she murmured. "Poor poor dear! My husband would have treated you successfully. He was the richest—"

Even as the busy-footed one mopped, she mumbled, *"Don't get any funny ideas now. I'm just trying to be hospitable."*

The bogus PM took the handkerchief from the red-wigged lady. "I'll do very well, Madame," he assured her graciously. "Thank you very much."

Virginia Oregonia Washington the Third took her

seat again and promptly began to play footsie with his leg again beneath the cocktail table. Another young-ish woman, strikingly handsome in the extreme, tall, majestic, burnt-brown-toast of skin came into the room and sat in the chair recently vacated by the venerable judge. Jimmy Jay was suddenly alerted. He thought her face familiar. He felt a familiar response to her deeply in the middle of him, warmly, in the middle of him. Her eyes were large and dark and wide and knowing, her mouth was fully lipped and firmly confident.

The bogus PM addressed his remarks to all of them, who looked to him now as if he were the second coming of the Long-Predicted One, now suddenly ar-rived. He knew his Negritude severely now and felt an awesome responsibility on his shoulders, somewhat like he imagined Jackie Robinson must have felt every time he came to bat in the last game of the World Series with the bases loaded with two outs and the Dodg-ers trailing seven to four, the responsibility of the entire race upon his slender shoulders. "Hit that ball, Jackie! What you say!" With grateful apologies to Flip Wilson. He felt the awesome lonesome responsibility he imagined Jackie must have known as did the great Paul Robeson and Willie Mays and Rosa Parks and Mary Bethune and all the other ones who blazed the trail, so long and awesome and alone. He felt the tears for them collecting on the other side of his eyes. Harriet Tubman, Frederick Douglass, Fannie Hamer. He blinked his eyes and blew his nose. His Negritude and his Pan-Africanism collided now, blending, clashing, and he would never regard his ministership primarily as flippantly as he had before. He reached around in his excited brain to say something of significance to his sisters and his brothers. "It seems to me, sisters and brothers, that the grave question before us is how can we as an African people inoculate ourselves with the serum of Pan-Africanism. I am an avid student of Pan-Africanism. My specialty is Afro-Americanism. As you know I lived for five years in this country. We as a people must come to understand that—"

The red-wigged footsie-playing lady, Madame Virginia Oregonia Washington the Third, interrupted him with, "*My late-departed husband knew niggers backwards, forward, upside down, and sideways. He was a specialist on them.*" She took a handkerchief from her pocketbook and began to dab her beady eyes. "I'm so happy that they died before he killed them. Or vice versa." She corrected herself, hopefully. She paused and blew her nose and looked around her. "He was too militant for them to live." The lady had been drinking.

The youngish majestic familiar-faced woman with

the burnt-brown-toasted skin stared at the red-wigged one, incredulously, impatiently. She addressed the fake PM directly. "What can we as African Americans do to bring our people closer together as an African people lost out here in this vast diaspora—" Jimmy Jay stared at her unbelievingly. He'd known what she would sound like before she had spoken. It was weird. It was unreal, a case of eerie déjà vu.

The red-wigged one said, "Ain't no way in the world to get rid of niggers. There are niggers when I came into this world and they'll be here when I leave it. They multiply like rats and roaches."

"Your Excellency," the burnt-brown-skinned beautiful lady with the face and voice that was familiar began again.

But Virginia Oregonia Washington the Third continued unabated. "I know niggers. My husband was a nigger specialist, the richest in the District of—The most militant—and revolu—"

The lovely burnt-brown youngish woman said, "Go on, Your Excellency, you were saying."

Apparently the red-wigged one thought the beautiful familiar-faced one had designated her as "Your Excellency." Virginia Oregonia Washington the Third continued. "As militant niggers, we must demand to be invited to the White House—We must—we must—" Ms. Red Wig paused to pour herself another drink.

The bogus PM leaped headlong into the vacuum. "We who are sons and daughters of Mother Africa must make the connection and let nothing dissuade us. We must be guided by an African value system, that places human beings ahead of things." He felt inspired, as though some other entity spoke through him. He was on automatic pilot now. "We had a communal system long before Karl Marx was born. We always believed that the earth and the fullness and the goodness thereof and therein were God given and belonged to all the people. We were—"

Ms. Red Wig of the dynamite footsie interrupted him with, "We must prove to the white man without a shadow that we're the same as him. We are human beings just like them. My hus—"

"That's where you are absolutely wrong," the familiar-faced one interpolated. "We are *not* like them. They are not human beings. They landed on this earth like thieves in the night, with the wheel. That's why and how they outdistanced everybody. They came with the wheel, and they've been wheeling and dealing ever since." She paused as she stared at the PM and his perspiring forehead. Then she said, "Why do you think they spent all of those billions for that first trip to the moon? They're getting things ready for them to go back where they really came from. And I wish them *bon voyage*. Because if they stay here much longer, this planet is going to be just like the moon. Empty. Lifeless. Just like they left it in the first place." She was smiling now.

Ms. Dynamite Footsie was left speechless, momentarily.

With a big grin on his face now, he heard himself say, "You may just have something there, Thelma Powell. I—" Then he thought, Where did I get that name from? He was sweating all over now, perspiration pouring from him. He had exposed himself, irrevocably.

When he heard her say, "My name is Aisha Umulubalu. I—"

He didn't hear the rest of it. She'd been Thelma Powell when he'd known her as a student at the university on Georgia Avenue. Why had he not recognized her instantly? They had been close friends, sweethearts, lovers, bosom buddies. It was her close-cropped Afro that had transformed her, embellished the latent beauty of her. She used to be pretty, with long black gleaming hair that came down to her shoulders, her pride and glory. No longer was she pretty. She was outrageously, defiantly beautiful. Dark eyes, deeply dark, a rich curvaceous African mouth. Her voice was possessed with more assurance than before. The Minister Primarily felt Maria Efwa's dark eyes staring warmly at him, as if she sensed the strong vibrations between His Excellency and Aisha Umulubalu.

Ms. Red Wig's nervous left foot was halfway up the PM's leg by now, her green eyes blinking a mile a minute. "I don't believe there is no such thing as a Klu Kluck Klan." Apropos of God knows what. "It's nothing but a publicity stunt to scare the hell out of Jews and Niggers. My late beloved husband wasn't no American Negro anyhow. He was an Indian."

"An Indian?" the winsome youngish burnt-brown woman, Aisha Umulubalu, asked her, suspiciously. "What kind of an Indian, Lord help us, and from what tribe?"

"A West Indian from Trinidad. He wasn't no American Negro. He was a British subject all the way, and the Klu Kluck Klan is nonexisting."

Aisha Umulubalu, a.k.a. Thelma Powell, was growing impatient, burnt-brownish skin, wide, beautiful, dazzling dark-brown eyes and all, gradually, at first, now rapidly and all at once. She turned to the fake PM again. "Your Excellency, you were saying."

Maria Efwa's warm dark eyes were taking note of everything going on between Jimmy and Aisha. Not that it mattered to her, personally, but her concern was with how it affected his role as the so-called Prime Minister of Guanaya. After all, she was not in the least emotionally involved with Jimmy Jay.

"We are all of us Africans," Jimmy Johnson said, importantly, in his very special theatrical voice à la Sidney Poitier, who was his model and his patron saint, next to Robeson and Du Bois and Rosa Parks and Douglass and Nkrumah and Nzinga and Nassar and Mary Bethune and Belafonte, Gil Noble, ad infinitum. "We are not a minority and we have a common destiny. None of us will be free until all of us are free. From Brazil to Ouagadougou, from Cairo to Hattiesburg to Johannesburg, to Port-of-Spain to Kingston, from Timbuktu to Boston, Mass. We must not allow ourselves to disunite. Freedom is indivis—"

The red-wigged one said, "I'm so indivisible I don't know what to do with myself sometimes. I—"

Aisha Umulubalu interrupted. "Keep talking, Your Excellency. Keep talking. Keep talking!"

Maria Efwa could never become emotionally involved with macho Jimmy Jay, she told herself.

"My husband was a revo—"

"Go ahead, Your Excellency. Keep talking. Keep talking. Don't let her—" Aisha Umulubalu was losing patience.

Jimmy felt the sudden urge of nature. He excused

himself and went toward the door to the powder room, to check the plumbing. As he opened the door, he almost poked Ms. Red Wig of the hyperactive foot and mouth in her breast with the doorknob. It was obvious to His Excellency that she meant to follow him inside the fashionable toilet with aquamarine bidet. "Madame," he said in a resonant voice that filled the room, purposefully. "Would you mind terribly if I took a pee in private?"

She replied, undaunted, "Oh don't pay me any mind. I used to be a doctor before my husband who was a militant nurse adapted, I mean, adopted me. I mean, I used to be a nurse before my militant doctor married me. I've seen all sizes and denominations, all races and religions." She hiccupped. "Like the man said, a rose is a rose is a rose, in the words of William Shakespeare."

Then he heard another voice entirely, that reminded him again of the girl in *The Exorcist*, in a kind of sotto voce, rapid-fire basso profundo. She whispered foggily. "*I know you're married, pretty baby, but everybody likes to play around every now and then. And Mother really do know how to play around from all angles and positions. Don't pay this strawberry wig no never mind. I'm a real Afro-American militant and a revolutionary.*"

"I believe you're quoting Gertie Stein instead of

Shakespeare. Notwithstanding, Madame, in my country, prime ministers simply do not piss publicly. It is not the custom or tradition in Guanaya. It would be considered gross. Totally undignified." He closed the door determinedly in the outraged lady's face.

Just as His Excellency came out of the powder room, he noticed uneasily a new person in the Tavern Room, one he had not remembered being present when he had gone to check the Tavern plumbing. He was dressed in a long flowing robe and was possessed of a long body and long face and long flowing beard, with a turban atop his wooly locks, long sideburns, everything about him of lengthy proportions. He was obviously an Arab, probably, but was apparently at the moment facing a severe identity crisis. He was confused as to his ethnicity, since before the fake PM could react, the strange one sailed through the air like he had supersonic wings, horizontally and lengthwise over the heads of those seated, dagger drawn and flashing, aiming directly at His Excellency, and screaming like a banshee and a karate black belt champion.

"Aaaaaaaaaaah!"

But His Excellency's footwork was swifter than the accuracy of the Nippon-Arab assassin's aim. The bogus

PM sidestepped the would-be black belt fellow and Black Belt's cranium went headlong into the doorknob of the powder room. He went crashing to the floor, mumbling.

"Death to Jaja! Death to Jaja!"

As immediately he lost touch with his consciousness.

Suddenly and definitely, it was time to terminate the party.

17

On the following morning they flew to the City, along with their escorts, Parkington and Carlton Carson, and the colored government chauffeur, Horace Whitestick, who had been assigned to them to drive them wherever they went, including crazy, as he told them jokingly. But he meant it, doggedly. All the way to New York, Secret Service chief Carlton Carson, born in Lolliloppi of the 'Sippis, Near-the-Gulf, had tried in vain to convince the bogus PM that he did not really want to go to Lolliloppi, Mississippi.

"You don't really want to go down there, Your Excellency."

"Can you say *Mister*?" the PM asked him innocently, apropos of nothing in particular, apparently.

The jet hit a heavy air pocket and bounced Jimmy

Jay's belly like an erratic football. Carlton Carson went white as a soda cracker; saltless, that is. "Can I say *Mister?*" he repeated two minutes later.

"How would I know?" the fake PM said. "If I had known the answer, I would not have asked the question."

"What question?"

" '*Can you say Mister.*' "

"Of course I can say *Mister.*"

"Can you say 'Mister Prime Minister' instead of 'Your Excellency'? Most people call me Mister Prime Minister."

Secret Service chief Carlton Carson of the 'Sippis swallowed his own bitter bitters and looked around for Parkington, but Parkington was preoccupied with his Guanayan counterpart, Foreign Minister Mamadou Tangi, and the only person's face he saw was the smiling Black face of the presidential chauffeur, Horace Whitestick, a dark-brown face that forever held an improbable mixture of servility and sarcasm. Whitestick Horace was always like a bulldog that growled and wagged his tail in the selfsame motion. Carlton Carson looked back at His Excellency. He opened his mouth and finally the words issued forth. "Yes, Your Excellency. I can say Mister Prime Minister."

His Excellency smiled. "Don't you mean 'Yes, Mister Prime Minister'?"

"Yes, Mister Prime Minister," Carlton Carson mumbled weakly. Then he got back on the track from which he had been derailed, expertly, momentarily. "You don't want to go to Lolliloppi, Mississippi, do you?"

"Do I what?"

"Do you, Mister Prime Minister?" Carlton Carson was sweating chinaberries.

"And why wouldn't I?"

"Well—it's so hot down there this time of the year."

His mind had wandered, remembering. And his memory sent a warmth throughout his body, remembering. A gentle warmth as he recalled the essence of her, Thelma Powell, n.k.a. (now known as) Aisha Umulubalu. In the confusion that followed the attempted assassination, she'd come close to him and whispered, "Your secret is entirely safe with me. Whatever you're up to, I know it's for a worthy cause. And, sweetheart, it had better be." She slipped to him her business card. He wiped the perspiration from his brow and felt Maria's large wide eyes heatedly upon the two of them. When he'd looked at it later, he'd read: AISHA UMULUBALU, COUNSELOR AT LAW, US DEPARTMENT OF JUSTICE, CIVIL RIGHTS DIVISION. Damn! he'd thought, and double damn!

Coming back now from his stream of consciousness, the bogus PM stared at carrot-colored Carson and laughed uproariously. Then he said, "I'm used to the hot weather. Bamakanougou is near the southern edge of the desert. As you down south folks would say, I'd be like a rabbit in the briar patch."

Carlton Carson tried again. "And furthermore, the people ain't used to Africans down there. They've never seen any."

Horace Whitestick erupted with a loud and raucous laughter and stared at his comic book. Not because he was an arrogant colored man, but because his sense of humor would not hold still, could not withstand the irony of Mississippi people being unused to Africans. It *was* a bit much. And so, he laughed till his stomach hurt him. Then he quickly assumed his servile posture. He always carried a Pogo comic book around with him, so that when he wanted to laugh at the ridiculous ways of white folks, white folks could never be absolutely sure that they were being laughed at. Pogo served his purpose admirably. Pogo was a tried and trusted friend of Horace Whitestick.

It was like the legendary laughing barrels they used to have down home at each corner in the downtown districts in the little cracker towns, in Georgia, 'Sippi, Alabama, and points south. If Black persons saw, heard, or even thought of something humorous, they would have to run like hell to the nearest corner and stick their heads in the barrel and laugh their fool heads off. Black public laughter was against the law. Strictly prohibited and seriously enforced.

"You mean there are no African Americans down in Lolliloppi?" the PM questioned Carlton Carson, searchingly.

"Well, only a few from time to time," Carson grudgingly admitted.

Horace Whitestick flipped a Pogo page and began to giggle his crazy giggle. "Te-he-he-he-gi-gi-gi-gi-qua-qua-qua—"

"What percentage of Mississippi is African American?" the PM inquired, as he reached for a book obviously titled *Population Breakdown in the Southern USA* and began to flip the pages. "'Sippi!" the bogus PM shouted softly, as if he had just struck gold, or diamonds.

Horace slapped the comic book and giggled loudly at old Pogo. "You got him treed, Pogo," Horace exhorted excitedly to the comic book. "You got that sucker up a tree!"

Carson carroted behind the ears. "About twenty-five percent." Carlton Carson turned and stared at the giggling comic-book-reading chauffeur and his white neck carroted. Carlton's white neck, that is.

The PM looked from the book to Carson and said aggressively, "How many?"

The giggling signifying chauffeur's black neck could not possibly redden.

"About fifty percent," Carson admitted, collecting heat around his collar.

"Gi-gi-gi-gi-gi-gi-gi," Horace giggled at the possum. "Git him, Pago, git him! You know all his tricks. You're a possum your own damn self."

"The Southland is where my heart is yearning ever," the fake PM said. "Where folk of African descent are happiest in this fair country."

"Yes sir, Mister Prime Minister," Carlton Carson agreed, exuding nostalgia for the good ol' days.

"Like we see in all your movies like *Gone with the Wind*." Jimmy closed his eyes nostalgically. "Cornbread and black-eyed peas and that's what I like about the South."

"Yes! Yes! Amen and halleluyah!" Carson was on the verge of tears. And he had been suspicious of this wonderful African.

"Where the living is easy and all the darkies ama weeping with plenty of nothing when old mass'r gets the cold cold ground that's coming to him. Way down upon the Swampy River. And also, where my heart is burning ever. It must be that greasy cuisine."

Old tough-hided Carlton Carson wiped his eyes unashamedly.

"Carry me back to Old Lolliloppi." Jimmy Johnson was carried away now, almost singing. "That's where the lady folks are never ever sloppy!"

"Mister *Prime Minister, Your Excellency, please Sir*!" Carson said in a voice chock-full of deeply felt emotions. "I never dreamed you were so fond of dear old Dixie. You know so much about the true nature of our Southland. You know the Southern soul."

"I am a student of Dixicana," Jimmy Jay responded with a very British accent. "It's as if I actually lived it." He closed his eyes in an overflow of ecstatic nostalgia. "I received my doctorate in Dixicology at the University of Bamakanougou. I can speak a Southern accent even, when the urge comes over me," the fake PM said with a long thick Southern drawl, that came dangerously close to being too authentic, he realized belatedly.

Carlton Carson could not believe any human being could be so wonderfully naive. But somehow he managed to believe it anyhow. He shook his head from side to side. His red face beamed. "Your Excellency, Mister Prime Minister Jaja Okwu Olivamaki, please Sir, you are a great man. You have a black skin, but you have a soul as white as newly picked cotton!"

"That is why we must go to Lolliloppi," the bogus PM said quietly.

And how could old dyed-in-the-cotton-patch Mississippi-born Carlton Carson fight such beautiful glorious sentiments? He got up from his seat and went reelingly to the powder room for whatever purpose.

Before Carlton Carson's seat got cold, State Department Parkington parked his carcass in it. Jimmy was staring across the aisle at Horace Whitestick, who had a nervous habit that he had developed, intentionally or otherwise, in addition to reading Pogo, of winking his eye when white folk's backs were turned, and crossing his fingers when he talked, again when white folk's backs were turned, and sometimes when they were not turned. Jimmy had a funny feeling that Horace Whitestick saw through him completely and even beyond him. He was forever winking an eye at Jimmy and crossing his index-and-his middle fingers. He told Jimmy one day, "When I, Horace Whitestick, talk with Mister Charlie, you better believe me, I got my fingers crossed, my eyes crossed, and my toes crossed. Sometimes my balls are even crossed, just to make sure everything is safe for democracy." The PM had stared at the little Black man and had wanted to roar with laughter. He had wanted to throw his arms around the man with the little angry eyes and tell him he dug him the mother-mucking most, but he had to pretend he didn't dig, dignifiedly. These days he had always to pretend he didn't dig. He was after all, the great pretender.

Parkington of the State Department broke into the phony PM's meditations. "I couldn't help overhearing your little chat with Mr. Carson, Your Ex—I mean—Mister Prime Minister, and I must tell you—your idyllic picture of the Southland is not entirely without a few, shall I say, fallacious impressions. Everything is not quite as rosy as Mr. Carson would have you believe." Parkington was as gentle and as graceful as a well-bred boa constrictor, highly polished, well conditioned.

"What do you mean?" the PM demanded, innocently. Beyond Parkington, Horace Whitestick had the fingers on both of his hands crossed and double-crossed, arms crossed, and he winked at the PM the most outrageous wink Jimmy had ever in his whole life witnessed. When the wink subsided, even his eyes were crossed, and an expression took over the Pogo-reading chauffeur's face of rare satirical obsequiousness. Horace was a *militant* in the weird disguise of an Uncle Tom, or vice versa. What worried Jimmy most of all was that one day soon Horace would be caught by the white folks in his Pogo-giggling finger-crossing eye-winking act and that he, the PM, would be implicated. But what worried Jimmy even more than most-of-all was this unspoken simpatico Horace had gratuitously established with His Most Esteemed and Dignified Excellency and from the very moment they had met.

Parkington stammered. "I mean, sir, that the southern picture, frankly sir, is not quite as white as Mr. Carson painted it."

Jimmy said, "Oh I understand, Parkington, that there are millions of Blacks in the southern picture, and even a few honest red men still on the old reservation. I know that much about Dixicana."

Parkington said, "Yes, quite. But what I mean is, that southerners are a bit backward, when it comes to race relations. They are—"

"What do you mean, Parkington?" His Excellency demanded, indignantly. "Are you casting aspersions on my people? My hackles are up, sir."

"Your people, sir? Your hackles?" Parkington was obviously bewildered at this point.

"The people of African descent, sir, who make up more than half of your population, in the State of Mississippi, for example. You were saying they are backward—"

Horace Whitestick began slapping his Pogo comic book. "Whoo-whee! You got him where you want him, Pogo. He way out on that limb. Donchoo let him get away! Whoo—wheel Ah-gi-gi-gi-gi-gi-gi-gooh! Ah-gi-gi-gi-gi-gi-gi-gooh!"

The bogus PM found it almost impossible to keep a straight face.

Jimmy fastened his seat belt and turned on an angry look of scorn, partially pretended, partially felt, upon the softhearted liberal-minded Parkington. "You are repeating Communist propaganda, Parkington, and I'd rather hear no more of it. You mean to tell me there is some place in this homeland of the brave and free where a man from Mother Africa would not be welcome? I do not believe you, sir. People from our great continent helped to build this mighty land of yours and especially in dear old Dixie, and you are telling me we would not be welcome?" Tears stood in the PM's eyes. "You are telling me I wouldn't be welcome way down upon the Swanee River?"

Horace Whitestick slapped the comic book repeatedly. "You got him, Pogo. You got that sucker where the short hair grows! Don't turn that mama jabber loose!"

"The Suwannee River is in Georgia, Your Excellency."

"Never mind," the PM said with deep indignation, partially felt, partially faked. "Don't change the subject. Mississippi is where the darkness is on the delta and all of God's children got someone to love. And you, sir, would rob me and my colleagues of visiting the land of William Faulkner and Hattie McDaniels and—" His voice choked off. It was one of his great performances and he must not overdo it. Mr. Lloyd thought he *had* already. Jimmy heard His Wife's Bottom clearing his scratchy throat as if he would scrape it through his mouth out onto the floor of the jet airliner.

Parkington was helpless before this kind of approach. "I'm not prejudiced, sir. That is why I want to be honest with you—"

"Try telling the truth then and cease at once this treasonous anti-American garbage! I'll report you to the President myself. All of the ambassadors from your country to my country, all reliable State Department people, Black and white, have consistently assured me of the wonderful progress between the races, in this arsenal of democracy—this—this—this Bulwark Against Communism, leader of the Free World. And you, you, you, sir, in whom I had more confidence than the rest of them—well this is a shocking revelation, and you don't even have a Russian accent either."

Parkington withered. He could only stammer at this point.

"You don't even have a southern accent, sir," Jimmy repeated. "I relaxed with you, Sir. I thought you were out of the same progressive mold as Roosevelt and Ken-

nedy and Eisenhower—and Johnson—and Adlai—and
Hubert and—I didn't even look upon you as a white
man. I said to Mr. His Wife's Bot—I mean Mr. Lloyd
just the other day, I said, 'His skin is white, but, by
the Holy Gods of Africa, he has a heart as black and as
beautiful as the nights of Bamakanougou. I was completely deceived by you, Sir!"

"I am—I have, sir—Indeed I am—Indeed I have—as
Black, I mean It's just that—"

Jimmy took one quick glance at the blankety-
blank, blinkity-blink, eye-crossing, finger-crossing,
Pogo-reading Whitestick and almost cracked up with
laughter, which is why he looked swiftly toward Carlton Carson, who had come back from the powder
room and stood nearby listening with his eyes and ears
and nose and throat. So engrossed was Carson he had
forgotten to sit and fasten his seat belt. The airplane
dropped straight down through several hundred feet
of clouds and stretched him out onto the floor, but
still he got up from the floor engrossed in Parkington and the Mister Prime Minister, His-Most-Noble-
Esteemed-Excellency.

Jimmy turned to Carson. "Mr. Carson, you're a
southerner, aren't you?"

"Born and bred in Mississippi, sir, Mister Prime Minister, Your Excellency. Please ma'am, and please sir!"

"Where are African Americans happiest in this country?"

"Mississippi, Mister Prime Minister, Your Excellency, sir."

"That being the case, is there any reason why an African should not visit Lolliloppi?"

"I can't rightly say, Mister Your Excellency, please sir."

Jimmy turned to Parkington triumphantly. "There you are. You see, Mr. Parkington. Carlton Carson is the true voice of the South, which is the true voice of America. So please, sir, no more of your subversive propaganda."

The plane made sudden contact with the earth, and Carson went smiling sprawling on his arse again, and Parkington hung his head in great confusion. Mister Prime Minister stared beyond him at the grimacing Horace Whitestick, and suddenly the ersatz PM's hands went up in a kind of Eisenhower-type victory salute with fingers crossed on both hands, and his right eye did an outrageous wink, à la Mister Horace Whitestick. And Whitesticked Horace cracked up laughing over that crazy possum.

They were getting off the plane now with the sound of music and gun salutes and the crowd of thousands gone completely mad, especially the young and middle-aged and elderly diddy boppers. Ooohing and aahing and screaming and screeching, they broke past the tight police guard. They mauled them and knocked them down and trampled them under, the poor downtrodden New York's Finest. The mayor and borough presidents never had a chance. Not even the newly elected colored borough president. The first girl who reached the PM was a redheaded-blue-eyed one, about sixteen or thirty-five years of age, give or take, mostly give and chiefly take. She stripped off her clothing as she came toward him screaming, stripped down to her natural red-haired birthday suit.

"Take me! Take me! For I am guilty, and I want atonement! I am guilty! Guilty! Guilty!" the strawberry-crotched one screamed to our frightened-shitless hero from the wilds of good ol' 'Sippi. "Take all of me, you noble savage! I want Black roots! I want Black roots! I want Black roots! I want—"

He sidestepped the dear girl and made a mad dash for one of the long Cadillac limousines that were waiting nearby. He jumped into the driver's seat and drove off leaving everybody, as the mad crowd chased him down one of the busy landing strips. He dodged in and out of the path of airplanes taking off and landing. Another limousine with sirens blasting caught up with Jimmy just as he was about to take off for the wild blue yonder out at the end of the strip, as if he thought the hog had wings.

One of the colored newspapers, in describing the incident of the PM's landing in New York, commented in typical-tongue-in-cheek African American fashion, on its front page, and we quote:

"OLIVAMAKI FALLS IN BIG."

Which was the understatement of nineteen hundred and eighty-something.

But in the words of the Duke of Ellington, "Our man Jimmy Jay was nonchalant!"

18

It had not been easy. To change drastically the parade route of New York's welcome to the Minister Primarily, the famous ticker tape parade that would go down in history as the greatest ever, even excelling in quantity and quality the welcome to the Iranian hostages and those valiant men who came back from the moon. It had been difficult, damn close to impossible.

Carson and his SS men, along with New York's Finest, had outlined meticulously the route of the PM and his entourage. They would be met at Kennedy Airport and be helicopted with adequately helicoptered SS escort to the northern end of Central Park at Fifth Avenue and 110th Street, where the parade would begin. Then down Fifth Avenue to Central

Park South or Fifty-Ninth Street (whichever), right on Fifty-Ninth, then left on Seventh Avenue, down Seventh Avenue through Times Square to the point where Seventh Avenue confluences into Broadway, down Broadway to City Hall, stopping for a brief ceremony in which Hizzoner would give to the Minister Primarily the key to the Big damn Apple, then down to and through the Wall Street area to the Battery. Someone had suggested that they take a boat out to the Lady of the Island.

The fake PM had laughed aloud at this suggestion. He could not restrain himself, since he remembered vividly when he and a group of artists including Poitier, Belafonte, Odetta, and Killens (Killens's wife, his mother, and his children included) had been part of a contingent that made a pilgrimage to the green-gilled Lady of Liberty in a demonstration for civil rights back in those old but unforgotten days. Anyhow and furthermore, he huddled privately with his cabinet before they left Washington and attempted to convince them to adopt a different plan. He argued that to begin the parade at the foot of Harlem and move southwardly away from Harlem would constitute an insult to all men and women of African descent throughout the entire nation. "Where is your

Negritude?" he demanded of his cabinet. "What happened to your Pan-Africanism? Your native-born socialistic tendencies? Your racial pride?" he shouted at the timid Mr. Lloyd, His Wife's Inevitable Bottom. "If you're so quickly willing to sell your people short, what the hell am I doing in this charade?"

Foreign Minister Mamadou Tangi saw the point immediately, as did Her Excellency Maria Efwa, pridefully, as did Barra Abingiba. Ultimately, His Wife's Bottom got a brief glimpse of the light that shined brilliantly in the darkness of Her Excellency's eyes.

Here is the plan they presented to the SS men of Washington to be conveyed to Hizzoner up in New York. Helicopter from the Kennedy Airport all the way to City Hall, there to receive the keys to the Big Appled city. Begin the parade there, proceed up Broadway against the one-way traffic, around the southern end of Central Park and up Fifth Avenue to 110th, left on 110th to Seventh Avenue, and right up Adam Clayton Powell Boulevard, ultimately to end in a big meeting at the 369th Armory. After they reached Seventh Avenue, it didn't matter how they got to the armory, so long as that is where they ended up.

Well sir! I mean Well-Sir-ree-bob! or prosaic

Southern exclamations to that effect. Brother Carson of the delta-ed 'Sippis and the SS almost had a shit hemorrhage. "It ain't correck!" Carlton Carson sputtered. "It ain't protocol!" Carlton Carson declaimed vehemently. "It ain't a goddamn whole heap of other things I can't even think of right now, and it's downright un-American!"

"It might very well not be a whole lot of other things," the fake PM acknowledged, "but it is very proper and respectful, and it's dignified." The bogus PM spoke nonchalantly. "What's wrong with paying our profound respect to the brethren and sorors of African descent?"

Carson answered, "It just ain't the way we do things in the good old USA."

His Excellency turned angrily to his Foreign Minister, Mamadou Tangi, and went into one of his typical tirades of daddle-do Hausa all mixed up with drips and drabs of Afro-Americanese. When he ran out of steam, Tangi turned to Carson and said firmly, "His Excellency says that is the way we do things in the old countree, in Africa, and specifically in the Independent People's Democratic Republic of Guanaya."

Carson argued, "Our nigrahs are different from 'all nigrahs.'" Then he remembered Parkington's wise admonition, and thus he waxed philosophical, confidentially. "Y'all ain't no nigrahs nohow. Y'all dignitaries. We start putting *our* nigrahs first and things would surely git out of hand. God in Heaven knows where it would lead to. And besides the mayor of New York would not stand for it."

His Excellency almost went into a temper tantrum. He pounded his right fist into his left palm and raged and ranted in some raggedy-arsed Hausa. He waved his hands above his head. Carson cowered beneath the PM's wrath. Tangi turned to Carson and said calmly, "His Excellency says if we cannot have the plan this way, we will change our schedule and proceed forthwith to Lolliloppi, where they know how to treat men and women of African descent."

His Excellency growled in rapid-fire Hausa one more time. "We will go forthwith and immediately to sample some of the good old southern hospitality," the Foreign Minister interpreted.

Carson paled visibly, as the saying goes, but actually he turned carrot colored. He was withering in the heat of the bogus PM's wrath, even though the place was air-conditioned. He said, "Perhaps the route of the parade can be altered. I see His Excellency's point, I reckin."

His Excellency said, "Thank you very much."

And now he had received the keys to the city from jovial-faced Mayor Harold Funkley, made his brief speech of acceptance, and was heading uptown. Ticker tape and confetti floated down from the windows like snowflakes in a driving blizzard, as they drove through the canyons of steel and stone and brick and glass and concrete. The fake PM sat on the back end of the open limousine, his handsome head almost entirely covered with red and white and blue confetti. He thought smilingly, Uptown it will be red and black and green. He stared up through the man-made Technicolored snow at the tall stone-and-brick-glass-and-concrete buildings. Smiling, waving back at the crowds at the windows and those who thronged the sidewalks. Hawkers all along the route, in the spirit of free enterprise, were selling buttons and sweatshirts with the PM's picture emblazoned thereon. Every now and then a woman of the pale complexion would come out of the crowd and turn her back to the PM and flip her dress up to show the fake PM her flat and plump and pink behind, as if she thought her orange-sherbet-colored arse was a shuttered candid camera. All the while our man from 'Sippi was thinking that any moment some hit man-woman-person with a contract would emerge from the crowd with his *roscoe* (handgun) aiming at the PM point-blank. The image of John Fitzgerald Kennedy and Dallas kept unfolding itself before his consciousness. And Malcolm X and Medgar Evers and Martin Luther King. Now and then he would imagine he saw a strange object protruding from a window high above him. Nothing of the sort would happen to him, he assured himself, without conviction. It happened only in spy novels and films of the James Bond variety, he told himself, but then he remembered John Fitzgerald Kennedy again and again and again. And Martin, Medgar, and Brother Malcolm. He had been active briefly in the Organization for Afro-American Unity. He felt a queasy premonition in his stomach that refused to leave him. He told himself to think positively. And yet at any moment it could happen, the entire world could end for him in one split second. It could all be over for the Minister Primarily.

They were going up Fifth Avenue now with Central Park to the left of them. The excitement building every moment, every ticktock of a second, he could feel it building in his heartbeat, the color of the sidewalk changing now, peoplewise, blending now, white-black, black-white, Black-brown, brown-Black, light brown, beige-brown, yellow-brown-Black, his people, homecoming, the feeling building in his shoulders up into his throat now filling up his foolish sentimental face. A thrill dancing back and forth across his shoulders, tears spilling from his shame-faced eyes. Forgotten were his premonitions. Nothing could happen to him. Within minutes he'd be home! Home to Harlem! All praises due to Claude McKay.

They had passed 109th Street. Approaching 110th. As they turned leftward at the northern tip of the park they were met by a group of young folks, Wilbert Burgie's Cadet Corp, with fife and drum already yet. They fell in line in front of His Excellency, as did a contingent of Black Masonry and Elks and Muslims, the Sons and Daughters of Marcus Garvey, and the Grand Lodge of this and that and especially the other. Just as he had anticipated, the confetti from the windows now was black and red and green.

He could hear the chanting clearly now.

"JAJA!—JAJA!—OLIVA-MAWKEE!"

"JAJA!—JAJA!—OLIVA-MAWKEE!"

The chanting now building into a wild climax. The tears spilling freely down his cheeks. It wasn't dignified, he thought. A prime minister from Africa weeping, as slyly he blew his nose and wiped his eyes. He felt the softness of a hand reach out and take his hand and squeeze it warmly. And then release it.

They had turned rightward up Adam Clayton Powell Boulevard, a.k.a. Seventh Avenue. Photographers were everywhere. Television, ABC and CBS and NBC and all the others vying for advantageous points of view. There was dancing in the streets. Premonitions gone forever. Nothing could happen to him now, baby. He was home! Home to Harlem! Relax! You're home! Laid back for all eternity, *for days*. Home! Home! Safe and sound! Perspiration of relief poured from him. Then suddenly it happened.

"*POW! POW! POW!*" The sound of gunfire from the crowded sidewalk. Shouts and screaming filled the air. "Lord have mercy! They've killed him! Killed him!" . . . "Somebody done killed Jaja!"

"Jesus save us!"

"Lord have mercy! Don't let him die!" . . . "Don't let our Jaja be dead, Jesus!"

SS men rushing here and there, stumbling over one another.

"He's dead! He's dead!"

But the fake PM did not feel dead, even though he almost put a small pool in his underwear.

They rushed toward the crowd whence came the shooting. And there was a drunken bearded brother of the middle ages dancing among a group of folks, shooting up into the empty air and shouting.

"JAJA!—JAJA!—OLIVA—MAWKEE!"

SS men seized him and disarmed him and began to rough him up and were dragging him away when the PM got himself together and leaped from the limo and got to the happy drunken brother. "Turn him aloose," the PM ordered. "Leave him alone. He's harmless. Let him ride with us."

The bewildered SS man in charge asked, "Are you sure, Your Excellency?"

"Of course I'm sure," the Minister Primarily answered. "He's a friend of mine, part of the welcoming committee, aren't you, comrade?"

The drunken comrade hiccupped. "What can I tell you, Your Highness?"

"You see?" the bogus PM said to the one in charge of the Secret Service. "He agrees with me completely."

"I don' know about all this 'comrade' business. Sounds too much like Commonism."

"That's the trouble with you democratic capitalists. Everything halfway decent and humanistic, you attribute to communism. You sure give them a lot of credit. It's a wonder that more Black people don't join the Communist Party."

By this time, the PM had his inebriated brother seated in the limo with him. No matter, it took them a little over half an hour to get the procession started again. As they passed the world-famous Hotel Theresa, where Fidel took his lodging, and were crossing 125th Street, the folks were shouting. Bars and churches and funeral parlors lined the boulevard. At least one of each in every block. Bars and churches and mortuary establishments.

"VIVA JAJA!" "VIVA JAJA!"

It was clear by now to everybody; His Excellency had not been assassinated. All the way up the boulevard, the crowd grew larger and larger and noisier and noisier. They turned right into 143rd Street toward the 369th Armory, where a veritable Black army four persons deep ringed the entrance to the fortress of a building.

Thousands of Black humanity were there waiting for the PM's entourage. Sidewalks, stoops, porches, windows jammed with Black folks. As the PM and his retinue came in sight a deafening roar of cheering began, gaining in crescendo every second.

"JAJA! JAJA! VIVA JAJA!"

"JAJA! JAJA! LONG LIVE JAJA!"

A tunnel of Black men and women had been formed extending from the ringed entrance all the way out to the sidewalk. When the limo with the PM stopped, two

Black men wearing black and red and green armbands stepped forward, militarily, from the waiting ranks to escort His Excellency through the human tunnel to the entrance. Four SS men leaped from the custom-ordered running board and blocked the Black men's progress. A brief scuffle ensued, which would have reached serious proportions had not the PM also leaped from the car and intervened.

"It's all right," he assured the SS men. "Everything's under control. They're also friends of mine," he lied. "I was expecting them. Everything was prearranged."

They marched in a military fashion, the two Black men in the lead and the four white SS men bringing up the rear. As they came closer to the entrance, Jimmy Johnson saw the fiercely proud Black folks, men and women, begin to close ranks, as they crossed their arms in front of them and joined hands with one another all along the line. Jimmy thought, WE SHALL OVERCOME SOME DAY. He imagined he could hear them singing. They had reached the entrance now and nothing barred their path except the great phalanx of Black humanity. He thought now he knew what was meant by "Black and beautiful" in the profoundest sense and context.

There was a brief and earnest discussion at the entrance between those Blacks who obviously were in charge and the white men of the Secret Service. Ultimately it was clear that the Blacks had no intention of allowing whites to attend their welcome rally.

The SS men explained to them with extreme patience that as long as the Prime Minister was in the country the Secret Service was responsible for his safety, absolutely, *positively*. The Alliance of The Sons and Daughters of Garvey, the Elks, the Muslims, and the Greater Grand Lodges of New York were equally and patiently adamant that no white folks were entering the Armory on this bright day in late September. They had a standoff. Even the glib ersatz PM could not persuade them away from their position. What to do? What to do?

There was running back and forth, gesticulating. Finally, the SS man in charge pointed to the fact that there were SS men armed to the teeth and at the ready with their telescopic machine guns at the chimneys on every rooftop in the neighborhood. "So, you see we have y'all covered."

Whereupon the Alliance chief responded, "Kindly observe also that beside every Secret Service storm trooper you will note, if you look sharply, there is an armed member of the Black Alliance."

The red-faced SS man in charge turned about and

kindly noted and observed. His face and neck became lathered with sweat.

"We simply cannot have a race riot here with His Excellency here and everything, and the whole world watching. And furthermore—"

The Black Alliance Chief agreed. Calmly smiling. "Precisely. So why don't you stormtrooping peckerwoods get back downtown. We are perfectly willing and capable of taking care of our own up here."

"It simply cannot be handled like this. It isn't protocol, and besides, we are under orders of the Commander-in-Chief of this entire nation."

"That's your problem," the Black Alliance Chief responded. He was ebony of color, medium height, broad shouldered, darkly wide of eye, fortyish, and exuding dignity, fiercely.

Back to the head car went the SS man in charge and finally after frenzied discussion by phone to Washington with officials at the Department of the Treasury, the Secret Service, after the State Department, after the FBI, after the CIA, after the this and the that and especially the other, the perspiring SS man in charge ultimately got through to the big man in the Big White Mansion.

"What in the hell's the matter with you, Carson? You can't handle a little problem like that without bothering the president of the United States? I got a goddamn fucking nation to run."

Carlton was sweating bullets. "Yes sir, that's what I'm saying, and I've been trying to get to you, Mr. President for the last forty-five minutes. I'm not dealing with dignitaries up here, Mr. President. I'm dealing with our own nigrahs."

Just a little more than two hours later, the skies above Harlem were dark with helicopters, as if uptown were under siege. A sudden deafening roar of silence lay upon the land, despite the droning sound of the copters, as people crowded into the streets, necks were craning, and all eyes were focused on the skies above them. They watched silently as the copters circled like predatory vultures and landed on the roofs, a couple of them coming down into the street, as the people watched in a solemn awesome quietude. Armed Black men from the Alliance aimed their guns upon the copters. Jimmy Johnson felt a queasy uproar in his belly and his buttocks. Things were getting out of control, as were his bowels. The word seemed to spread out through the crowd like a contagious and dread disease. Black folks came running toward the center of the conflict as if drawn there by a magnet that was irresistible.

The battle cry went up with shouts of "The shit is on! The shit is on!" People who had been watching the proceedings on TV clicked off their sets and hit the streets. Others did not take the time to click them off. If the excrement had indeed come into sharp contact with the air-conditioner, or in the poetic vernacular of the mean and happy streets, with all due respect to Piri, "if the shit had indeed hit the fan," they wanted to make sure it flew in the right direction and into the proper and deserving faces. Can you dig it? Meanwhile the rest of the world held its breath on television.

When out of the first copter, then the second, third and fourth and fifth stepped men and women of an African descendency. A deafening roar went up, as if the ultimate bomb had been exploded. Windows detonated. Ears were damaged permanently.

"RAAAAAAAAAAAAAY! RAAAAAAAAAAAAY!"

Some wisecracking Harlemite was reputed to have quipped, "The Maroons have landed, and the situation is well in hand! Everything is copasetic!"

Which was apparently no overstatement, since the white SS withdrew discreetly, though hurriedly, and now the PM and his entourage and his honor guard of the Black Alliance and Black persons of the Secret Service proceeded to move jauntily toward the entrance of the Armory. As they gained the entrance and moved toward the platform, the roar of welcome increased. Before they reached the platform, the rafters were actually quaking with applause and cheering.

Rhythmic handclapping to the beat of:

"JAJA! JAJA!"

"LONG LIVE JAJA!"

CLAP CLAP—CLAP CLAP CLAP!

"JAJA! JAJA! LONG LIVE JAJA!"

CLAP CLAP!—CLAP CLAP CLAP!

Whistling, stomping. More than fifteen minutes passed before quiet could be achieved. Then a deafening din of expectant quietude. The mayor of Harlem introduced the Minister Primarily. And then another bursting forth of uproarious welcome as he strode to the podium.

Jimmy Johnson stood before the mic now with both arms upraised. Ultimately there was silence.

"Sisters and brothers—"

An equal mixture of sighs and applause. He'd never thought his voice was sexy or even sensual. He held up both arms again.

"Sisters and brothers. This is homecoming day for me. I feel somewhat like the prodigal son. As you probably know I spent many months going down these mean and beautiful streets, all praises to Brother Piri Thomas. I feel that you *are* my family, my sisters and brothers, my mothers and fathers, and I love each and every one of you. I said I felt like the prodigal son, but I don' need a fatted calf, because this is a feast of love, and I am filled up with the love that pervades every nook and corner of this vast auditorium. If we could sustain all the love we feel for one another in this room this afternoon, if we could preserve this precious moment, we would constitute an irresistible force and there is no immovable object on this earth that we could not set into motion."

"*RAAAAAAAAAAAAAA!*" Shouts of "TEACH!— TEACH!"

"I love you and I want you to know that the people of the land of your ancestors love you, and we also want you to know that anytime you wish to come home the welcome mat is waiting for you. We believe in you. I bring you expressions of solidarity to you from the Mother Continent, in your struggle for liberation, which is a statement perhaps not tactful or diplomatic of me, coming as it does from a leader of another country. But I say it to you from the heart, we extend our hands to you from across the wide Atlantic."

He had been speaking for almost an hour, looking down upon a sea of upturned faces. Those faces were more like a lake than an ocean in the tranquility of their countenances, taking in every word, as if they drank spring water from the depths of an everlasting spa. He knew that there were some unattractive Black folks somewhere on this earth, but today as he looked down upon their faces, they seemed the most beautiful people he'd ever gazed upon. Beautiful people. Classy people. It had nothing to do with how nicely they were dressed. He'd seen ugly well-dressed people.

It was a sense he had of how they felt about themselves and of each other. He felt their love for him deeply, and likewise his great love for them flowing to and fro across the distance between the audience to the podium. At the same time, he felt an awesome responsibility to them. He felt humbled by their love for him. Then against his conscious will the prescience of great danger began to grow inside him, a premonition he fought valiantly against, but it persisted, as he remembered Malcolm and that fateful day at the Audubon Ballroom. He continued speaking but his mind began to wander. For he had learned his lesson, painfully, the folly of ignoring his premonitions. He fought fiercely to recapture the precious-to-him moment of the love he had been overwhelmed by. When over to the left of him, down in the audience, a scuffle began, he thought immediately again of Malcolm at the Audubon.

A Black man jumped up screaming, "Get his hunkie motherfucka outa here!" A diversionary tactic. Obviously.

His Excellency stood there wanting to duck behind the podium but thought it would not be dignified. It would be cowardly, unbecoming an African prime minister. He need not have worried. Before he could react, four of the Black honor guards from the Black Alliance came swiftly from four edges of the stage and surrounded him. Meanwhile down on the floor, other security men and women moved hurriedly toward the center of the great diversion, where they were dragging the "hunkie motherfucka" from his seat, until one of the security men of the Alliance said in a loud, baritone, and definite voice, "Hey, I know that brother. He ain't no hunkie. He's Black like us."

The embarrassed Black brother released his victim reluctantly.

One of the brothers in the conflict said, grudgingly, "Well if he isn't a hunkie, he ain't got no business looking like one."

When he got their attention again, Jimmy Johnson asked, "What is Blackness? Is it the color of the skin?"

Most of the audience answered:

"IT IS NOT THE COLOR OF THE SKIN."

"Was anybody Blacker than Big Detroit Red, better known as Malcolm X?"

"NOBODY WAS BLACKER THAN BIG RED!"

"Well all right then. I think you get the point I'm making. It isn't about who has the darkest skin. It's about who has the deepest commitment to the people."

"Teach! Teach!"—"Talk pretty for the people!"

The PM smiled at them. "All right now. Understand that you African Americans are the most beautiful people on the face of this earth. Look around me if you don't believe me."

They looked around at one another, their faces beaming.

"You are the greatest people on this earth, the Afro-American and Caribbean people, Central American, South American, English speaking, Spanish, French, Portuguese. What matters the language spoken by your slave and colonial masters?"

They shouted, "Teach!" . . . "Teach!" They applauded and they shouted, "Tell it like it is!" . . . "Talk pretty to the people!"

He continued, "Greatest, not because God, Allah, Buddha, Jehovah, or nature ever made one race superior to another, but because you are descendants of ancestors who were the *crème de la crème* of a great continent. When the most horrendous holocaust known to human history was perpetrated, they snatched away from Mother Africa her greatest and very finest sons and daughters. Those who were not great and strong enough did not survive the horrors of the Middle Passage, in which more than a hundred million souls were sacrificed." A shocked expression on most of their faces. An angry and an anguished murmur.

He went on. "How else to explain the magnificence and the fortitude of Frederick Douglass, Harriet Tubman, Sojourner Truth, Elijah, Robeson, Du Bois, Garvey, and Hugh Mulzac? How to explain the physical and athletic prowess of a Jack Johnson, a Joe Louis, Muhammad Ali, Kareem Abdul-Jabbar, Jim Brown, and Paul Robeson, again. The creative and artistically gifted ones like Richard Wright, Margaret Walker, Langston Hughes, Aretha Franklin, Lena Horne, Belafonte, and Robeson again. The magnificent Leontyne Price, the late Roland Hayes, and the incomparable Marian Anderson. The aristocrats of indigenous American music, Lady Day, the King of Cole, the Duke of Ellington, the Count of Basie, and the Earl of Hines." He paused for their appreciative laughter, their shouting and applause. Then he continued. "Never to forget the comedic genius of Richard Pryor, who doesn't call us niggers anymore." The Armory detonated with whistling and applause and cheering. "Thank you, dear Richard, beloved brother." He paused again. "And how to explain the indomitable courage of Rosa Parks, Daisy Bates, and the children of Little Rock, Malcolm, Medgar, and Dr. King. And who would deny that Paul Robeson is the authentic protagonist of the twentieth century, along with Jesse Jackson, Fannie Lou Hamer, as were Tubman and Douglass of the nineteenth century?" He paused. He smiled with pride.

"You African Americans are much too modest," he told them. "If you really understood how truly great and beautiful you are, you would turn this old earth upside down."

He turned from the podium and started toward his chair on the stage amid deafening applause. Standing, cheering, stomping, whistling, clapping.

As one thundering voice, they shouted:

"JAJA! JAJA! LONG LIVE JAJA!"

"JAJA! JAJA! LONG LIVE JAJA!"

He turned again and strode back to the podium. He held up his hands, and the clamorous ovations slowly subsided.

"Sisters and brothers, I was feeling so good, I felt so much love coming from you to me and going from me to you, I almost forgot to introduce to you the people who lead the Independent People's Democratic Republic of Guanaya. It would have been a terrible egotistical faux pas."

He introduced each in their turn as they were seated on the stage, deliberately skipping over Her Excellency, who was seated in the middle of them. And then he turned to her and said, "And now the high point of the afternoon, I introduce to you one of Africa's most beautiful of daughters, physically, intellectually, and spiritually, Her Excellency the Minister of Education of the Independent People's Democratic Republic of Guanaya, Miss Maria Efwa!"

She stood, her lovely face abeam with smiling. She heard murmurs and sighs of admiration and then applause that made the building shudder. He came to her and took her by the hand and led her to the podium, holding up his hand for silence. The shouting and the cheering slowly died away.

It would be more accurate to say that, with her statuesque construction, she glided to the podium and

the microphone. In a voice that was like violins playing and soft summer rain, *à la* Miriam Makeba, she
told them:

"*I love you. I love you. I love you!* In this Armory,
like His Excellency, I also feel I am at home. I am in
Africa, among my people. You are my people. Wherever you are together like this, a hallowed place like
this suddenly becomes Africa. You are Africans, the
sons and daughters of the African people. His Excellency is right. You are our greatest sons and daughters.
And I love you. I love you! I love you!" She felt the
tears spilling down her cheeks; she did not bother to
wipe them away, and as she turned to her bogus Prime
Minister, she saw that his dark eyes were also filled
with wetness. They went toward each other and into
each other's arms, and they kissed each other briefly,
deeply, as the people stood and applauded wildly.

Through the standing clamorous ovation, they dimly
heard the voice of Foreign Minister Mamadou Tangi.
"Your Excellencies have forgotten you are first cousins
and leaders of a country!"

Over in a corner of the auditorium, a lovely young
brown-skinned brown-eyed Black woman sketched
hastily on a pad of drawing paper an imagined picture
of His Excellency, the Prime Minister—without a

beard. She shook her head in disbelief. No matter, she believed it. More than that, she was convinced. His Excellency Jaja Olivamaki of Guanaya and Jimmy Jay Leander Johnson of the 'Sippis were one and the selfsame person.

Back downtown at the presidential suite at the Waldorf, they were still high under the intoxicating influence of the uptown meeting, the festival of love, as the Minister Primarily would always remember it. It was a happy enervating high that had them three or four sheets in the wind. The doors closed, locked, the outside world locked out, he took off his phony beard and threw it across the room. He saw her come toward him as if in a dream he'd dreamed too many times for it ever to come true.

"Your Excellency! Your Excellency!" she murmured. "You were magnificent, and I love you, and I'm glad I love you. I do. I do. I truly do! And I don't care. I do! I do!"

She was in his arms now, and her rich mouth went up toward his mouth in a joyous and receptive mood. Her mouth opened as their lips met. No one existed then for them in time and space save them, even as the members of the cabinet of the Independent People's Democratic Republic of Guanaya stood there in shocked amazement. They were brought back down to earth from their outlandish high by the clearing of ministerial throats and the gravelly voice of Mamadou Tangi.

"Your Excellencies—please!"

Flush-faced, they moved away from one another. Maria Efwa's face was flaming. She turned away and went swiftly out of the room and down the hall to her private quarters.

They sat the bogus PM down and spoke with him heatedly about his relationship with Her Excellency. Cousins did not conduct themselves like this in Guanaya, especially in a family like the Olivamakis. It was not traditional. Unheard of, even. Especially in public places, and never ever privately.

He stared at them, smilingly and smug. Like the cat that had drunk up all the milk, or did he swallow the canary? And yet there was plenty more where that came from. He looked around him at "his" cabinet. Mamadou Tangi was pissed off, for days. His Wife's Bottom was scratching and clucking his forever itchy throat, disapprovingly. Mr. Tobey's countenance was deeply lined with worry. Abingiba was smiling at them.

Jimmy Johnson laughed at them. "But Her Excellency is not my cousin," he reminded them, with relish.

He figured he was in the catbird seat. And loving every minute of it.

"Well," Mamadou Tangi declared, "we will just have to see that you two are not together any more than is absolutely necessary."

"But you forget, comrades in the struggle, that we have to spend every moment that's available together, teaching me the history and the folklore of your people." He smiled at them. (It was more smirk than actual smile.) "I appreciate your deep concern for me, comrades, but look at it this way. It's all in the line of duty. For the cause of African liberation."

19

By crook or by hook, or even vice versa, whichever, the bogus PM was determined to get Horace
Whitestick into the inner-circle sanctuary of the Independent People's Democratic Republic of Guanaya
cabinet in the executive suite of the Waldorf-Astoria,
and likewise Hubert Herbert Hubert was equally determined to have the same Horace Whitestick worm his
way into the confidence of the cabinet of the Independent People's Democratic Republic of Guanaya. Horace
Whitestick was all manner of things to all kinds of
people; truly he was a man for all seasons and reasons.
An Uncle Thomas to the beloved Prexy, an avowed
Black Nationalistic Pan-African loyalist to the Minister
Primarily.

"You must win their confidence," the President declared to him, "by any means necessary, and report to us daily about their conversation. I want to know every thought they ever think they thought. Act stupid. Draw them out. You can do it easy."

"Yassah," Horace Whitestick answered obediently, head down, with both hands behind his back and all his fingers crossed, and even double crossed.

"That's a fu-fu-fucking good boy," the President exhorted him. "You'll be doing your fucking duty to God and your fucking country and a credit to your fucking race."

"Yas—Sah!" Horace did his damndest to cross his testicle. His eyes were already cocked and crossed.

The Lord works in mysterious fucking ways, Horace Whitestick thought, when three days later His Excellency ushered him past the two sentries at the entrance to the executive suite of the Waldorf.

Now they sat in the vast and very plush living room drinking Scotch and water. The PM stared across the room at the little man with the dark shifty eyes. The members of His Excellency's cabinet stared askance and aghast at both of these Africans lost out here in the diaspora of the Americas, as the saying went in those wild and wooly Western days, wondering what in God-or-

Allah's name Jimmy Johnson was up to. Had he suddenly lost touch with his African reality? Had the stress and strain of the grandiose impersonation proved too much for poor exhausted Jimmy? Had his mind suddenly gone crackers?

Jimmy gave Horace Whitestick another drink and gave himself another, then sat back in his easy chair, relaxedly, laid back, and stared intently at old Horace. How much did this little man already know? How much had a crafty one like him already figured out? Could he be trusted? Jimmy Johnson wanted terribly to trust him. He wanted painfully to open up to him entirely. He felt, desperately, the need of the confidence of another African-diasporated-American.

Meanwhile they sat staring at one another, when suddenly the little man burst forth with laughter.

"Qua-qua-qua-gi-gi-gi! White folks is just about the mama-jabbing most!" He laughed now until the tears streamed down his cheeks. When he finally stopped laughing, he got himself another drink. And then he told Jimmy and the astonished cabinet about his conversation with the President. "That cracker President wanted me to spy on my own people, and he thought I didn't have no better sense than to do what he suggested."

Jimmy Johnson joshed him. "What do you mean—your own people? You're no Guanayan, you're an American. You're no African."

Which was when he thought he heard the little man say, "You ain't no Guanayan neither."

Then he knew he heard the little man say, "If I ain't African, you ain't Guanayan, the pope ain't Catholic, grits ain't groceries, and Mona Lisa was a natural lesbianese faggot." He began that crazy contagious laugh again. Before he knew it, Jimmy found himself laughing now without restraint, as were the members of the cabinet of the Independent People' s Democratic Republic of Guanaya, albeit tentatively. The living room erupted with their laughter. Jimmy Johnson laughed so hard he snatched off his phony beard and threw it on the floor. Suddenly there was a roaring silence in the room.

Whereupon Horace Whitestick began to shout, "I knew it! I knew it! I knew it!"

"What do you mean, you knew it?" the fake PM demanded, after he had gotten himself together and donned his phony beard again.

Horace began to slap his thighs. "I knew there was something about you damn familiar. I just couldn't put my fingers on it. Your walk, your voice. I just couldn't place it. Then when you asked the President could you go to Lolliloppi, I knew there was something about you Lolliloppian. I'm from Lolliloppi my own damn self, Hot Shot. I mean Mr. Prime Minister, Your Excellency, sir." And he began to laugh that crazy laugh again.

"Hot Shot?" The fake PM almost went into shock. He rose from his chair and went over to Horace Whitestick and shook the little man by his shoulders. "Where did you get that 'Hot Shot' bit from?"

Old Horace said, "When I saw you without that shit all over your face, I knew where I knowed you from. Excuse my French, Miss Efwa, please ma'am. Out at the golf course when they used to call you 'Hot Shot.' After you cut from Lolliloppi, I got the job as caddy for old Hubert Herbert, better known those days as 'Snot Rag.' When he got elected to the White House, he brought me to Washington with him."

"Snot Rag?" Jimmy cracked up laughing. "I had forgotten old Hubert's nickname. 'President Snot Rag Hubert!'" He began to laugh again. He couldn't stop laughing, tears streaming. Between the fits of laughter, he explained to Horace all about the Minister Primarily caper, the whereas and the wherefore and the how come, even, of this outrageous escapade. He swore his fellow Lolliloppian to absolute secrecy.

"Don't worry about a thing. If I were to betray my

African brothers, I hope that my right hand loses its cunning and my tongue be cleaved to the roof of my mouth." Even in his great joyfulness, the PM noticed that the more the little man relaxed, the more he spoke in unbroken English—Afro-Americanese, that is. They gave each other the African handshake, with hand and thumb and elbows, and finally he embraced old Horace and kissed him on each side of his grizzly cheeks. It was as if he had at long last found his father.

He turned to the doubtful faces that belonged to the cabinet members. "Don't worry about a thing," he said offhandedly. "Everything is copasetic."

No matter, the Guanayan cabinet of the Independent People's Democratic Republic was definitely worried.

That night old Horace called the special number that connected him directly with the President in the White House. "Everything is copasetic, Mr. President."

"Copasetic?"

"Everything going according to plan. I'm going in the executive suite with them now. I'm in their confidence already."

"Good fucking boy! I knew I could depend on you to fucking outfox them fucking Africans."

Horace Whitestick said, "God bless fuh-fabulous America."

Between Horace and the bogus PM, they figured out a plan to sneak out of the hotel without his bogus beard. It took a lot of convincing to get his cabinet to go along with the plan.

Finally, His Excellency put it up to them. They either went with him or he and Horace went alone, together. Faced with these alternatives, they decided to go along. You would have thought they still didn't trust our hero.

In any event, one early afternoon, they piled out of the executive suite with the PM in the midst without beard and made it down a back elevator and exited on Lexington Avenue. They were dressed up like Americans. Even His Wife's Bottom was. It was the day Maria Efwa was in bed with a slight temperature. They left her in the care of an official nurse who had come with them from Guanaya.

"I'm going to take you cats to see the greatest show on earth. I'm going to Americanize you, culturate you."

"I know what you mean," His Wife's Bottom boasted. "You mean the three-ring circus." He bragged proudly of his obvious sophistication. "Three-ring circus. Bailey and Barnum."

Jimmy Johnson said, "Three-ring circus is absolutely

right. But this one is not underneath a tent. This is in the natural streets. This is the avenue I'm taking you to," he sang. Ever since he had reached the Big Apple, he had wanted to see Times Square one more time. He wanted to compare it with Piccadilly Circus.

They caught a bus and went across town to the West Side on Forty-Ninth Street. "Use the transportation of the masses." They got off the bus near a sign that said on one side of the street, BROADWAY and TIMES SQUARE on the other side.

"Is this it?" His Wife's Bottom inquired, nervously.

"We're getting warm." His Wife's Bottom's eyes were as large as saucers, the flying kind, UFOs. It was a madhouse. Everybody and his grandmother's grandmother were out on the streets. They halted in front of a demurely gaudy place, the *Rue de la Femmes*. The cabinet members hesitated. Then Jimmy Jay grabbed His Wife's Bottom by the arm. "All right, come on, country cousin. Might as well—"

Inside there were winsome young ladies dancing on a long counter. It wasn't till they reached the counter that the Vice-PM realized that these women were dancing in the attire of their nativity. Even then, he thought his eyes must certainly be betraying him, deliberately. Surely, he thought, they must have some of those skin-tight skin-colored things on. They wouldn't be stark naked. Not even in New York City! Men were seated on stools with the supposed-to-be naked young lassies dancing innocently above them. They looked so virtuous and guileless, these soft-faced demivirgins, so sweet, so pure, so white as the driven snow, and it wasn't even snowing outside. His Wife's Bottom just knew they couldn't possibly be naked. After all, wasn't that a blue-suited member of the New York constabulary standing calmly at the entrance?

A long-legged, blond, gentle-faced lady danced in front of a bearded gentleman seated at the counter next to the Vice-PM, drinking beer. She was grinding and twisting her seemingly nude backside in front of the gentleman.

If he'd been naive and easily fooled, he would have sworn that the lady was naked. But His Wife's Bottom was too worldly wise to be beguiled so easily. He turned to Jimmy Jay and boasted, "I'm too sophisticated to be deceived by an optical illusion. I knew she's wearing some of those skin-colored undergarments."

Barra Abingiba said, "Tell me about it. Say it isn't so. Talk that talk!"

Jimmy Jay stared at His Wife's Bottom. "Hey! My

man is the hippest dude that ever came out of Ba-makanougou! How you get so hip so quick? You is the horse's ass. You just can't shit running."

His Wife's Bottom smiled broadly, proudly. "I always was sophisticated ever since I can remember."

The blushing fair young maiden squatted down in front of the Caucasian gentleman with his head between her legs. He flicked out his devilish tongue. The lady said, "Naughty-naughty! Mustn't touch. Mustn't touch. A snake might bite you."

The Vice-PM could not believe his ears let alone his eyes. He imagined he heard the sweet young lass say, blushingly and playfully, "It'll cost you a dollar to feel my pussy." These people in New York City talked so swiftly and with such strange accents. He could not have possibly heard what he was absolutely sure he heard.

The Vice-PM knew he must be mistaken, but his eyes almost popped out of their sockets, when he saw the gentleman next to him reach into his pocket, give the winsome lass a dollar, and saw his hand disappear along with the green stuff of the realm somewhere between those glowing nubile thighs and just beneath the mound of her downy blond profusion. An upside-down triangle of it.

He looked up and around and noticed another lady

just above him who also seemed to be unclothed. She was petite, brunette, and as pretty as a sunset out on the faraway horizon just outside Bamakanougou. She squatted down above him and almost concealed his perspiring head from view. And he could smell the perspiration exuding from the middle of her, like fresh shrimps right out of the open sea. He thought surely he would suffocate. He began to cough and sneeze. "*Aaa-chew!*" Spraying the lady's in-between. "*Aaa-chew!*" He sprayed the lady one more time. He was perspiring. And he was finally convinced that the lady was totally ungarmented because he could see the darkly sprinkled dewy down of her pubescence stick out from between her legs as it hadn't seen a comb or hairbrush for several fortnights. His Wife's Bottom was utterly speechless. Jimmy Jay's stomach was in an awful hurt, as he fought to keep from breaking up with laughter.

"How y'all doing, handsome?" the blushing lady asked the Vice-PM in a strong southern accent.

"Just fine," Jimmy answered, for His Wife's Bottom, as he pulled the perspiring HWB from beneath the funky dewy down, and he looked back on their way out of the door. His cabinet members came behind him, hurriedly. His Wife's Bottom seemed in shock.

"What's the matter, His Wife's Bottom," Jimmy

teased. "You scared of white women?" Sometimes he called the Vice-PM "HWB."

"Those ladies are a little on the swift side, don't you imagine?"

Jimmy Jay stared at Mr. Lloyd with feigned amazement. "Now whatever on earth could have given you such an idea, HWB?"

"Well I didn't say the young ladies were harlots or anything like that, but after all—"

Jimmy Jay said, "Those ladies are in the very finest tradition of southern womanhood. That was a southern nudist colony."

Horace Whitestick began his crazy giggle. Barra Abingiba laughed aloud.

HWB said, "But—"

And that was as far as HWB got, because they had been walking while they were talking, and there on a corner was a chocolate-brown-skinned Black man with a crowd of people, mostly white, surrounding him, and Jimmy thought, Lynch mob! . . . race riot! But as they came up close, they saw that the brother was some kind of a magician.

He seemed to be pulling handkerchiefs out of his fingernails, but Jimmy Jay knew better than that. The hand's quicker than the eye, right? He obviously had things up his sleeve. The only trouble, the cat was wearing a short-sleeved shirt.

The throng was staring at him owl-eyed as he chattered away and did his thing.

"You can do it too; you can do it too. Just a little legerdemain. Just a little old legerdemain. My father taught me, way down yonder in Chittling Switch, Louisiana."

A white boy in the crowd asked, "What's legerdemain, sir?"

"Just a little old Black magic, but you can do it too. Black magic. No racial implications implicated. All men and women are equal, legerdemainwise. If I can do it, you can surely do it too."

They were walking away from the crowd now. Jimmy Jay said to Horace Whitestick, "Damn, my man, I'm a little old country boy myself, but I know sleight of hand when I see it. Don't these so-called hep New Yorkers know the hand is quicker than the eye?"

Old Horace said, "Yeah. But they don't know which hand to watch."

Jimmy said, "That's easy. Watch both of them. That's what I was doing."

Horace came back with, "Now that's just where you're wrong, bro, Your Highness, Hot Shot, Himself, or whatsoever. My man had ten hands or twenty or maybe even thirty working for him, that nobody was watching. You dig? I know what I'm talking about. I'm up here every time I get a day off, digging on this crazy scene. The Apple is a mama-jabber."

Jimmy had been learning all that brand-new jive talk. So he said, in real hip rhythm, "That's heav—veee!"

Horace agreed, "They are some heavy-handed mama-jabbers, but they are light-fingered too. You dig where I'm coming from?"

Jimmy Jay said, "I dig where you coming from, I'll be damn if I know where in the hell you're headed. What is all this heavy-handed light-fingered bullshit all about?"

His Excellency's cabinet members were completely out of it as far as this crazy heavy-handed light-fingered conversation was concerned. And they'd thought they knew the English language.

Horace broke it down for Jimmy. "While the masses are watching both of my man's hands, three or four or five of his com-rads are picking pockets like a mama-jabber—for the revolution," Horace added with a roguish grin.

Well. After the southern nudist colony at the *Rue de la Femmes*, who knew what to believe?

Horace said, "I figure they average about two or

three hundred of that green stuff every day a goose goes barefooted." Then he added, "For the revolution." Then, "It sure ain't for to buy the goose no new pair of shoes."

Jimmy Jay looked around at his astonished cabinet members. "You all getting hungry?" They were silent, shell-shocked. He guided them across the street to a place called NATHAN'S. "Take you over to eat with the masses." A dollar and fifty cents for a hot dog? But they're the best dogs he'd ever tasted. Mustard relish, coleslaw, everything including the kitchen sink. After the warm canines, they went downstairs and downed a couple of stiff ones. After that, they were ready for Freddy.

By the time they came out of NATHAN'S, there was a colored lady outside preaching the word of God, like they did down there in Lolliloppi. She was a real fine sister. Constructed like a brick shed house, Jimmy Jay thought, when bricks were inexpensive. Many years before inflation.

"Bring your burdens to the Lord and leave it there. Come, before it's too late. Jesus is your only salvation." The lovely sister was marching up and down.

"Only He can save you. Open your arms to Him and he will take you in and save you. Let Him be your lover." Her eyes were closed now. Breathing deeply.

She had gotten carried away now by her own gospel rhetoric. "Jesus is my lover." She was in the arms of Jesus now. "Let Jesus be your lover! Let Christ be your lover. Walk in the Garden alone with Him, while the dew is still on the roses." She was swaying from side to side in the throes of ecstasy.

"You've tried whiskey. Did it save you? Ah-hanh!" She moaned.

"You've tried grass. Did it help you to get over? Ah-hanh!" She groaned.

"I know it didn't, cause I tried it too. Ah-hanh!" Breathless.

"But I tried Jesus and look at me now."

A brother from the gathering crowd said, "You don't look so cool to me. If you're all that together, what you doing out here in Times Square bullshitting?"

"That's an easy question, brother."

"Answer it then."

"I'm out here because Jesus teaches us not to be selfish. Didn't he teach us to go into the highways and byways preaching the word of God?"

"Did He?"

"Didn't He give his own life for us?"

"Did He?" The Afro-bushed brother stepped closer to the sister.

"Sister, are you advocating Christian faggotism?

What I look like letting Jesus be my lover? JC dug women the natural most. How you sound? Jesus was a revolutionary, a wino, and a womanizer. Mary and Martha almost came to blows over the dude. Why you think he changed all that water into wine? Check it out. He was a wino and a lady's man. A man of the people. Furthermore he was a soul brother. The Bible states it plain as the nose on your face or anybody else's face. He had hair like lamb's wool. It's right there in the Good Book. Old JC had to be a man of color. Why you think they did him in? The only Caucasians in that part of the world were the Roman colonizers. What does that make Jesus? A nappy-headed freedom fighter."

The crowd was giggling and laughing now.

"Teach! Teach!"

"Right on!"

"Tell it like it is!"

"A nappy-headed freedom fighter—damn I reckin!"

The sister began to preach again. "He died to save us from sin and damnation—Yes! Jesus died to set us free from the evils of reefer and poppies and acid—Yes, he did! And whiskey—Onh-honh!"

Her asthmatic histrionics reminded Jimmy of a Black Baptist preacher at Big Meeting time in the little old country towns in the backwoods of old 'Sipp. Her rhythms and the way she drew her breath at the end of every sentence.

Jimmy told Horace, "That lady can preach her ass off."

One of her lovely disciples came over toward Horace, a slim pretty brown-skinned lady with a mouth full of thirty-two pearly whites, and they all looked like they belonged to her, originally. She came toward them, smilingly and Jimmy Jay knew a sudden fearful sense of déjà vu. She was some lovely body out of his past who recognized him. He sweated; his stomach percolated. Instead of speaking to him, however she said to Horace, "How you doing, my main man?" It was obvious that Horace and the lady were at least on speaking terms.

"What's happening, brother?" Even as she spoke to Horace, she was sizing up the Minister Primarily.

Horace Whitestick answered, "I'm happening, baby. I'm the only thing that's happening."

The slim pretty bright-eyed sister, staring at nervous Jimmy Jay, came back with: "You're not happening, brother. There isn't but one happening, and that's the Lord God Jehovah. Do you want to find the light?" There was definitely something familiar about the pretty lady who eyed Jimmy Jay up and down even as she ran her dialogue with Cool Horace. Jimmy panicked momentarily. Was she one of the chickadees of his former iniquitous existence come home suddenly to roost? Then he got himself together. He was letting his imagination get the better of him. The stress and strain of his Prime Ministership primarily was getting to him. He told himself, Be cool! Be nonchalant! But the squeamish feeling in his queasy buttocks would not leave him.

Cool Horace said, "How you know I haven't already found it?"

The sister answered, "If youda found it, Jesus would've put a glow in your face like the one he put in mine."

Her Main man said, "I thought some good pot made your eyes shine like that."

Her eyes lit up even brighter now with recognition, as she still stared at Jimmy Jay. He fought hard to keep himself from leaving, conspicuously and suddenly.

"Uh-uh!" From the signifying gathering.

The sister moved away from Horace. "The Lord will not bless you talking disrespectful to one of his disciples."

"Bullshit!"

As they walked bug-eyed across the street and turned left, Horace was telling them how he knew the sister who was one of the Lord's disciples. "The last time I saw that chick she was a natural fox. She was a model with a couple of minks, one of which she used to wear in the middle of July. I used to see her at all the parties, and she would always be tripped out, on pot or booze or pills or something."

Jimmy Jay was breathing naturally now. He said, "She's still tripping out. She went from one trip to another."

Her Main man said, "Didn't she?"

They walked one block and turned right, the eyes of the members of His Excellency's cabinet growing wider and wider, like people in perpetual stupefaction. Jimmy Jay said excitedly, "Here it is! The greatest show on earth! This is the center of it, the big damn tent."

When he finally caught his breath, HWB said, "So this is Forty-Second Street!"

Jimmy Jay sang, "The avenue I'm taking you to."

HWB said, "The greatest show on earth!"

Even cool Horace Whitestick sounded excited. "Believe me when I tell you."

On the corner of Forty-Second and Seventh Avenue two nicely dressed young men in bow ties and very very closely cropped Afros were selling newspapers. "Get your *Bilalian News*, brothers and sisters. Get your *Bilalian News* right here."

They approached cool Horace. "I get it delivered to my domicile," he told them.

"Good, brother, good!"

Jimmy Jay said, "*Bilalian News*? What happened to *Muhammad Speaks*?"

Cool Horace made with the burlesque. "That's right, Bro. You ain't no Afro-American no more. You ain't no African neither. You ain't even Black. You *is a* Bilalian."

Jimmy Jay said, "The hell you say."

"The hell you say is right."

"Where is Bilalia?"

Well?

About ten or eleven steps from the closely cropped bow-tied nicely dressed Bilalians, a Black man cleanly decked out in a pale green suit like it had been ripped off of a table in a billiard parlor and a pale green polka dot sport shirt was preaching the word of God, calling on the wayward brothers and sisters to "Come to Jesus just now." A disinterested crowd was gathering.

The cabinet lingered. Jimmy pulled at HWB. "Come on, country cousin." They continued, awe-eyed down the honky-tonk boulevard.

Cool Horace told them, "If ever any one of you cats finds yourself alone on this mama-jabbing street, like you're on the way to catch a bus down at the Authority, just walk straight ahead and don't say nothing to nobody. Don't look to your right or left. Anybody say anything to you, make tend you're deaf in one ear and hard of hearing in the other one. Don't give anybody the time of day, or nothing."

The awe-eyed cabinet members looked from Horace to Jimmy for a translation of what sounded vaguely here and there as having a slight kinship with the English language.

Jimmy gave them a rather broad interpretation. "Like keep your eyes and ears open and your good hand on your wallet. I was walking down this mother one day, and cat bumped into me, and I said excuse me. He said, 'Don't mention it, brother.' And like a conditioned reflex, I reached back to pat my back pocket. My wallet was gone. By the time I looked up again that mama-jabber that picked my pocket was long gone— around the corner . . . So, watch it!"

Barra Abingiba and Jimmy Jay slapped palms. "Hey! But you don't have to worry about a thing. I know you brought your protection with you. I hipped you to that shit in front." Barra Abingiba was the hippest African the fake PM had ever known or even heard of. Barra even walked with a Lenox Avenue limp.

Somewhere along the avenue, HWB had lost his way. He inquired timidly, frightened, "But what is, I mean, how can one walk down one's mother and how big are cats that bump into you and pick your pockets and then speaks English?"

Mamadou Tangi said, "His Excellency obviously speaks in similes and metaphors and symbolisms."

His so-called Excellency said, "Exactly so."

Barra said, "You got it."

They walked cautiously down the thronging throbbing boulevard with their left hands rigidly on their hip pockets. Somebody stuck his or her head out of a third-story window and shouted, "Jimmy! Jimmy Jay!" And the Minister Primarily almost jumped out of his trousers and simultaneously wet himself, almost, ungentlemanly. His breath came now in brief swift blasts.

But then a dude down on the street looked up and answered. He was not the only Jimmy Jay on the one and only Great White Way, for which he was profoundly grateful. Undaunted, they continued down the honky-tonk boulevard.

They stopped and stared at the advertisement of naked white women on the marquee outside of a theater. Cool Horace gave Jimmy Jay an elbow in the side, and Jimmy turned and watched, surreptitiously, a tall blond lady strutting by. She was wearing very high-heeled shoes and a miniskirt that "came up to her mustache," in the words of Horace Whitestick. Didn't quite cover the cheeks of her buttocks. She dropped her hanky, ladylike, and when she stopped to pick it up, you could tell what the dear girl ate for breakfast.

Thousands of people were out on the streets. Mamadou Tangi said to His Excellency, "This is truly the greatest show on earth. The rise and fall of Western civilization, hopefully."

His so-called Excellency said, "Exactly so. But don't make book on it."

Now they stood near an art theater advertising a picture that was the last word in artistic cinematography with the provocative title of *Guess Who's Coming.* "Hard-core porno." ". . . Mixed Combo." They could not help overhearing a great big voice.

Jimmy turned and standing very near him talking to another cat was a little-biddy Black dude who looked like a stand-in for Woody the Woodpecker in the very last stages of tuberculosis, profiling underneath a wide black hat so wide you could hardly see him. The sun couldn't get to the dude and he was obviously turning pale for the loss of sunlight, visibly, every ticktock of a second.

In a froggy voice he proclaimed to one and all, "I know I'm a pretty motherfucka cause the whores tell me so!"

HWB asked timidly, "I say, do so many of the people have sexual relations with their mothers? I mean, habitually?"

Horace Whitestick cracked up laughing. Then he hunched Jimmy Jay again. "Look what I see yonder coming."

A tall redheaded genteel lady, double breasted, was strolling down the avenue in a low-cut blouse, cleavage exposed entirely, nothing below it but some pinkish flower-patterned see-through panties. Her pubescence seemed afire. She was walking up the street unnoticed. Perhaps there were at least a hundred thousand on this block.

Now they saw a couple of Black clowns limping down the avenue in high-heeled sneakers, underneath wide-brimmed hats with built-in processed sideburns. Even hip Jimmy Jay found himself mumbling, "I can't believe it! I can't believe it!"

Cool Horace said, "There are clowns in every circus, and like you said in front, this *is* the greatest show on earth."

And Jimmy Jay repeated, "The greatest show on earth—at least."

Cool Horace improvised. "It is the most—at least."

Barra said, "Believe me when I say so."

They crossed over in the middle of the block to the

left side of the street heading toward the Hudson River, according to Cool Horace. They stood there near the corner in front of the SUPERFLY BOUTIQUE, digging the wild and crazy scene. A dude was conferring with a couple of blonde-wigged bouffant-Afroed high-heeled Black women. This dude had curlers in his process with a red kerchief atop. Reading the riot act to tie genteel ladies of the boulevard.

"I don't want to have to speak to you bitches about that shit again!"

Jimmy Jay, usually the cool one, lunged suddenly toward the big hair-curlered bastard. Cool Horace had to restrain him. He pulled Jimmy Jay away, and they continued down the street. "Baby, you were about to get yourself all messed up."

Jimmy grumbled, "Goddammit, I hate to see womenfolks mistreated like that, especially Black ones, and by a Black man. I'd like to beat the shit out of the no-good bastard!"

"The only trouble with that is all three of them would have probably ganged up on you."

"What's his story, anyhow?" Jimmy asked, rhetorically. Jimmy Jay wasn't stupid.

"The same as that mama-jabbing road runner over there on the other side."

"And—?"

"Both of them are ladies' men. Mama-jabbing pimps."

Jimmy Jay said, "Both of them ought to be shot with shit and put in jail for stinking. A pimp could crawl underneath a sleeping rattlesnake without waking up the motherfucka!"

"Wouldn't be no pimps if there weren't no whores," Cool Horace philosophized.

It was 12:25 by the clock on the corner, where the madness continued, unabated, intensifying. The theater listings on the marquees were not to be believed.

"PUSSY GALORE!"
"MEAT PACKERS CONVENTION!"
"BIG DICK RICHARDS!"

Near the corner in front of BIG DICK RICHARDS were gathered the faithful Onward Christian Soldiers of the Salvation Army with saxophone and tambourines just finished now with BRIGHTEN THE CORNER WHERE YOU ARE and moving blithely and determinedly into WHEN THE ROLL IS CALLED UP YONDER. Dressed they were in their blue uniforms and caps, trimmed in red. Except that two of them, young ladies, integrated (Black and white), stood there in the midst of them, singing loudly, clearly, and sincerely, in a different kind of uniform underneath outlandish auburn wigs, and wigged they were by unusual spirits, very very highly heeled, in skimpy skirts, that were also high almost above their bouncy buttocks. The tears streamed down the wigged ones' eyes as they sang—

WHEN THE TRUMPETS OF THE LORD
 SHALL SOUND,
AND TIME SHALL BE NO MORE—

The Minister Primarily and his cabinet stood there for a moment, fascinated; tenderhearted HWB in tears for the wayward girls who had lost their way, and had clearly found themselves again. Their souls had been obviously converted.

One of the high-hipped auburn-wigged ones wiped the tears from her eyes and blew her nostrils and winked a smiling wicked wink at the Minister Primarily, who naturally returned the compliment. Who said that chivalry was dead?

They turned rightward now, across the boulevard, heading north up Eighth Avenue. In this block there were more whites than Blacks. Hustlers, pimps, whores, hopheads, the whole magilla. Frowsy-looking outrageously wigged funky-looking ladies strolling down the avenue, some white women in Afro wigs. Fat ones, skinny ones, and all in between. ALL MALE NUDE SHOW, ALL GIRL NUDE SHOW. LOVE TEAMS, TOPLESS—BOTTOMLESS. Art theaters all over the place. A veritable conclave of the thriving arts. Broadway Renaissance overflowing on Eighth Avenue.

HWB ventured timorously, "This certainly is an artistic community."

Jimmy stared at HWB, questioningly. Surely Mr. Lloyd was being sarcastic. Cool Horace started his crazy giggle.

Barra said to his very proper countryman, "You got to be putting us on."

"Putting you on what?" HWB inquired.

A bearded dark-haired white gentleman walked up to HWB and tugged at his jacket. His voice was like a foghorn in disrepair. "I want to hip you to something. Whole bunch of white bitches do anything you want them to. Fuck you, suck you, lick you in the arse. You Black boys will surely love it."

This time it was Cool Horace losing his cool. "Take your hands off the man's dry goods, motherfucka!"

This time Jimmy Jay pulled Horace away. "That's Mafia, fool!"

"What is he, a Jew?"

"Hell naw."

"Eyetalian?"

"He is not an Eyetalian."

"What the hell is he then. He damn sure ain't no Irishman."

"He's an Englishman," Jimmy responded, "an Englishman of the first generation." Jimmy thought of the teddy boys in Piccadilly Circus. He remembered Old Blue Eyes at Daphne's London party.

"No shit?"

"I'm like Professor Higgins. I'm an expert on brogues and accents. For example, I can tell from the way you speak that you came from a little old bad cracker town in 'Sippi."

All Horace answered was "No shit?"

They were standing in front of an "Art Cinema," which proclaimed to one and all: "An Art Cinema of the Esoteric for Discriminating People of Distinction." Jimmy Jay walked up to the ticket booth and purchased tickets and conducted them inside, burlesquing, "We is discriminating, esoteric peoples of distinction."

It was so dark and funky inside he almost broke his ass several times as they stumbled toward the front. The crowd was getting restless, whistling, and stomping. Finally, the music started on the stereo loud and ear-drum-blasting. *Black and Tan Fantasy.* The venerable Duke of Ellington.

They walked into a row near the front in front of

white folks stepping on feet and mumbling, "Excuse me," and now all of them were seated.

HWB looked nervously around him. "Don't any ladies of distinction attend the esoteric cinema?"

No one bothered to answer His-Wife's-Unsophisticated-Bottom. Okay now, the show was ready to begin. An electronic New York voice announced, "Ladies and gentlemen, we welcome you to the Art Cinema of the Esoteric. This is an art theater of the highest cultural attainment. Our policy is never to lend ourselves to the encouragement of prurient tendencies or instincts. This serious adult art theater is for the cultural uplift of humankind. Art for art's sake is the ultimate of all human endeavor. It is in this tradition and spirit that the Art Cinema of the Esoteric for Discriminating Persons of Distinction proudly introduces, direct from one year's engagement in Las Vegas at the Follies Bougerre Brothelle Magnifique, the only show of its kind in the Big Apple. Again, we proudly present the female portion of that famous love team of Pussy Cat O'Malley and Big Stick Pritchard, give her a big hand, ladies and gentlemen. If anything at all in this presentation offends you, be sure to tell your friends about it."

No applause.

The lovely lady with the long little-girl blue-ribboned pigtails danced slowly onto the tiny dusty stage with its encased electric fans blowing from each side. She was sweet faced and angelic and as innocent as a newborn infant. She was thinly clad in a tight-fitting dress with a long slit down the middle of her. The angel-faced one was twisting and grinding more or less to the beat of the music, which was blasting eardrums from the stereo establishment. Now it was playing I CAN'T GIVE YOU ANYTHING BUT LOVE, BABY.

By the time the piece was over, Angel Face had discarded her outer garments and had taken off her bra. The lovely Goldilocked maiden was not consumptively breasted in the least. Cool Horace made such off-the-wall remarks as "She keeps that up, she gon catch her death of dampness."

There was a loudmouthed dude of Caucasian ancestry underneath a Texas hat several rows behind them, yelling, "Take it off, bitch! Take it all off!"

Jimmy Jay said to Cool Horace, sarcastically, "Somebody ought to teach that fool some table manners."

Cool Horace said to Jimmy, "Don't you recognize that idiot?"

Jimmy turned around and got a good hard look. "His flap ears look familiar, but his head and face have grown beyond my recollection."

"That's Senator Bobby Lee Badcock from Lolliloppi County, Hot Shot, Mr. Prime Minister, Himself, Your

Excellency, sir. He's from Daddle-Do, Mississippi, about fifteen miles north of Rareback. Between Rareback and the county seat in Lolliloppi. He's the knight in shining armor, defender of the Ku Klux Klan and the honor of southern womanhood, and especially whatnot. The baddest cracker in the US Congress. Just last month, he introduced a bill to send all the quote unquote 'niggers' back to Africa. I sure do wish I had a camera."

The fake PM said, "I wish I had a goddamn pistol."

The stereo establishment was detonating eardrums now with I DON'T WANT TO BE LONELY. By the time LONELY was done, Goldilocks was down to her natural clothing, wearing nothing but a beautiful smile. And it was plain to see she was a natural blond all the way down to the dampish downy just above her in-between.

The bogus PM leaned over to His Wife's Bottom and whispered, devilishly, "She sure has got some pretty blue eyes."

Barra whispered, "She's got a very intelligent face." *Sotto voce.*

Meanwhile she was wiggling around innocently in her altogether more or less to the rhythm of the music, as if it really mattered.

HWB whispered back to Jimmy, "She is not an excellent dancer, I think, perhaps."

The idiot senator from the old home state was still

shouting. "Take it off, bitch! Take it all off!" What in the hell did he want from the lady?

The music changed again, and Big Stick Pritchard entered upon the stage. He was a big handsome soft-faced Black man. Sweet Face danced over to him and they engaged in a long-protracted kiss. Jimmy Jay looked around him uneasily for the pyramidal-headed bastards of the KKK. Miss O'Malley unbuttoned and pulled off Big Stick's shirt, affectionately, still squirming and twisting more or less to the beat of the music. HWB transfixed, watched a cockroach crawling calmly up Big Stick's trousers. Tenderly she unbuttoned Big Stick's fly, pulled his pants down. The cockroach by then had disappeared. Kneeling now, she cupped his crotch with her hand. The bigmouthed senator was quiet now. Jimmy Jay stared back at him. He was slobbering now; his lips were dripping. Big Stick stepped out of his trousers. Lovingly, she cupped the great bulge of his crotch again in all five of her gentle pinkies.

Barra Abingiba loudmouthed, "Such a tender and heartwarming scene. So poignant and romantic."

Jimmy Jay could not believe his eyes. He, who thought he had seen everything. Slowly Miss O'Malley, of the angelic face, the blue-ribboned pigtails, pulled down his jock underwear displaying now for all to see his great big black protrusion, which she caressed gingerly, momentarily. The cockroach crawled out on Big Stick's big black member, nonchalantly. The lady slapped him (or her) off impatiently. Then daintily, she put the big black thing in her mouth and went to work on it, hungrily. Like poor little Cinderella starved for affection. Poor poor thing.

Cool Horace whispered jokingly to His Wife's Bottom, "What you say, Mr. Vice–Prime Minister? She can't dance worth a shit!" Horace giggled quietly.

Now they were on the funky-looking bed and Big Stick was shoving it into the Caucasian lady with adequate gusto, with a bored expression on his face. Jimmy Jay expected the police to break into the art theater of the esoteric any moment and take them all to the slammer. And the Republic of Guanaya would be disgraced forever. He had let his sense-of-humored escapade-oriented nature get the best of him again. All of a sudden, the senator found his voice again. "Sock it to her! Sock it to the bitch, you black motherfucka!"

The bogus PM thought his eyes and ears had gone completely berserk. He was not seeing what he thought he saw. Nor was he hearing what he thought he heard. But, seated down front with the great fans blowing, he knew he was smelling what he thought he smelled.

"Sock it to her, I say. Sock it to the bitch, you black motherfucka!"

Big Black Stick Pritchard raised up from the genteel lady. "Who the hell you calling a motherfuca motherfucka? Did you ever see me fucking your clappy mammy?"

The bogus PM figured it was time for them to split. Mamadou Tangi had begun to mumble to himself. "And they call us savages! And they call us animals and savages!" Jimmy got up and moved with them swiftly out of the Art Cinema of the Esoteric. Out on the street they walked in shell-shocked silence except for the quiet mumbling. "And they call us animals and savages!" They walked like zombies toward the subway in a state of stupefaction. Past the hustlers, past the winos, past the joyless hookers. Before they realized it, they had crossed Forty-Second Street and had reached Thirty-Ninth. Signs were plastered on the buildings all along the way. Young lads at the corners distributing throwaway advertising:

BIG PUNK ROCK FESTIVAL!
MADISON SQUARE GARDEN FELT FORUM
MATINEE PERFORMANCE—3 P.M.

Jimmy Jay looked at his wristwatch. It was 2:39. He thought, Why the hell not? They were already in cultural shock. He might as well take them all the way.

The Americanization of Oooga Booga. Hugh Masekela. They continued to walk. HWB and Mamadou Tangi were mumbling to themselves. By the time they reached Thirty-Third Street, he saw a line of people extending from Seventh Avenue across Eighth Avenue all the way over to Ninth Avenue and possibly beyond. Stopping the flow of traffic, horns honking, shouted cursing. If he started at the foot of the line, by the time he got to the box office, if ever, the damn show would be over. He paused and pondered. Not to worry. He gathered his flock and headed straight for the front of the line.

Outside the Garden, bona fide versions of born-again Christians were picketing, heatedly, the punk rock festival.

"INSIDE THIS DEN OF INIQUITY IS THE HELL
THAT GOD PREDICTED,
THE FIRE AND THE BRIMSTONE!"

and

"ARMAGEDDON IS AT HAND!
THE RIGHTEOUS ARE MARCHING IN THE
FINAL BATTLE AGAINST THE EVIL DAYS
THAT ARE FINALLY UPON US.
JOIN US IN THE STRUGGLE BEFORE IT IS TOO LATE!"

Over in front of the big hotel were a group of Hare Krishnas jumping up and down, off the beat, as usual. Chaos all around the place. Pickets were picketing pickets picketing pickets who were picketing. It could even get confusing if you really put your mind to it. It was difficult to figure out who was who and what was what, and who was for what, and how come? Another group of avid democrats had their own thing going.

"PUNK ROCKERS ARE THE TRUE FREEDOM FIGHTERS!
WE ARE THE ADVOCATES OF FREE SPEECH!"

Friendly fistfights breaking out all over the place with alarming frequency. Women's Lib were out there with their picket signs.

"SEXISM ON THE RAMPAGE!
DOWN WITH MALE SUPREMACY!
THE MOTHERFUCKERS ARE MASCULINE IMPERIALISTS!"

When he got near one of the ticket booths, he dropped a coin, seemingly by accident, and he reached down to pick it up, and by the time he stood up he was directly in front of the ticket window, with his phony beard in place. He spoke in an African accent. "Please to excuse me, but I am desirous of giving my retinue of cabinet ministers a true American cultural experience. And I'm afraid that if we stand in line, I will be recognized, which might very well cause an incident, a stampede, and so on, the way things are. You do understand?"

The ticket seller's eyes popped out with surprise and recognition.

Jimmy Jay could hear people behind him grumbling and cussing.

The dark-haired ticket seller looked around him. "I quite understand, sir. How many tickets do you require?"

Jimmy Jay said, "Seven. How much would that cost us?"

"No cost at all, sir. With our sincere compliments."

"Thank you very much. You do understand of course, we are traveling incognito. Please to help us keep our presence secret."

"But of course, sir. Understandably."

Once the bogus PM received the tickets, he took off his phony beard much to the astonishment of the ticket seller, whose mouth flapped open, as Jimmy motioned for his retine to follow him.

Inside now, down near the front in the jam-packed Forum, they had, for a couple of hours, been entertained by THE SAVAGES, THE ANIMALS, THE PRIMITIVES, THE FLAMING FAGGOTS, and "last but far from least, the *pièce de résistance* of the afternoon, the treat you've all been waiting for, the internationally famous MOTHERFUCKERS!"

They came on electronically, guitars plunking electrifiedly, saxophones honking, jumping up and down, cacophonously. After a couple of endless moments of discordant sounds and antics, they began to sing, and jump about, off the beat like inebriated Hare Krishnas.

Singing, screaming:

Eyes right—assholes tight!
Cankers to the rear.
We're the motherfuckas of Punk Rock U,
And we all got gonorrhea
Rear rear rear—
We're the heroes of the night
We'd druther fuck than fight.
We're the boys of Punk Rock U.

They repeated the tender little lyric one more time, and then they began to bang their expensive electronic instruments on the floor. A red-haired straggly headed "motherfuckering punk rocker" threw his guitar down on the stage and began to jump up and down on it.

Another darker-haired one took his guitar and began to beat another on the head with it, until his head and ears were bleeding, as the audience applauded boisterously, wild with frenzy and approval.

Now young ladies from the audience converged upon the stage with shouts and screams, stripping off their clothing; they leaped upon the stage, by which time the blond-headed straggly-haired leader of the MOTHERFUCKERS had stripped down to his bare essentials and was beating himself in the head with his own guitar. Then he put the guitar between his legs and jumped around the stage like he thought he was the Lone Ranger riding Silver.

His Wife's Bottom shouted feebly, "What does it mean? What does it mean? What are the metaphors and symbolisms?"

Jimmy Jay said, calmly, and with infinite patience, "It simply means the young people of the USA are rebelling against their great-great-grandparents. It's the democratic way. It's like true Americanism. Freedom of Expression. It's their dramatic way of pleading the First Amendment."

"It means," Mamadou Tangi stated even more calmly, "that we are witnessing the final gasping symptoms of the decline of Western civilization." He turned to the bogus PM and said, "Your Esteemed Excellency, we have you to thank eternally for this historic opportunity, for which we are grateful everlastingly."

"Oh, think nothing of it," His Excellency responded. He stared up toward the ceiling, all brightly lit and everything. He mumbled solemnly, "One nation indivisible."

Barra said to Jimmy Jay anxiously, "Get yourself some protection in a hurry."

20

A couple of before-day-in-the-mornings later, in the neighborhood of four thirty a.m., the direct line into *Himself*, the so-called Prime Minister's bedroom, rang again and again persistently as the Minister Primarily lay there half-awake, hoping desperately that the ringing would go away somewhere and get lost forever, and a couple of centuries thereafter. He wanted it fervently to be a dream he was dreaming, but the ringing phone went on and on and on and on, interminably. He stumbled out of bed and took one of the pillows and tried to smother the ringing phone, but succeeded only in knocking it from the night table to the floor. He put it back in its cradle and back onto the night table and crept stealthily back into the bed, and settled into its seductive solace, and forced a comforting snore, psyching himself off on a peaceful journey into the land of nod, just as the phone began to ring again.

He called the phone all varieties of obscenities, he cursed, he swore, very un-Prime-Minister-like, even as he picked it up again. "Hullo—goddamn—goodbye." And started to bang it down again when he heard an unfamiliar voice:

"I have a collect call from a Mister Horatio White-stalk. Will you ac—"

A quivering voice interrupted. "Whitestick, nu-nu-not Whitestalk! Huh-huh-huh-Horace, not Hu-huh-Horatio. Huh huh-Horace Junior Frederick Whitestick!"

Jimmy was still half asleep. "Operator, do you realize what time it is? Tell them to call back later."

At which time he heard a strangely familiar voice, getting more familiar every moment making its way into his slowly awakening consciousness. It was more-over a voice of unquiet desperation.

"Hey! Please! Don't hang up, Hot Shot, Himself, I mu-mu-mu-mean, Your Excellency, Please, sir!" The half-asleep Minister Primarily recognized the desper-ate uncool voice of the Cool One, the one and only Horace Frederick Whitestick. It was difficult to under-stand him. It sounded like his teeth were chattering. Like dice dancing around in an empty tin bucket.

"I'll take the call, operator."

"Cu-cu-cu-come and gu-gu-gu-gu-get me!"

"Where in the hell are you this time of morning? Where's the car?"

By now, his teeth were making like castanets.

"Cu-cu-cu-cu-catch a cab and cu-cu-cu-cu-come and get me. I'll explain everything when you gu-gu-gu-gu-get here."

The shivering Cool One said he was somewhere in Jamaica, Queens, somewhere just off Sutphin Boulevard near the corner of 359th Street in a "fu-fu-fu-fucking phone booth." Bring him some clothes and bring an overcoat, "inclu-clu-clu-cluding some underwear. I'm freezing my fu-fu-fu-fucking ass off!"

Shucking to himself, the Minister Primarily stumbled around his bedroom, sleepily dressing, washed the sleep out of his eyes, his drowsy mind trying to create an image of Cool Horace's predicament. He went tippy-toe down the inside corridor to HWB's bedroom, woke him up, and got some of his clothes together, including underwear and overcoat. He figured they were about the same size, HWB and Cool Horace. The two of them stole past the sleeping snoring guards. Jimmy Jay picked up one of the rifles from the floor where it had fallen. Put it back in the sleeping sentry's lap. Then went down the hall to one of the back elevators and out on Lexington Avenue into the lifting darkness, where day was slowly breaking all over the eastern skies. New York City was finally fast asleep, almost.

They stood there for fifteen or twenty minutes, as cabs would pull up to the curb, stare at the two of them, and pull away with "Sorry, I'm heading home." . . . "Been out here all night long." . . . "I'm going the other way, sorry about that."

He remembered years ago when he used to run with great Black cats like Lonne Elder and Belafonte and Godfrey Cambridge, Sidney, Ossie, Ruby Dee. Such a long long time ago, it seemed. Godfrey, when he answered you via the telephone: "Cambridge residence. God speaking." He stood there smiling through his anger. Himself had appeared at the Vanguard and at the Village Gate under Belafonte's sponsorship. Lonne and God and Bobby Hooks. His truly wild and crazy days. Julian Mayfield. The cabs would pull up, and when the driver saw they were Black, would pull away again. Sometimes they threw bricks at the taxis (alley apples). He stood there feeling a sense of déjà vu. The night Himself and Harry B. stood in front of the very same Waldorf, where Harry was appearing in the Empire Room. The cabs would pull up, then pull off again. Harry was fuming, livid. He was the very biggest in show biz. Mr. Big, himself. Our very first Black movie idol.

He'd laughed bitterly at Mr. B. "I'm glad it's happening to you, booby. Keeps you honest. If it can happen to a great dude like you, what do you think happens daily to us ordinary people?" In his hoarse voice, Harry B. said, "Yeah."

Finally, the Minister Primarily went, uttering unmentionable curse words to himself, followed by bewildered HWB, sleepwalking through the by-now-awakened hotel lobby to the front entrance. Jimmy Jay walked up to one of the white bellmen near the front and demanded belligerently that goddammit he hail them a cab.

"Certainly, sir."

Now they piled into a Yellow Cab, HWB nervously, His Excellency aggressively. "Queens, I think it's Jamaica, or something. Three Hundred and Fifty-Ninth and Sutphin Boulevard."

"Queens? Jamaica?" the white cabbie mumbled irritably. "How do you get there?"

"How in the hell should I know?" Jimmy Jay growled. "You're the cabdriver. You're supposed to know the city forwards and backwards."

"Sounds like a very expensive trip. I tell you in front."

"Don't worry about it, buddy boy."

The white cabbie mumbled under his breath and

started up the motor and shot off down Park Avenue, through the early-morning traffic, which was getting busy and frenetic already, horns honking, even at the traffic lights. About fifteen minutes later they were on the parkway, going along at a lively clip, dipping from one lane to another like a halfback broken-field-running for a touchdown. The sky was an almost cloudless and translucent blue, one of those chilly clear October days when you could see forever, that is, if you were that full of curiosity.

The bogus PM leaned forward, speaking with a very British accent, "I say, old chap, it's damn hospitable of you, a free trip to Jamaica, is it? A new courtesy you extend to distinguished visitors to the city. Quite sporting of you. It's quite civilized, really."

"What're you talking about?" the cabbie responded, nervously, irritated.

"I see you don't have your meter going, so I imagine you're taking us out there for nothing. Gratis. Thank you very much."

The cabbie cursed aloud this time, as he clicked on the meter.

"The first few miles you gave to us for nothing," HIMSELF rambled on with great enthusiasm. "That's really quite Black and sporting of you, old boy, I really mean it. It's civil of you." The PM kept up a continuous chatter in praise of New York cabbies, that extraordinary hospitable breed, practically unheard of in the Western world, how incredibly nice of them. "One might say it's almost African of you." Who said New Yorkers were not warmhearted people? And absolutely free they were of stupid racial prejudices. Such unheard-of civility and generosity, eh? Hearts of gold, and so forth and so on, even as the cabbie continued mumbling curses to himself. Finally, the cabbie cried out for mercy. "Please! I mean, would you mind if, I mean, I'd appreciate it greatly for just a little bit of quietudeness. I mean I really hung one on last night. I got a terrible headache this here morning."

"I quite understand, my boy. I shan't say another word. I'm a firm believer in the axiom that silence is absolutely golden. Silvery and diamondy even. I shan't utter another sound, so help me, Martin, Malcolm, Medgar, and all the patron saints of Africa. You should have spoken up at once, old boy. Knowing what a lonely and reflective life a cabbie leads, I thought to keep you company for your kindness and your unheard-of civility. I had no idea, sincerely, I did not. I am usually the silent type. A very private person am I, and always was. I was just so overcome by your hospitality, your generosity, which is legendary, and actually incredible, so to speak, as the saying goes, if you get my drift, old boy. However, and nevertheless I shall not utter another word, not one solitary sound, excepting to observe that we have passed this corner at least several times in the last few minutes. Sutphin and Three Hundred and Fifty-Ninth. Turn here, right here, mate. Here we go now—" Jimmy Jay said pleasantly, as the angry cabbie braking madly, screechingly, turned the corner on two wheels.

"Sonuabitchin'—!"

"Right here, sir," Himself sang out cheerily. "Right over there near—that phone booth on this end of the quadrangle where the police cars are . . ." His voice trailed off, as he saw the three squad cars gathered near the phone booth and watched two policemen leap from their car and hurry toward the phone booth, which was obviously occupied. The Minister Primarily hastily donned his phony beard, which he kept with him for all occasions and especially emergencies. Cops were leaping from every squad car now, revolvers drawn. HIMSELF leaped from the cab, pulling a woefully bewildered HWB along with him, gave the astonished cabbie a twenty-dollar bill and waved for him to keep the change. The cabbie pulled off his cap and scratched his head and murmured, "Goddamn!— It's Olivamakeee!"

Jimmy Jay hurried over to the phone booth where the cops surrounded a shivering Cool Horace, as he stood there in the suit of his nativity, as naked as a jaybird in whistling time, as they are wont to say back in old 'Sippi. Goose-pimpled, Cool Horace was, from head to feet. The Minister Primarily fought hard to keep a straight face, as he threw HWB's overcoat around the Cool One's quaking body. The cops had already pulled him naked from the phone booth.

"Your Excellency, she-she-she-she pu-pu-pu-pulled a gun on me and put me out bu-bu-bu-buck naked."

Two of the policemen were Black, and they doffed their caps, as they recognized they were in the august presence of the legendary Prime Minister of the Independent People's Democratic Republic of Guanaya. "Your Majesty!" the lanky Black policeman exclaimed, worshipfully.

The Minister Primarily took the two Black cops aside, and he explained the embarrassing predicament his official chauffeur found himself in, and, grinningly, they told him that they understood. They huddled hurriedly with the four white cops, and the tall Black cop came back to Jimmy Jay, along with the other one, and said, "Everything's cool, Your Excellency. We'll escort you back to town."

The Minister Primarily said, "How can I ever thank you brothers? Surely you understand the importance of keeping this incident hushed up. You can see how embarrassing and destructive it would be for the image and the dignity of our country and all of Africa."

They assured him that they understood. "Mum's the word, Your Highness, sir. We'll wait until your chauffeur gets dressed inside the car, and then we'll escort you into town, in style."

"Thank you very much. And you have a standing invitation to visit our country, anytime your heart desires. The welcome mat will always be there waiting for you." He gave each of them his card.

They saluted him. "Your Majesty!" He returned their salute, smartly, and they went to their car and waited. The white policemen drove away.

Cool Horace's lips were bluish white with chill, as he dressed, trying at the same time to explain what had happened to him, teeth still chattering all the while. He got behind the wheel, started up the motor, but his hand was so chilled it could not take firm hold of the steering wheel. Jimmy Jay got out of the car again and went around to the other side of the long black limousine, and told Cool Horace to move over, he would drive. Jimmy got behind the wheel and signaled to the cops that they were ready to roll. They went through early-morning Jamaica, sirens blasting. "First time I ever chased a policeman's car," the PM remarked, sarcastically.

Cool Horace trying to explain. "Mu-m-muman, she was my old lu-lu-lady, and I truly lu-lu-loved that woman. Thu-thu-thu-that's how come I come up here to the Apple so damn often. She-sh-sh-she ain't never acted up like this before."

"Does she know you're married?"

"Of course," he declared, with indignation. "I'm an honorable man, even though I am a lady's man. I can't help it if I'm ir-ir-ir-resistible."

"You're an honorable man," His Excellency agreed.

"An honorable man," His Wife's Bottom repeated, distinctly, instinctively.

"An honorable man," HIMSELF repeated. He could not restrain a snigger.

"Yeah," Cool Horace maintained righteously, "and I promised that woman I was going to get a divorce and do the right thing by her, as soon as I could spell able, for the longest kind of time, I told her. And she ain't never acted up like this before." Cool Horace was heating up now with a righteous indignation.

"What happened, my main man?"

"We-we-we had been out on the town, had dinner

at one of them fine and fancy, what-I'm-talking-about, expensive Eyetalian restaurant, went to a club down in the Village, dug on *bad* Max Roach, came home, and she went into the bathroom and took her shower like she usually do, and she got into the bed just like she usually do, and me I got undressed just like I usually do, and she pulled a pistol out from under her pillow—"

"Like she usually doesn't do." Jimmy Jay could not resist.

"And put my bare ass out in chilly weather. Told me not to come back till I brought the papers with me. I—" The Cool One's eyes and nose were running. He blew his pitiful nostrils.

The Minister Primarily had felt the laughter building up inside him and now the tears were streaming down his cheeks. The car had begun to swerve from side to side in the crazy morning parkway traffic. Horns were blowing, drivers cursing. Up ahead the squad car with its siren blasting. He could not control the car for laughing. "Hold it, Horatio, I mean Horace, please, man. I can't drive the . . ." He swerved into the middle lane and barely missed another car.

"I don't see a damn thing funny," Horace mumbled. And he was no longer cool. "I mean she wouldn't even let me get my clothes and put them on." Cool Horace was no longer chilled. He was heatedly indignant.

Jimmy Jay began to bang upon the steering wheel with laughter. "Please! No more! If you don't want us to have a smashup on the Parkway. Save it till we reach the hotel. Please!"

His Wife's Bottom's only quiet comment was, "Quite obviously. An honorable man."

Cool Horace, who (repeat) was no longer cool, repeated, "I don't see a damn thing funny." Which made the PM roar with laughter, dangerously.

When they arrived back at the Waldorf, the hotel was surrounded by squad cars. SS men were everywhere. TV folks all over the place. He recognized Bob Teague, a Black TV reporter who used to be an anchorman, whom Jimmy Jay had always admired for the dignity with which he enhanced the job of TV anchoring and reporting. The newspaper and TV folks surged toward them.

"Where were you?"

"What happened?"

"Were you abducted?" "Kidnapped?" "Assassinated?"

"No comment," he repeated over and over. Then finally he told them, "I was abducted, kidnapped, and assassinated," as he was escorted forcibly by SS persons. As he was passing Bob Teague, forgetting who he, Himself, was, or was supposed to be, he reached out and shook his hand. He put his arm around Bob Teague's shoulders, and he mumbled, "My main man."

When they reached the executive suite, the place was bedlam, two times over. The others of the cabinet bombarded them with questions. They had awakened as usual for regular chitchat before breakfast, for a run-through of the program for the day. When they missed His (so-called) Excellency and His Wife's Bottom, they had checked with the guards outside, who were ready to swear on a stack of Bibles that no one had come past them. They had not known what to do. Finally, they had had to notify the police that the Prime Minister was missing. And then the deluge. Panic! Hey!

"How could you do this to us?" Maria Efwa angrily demanded.

"Totally irresponsible," Mamadou Tangi asserted, firmly, agitatedly.

Meanwhile His Excellency had thrown himself upon the silken downy couch, unrestrained laughter erupting from him. "Now," he said to uncool Cool Horace when he could get himself together. "Begin all over again and tell us the story from start to finish." As again he burst forth into roars of laughter. Amidst the bedlam of excited talking and intermittent eruptions of laughing, Cool Horace told, unsmilingly, his tale of aggravated woe, *seriously.*

It seemed that his lady friend, his New York mistress, if you please, the really great love of his romantically eventful life, and he had had a healthy uncomplicated ongoing love affair, him and his lady, for four or five years, much to their mutual joy and euphoristic satisfaction, until recently, perhaps about a year ago, when his "old lady" began to raise the question of getting married every time he looked around, knowing all the while that he was a married man already, with several children. By now they were no longer children; all of them were graduated by this time. Perhaps it was when the last boy reached twenty-one when his "old lady" really started to get marriage happy.

"But you know how it is. Like I was always on the up-and-up with Sherry Charlene Jamison. That's my old lady's maiden name. She's a widow woman."

Jimmy Jay began to snigger.

It was more than a whole year, Cool Horace grindingly admitted, that he had promised the lady that now that the children were up and out of the way, he would do the right thing by her. Just give him time and take it easy. What with first one thing and then another, being awfully busy and whatnot, he had never gotten around to doing anything about it. Giving her one excuse after another. Every time he saw her here lately, she seemed to get seriouser and seriouser about it. She began to hint about things, and signifying, saying things like "Fish or cut hook" or "Piss or get off the pot." And time before last she'd told him flatly, "Shit or get off the goddamn pot!" Which was not like her to use that kind of language. She was a lady up and down. Went to church every Sunday and prayer meeting every Wednesday night. A deaconess, don't you know, chairperson of the deaconess board, she was. And so he still didn't pay her much never mind, because all he ever had to do was to throw some sweet talk at her, she would always get weak for him, when it got down to the nitty-gritty. He was irresistible when he started his sweet-talking. He was a natural rhapsodizer. Always had been. Anyhow, last night, after they'd did it up, the town that is, they got home about three thirty in the morning. "My old lady took a shower like she always do, came back and got between the sheets, as usually. She watched me as I took off my clothes and stood in front of her buck naked, like I always did, profiling, don't you know, and letting her dig my physique, get her kicks, turning my old lady on as usually. Just as I was getting into bed, she pulled a pistol from under her pillow and pointed it dead at my whatsoname. She says, 'Where's the papers?' I say, 'What papers, baby darling?' And she says, 'If you don't know what papers, get your black ass outa my apartment.' Then I says, 'You got to be kidding, sugar pie.' But her eyes told me she won't kidding, not a pound. Her eyes were closed almost, but she could see me, cause they were flashing like a tiger's eyes. I grinned at her and started to get into the bed, when she cocked the pistol in my face, a long black roscoe with a silencer already. I knew the lady was as serious as a massive heart attack. I started to the other side of the room to get my clothes. 'I want you to get your ass outa my apartment just like you came into the world, in your natural birthday suit.' Then I says to her, like sugar wouldn't melt in my natural mouth, I says, 'You have got to be kidding, sugar dumpling.' And kept on walking to my clothes. That's when she started shooting up the lint from the carpet 'round my feet. Came so close it gave me a hotfoot. I looked down and saw the smoking holes in the rug. I could smell the carpet burning. I says to her, 'It's chilly out there, honey bunch. Have pity on poor me. Jesus Himself says always have mercy.' She says, 'Vengeance is mine sayeth the Lord.' I says, 'I just know you gon at least let me put on my drawers. A sweet little woman like you wouldn't never be that hard-hearted. After all we been to one another.' She smiled and I knew I had her going my way then. I reached down for my underwear again. Then she says, 'You won't born with no drawers on. Let the doorknob hit you where the bad dog bit you.' And kept shooting down around my feet. I says, 'But ain't no bad dog bit me, darling.' She says, 'This bad dog I got in my hand gon bite you, you don't get your black ass outa here, I mean in a hurry.' And she started shooting all around me. For some reason or other, all of a sudden, I found myself outside the door in the hall, and hear her inside putting all of them locks on the door, about a dozen of them. Here I am out there naked with my bare ass out and knocking on her door begging her to let me in and at least let me get my clothes and put them on. People started opening doors and looking out in the hall at me buck naked. I ran to the elevator, but it looked like it was never coming up. Finally, I gets on the elevator with no clothes on, and look like to me the damn thing stopped on every floor from the tenth floor all the way down. The door would open, and people would start to get on, and see me naked and step back off and run down the hallway screaming like hell to beat the band. Three or four times it was womenfolks dressed up like they work in service. It was a holy mess, I'm telling you. When I finally got downstairs, I had to go outside in the chilly weather and walk buck naked clear across the quadrangle about a block long, I mean I was naked as a ragged-ass jaybird all the way to the phone-damn-booth. I mean, my ass was freezing. Wasn't long before the police come."

By the time Cool Horace finished his tale of agonizing woe, the Minister Primarily had fallen off the couch with laughter. Even dignified Maria Efwa broke up with laughter. Abingiba was also on the floor kicking up his heels and howling.

But Cool Horace could not see a damn thing funny.

21

A new thing was developing. Every time he came outside the Waldorf, there were thousands standing there in wait, just for a fleeting glimpse of Himself. Indeed, some actually sought and fought just to touch the hem of his garment. His immaculate boubou.

White and Black, they dearly loved His (so-called) Excellency. The uncanny aspect of it was that they seemed always to know each time he had an appointment that would require him leaving the hotel. They would begin to collect about an hour ahead of time. They would begin to gather slowly, at first, then more and more, ultimately pouring from the buses and the subway, a feverish and disgorged humanity, flooding the streets across Park Avenue, jamming the traffic. Horn blowing. Shouted oaths. You could set your watch by it. You could make book on it. An hour or so after the crowds began to gather, about the time the street was jammed with people, Himself, as Abingiba had begun to call the Minister Primarily regularly, affectionately, would make his appearance, or disappearance, if you will. It was eerie how they gathered in anticipation. It sort of got to Himself, who, no matter how they loved him and adored him, no matter also that the venerable *New York Times* called him the most urbane, the most articulate, the most debonair head of state it had been their good fortune to encounter, with all that *savoir faire* to spare, notwithstanding, he was no more no less, at his heart of hearts, a country boy, a strapping rustic from the backwoods of the 'Sippis. And like the man said, you can get them out of the country, but you cannot get the country out of them. Face it, it got to our man, and why shouldn't it? Then suddenly all that changed, and qualitatively.

One early afternoon, he was due to leave for La Guardia Airport to take a quick trip southwardly as the crow flew for a meeting with the President. This time he went out of a back entrance on Lexington Avenue. It made no difference. His adoring public was out there in force. Somehow, they knew he would try to sneak out the back way unnoticed. And then he saw something slightly different from all that had transpired before.

Across the street on the edge of the crowd about a dozen men all dressed in white-sheeted robes had gathered, and somehow, they did not look like angels to Himself. They were red-blooded, Mayflowered, superpatriotic born-again-Christian members of the Ku Klux Klan. For some unfathomable reason, Himself felt they had not gathered to adore him. With their pyramidal hoods covering their heads and faces, which made their heads to be shaped like steeples. He thought uneasily of them as the "steeple-headed people." Three days later they gathered again and in larger numbers, this time with picket signs. Men, women, and even little children.

WAKE UP WHITE AMERICA!
STOP KISSING THIS NIGGER'S ASS!
OLIVAMAKI IS A SAVAGE!
BLACK BABOON, YOUR DAYS IS NUMBERED!
BEWARE JAJA. KKK GOT HIS EYES ON YOU!

It almost made Himself, himself, feel unwanted. Two days later members of the Black Alliance were out there also in force and ready for combat duty, as were hundreds of New York's very very finest along with the Feebies (FBIs), the Alliance Blacks with gloves and mitts and baseball bats with picket signs and other items of amicable weaponry. The picket signs were memorable evidence of consummate artistry and esoteric subtlety.

WE LOVE YOU, JAJA!
LOVE YOU MADLY, JAJA!
THE KKK BETTER KEEP THEIR ASS AWAY!
IT'S ASS-KICKING TIME DOWN ON THE DELTA!
YOU AIN'T IN 'SIPPI NOW, HUNKIE!

The Black Alliance was not entirely Black. Here and there were sprinkled whites among the Black Alliance, with Afro-ed bouffants, yet, a few truly good white folks, like those who down home were known historically as "Freedom Fuckers," in the glorious Movement of the sixties. Each time he left the hotel now there were small-size race riots, large-scale ones barely averted. The law-and-order folks kept cracked heads to a minimum. Nothing serious.

The *New York Times* ran an editorial expressing its shame that such a thing could happen in this city of cities, this democratic melting pot.

But in any event, it demonstrates unequivocally the absolute freedom of the First Amendment, that could happen only in a democracy like the USA. And in any other event, let no one misunderstand these unfortunate happenings and infer that these incidents are racially motivated.

Perhaps, another daily newspaper which shall be nameless, suggested, His Excellency should move his circus away from the classy Waldorf. It was scandalous that these things should happen outside the vaunted Waldorf-Astoria in the equally vaunted affluence of Park Avenue.

Whereupon Himself called a press conference and threatened to do the Castro on them and move his operation uptown to the Theresa. But of course, the Theresa no longer existed, as a hotel. "We wouldn't be treated like this in the USSR," His Excellency clearly enunciated his great displeasure. "Perhaps that is where we should have gone first in the first place," he declared menacingly, and redundantly. "If there were not so many of us, we would do like Brother Jesse and go and live with our sisters and brothers in the projects."

Barra Abingiba kept reminding that he would have had nothing to worry about, had he taken his advice and gotten himself some "protection" before leaving the Motherland.

One night they went under the protection of his own security people and the Feebies and the SS and the

NYPD to a secret meeting at a hotel near the United Nations. When the meeting ended, they went down the back elevators to the basement of the hotel, then up a short flight of stairs out into a dark alley. Himself walked gingerly through the moonless midnight darkness in the midst of his security. He was so secure he could hardly catch up with his breath. There must have been more than fifty of them, stumbling over one another. It did not make him feel overconfident regarding his security. It was so black-dark he could not have seen a lightning bug had it been blinking directly on the tip of his nose. He walked carefully, putting one foot in front of the other like a blind man. Then suddenly his feet went out from under him, as he felt himself being rudely pushed forward. As he fell, a muffled shot went zinging by his ear so close that his ear was hot and tingling. The alley had been flooded instantly with light, then suddenly went out again. Several hands pulled him roughly from the ground and ran him toward the end of the alley. He could not see who held him. He hoped the hands were friendly ones. He didn't even know who had pushed him. He suspected it was Abingiba. They made it to the end of the alley and into one of the waiting limos and sped off down the avenue. Himself was out of breath and leaking perspiration. Barra was seated next to him.

"How did you know?" he asked Barra when he got his breath together.

"I had my Juju working. I got a sudden message from the Man from cross the ocean. You are well protected," Barra boasted, "whenever you're close to me." Barra began to laugh uproariously. Himself didn't see a damn thing funny. He longed now for his own and personal "protection."

He learned the next day that two SS men had been wounded. The KKK phoned him and the police and took full credit. They warned him that the worst was yet to come. The newspapers were appalled, but not appalled enough, Himself thought angrily, and with indignation, even. Later that night he'd gotten more than a dozen "crank" phone calls from different voices who knew his private phone number, the one that went directly to his room and bypassed the Great Waldorf switchboard. It was a number he hardly knew himself. He never could remember it.

"Next time we won't miss," a growling drawling voice promised faithfully. "You can't keep a secret from us. We see all you do. We hear all you say. The FBI and Secret Service can't save your Black ass, cause we got them all infiltrated. We even got the Black Alliance covered. We're the invisible government." A Voice that made his belly double into knots.

Another said, "We got your number, nigger, and your days are numbered." Fear was making a gluttonous picnic of his entrails.

Another: "Prime Minister some stew beef! We know who you really are!" Live crabs clawed at his intestines. They knew who he really was!

Himself was getting rest broken and paranoiac. A nervous wreck, a living smashup. Day and night, every time the telephone rang, he jumped, as if the rings were pistol shots, as if Ma Bell could actually assassinate him.

At the President's insistence, he spent a couple of nights at the White House. "Where could you be safer?" the President asked, rhetorically.

They had sneaked out of the Waldorf at four a.m. and flown from La Guardia down to Dulles Airport in Virginia. They had been helicoptered from the airport past the ominously white buildings of the Pentagon and the Central Intelligence Agency, past the greatest of all phallic symbols on this earth, the Washington Monument, symbolic of the man who fathered an entire country, Himself thought, ironically, smilingly, and who fathered a whole heap of 'cullud younguns.' (How many white Washingtons do you know?) Losing altitude now, passing over the virginally white buildings glowing so lovely in the mellow moonlight, and finally alighting on the helicopter landing pad in the backyard of the White House. Then furtively they were ushered across the South Lawn and into the big and awesome White House.

"That's the Diplomatic Reception Room," one of the Afro-American security guides whispered to His (so-called) Excellency, as they moved through the entrance. Himself made, secretly, the sign of the cross. He felt like genuflecting.

And now they had met all day long, working out the details for a mutual understanding on who would get the cobanium out of the earth of the Northern Province, and how much would go to whom. Foreign Minister Mamadou Tangi was a tough negotiator, as was the gentle-voiced Minister of Education, Maria Efwa. They insisted that the cobanium would be equally divided between the four great powers, the United States, the Soviet Union, the People's Republic of China, and the People's Independent Democratic Republic of Guanaya, then to be further divided equally among the "First World" countries, according to their population. The allotments would be overseen by the Guanayan government. Also, a treaty would be drawn up in which each nation receiving cobanium would have to agree to use it for peaceful purposes only. The President and his negotiating team had never encountered such impertinent *noble savages* in all their born and unborn days. It was unheard of. It was scandalous. It was un-American. It ultimately became a question of when and how the arrangements would redound to the benefit of all parties concerned, especially Guanaya.

After debating the question back and forth, it was clear that the Foreign Minister and the Education Minister (or is it Ministress?) were chief spokespersons for the Guanayan negotiators. Mamadou Tangi and Maria Efwa were the center of gravity. Where they led, His Excellency and the others would surely follow. The more he saw of them and discussed affairs of state with them, the more the President of the US became convinced that a change of strategy was required, if they were to win the Guanayan leaders' confidence.

So that at one point during the discussion the President rose and said, "Well, lady and gentlemen, I think this has been a fruitful meeting. I believe in the capitalistic democratic law of diminishing returns. We've been at it all day long and far into the night. So why don't we retire to the Diplomatic Reception Room, and drink to our mutual friendship and good health and to peace on earth and whatnot."

Himself said, "Especially to whatnot."

At which point they retired to the Reception Room and began to drink to everything under the sun and beneath the moon and likewise the stars. And stripes.

Essentially a "country boy," Himself could not help himself from staring, slyly, almost clandestinely, at the decor and the color scheme of gold and white, and beneath his feet, the deeply plushed and woven oval rug, also of gold and white and pale blue, with the emblems of the fifty states incorporated around the carpet's border. He could not help from staring openly at the panoramic mural on the wall of "Scenic America," with Boston Harbor and Blacks in slavery-time attire and at what he assumed was Plymouth Rock. And the gleaming Regency chandelier above him. He thought, This is me, myself and I, from the Big Damn 'Sipp, Himself. He thought, This is the Biggest of all the Big Damn Houses. Big and white and awesome House. He could not keep himself from laughing. And he laughed aloud. They stared wonderingly at His (so-called) Excellency, who had not been tippling and toasting with them, yet.

"To the brotherhood of man!" From the tippling toasting President.

"To the womanhood of sisters too!" Himself suggested raucously.

They had been going at it steadily for more than half an hour, when Himself caught on to the fact that the

President only pretended to be drinking. He was holding the liquor in his mouth. Himself was also faking it. Each of them had caught on to the other and was aware that the other was faking and each was aware of the other's awareness. It was the surest way on this earth to get completely stoned out of your skull. Except that Himself was only faking that he was faking. It could really get confusing. Somewhere along the way the President slyly signaled his extra VIPs to depart surreptitiously and without fanfare. But Himself's retinue did not leave, reluctant as they were to leave Himself in the clutches of the most powerful personage on this earth. After hints and signifying did not suffice to get rid of them, Himself finally became indignant.

"And whasamatter with you sisser and brussers? You don't truss your Prime Minaceter? You don't think I can hold my own with this old presdence here? This old precidence of the Uniney Snakes? Hohn? Answer me quession. You don' truss me, why you lect me?" He leaned over and whispered aloud to Abingiba, "I gots my jug working, Bro. You think I come way over here in this Uniney Snakes of a Milk The Cow without going to see my head bad Juju man? I'll juju the shit out of him, he try mess with me. He snice fella anyhow. He's very snice man." He lowered his voice and winked his eye at his buddy, even as his tongue grew thicker, even also as he insisted he had not been drinking. "Smatter with you sissers and brussers. Oh, you of little face. If you all have so little face in me, I'm going to tender my resignation tomorror mornin', to become 'fective as of the day before yesterday, *ex post facto*, retroactively, *redundantly*!"

He came so close to Abingiba's ear he almost nibbled it as he whispered. "He thinks I've been drinking, but I've been only pretending to be drinking, like he's only pretending. He's been trying to hold all that whiskey in his mouth, which is impossible, while I've been pouring mine in this spittoon down here beneath the chair. The President must be a modern hipster. He dips snuff like all the young folks do these days. Snuff-dipping is hip. The President's getting as drunk as a skunk in the 'Sippi bayous." Himself's eyes were crossing. Maria Efwa stared at Himself, anxiously. Obviously, some of the whiskey he'd been drinking did not get poured into the hip spittoon. In the tradition of Cool Horace, the fingers of both of Himself's hands were crossed.

In any event and notwithstanding, Himself's retinue was finally convinced that Himself would be perfectly safe in the Lincoln Bedroom in the White House. "What place on this earth can be more safer than the White House in the United States?" the drunken President demanded indignantly. They grudgingly agreed with the President. So far as they knew, in the entire history of this whitest of white houses, no would-be-assassins had ever reached the upper floors of this historic edifice. They were overawed by the sense of history and Caucasian power, the like of which the world had never known. And if they had known, they had certainly forgotten. Or wouldn't dare to mention, even to themselves.

And so, they watched Himself and the beloved President go (arms around each other's shoulders) and get swallowed up by the presidential elevator. They were escorted out of the big White House across the way to Blair House for their diplomatic lodgings.

"You're going slip in Lincoln's Bedroom. It's very pissful place to slip in there with Lincoln. Its room I always slip in when Mrs. Hubert is out of town visiting her ailing mother, or whatever. I always feel at piss with myself in old Abe's bedroom. Mrs. Hubert can't stand the place. Her pappy was a slave master." They were in the hall in front of the room where Lincoln slept. The drunken president put his arms around Himself's shoulders again and started singing, off key.

Pish on earth and mushy mile,
God and sinners rest awhile—

He hiccupped and giggled. "If it wasn't for ol' Abie boy, you might've been my slave, Your Excellency." He stated it almost wistfully. "How about that?"

Himself feigned a drunken hiccup. "And I might have done a Nat Turner on your arse and slit your presidential throat."

The President put his hand around his throat and howled with laughter.

It was not easy for Himself to fall asleep, sleeping there in Lincoln's bed. The bedroom smelled anciently and moldishly of olden times, of civil war and intrigue and chewing tobacco and presidential nightmares; it was redolent with age and historic frames of references. He knew that the ancient smells were more figments of his imagination than real, since it was obvious that they kept all the landmarks in the White House sterile and immaculate. Notwithstanding, the imagined ancient smells were overwhelming to his senses. In fact, the knowledge that his imagination was playing tricks on his senses made the situation even more frightening. Himself did not believe in ghosts, and yet he wished fervently he'd taken Barra Abingiba's advice and gotten himself some real "protection" before he'd left the Motherland. Himself was a young man inordinately awed by history and by myth and legend. And he was lying there in the same bed slept in so many many times by the legendary Great Emancipator.

He, an orphaned Black dude from the cypressed swamp woods of the 'Sippis! How in the hell could he be expected to fall asleep easily behind all that heavy history? He told himself he was too hip, too irreverent to be awed by old Abe Lincoln. "I got my shit together," he told himself. "I hang too tough to be impressed." And yet he wished now he had actually been drinking all that booze instead of faking it, pouring it into that goddamn spittoon! In which case he could have slept it off. He lay there staring at the terrifying darkness. "Let old Abe come. Let him come! We'll see who's *bad*!" He heard noises that he didn't hear. He'd show Abe Lincoln who was boss. He imagined he heard somebody breathing deeply, laboredly, asthmatically. Perhaps the Big White House itself had been infiltrated, he thought, Lincoln's bedroom. Perhaps the CIA had hired a Juju hit man to scare him so badly his heart would cease to function. A Juju hit man! With the heavy breathing and the wheezing. A clear case of assassination, clear and clean, leaving no traces. Ghosts never did leave fingerprints. The perfect crime! Then again, he thought, perhaps it was himself he heard, his own frightened bated breathing. He tried to think of funny things to amuse him out of the nonsense of his nervousness, to exorcize his stupid fear, so he could fall asleep. He made himself remember a funny little ditty.

> *The other day upon the stair,*
> *I saw a man who wasn't there.*
> *He wasn't there again today.*
> *Gee, I wish he'd stay away.*

He smiled to himself. It hadn't helped exorcize the ghost who wasn't there. The heavy labored breathing started up again. Probably lanky Lincoln in his death throes. Breathing, gasping. He wasn't scared, he told himself. Hell no. He started whistling Dixie. He wasn't scared. Hell naw. He was terrified! He swallowed the imagined thick decaying smell of the ancient bedroom. Then he remembered Lincoln had not died in the White House. The knowledge of it didn't help. Ghosts were never noted for being logical. It was not one of their stronger points. The breathing continued louder than ever. Trembling chills moved over his shoulders back and forth. He sat up in bed with his fists balled up. He wasn't scared. His body was raining perspiration. He got up and fumbled around the room looking desperately for the light switch. Forgotten completely were the lamps on the night tables on both sides of the bed. He tried to remember where things were in the carpeted room. His mind was able to fashion the carpet with its patterns of apricot and bright olive colors, even as his knee came into sharp contact with the marble-topped rosewood table in the middle of the room. "Shit! Damn! Hell!" The pain shot through his knee and down his leg, as he limped about blindly and fell upon the now-remembered apricot-colored love seat.

He got up again and put his hand before him till he reached the treacherous marble-topped rosewood table again. Stumbling around there in the darkness, he expected that any moment something would reach out and touch him on his shoulder. And when it happened, he knew he would disgrace the executive pajamas they had provided him.

Ultimately, he found the wall switch. The lights were on now and he looked furtively around the room. Nobody was there for him to see, because it was common knowledge that ghosts always disappear when the lights come on. He stared at the imposing awe-compelling rosewood bed with its bedclothing of yellowish pink, the antique rocker and boudoir chair on one side and the green upholstered antique chair on the other side. The walls of pinkish yellow with pictures, he imagined, of past presidents whom he did not recognize staring at him from all sides. He switched off the lights and made his way back to the bed.

He lay there now in Lincoln's rosewood bed, thinking, if old Abe was the Great Emancipator, how come he didn't feel emancipated? He turned and twisted, got entangled in the bedclothing. And wrestled with a ghost who tried to give him death by strangulation. Ultimately, he fell asleep from sheer exhaustion. A presence in the room awoke him shortly afterward. It was a presence more felt than seen, but no less a presence notwithstanding. A frigid presence. His entire body knew a chilly perspiration, as the icy presence slowly materialized into a visible apparition clothed immaculately in white. He knew a prickling in the nape of his head "back in the kitchen," where the baby hair grew, and his being knew a vertiginous sensation, as the gliding apparition loomed nearer and nearer clearer and clearer. Hovering above him now. All in white. He closed his eyes momentarily, and he imagined the unearthly apparition got into bed with him. His sense of humor won out over his great fear, as he thought, Damn! That's one part of the Lincoln legend they left out about old Abe, the switch-hitting aspect. An AC-DC gentleperson. How about that mess! He was immobilized by fear, or else he would have told the ghost, "I don't play that he-ing and she-ing shit." It was not in his repertoire. Definitely it was not. He swung right-handed all the way. Then suddenly he came back to earth thinking that the hands of ghosts were supposed to be bony and without flesh. But these were soft and gentle hands that made contact with his perspiring body. Was he dreaming? Were ghosts tactile? Did they possess physical ties that were tangible? He'd never slept with a ghost before. And he wished for his African "protection," but vainly and belatedly.

The tingling sensation started again when he realized this particular apparition obviously believed in faith healing and the laying on of hands, soft and gentle hands, powerful juju, soothing juju, overcoming fear and trepidations. Moving ever downward toward his supple nervous and witch-crafted member (of the wedding), this apparition, murmuring now in unknown tongues fluttering sounds of desires fulfilled and excitation. The ghost was purring like a pampered kitten. And suddenly he realized his apparition was softly round and amply breasted, and of a decidedly different sexual construction and proclivity. He was not abed with old Abe Lincoln! Perhaps this was an ethereal visitation from one of old Abe's young mistresses!

A fact that was verified when his apparition spoke. "Oh, my my my!" She held his member ever so fondly.

"Honeybunch has grown to be a great big boy now!" She had opened his pajamas. She began to kiss his body all over, murmuring sweetly as she went. "Oh, my my my my! Daddy won't need no dildo tonight. But how can him be so big and still so soft? Was him had too much to drink?"

Him was wide awake now and very much alive, leapingly. Himself said groggily, "There must be some mistake here." As he reached toward the now-remembered night table and clicked on the bed lamp.

She began, "Mr. President, you are so formal, so unlike yourself, I mean—your voice—Oh my my my mymymy! There really has been a mistake. And a very very big one and thank God for all the big mistakes in life. You are His Excellency?" She had released his member quickly as if it were a thing too hot for her to handle, as if a deadly snake had bitten her. Then on second thought she fondled it again. "Oh well, the Lord works in mysterious ways his wonders to perform. I thought at first a miracle had been performed. So beautiful and big! And who's to question the reason why? And I wonder if His Excellency's excellency can rise to the occasion. What's a poor little country girl from Texas supposed to do in a situation such as this? Mama never said that there'd be days like this. She just told me, 'If you see something you want, go after it.

Take it in hand.'" She sighed philosophically, as bravely she took matters in her gentle hands again.

Himself panicked, momentarily. He thought, *Jail bait!* Can't be more than fifteen years old, if that much. Straw blond, innocently blue-eyed. The eyes of *Texas?* Statutory rape in the White-damn-House! One hundred years of solitude and hard damn labor. He'd be a disgrace to the African profession, no special thanks to Ossie Davis. But then that part of him influenced by the devil, which was always in him, sometimes cat-napping, woke up and exhorted him. "What a prank-ish escapade, what a caper, to make it with the child mistress of the President of the United Snakes!" the devil whispered loudly to him. His member must have eavesdropped him, as it responded gleefully, boldly in-stantly steeling itself, rising to the grandiose occasion, firmly, nobly, dignifiedly. The dear girl's face blushed rubescently with the greatest expectations.

The darling girl explained, "He told me to meet him here after midnight, and everything would be on the up-and-up. He must've forgot. He's freakish for young girls, you know, and they must always wear red rib-bons in their hair and be dressed in white, suggesting their virginity. He always sings 'Scarlet Ribbons' when he's doing it to me. Sometimes he makes me put tomato ketchup in my doohickey.

"Oh, my my my mymymy!" she shouted quietly and gleefully, philosophically. "Perhaps he had you in mind, Your Excellency. You're certainly on the up-and-up and getting more so every second.

"Oh well," she sighed resignedly. "Like my mama always said, what's a poor little Texas country girl to do in a case like this?" Now she watched the him of him leaping playfully about, completely out of control now. She cooed and murmured. "My my my mymymy! Him thinks him a toady frog!" She giggled and she fondled.

Himself answered, "You're going to get the hell out of here and in a hurry, that's what you're going to do, and let me get myself some sleep." The dignity of his Africanness had asserted its priority over his horniness and deviltry. He could feel his member dwindling in agreement with his Pan-Africanism. Who said a stiff one had no conscious? At which point there was a knocking at the door. At which other point Himself closed his eyes tightly and began to snore. He heard the President's drunken voice.

"Are you 'sleep Misher Prim Minster?"

"Hell yes!" Himself shouted back. "Can't you hear me snoring?" He clicked off the night table lamp.

"May I come in?" The President was already entering the bedroom. He switched on the overhead light. It was only then that Himself remembered the President's child-mistress, the scarlet-ribboned demivirgin. He closed his eyes waiting for the President's outcry. All he heard was silence and a quiet giggling from beneath the bed. It was the kind of giggling that seemed on the verge of erupting into hysterical laughter.

The President looked around the room. "You're sure you're 'sleep, Misher Prim Minster?"

"Of course I'm sure. I'm only dreaming that you woke me up."

The President came in and sat in the ancient rocker near the bed. Himself kept his eyes shut tight.

The President rocked back and forth. Himself could hear the squeaking rocker. It needed lubricating. "You know, Mr. Prim Minster, I've really taken a liking to you. I seems like I've known you for the longest time. Like we grew up together or something." The President's voice was slurred. "Of all the stinguished visiters to the outhouse. I mean the White House, I've never taken to anyone as mush as I've taken to you. You are magnicifent, Mish Prim Minster. I like you very mush."

His prankish nature was surfacing again. He thought, What if I called the President "Snot Rag"?

What would happen? Then he tensed again, as he imagined he heard the giggling underneath the bed clearly now, and he thought, The President must surely hear it also. He began to perspire. Perhaps it was a game the two of them were playing with him. He imagined the girl underneath the bed was laughing raucously now. He closed his eyes even tighter than before and began to snore deliberately, boisterously.

"Whatsamatter, Misher Prim Minster? You got a girl underneath your bed?"

Bullets of perspiration covered his forehead, leaked from his armpits. He began to snore louder than ever. To drown out the laughter coming from under the bed.

The President said, "I really do like you a lot. I don't understand it. You're just like a long-lost buddy."

Himself said, "Thank you very much," and continued to snore.

Suddenly it became fearfully quiet in the bedroom, except for the giggling beneath the bed, an awesome silence, which acted as an amplifier to the noise beneath the bed. He opened, tentatively, his eyes and sneaked a peek at the President. He had to find him first. His eyes took in, at first, the tall windows with the white lace curtains flanked by dark-green silken drapes tied back and trimmed with golden edges and topped by swagged valances. (Where was the President?) Surely he could hear the giggling now amplified as if she giggled through loudspeakers. He finally located the portly gentleman standing before the antique vanity staring at himself before the mirror at the dressing table. He thought he heard the President mumbling to himself.

"You've come a fuh-fuh-fuh-fucking long ways, baby. You and old fuh-fuh-fuh-fucking Abe Lincoln." Himself closed his eyes again, but he still heard the President. His speech was louder, clearer now.

"They used to call you Puddin' Head Jones in school, said you was fuh-fuh-fuh-fucking fat and funky. You wasn't smuch to look at, allergic to book learning, made you breakout in spots. But where're they? And look at you now. Smost powerful somebitch in the whole fuh-fucking universe, 'eluding the moon. Have the prettiest women in the world at your becking and calling. You smost powerful somebitch in the whole wide world. You can get more pussy than Jack Fitzgerald Kennedy. You can snap your pinkies and end life on this fuh-fuh-fuh-fucking earth in sixty seconds. You the fuh-fuh-fucking Presidence of the Uniney Stace!" He was screaming at the mirror now. Then everything got quiet again. Himself could hear the giggling clearly now underneath the bed, and he could feel the drunken President moving toward the bed, and he could hear his own heart beating up in his sweating forehead like an exaggerated stethoscope.

The President stood at his bedside now, hovering above him. "You're sure you don't have a pretty lady underneath your bed?"

"What the hell would I be doing with a woman 'neath my bed, when I'm fast asleep? Can't you hear me snoring?" He began to snore louder than ever, snoring, snorting, wheezing, spitting.

The President started to squat down to look under the bed, but it required too much effort, physically. His (so-called) Excellency could hear the Prexy's bones creaking like a squeaky gate that needed lubricating. Like the rocking chair beside the bed. Instead, he straightened up and said, "All right then. You take care. I'll leave you alone with the Great Emancipator, hear? Sleep tight. Don't let the fuh-fuh-fucking bedbugs bits, as they used to say where I come from."

Himself repeated, "Thank you very much. And do me a favor old buddy. Turn off the light as you leave the room."

The room went dark as the President departed. And the young mistress rolled out from under the bed breaking up with laughter. She jumped into the bed of the Great Emancipator. Between the giggling and the raucous laughter, Himself heard her say distinctly: "I want to be emancipated! I want to be emancipated!" Excitedly.

Why not? Himself thought. Why not emancipate the poor little scarlet-ribboned demivirgin from the Long Star State? His missionary spirt was aroused with Quaker pity for the girl. The devil in Himself demanded, "Why the hell not? Why not make it with the President's young mistress with the scarlet ribbons in her yellow hair?!" He could almost hear his member (of the wedding) giggling at the idea of it. Even as she held his stiffening member in her tender and caressing fingers, the devil in his prankish member advocating. To cuckold none other than the Prexy of the Caucasian-powered USA. He thought he heard his swollen member laugh uproariously.

But then he knew that Lincoln's room was haunted when he heard his member speak to him distinctly now. "You are the Prime Minister of the Independent People's Democratic Republic of Guanaya. You are a great man of enormous dignity and commitment. And what makes this little blond chit think you have a craving for her alabaster body?" He was frightened witless for a moment, to hear his member speaking to him thusly. His entire body lathered now with perspiration like Seattle Slew coming into the home stretch. But then he Himself felt indignant and insulted, remembering Daphne Jack-Armstrong, and her "big black stud" named Jimmy Jay Leander Johnson of the 'Sippis, and it was like a thousand years of experiences ago, a person he no longer knew, hardly remembered. Even his member (of the wedding) had acquired a new intelligence, hardly recognizable, from the other fellah he had known, which is probably why he felt it dwindling now, losing interest at the moment.

He switched the bed light on and got out of bed and took Scarlet Ribbons up in his arms, as she held on for dear life to his softening member, even as she kicked and squealed.

Scarlet cried out, "What y'all doing?"

"You'll find out very shortly," the devil in him advocated.

Scarlet gigged now, delighted. "Oh!" she said, "a good idea! I should have known—all nigger men are kinky! You want to do it on the floor! You want to do it on the floor!"

"You got it, girl," His Excellency responded. "On the floor, outside the door. On the floor, outside the door," His Excellency repeated.

And that is where he left her, on the floor outside the

door, kicking, squealing, cussing, as he quickly closed the door and turned the latch and went back to Lincoln's rosewood bed. *How dare she take for granted the dignified prime minister of the Independent People's Democratic Republic of Guanaya?*

Back at the Waldorf the KKK kept up their continuous vigil, and likewise did the Black Alliance, along with the well-intentioned "Freedom Fuckers." The Grand Coalition was ever ready in the Combat Zone. The crank phone calls increased, along with letters and telegrams threatening Himself's immortality. He was becoming a piece of nervous wreckage. He jumped at every sudden sound. One day he had all phone calls shut off, except his private line. He gave instructions to the main switchboard. "No more phone calls until we leave for Lolliloppi."

It was drawing close to the time when all this would be ended. His feelings were one great twisted bundle of agonized ambivalence. Was he ready to give up all this phony power, this undreamed-of popularity, this adulation, this unheard-of celebrity, this outpouring of love his people gave unstintingly to him? Sometimes he told himself the love they gave to him was to Himself and not to his Prime Ministership. And he wanted desperately to believe it, almost made himself believe that this outpouring was for him and him alone. He told himself he wanted to finish his schedule, which included the trip to Lolliloppi and a speech to the United Nations General Assembly afterward, and then get back to the Old Country, and to be himself Jimmy Jay Leander Johnson, and the masquerade would be over *for all times*. But nobody could ever take this couple of weeks away from him. Sometimes he thought they should forget about the trip to Lolliloppi. It was fraught with too much danger. It was crazy. It was idiotic. One day he told his group they would not go. Who needs it? he demanded. He saw the relief flow into their faces. It had been said that Lolliloppi was so damn deep in the darkness of the delta, the Supreme Court decision had never reached them. Lynching Blacks was fashionable, chic. James Crow was in the driver's seat, ensconced forever.

He said, "I know all of you are keenly disappointed at not getting a chance to see the dear old Southland of William Faulkner and Tennessee Williams and Carson McCullers and the Confession of Willie Styron." He went deep into his Southern accent. "I was going to show you that cat sitting on a hot tin roof and that streetcar named Desire, where all the darkies ama weeping, when ol' Masser gits the cold cold ground that's coming to him." He got out his brand-new guitar and began to plunk on it, singing à la Al Jolson:

How I love you, how I love you.
Dear ol' Swampee—

Then he went into

Summer Time—
And the cooking is greasy—

He was perspiring freely now, with a mad gleam in his eyes. It frightened all of them excepting Horace and Abingiba.

Way down upon the Swampee Ribber—

He stared around at the frightened looks on their faces. Yet he knew they were relieved at his decision not to go. He said, "On the other hand, I wouldn't feel right depriving you of experiencing that fundamental slice of Americana. So historic, so nostalgic. So much like the real America."

His Wife's Bottom assured Himself, eagerly, "It's perfectly all right with us. We understand, and we agree—"

Himself was working himself into a bizarre frame of mind. His face wore a whimsical expression, his great dark eyes a twinkle. The prankster in him winning out again, as per usual. He was the devil's advocate and him personified. "Why the hell not go to 'Sippi? So, what if something happens out of the way down there? Suppose two or three of us do get lynched? It'll simply expose the deceitful mama-muckers."

His mind was leapingly alive. He saw his people now deep deep in the darkness of the delta of despair, heads bowed, cowed and afraid. If he could give them one brief moment with their heads up, one hundredth of a second of self-pride and assurance, it would be worth the trip, well worth the danger that would be involved. If they could glimpse their sisters and their brothers from across the ocean. See them face-to-face. Speak with them. Shake their hands. His brothers and sisters in the delta were more African than any others in the country, closer to their African culture, their African humanity. They were the honest-to-goodness diasporated Africans. With their mojo and their voodoo and their belief in "haints" and roots and their music and their churches and their shouting and their dancing.

He remembered now his last trip to Lolliloppi. Belafonte had subsidized a trip for him back home to research the folk songs of his people. He'd been taken by excited students from a school founded more than a hundred years before by the United Missionary Association, taken deep into the delta bush to this seventy-five-year-old great-grandmother who lived in a two-room cabin. She was a folk singer and guitarist with twelve children and twenty-seven grandchildren and God knew how many great-grandchildren. She was in strong voice and she sang for him, to him, and she told him ghost stories of things that hang about her bed at night, great big beasts that slid under and out of windows with them pulled down tight. She was born with a veil over her eyes, and she could see things others were unable to see. She told these stories with a profound conviction. It was only after he had been in Guanaya a couple of months and was reading everything he could lay his hands on written by African writers that he had come across a novel written by a Nigerian writer, Amos Tutuola, author of *The Palm-Wine Drinkard*. He had been reading from a scene in the novel that had a strange feeling of déjà vu. He read the scene again and again until he realized it was the same ghost story told to him by this illiterate Black Mississippi great-grandmother almost verbatim, word for word. It sent a shiver along his spine.

His Wife's Bottom said, "But surely—"

HIMSELF went on. "But surely, if I risk everything for the love of Africa, what was it you said, HWB? I might be exiled from my country, shot at sunrise, or is it electification in this country? I mean, the least you can do is to take this risk along with Yours Sincerely."

The next morning, he got a call on his direct line from the President of the Uniney Snakes! "This is the President of the United States, your good buddy, Mr. Prime Minister. I just want to say that we're doubling the security around you. We got word recently that there will be an attempt on your life by international assassins smuggled into this country from Africa and paid for by persons of your own country! So, don't you trust nobody's body, as my mama used to say. Furthermore, we have been approached by members of your opposition party offering us preferred status in the cobanium situation, if we would lend ourselves to your undoing." The President lowered his voice. "There were members of my cabinet who wanted to go along with the proposal. I had to put my foot down. I told them that, under no circumstances whatever must you be allowed to be murdered in my country. Let them do their fuh-fuh-fucking dirty tricks somewhere fuh-fuh-fucking else."

Himself wiped the perspiration from his brow agitatedly. He said in a froggy voice, "Thank you very much, Mr. President." No sarcasm was intended. The President's voice went down an octave even lower than before. Himself had to strain his ears to hear him. "I don't trust that goddamn CIA, so you be careful, buddy boy. And keep what I told you under your hat. Don't you tell nobody's body. You hear?"

Himself said, "You have my word, Mr. President. Everything stays under my hat, and my head stays where it's supposed to be, on top of my broad shoulders."

The President laughed and said, "Tata."

That very same night His Excellency got a call on his new, direct and private line. A gravelly flesh-crawling voice said, "Is this Prime Minister Jaja?"

Jimmy Jay said, agitatedly, "How in the hell did you get this number?"

The voice sounded like somebody scraping a blackboard with a rusty knife. "We just want you to know, Mr. Prime Minister Jaja, that we love you. We're out there every day, and we'll be protecting you with our own lives, if it comes to that. You're a great man, Prime Minister Jaja. You're in the tradition of men like Frederick Douglass and W. E. B. Du Bois and Robeson and Malcolm and Martin and Medgar and Elijah and Garvey and Touré and Neyrere and Chaka and Nkrumah, and also Rosa Parks and Harriet Tubman."

"Well," Himself said, lying back and relaxing now, "thank you very much. But I'm afraid I don't deserve to be compared with giants like—"

"Don't be afraid of nothing," the blackboard-scraping voice assured him. "You deserve it all right. All the praises given to you, and more besides. You're the greatest Black man on this earth. And for that matter, you're the greatest woman too. I am not a chauvinist pig."

"I'm overwhelmed—" Himself began.

"You're the greatest," the voice on the other end insisted, "and you are definitely the chosen one. And we will let no harm come to you from outside forces, over our dead bodies." He lowered his voice and growled the rest. "I repeat, you are the chosen one, and we have chosen you for martyr-dam. We are going to kill you and blame it on the American government in collusion with the Ku Kluck Klan, and Black folks all over this country and throughout the world will insurrect, and we'll have ourselves a real revolution. It's the only way. I just called you up to offer my congratulations. You'll go down in history. So, don't you worry about a thing. Nobody's going to harm one hair on your handsome head, I guarantee—"

Himself was enraged and sweating chinaberries. Crabs were staging a feasting orgy in his intestines. He knew a feeling close to vertigo. His voice was cracked and quaking. He forgot he was supposed to be a dignified African prime minister; he reverted to the jargon of the streets. "Excepting you, you simpleminded motherfucker! I recognize your voice," he lied. "And I'm going to put the word out on your ass. If one solitary hair is harmed on my head, you, your mother, your grandmother, if you got one, and your grandmother's grandmother and all your children and your children's children's children down to the hundredth generation will wish like hell they'd never been born. And as soon as you get your simple ass off the phone, I'm going to call the baddest Juju man in Africa and give him your name."

The voice on the other end went from gravelly to high soprano. It began to stammer, frantically, idiotically. "But-bu-bu-but, Mr. Pu-pu-pu-prime Minister, pu-pu-pu-please ma'am and pu-pu-pu-please sir. I mu-mu-mu-mean, cu-cu-cu-cain't you-you-you-tu-tu-tu-take a joke?" As Himself slammed the receiver back onto its cradle.

22

Through the years Jimmy Jay had grown to rely heavily on his premonitions, especially in times of extraordinary strain and stress, placed his absolute faith and confidence in his undeniable presentiments, trusted them to send out SOSs to him and throw up mucho danger signals. Perhaps it was the latent African in him, he thought whenever he thought about it. No matter, he looked religiously for omens, good and bad (Give me a sign, O Lord!); he wore his amulets religiously and more so now than ever since the experience of his African pilgrimage, in that highly civilized state of human being known as Bamakanougou in the Central Province of Guanaya. He thought, smilingly, of his erstwhile buddy Hugh Masekela. After four months in the old country, Jimmy had reverted to his roots like a bee-martin to his hole. Remembering Hugh Masekela again, he thought of himself as "The Africanization of Ooga Booga." Jimmy Jay Leander deemed himself defenseless without his premonitions, and they never ever failed him. But this particular day his prescience did him dirt, deserted him completely, caught him entirely with his guard down, with his trousers lowered, so to speak.

He'd awakened to a sun-blessed day. The meteorologist at radio station WLIB predicted a balmy one in a very late October of the decade of the eighties, of cloudless skies with no sign of any kind of precipitation anywhere in the Western Hemisphere all along the Eastern Seaboard. He'd awakened, that morning, hardened in the middle of him, horny, spry, and chipper, and had gone through his ablution ceremonies, relieved himself, becoming softer, memberwise, showered, brushed his pearlies, singing as he went—OH WHAT A BEAU-TIFUL MORNING, OH WHAT A BEAUTIFUL DAY—shaved, stared at the bathroom mirror, admiringly, at himself, at the clean-looking handsomeness of himself, profiling from the right side and the left, then frontally again, as if he still couldn't believe his own eyes. You vain bastard! he thought, even as he continued to observe himself, admiringly. Clear dark-brown eyes of burning brilliance that seemed to stare beyond the far horizon, singing IN THAT GREAT GITTIN' UP MORNING now, heavily eyelashed and eyebrowed, fully lipped and perpetually poutish. There had always seemed to be a hidden mischief in the eyes and mouth. He smiled openly now at his extravagant good looks. A mouth crammed full of gleaming pearls, proportioned evenly, except for the two upper front that were slightly larger than their other next-door neighbors, a sensuous mouth that seemed to have an avid appetite for life and living. "You're the vainest sonofabitch alive!"

Recalling now, nostalgically, his boyhood deep down in the delta of the 'Sippis. He'd been a boy of whom the little girls usually said, "Humph! He thinks he's cute!" He came out of his nostalgic narcissistic daydream, as he thought of Her Excellency Maria Efwa, and he remembered that he was His Excellency Jaja Okwu Olivamaki, Prime Minister of the Independent People's Democratic Republic of Guanaya, a.k.a. Himself, a.k.a. the Minister Primarily. He donned his phony beard, drifted into the communal and commodious living room, where they all gathered every morning, exchanging pleasantries, sipping coffee or tea, and munching English crumpets, discussing casually their program for the day. But first of all, he went, as usual, leisurely through the *New York Times*, front to back, section A (the front page), the Cold War heating up

again, as per usual. Israel and the PLO, Poland and His
Holiness, rebellion in South Africa. Bombs, rioting.
First World people acting up, ungraciously. Ingrates
all. After all white folks had done for them. Civilized
them. Christianized them. Then leafing through that
section unhurriedly till he reached the obituary page,
slowing down to a cruising pace now, perusing carefully names and pictures, then sighing deeply, relieved
that he did not see his own face or his own name listed,
which meant that he was still among the living. (He'd
get back to the editorial page later), then to section B
(with the sports, the Yankees in a very lengthy losing
streak; Mr. October was in Los Angeles; Billy Martin
acting up, hired again—fired again), then on to section
C (the Wednesday-morning living section, the arts,
books, plays, entertainment, a brief go at the morning
crossword puzzle), then back to section A and the editorial page. A letter to the editor caught his eye. He could
feel the wonderful dark-black eyes of Maria Efwa upon
him like the warmth of an African midnight. Perhaps
it was a figment of his tremendous wish fulfillment. He
felt the soothing of her midnight eyes pervading him
with a sweet and overwhelming warmth, as he read:

*"Dear Editor: The cowtowing of the American
government to the fascists of South Africa is a dis-*

grace to the American people and its international image. This country has become the buttress of every oppressive government on this earth. If this government withheld its support for one day only, every reactionary regime in the world would come crashing down so loud and instantly, it might very well cause an earthquake of grave and seismometric proportions on the Richter scale."

He paused and looked around him. He breathed deeply his approval. He mumbled, "Tell it like it EYE ESS is!" He read further.

"Instead of welfare, we have become a warfare state, the world center of munition makers. We are the White Marketeers for Death throughout the universe.

It is time for the American people to wake up and understand who is the real threat to World Peace and the annihilation of all life on this planet. Hooray for the courage of the Roman Catholics of the USA."

Jimmy Jay shouted softly, "Yeah! Bravo to the Catholic Church. More power to them. Blessed are the peacemakers! God Bless Jesse Jackson!" He had begun to read aloud, and he knew his cabinet was listening now.

"The Star-Spangled Banner has become a right-wing symbol for World Imperialism and counter-revolution, somewhat like the swastika used to be a symbol of fascism and despised throughout the world."

He stopped reading, momentarily. "Listen to this." He need not have worried. They were listening with every bit of their aural equipment.

"But back to the neo-Nazis in South Africa. If war breaks out in that unhappy place, and this government goes to war to save the world for "democracy" and against "Godless Communism," this government will be faced with some very severe and perhaps irreconcilable contradictions, due to the fact that the US Army is in the main a Black army, which will be called upon to go thousands of miles away from home to kill other Black folks in the name of freedom which they do not themselves enjoy back home."

He stopped and laughed and slapped the paper, and shouted mutedly, "Right on, brother, right on! Or sister, just as likely." He paused and wiped his perspiring and admiring face. "That's some dangerous stuff. They killed Martin for messing with their international devilment, and Malcolm too. That's why they can't stand Jesse. I hope the cat who wrote this is in another country by now, a million miles away from here. It won't do him any good. The CIA will hunt him down, even if he's up there on the moon."

"They might be able to get some of the Black Uncle Tom majors and colonels and brigadiers, nearing retirement, and bucking for one- and two- and three-star generalships, but the rank and file will say, 'Hell no! We won't go!' And if some of them are forced to go, the damn majors and colonels would be scared to give them armed rifles, not knowing which enemy they would train their rifles on."

"Goddamn! Goddamn! Goddamn!" the bogus PM mumbled. "The brother or sister is baaad! He's so bad it's a wonder he isn't scared of his own damn self." He continued to read, mumbling intermittently, "Right on!" . . . "Let it all hang out." . . . "Go on, with your bad damn self!" . . . "I sure hope the CIA never catches up with your ass. I feel sorry for you if they do!" He looked up at Maria Efwa. "Please ma'am, excuse me language."

He got up and began to walk the floor. They had never seen him so excited. He continued to read until he came to the signature, read it aloud, absentmindedly, at first. Then he read again, unbelievingly, "*James Jay Leander Johnson, Lolliloppi, Mississippi! . . .*" His voice trailed away.

"Goddamn! Goddamn! Goddamn! Goddamn!" He fell back in his chair. He was lathered all over with sweat, as if he'd been caught out in the rain in Bamakanougou, unexpectedly, without his British umbrella. He got up and began to walk the floor again.

"That's your name," Maria Efwa stated, worriedly.

"Tell me something I don't know," Jimmy Jay responded.

"Somebody is trying to get you into trouble," Her Excellency suggested. Her eyes were filled with great concern, larger, darker, deeply dilated now were they.

"Tell me something I don't know," His so-called Excellency repeated. He stared incredulously at his name in the paper, as if he thought to stare it into nonexistence. He threw the paper aside. He laughed. He said with exaggerated bravado, "What have I got to worry about? That's not my name anyhow. I'm not James Jay Leander Johnson from Lolliloppi, Mississippi. I am His Excellency Jaja Okwu Olivamaki, the Prime Minister of the Independent People's Democratic Republic of Guanaya." He looked around to them, desperately. He demanded, "Well, am I or am I not?"

"Yes, of course," she said. "However—yet and still—" Then she asked anxiously, "What are you going to do?"

His Wife's Bottom suggested, pompously, "Call them, the CIA people, and assure them that someone forged your name. Surely, with your prestige, Your Excellency, they'll believe—"

Jimmy Jay stared at HWB in disbelief. "What prestige has Jimmy Jay?" Then he said, "They did not forge *my* name. *My* so-called prestigious name is Jaja." Then in a quaking voice he said, "I'm the Pruh-pruh-pruh-pruh-prime damn Minister."

"Then you have absolutely nothing at all to worry about," HWB pontificated.

It all came back to him now. The signs were all there, the bad omens, the terrible premonitions. And he had been so wrapped up in *Himself,* and his smoldering romance with himself, and his unrequited romance with Her beautiful and most majestic Excellency, he had ignored the signs. It had not been a coincidence that he had come in late a couple of nights before and had watched the late-late show, titled *The Latter-Day Crusaders*, in which a man was being sought and tracked down in the dense rain forest of South America by the CIA. Robert Hedford had thought himself secure, had lived there for a decade with the kindly "natives." Nobody knew where he was, excepting his mother. He had managed to get word to her, clandestinely, through a surreptitious grapevine. She sets out to find her son, to lay eyes upon him one more time. She goes through the densest of rain forests, like A MESSAGE TO GARCIA, thick and feral and primordial, wild with crawling howling snarling treacherous venomous murderous beasts and reptiles, overcome by tropical heat. You could almost smell the sweaty funk come off the Tee Vee screen. She finally gets to him. He walks toward her overwhelmed with the shock and pleasure of seeing her once more, a thing he'd not dared to dream was possible. "Mother! Mother!" he shouts as she pulls a handgun from her pocketbook and shoots him dead. She, his mother, is the executioner sent by the CIA to dispatch her son to heaven or the other place.

That same day Jimmy had been given a beautiful book written by Counter and Evans, a couple of Black Harvard scientists who had traveled to the inner rain forest of Suriname to reach a tribe of Africans who had lived there for centuries, with their indigenous culture untouched by so-called civilization. *I Sought My Brother*, a beautiful book of text and pictures. He had been deeply moved. And that same night he had gone to sleep and dreamed. He had put the two experiences together in his dream, the scary movie and the beautiful book, and had come up with a nightmare that awakened him in a damp cold shivering sweat. In his dream, the Organization had tracked him down all the way to the dense forests of Suriname, where he lived happily with his people and Her Excellency Maria Efwa, who was his wife and also was their gracious queen. They had sought him out and found him, but when he faded into the landscape among the indigenous people, and they could not tell him from the other, they decided to wipe out the whole village, which they proceeded to do. He woke up shaking like he suffered from Parkinson's. He got out of bed and went shakily to the bathroom and took a sleeping pill and washed it down with Scotch and water, a thing he had never done before. And lay there for hours afraid to fall asleep for fear that his nightmare might return. But then the following day, the warmth of Maria's smile, the mere presence of her, her magnificence, had washed away his premonitions. So that what should have alerted him, the omens and the premonitions, the memory of the nightmare, had forsaken him, because he had forsaken them. Her Excellency was dangerous. Perhaps she was the Great Witch Doctor, the saboteur within their midst.

He turned to Barra Abingiba. "What in the hell are you laughing at? You said I had nothing to worry about, so long as you were with me. You said you had me well protected." Perhaps Barra was the ringer in their midst. All that time he'd spent in the States. "What in the hell do you know about the Brotherhood of the Bell?"

"I told you to get your own protection before you left home. But you wouldn't listen to me. You were a nonbeliever. What brotherhood of what damn bell?"

He listened carefully to Barra's voice, the blackboard-scraping voice that had offered "martyrdom" to him.

He couldn't believe he was having this stupid discussion with Barra Abingiba, even as he protested, "I am not a nonbeliever."

Barra laughed at him again. "You want me to get you in touch with the man?"

He had never noticed the rasping quality of Barra's voice before.

"What man?" the shaky so-called Prime Minister asked. He did not want to hear the answer.

"The Doctor," Barra asserted, raspily. "The Witch damn doctor if it pleases you. The baddest Black man on this earth. The CIA doesn't scare him. He'll take them on any day in the week. All you've got to do is just say the word." The grating Louis Armstrong voice was there for all to hear, and clear as scraping a blackboard with a rusty knife. His flesh crawled, repeatedly.

Jimmy felt an icy coldness in his mouth. "I'm saying the word. Goddammit, can't you hear me?" Sweat was pouring from all over him.

Her Excellency had never seen him like this, in such a state. She'd always thought of him as "super cool, laid back," as Barra Abingiba would have expressed it. She loved him now, albeit brotherly, even as she feared for him. It humanized him, made him more like everybody else. It warmed her toward him. Then she thought, It's a trick. He knows I'm watching him. And I almost fell for it. Stay on your guard, Maria Efwa. You are a married woman. You must be faithful to the one back home. Be faithful even in your contemplations. "As a man (or woman) thinketh, so is he and so is she."

Barra had picked up the telephone. "Operator, I wish to place a call to Bamakanougou in Guanaya. Bama-kah-noo-goo, operator, in Guanaya. That certainly is in Africa, operator, yes. No doubt about it." He put his hand over the mouth of the phone, as he stared at Jimmy Jay. "In fifteen minutes, you'll be surrounded by the baddest snakes on this earth. My man, the Doctor, does not play around. He's no small boy. He's serious."

A chill vibrated across the back of Jimmy Jay's body from ear to ear, shoulder to shoulder. The muscles in the back of his neck were dancing. He felt he teetered at the edge of a gaping canyon. He was vertiginous. The floor seemed about to move from under him. He sank back into the easy chair. He breathed with difficulty now. He spoke in a shouted whisper. "Snakes—snakes! I told you, goddammit, I'm deathly afraid of snakes!"

"They won't bite you, babay. They'll be there with you wherever you go, for your protection. I'm talking about mambas. They're deadlier than the cobra or the rattlesnake. They'll make the CIA wish they'd never heard of James Jay Leander Johnson of Lolliloppi, Mississippi." Barra laughed at the look on Jimmy Jay's face. A Black man turning as green in the face as tarnished copper. "You can walk through the valley of death and fear no evil, for the Doctor will be with you in the form of mambas."

"No snakes! No goddamn snakes!" Jimmy shouted limply. "I hate snakes! I hate snakes!"

Barra said, "You can't ask the Doctor for protection and dictate the terms of treatment. I mean the Doctor knows his business, and bad snakes are his most effective weapon. And you'd better keep your hatred of snakes a secret, I mean keep your feeling about them under wraps. These snakes are very sensitive. I tell you what I'm going to do. I'll tell him to send you some unobtrusive snakes, the quiet ones that don't be hissing all over the place."

He still could not believe that he, James Jay Leander Johnson, a.k.a. Prime Minister Jaja Okwu Olivamaki of the Independent People's Democratic Republic of Guanaya, the suave, sophisticated one, worldly-wise, with savoir faire to spare and even squander, was actually having this serious conversation about snakes and Juju. It was absolutely incredible. And yet he heard himself say, seriously, "There is no earthy way I could hide my distaste for snakes. Forget about the Juju. Forget about the snakes. Forget the Doctor." His voice was trembling.

Barra had put the phone back in its cradle. "You really mean that? You prefer to take your chances with the CIA than to deal with some friendly snakes, who are willing to lay down their lives for your protection?"

Maria Efwa said, "Leave him alone, Barra. He told you to forget it."

Barra said, "It is up to Himself, Your Excellency. He is the Prime Minister, after all."

Jimmy's voice had grown stronger. "I'm the Prime Minister, and I say, forget about it. Drop it." Perspiration still poured from him.

The telephone rang. Jimmy Jay's secretary, Mr. Tobey, picked it up. "Yes, this is His Excellency's suite. You're ready for that call to Bamakanougou?"

Barra took the phone from him. "Never mind, operator. Cancel the call to Bamakanougou. Terribly sorry about that."

23

Somehow, he knew this day would be entirely different. The premonitions were all there. The frightful dreams he dreamed all night. Perhaps he should have accepted the Great Witch Doctor's "snake" protection Barra Abingiba had so generously offered him. He had been awakened that morning by the staccato drumbeat of the rain against the pretty picture windows. Torrents of rain cascading up against the tall majestic glass encasements. Somehow, he thought, ironically, the executive suite of the famous Waldorf should have secured him from the ominous sounds of an autumn thunderstorm. He made his way to the window and stared down at the dreary Manhattan morning. The traffic down there looked like drowning vermin scurrying frantically around like rats and

cockroaches. He thought, Obviously the ship is sinking. An ominous omen.

He listened to the news on WLIB. David Lam-
pell and Carl Ferguson telling you where everything
was at. Judy Simmons would be along shortly. Pablo
Guzman later on. It was raining all along the East-
ern Seaboard. The traffic was jammed on the Grand
Central Parkway. Likewise, on FDR Drive as was the
Interboro coming out of Brooklyn. A smashup on the
Major Deegan had traffic tied up coming in from the
Bronx. Otherwise everything was cool. Nevertheless,
he somehow got through the rain-drenched morning.
A tea-and-crumpeted meeting with his delegation on
his upcoming trip to Lolliloppi. Breakfast. The *New
York Times*. He made his way through section A all
the way to the obit page. He sighed, happily, relieved
to see that he was not listed, which meant that he was
still among the living. The *Times'* obit page always
reassured him, unrealistically, of his continued immortality. What did he need with Barra's Juju man?

A session with Maria Efwa on Africa and southern folklore, the striking similarities. The growing
realization of his deepening involvement with Her
Excellency, emotionally. He thought of the Duke
of Ellington's I GOT IT BAD AND THAT AIN'T
GOOD. He imagined he could hear the voice of

Etta Jones. They went into a heavy discussion of the southern Black church and its dancing, its shouts, its hollers, its tambourines to glory and its drums and saxophones. He told her that one day before they went back to the Old Country, they must get up to one of those swinging shouting storefront churches on 125th Street in Harlem, which was African and southern at its very essence.

Then almost unknowingly, mesmerized by eyes and mouth and majesty, perhaps witchcrafted even, he watched Himself, with amazement, take her hands into his own and heard Himself say softly, fervently, "You are without a doubt, the most beautiful woman who ever favored this ungrateful earth with her queenly presence."

Her dark sweet face flushed, her lovely eyes almost in panic, fleetingly. "Your Excellency! We must never lose perspective regarding our relationship. Besides, you know I am a married woman. I'm married to one of the most revered men in Africa." Still bewitched, he took each of her darkly beautiful slender hands and kissed the fingers gently one by one.

Even as he said, "Forgive me. Truly I did lose perspective, for the moment. It isn't easy, you know. We are thrown together so very often. And you *are* extravagantly, outrageously, beautiful, and I am helplessly susceptible to beauty. I'm so hopelessly susceptible, I feel sorry for myself."

She conceded, matter-of-factly, "I'm aware it isn't easy. However, we must persevere." Then she said, more firmly, "There is simply no way there could ever be anything romantic or emotional between us. Please don't make it more difficult than it has to be. Promise me?" She was so damn composed, always in complete control of her emotions, her intellectuality.

His (so-called) Excellency promised, sorrowfully. He felt that time and circumstance were ganging up against him. Born to lose, and he was losing her before he had won her in the first damn place. Maria Efwa had grown on him like a sweet though dangerous addiction, bit by bit, moment by moment; she had cast a spell on him, and he had been powerless to resist it, even as he watched it happening and warned himself against it. If he could just take one sip, it would be the first and last sweet sip, because he was too strong and wise to allow himself to become a full-scale alcoholic, he thoroughly and foolishly convinced himself. It was the reasoning of all addicts, the way all addiction started.

First, he'd been consumed back there in his Bamakanougou hospital bed by the absolute perfection of her physicality, even as he desperately searched for flaws. Her ample and curvaceous lips. Perhaps they were too plentiful (thick fat lips were ugly lips he had once thought). Her wine-red lips were sensuous and sensual. Her eyes so deep and dark and intense, staring at you, penetrating. (He thought definitely her eyes were crossed. How could a cross-eyed woman bewitch Jimmy Jay?) He tried to find some imperfection in the way she walked, the way she carried, dignifiedly, this splendid miracle of architecture. Ah-ha! She was pigeon-toed! She was long-legged, she was high-assed, and she was slim and roundly structured. See how she stands wide-leggedly. A contradiction! How could one be slim and round? It didn't help poor Jimmy Jay at all. Even her so-called imperfections were absolutely perfect.

Secondly, he had been witchcrafted by her awesome erudition. She was a perambulating encyclopedia of knowledge, African folklore, infinite wisdoms; European presumptions, eternal idiocies, he learned from her. It was an erudition she felt no need to boast about. It was just there all sorted out and available, compartmentalized, waiting eagerly to be used by her, when the occasion called for it.

And then there was most of all the grandiose totality of her African spirituality. Put it all together, and she was Africa personified. Undeniable. Irresistible. Now he understood profoundly the meaning of WE SHALL

OVERCOME. He had gone there, a desperate lost and lonely pilgrim, looking for his Africa, and he'd found Maria Efwa.

Of course, he told himself he knew no one on earth was that close to perfection, physically, intellectually, spiritually. Not even the African gods could have wrought such a heavenly creation. The knowledge of it could not save him from the witchcraft with which she affected him. He was hopelessly mesmerized.

Later that morning he was going through his personal mail when he came across a familiar handwriting. His hands began to tremble. His heartbeat quickened; he heard a throbbing thunder in his earlobes. He swallowed hard and deeply, as he nervously took the letter from its envelope.

Dear Mr. Prime Minister, a.k.a. James Jay Leander Johnson:

I have watched your recent career with great interest, especially that aspect of it, i.e., His Excellency the Prime Minister of Guanaya. You were magnificent at the Armory, reminiscent of the era of the great Paul Robeson. I do recall though another time when you were Jimmy Jay of

Lolliloppi, Mississippi, sans beard, and we were rather close and even intimate here in New York when you had ambitions as a folk singer. I must discuss with you a matter of grave and paramount importance. I hope that we can handle this matter as discreetly as possible. I shouldn't like to take this to the media and cause an international embarrassment for you and your delegation.

Please call me at 950-8517. I shall await your call, but I shall not wait forever.

As ever fondly,
Love
Debby (Bostick)

His hand continued to shake, as he read the letter over and over several times. Every comma, every word, every sentence, every nuance, stubbornly remained unchanged. Wave after wave of feelings and remembrances washed over him like the rain outside his windows. Deborah Cassandra Bostick. Otherwise, the day of autumnal thunderstorm was uneventful until that evening after dinner, when a phone call came in on his direct line.

He heard a voice say, "Jimmy darling! How wonderful to hear your voice." He saw her face before him now. The deep and forever darkening brownness of her eyes, always brilliantly alive with mischief, the glowing reddish-ebony brownness of the darkness of her lovely face. Her skin tones, black on brown on ebony with deep burgundy overtones and undertones as if wrought by African sun–rayed afternoons. The eyes, the mouth, the soft oval face—Debby Bostick was the image of Maria Efwa, a fact he had not remembered till this moment. And was it an actual fact or a figment of his imagination? Even their voices were astonishingly alike, he thought, as chill after thrill after chill raced across his back from shoulder to shoulder. She brought him back to earth with "Jimmy! It's me— Debby Bostick."

He answered feebly, "I'm afraid there's been a mistake. I'm Jaja—"

As if she hadn't heard. "Jimmy! This is me! This is Debby! Debby Bostick. I don't know what this Prime Minister business is all about, but I do know Jimmy Jay Leander Johnson when I see him, and I saw you at the Armory, and I've got to see you once alone, *in person*, I must see you at least one time before you go back to Africa."

"But, lady," he began to mumble.

"I'm not a lady!" the lady shouted, excitedly. "I'm

Debby Bostick. Deborah Cassandra Bostick, and I'm going to have a baby, your baby! Our baby! I know you're just tickled pink. I—"

He was leaking perspiration now. "Madame, I have no idea what you're talking about. I know of no person by the name of Deborah Bostick. And pink I will never be tickled. It isn't possible, physically. I—"

"So that's the way it's going to be, is it? I'll have to go to the media after all. I'm a media woman, as you know, and I have connections with people in print, on television and radio, that is, if you'd prefer me to make a federal case of it." She paused to catch up with her breath. "I had thought we could have a quiet evening, dinner at my apartment. Talk about old times friendly like. But if you prefer me to go public, well—"

It was painful for him to try to brush her off like this, but what else could he do? "Miss, what did you say your name was? Deborah Bostick? Well, Miss Bostick, I'll get back to you on this matter of mistaken identity, only of course to spare you and my delegation unnecessary embarrassment. I'm sure we'll be able to clear everything up. But I have your phone number. And I'll call you later."

She said, "All right. Good night, Jimmy. Hear from you later."

He said good night and wiped the perspiration from

his forehead. He called the group together and laid the facts before them. Showed them the letter. Told them of the phone call.

"Well," Maria Efwa commented, after she had read the letter and listened to his explanation. "You certainly have got yourself into a proper mess."

"*We* are in a proper mess," he reminded all of them.

Mamadou Tangi asked, "Will she carry out her threat, or is she merely bluffing?"

"I don't think there is any doubt about it. She certainly can, and she surely will."

Maria Efwa smiled ironically, "A woman scorned— and about to have a child for you. I think the least you have to do is to make discreet arrangements to see the lady." She laughed lightly. "Clearly we selected a Casanova to be our acting Prime Minister."

Mamadou Tangi said, "Clearly." Sarcastically.

Barra Abingiba reminded them, "It wasn't his idea in the first place. You cats selected him. Remember? Nobody quizzed him on the state of his virginity or lack of it."

His Wife's Bottom said, surprisingly, "Exactly so."

Jimmy Jay said, "Thank you so much."

Mamadou Tangi said, "Well, Casanova, you'd better call her back and make the necessary arrangements."

The arrangements were made. A man about his height and build dressed as an Arab sheik in dark glasses visited them about five o'clock three evenings later. They sneaked Jimmy Jay out of the hotel dressed as an Arab emir about an hour later, dark shades and all and under heavy Guanayan security. Cool Horace drove him uptown under the cover of lowering darkness along the softly lighted streets past the taverns up Adam Clayton Powell Jr. Boulevard past the funeral parlors and the churches, crossing over 125th Street past the people thronging the avenue past more taverns past more funeral parlors and inevitably more churches, with a car full of Guanayan SS men in unobtrusive pursuit. There were already two security men in the car with His (so-called) Excellency. And a limousine in front of them. One might have gotten the impression that they were securing him against himself, preventing him from splitting the coop. But then, he thought, those in pursuit might very well be of American denomination. Now turning right at 135th Street going past the YMCA past the Schomburg Center at the other end of the block, now across people-thronged Lenox Avenue, thinking warmly of Margaret Walker's immortal FOR MY PEOPLE.

They dropped him off in front of the highly priced

high-rise apartments, Lenox Terrace, the very same apartment building that housed the famous Percy Sutton, formerly borough president of Manhattan and presently chairman of the board of Inner City Broadcasting. He thought of Claude McKay and *Home to Harlem*, and he truly felt at home, in Harlem. Cool Horace would wait outside in the car. "I'll be back in a couple of hours," Jimmy Jay advised. The two Guanayan SS men in the car with him escorted him to the elevator, and up to the eleventh floor, where they would remain outside the door until he came out two hours later.

Now he stood before the door where she lived. All over his forehead and his shoulders he had broken out into bullets of perspiration. Yet he shivered. He pushed upon the button lightly, as if he wanted no one to hear him. He thought, What the hell—and pushed determinedly the second time.

It felt like centuries before he heard a voice from inside. "Who is it?"

His heartbeat quickened. He almost answered, "This is Jimmy Jay." He thought, what if he was walking into a well-laid trap? What if the CIA or Carlton Carson and his Secret Service were there to leap out of a corner and lay hold of him? He was thinking, What if—what if, when the door opened and one of the most beautiful women who ever walked this earth was standing there, all five feet five of midnight eyes and dark-brown ebony textured skin, her face aglow with moonlit smiles, and saying simply, "Come in, Jimmy."

Her beauty rendered him speechless, momentarily, "A simple case of mistaken identity, I can assure you, Madame." He sounded phony even to himself. Unconvincing.

She closed the door behind him as he entered. Then she went into his arms and all up against him. And she could tell that he remembered, as Himself responded rigidly. "Oh Jimmy! Jimmy? Jimmy Jay! Jimmy Jay!" She put her softened hands around his neck and brought his head down toward hers, his mouth to meet her eager lips. Thrusting eagerly expertly with her agile tongue. For a moment he imagined she was Her Excellency Maria Efwa, and he wanted desperately for his imagination to unfold into reality.

She stepped back from him and she looked him up and down and began to laugh uncontrollably. "What on earth are you doing in that ridiculous getup? Halloween was last Saturday night. What are you supposed to be disguised as this time, the sheik of Arabee? Are you King Fahd's second cousin?" She began to laugh again and threw herself upon the couch with laughter.

He felt silly standing there in his turban and his long robe behind the dark shades, which had him walking blunderingly around the room like a blind man. He stood away from her. Even through his simpleminded shades, he could see the slimly womanish roundness of her, as she stood before him once again, daringly, seductively. Her pregnancy did not show at all.

She said, "All right, so I'm not pregnant. I had to do something to get you here. I didn't really want to resort to calling a press conference, whatever the hell you were up to."

He was overwhelmed with mixed emotions of disappointment and deliverance. His fatherhood of such brief duration. He was not sure which feeling dominated.

She reached up and took his dark shades from him. "Take those silly things off. I want to see those sexy bedroom eyes of yours." She took him by the hand and led him toward the couch and went into his arms again. Her lips sought out his mouth again. Her clever tongue busied itself anew. Her hands were busy too. Feeling the back of his neck, back in the kitchen where the baby hair grew, always and forever grew. She knew where every erogenous zone on his body existed. She knew how to turn him on. She nibbled an earlobe. Her hands on his back, caressing tenderly his spine, his buttocks, now a-flaming with desire.

He felt himself turning on, erecting shamelessly in the middle of him, even as he protested. "Now before we both get carried away, let us first be clear. I am not your Jimmy Jay, or whoever—I'm—"

She was so damn sure of herself. He tried in vain to resist and resent the contentment in her silken voice. "Okay, if that's the way you want to play it. It's all right with me." She rose from the couch and left him. "I'd better see what's doing in the kitchen." He watched her walk away from him, her high-assed slimly rounded buttocks swiveling subtly from side to side. He thought, Maria Efwa never walked seductively.

He looked around the spacious living room. The floor was covered with colorful scatter carpets arranged artistically around the place. Press work was the way she earned her grits and paid the rent, but painting was where her heart was. He looked around at the paintings on the wall, Tom Feelings and Charlie White and Ernest Crichlow, Romie Bearden, Otto Neals, Vincent Smith and Leo Carty, Izell Glover, a couple of her own, one an old portrait of him as Jimmy Jay, another very recent one of the Minister Primarily. There was a knotty pine make-it-yourself rectangular table in the dining area near the kitchen, which served as work space and was also a dining table. She came out of the kitchen. "Smells damn good, if I do say so myself, and I definitely do say so myself." She started clearing the table of books and portable typewriter and painting materials. He rose and came toward her to help her.

She said, teasingly, "As my darling Jimmy Jay, you are perfectly welcome to give a helping hand, but as Your Excellency, Prime Minister of Guanaya, it is my pleasure to serve you and my prerogative to have you patiently await my service."

Jimmy Jay continued to take books and typewriter from the table, "Nevertheless I am Jaja Okwu Olivamaki, and it is my pleasure to help you set the table and prepare for this memorable feast."

Now they sat there opposite each other at the table, staring at one another one moment and stealing glances the next, speaking with each other almost at cross-purposes. She reminiscing about the two of them as Jimmy Jay and Debby, and he speaking to her of the lovely country of Guanaya and the great and lovely people who lived there.

"Remember the time when we demonstrated at the Statue of Liberty with Harry and Sidney and Odetta and Killens and his wife and his mother and his children?"

He said, "I spent two years in a British prison in my own country for sedition against the Crown."

"I know you remember the time we went down to the March on Washington. Nineteen sixty-three? You were just about eighteen years old and just out of Mississippi. Hadn't gotten the cotton out of your head yet." She rolled her eyes. She laughed and shouted softly, "'Country!' You still smelled like collard greens. And I was nothing but a child myself. Came down there with my older sister."

"I remember the March on Washington; it was my first year at Lincoln University."

The kitchen and the dining area were saturated with appetizing and familiar odors of baked chicken with stuffing and candied yams and greens and buttermilk biscuits and a home-baked apple pie. He was getting high on kitchen smells. His head was getting giddy. He was stuffing himself like a boa constrictor.

"You had just done one year at Toogaloo. Football star. Thought you were the hottest stuff in town. We met at a party somewhere up near Howard's campus. I was with my sister. You and your guitar and your country music. You thought you were the second coming of Leadbelly, and that's when you met Belafonte. I was outrageous that night. Followed you around like your butt was made of chocolate candy. I was only ten years old, a precocious ten. The older people laughed at me and teased me, the way I followed you around. And did I have a crush on you?! It was awful. It was painful. The next time I saw you was ten years later. You were singing at the Village Gate. You didn't remember me from Adam."

The smells from the kitchen, the memories of her young fresh sweetness, tomboyish sassiness, all the good feelings came together and ganged up on him, caught him off guard. He said, "That wasn't country music. That was Black folk songs. I-I-I mean, that was the year I spent the summer in London."

She felt so good, so at home in this place with him, she didn't even notice, as she and His Excellency cleared away the food on the table. He insisted on putting on an apron and helping wash the dishes. There were sayings on the wall around the kitchen, satirical quotations, such as: "It's difficult to soar with eagles, when you have to work with turkeys . . ." "The light at the end of the tunnel is the headlamp of an oncoming train."

Now they were sitting on the couch together, sipping Scotch and ginger. She had gotten high and giggly. "Jimmy Jay! Jimmy Jay!" she snickered. "All the way with Jimmy Jay. That is what we used to say. All the way with Jimmy Jay."

He said, "I've got to be going. I really enjoyed the dinner. I'd love to stay longer, but we have a really busy day tomorrow."

She got to her feet and the room began to spin around and around, and she fell back into his arms. He repeated embarrassed, "I really do have to be going now. They're waiting for me outside." He disengaged himself from her and got up from the couch.

She got up with him. She said, "I got a buzzing on. Qoh! High as a Georgia pine. Would you do me a fuh-fuh-flavor, Your Excellency? Would you fu-fu-fix me an Alka-Seltzer, get it out of the kitchen cabinet?"

"My pleasure," the bogus PM responded.

He moved heavily toward the kitchen, which was when she suddenly came alive and took a pill from her pocketbook and dropped it into his drink. When he returned, she was stretched out cold on the couch. Her sweet-looking limbs had exercised her skirt up to her dark brown hips like an open invitation, the subtle skin tones of her thighs of brown and black and burgundy gently clashing, sweetly blending. He wanted terribly to believe that in fact she was Her Excellency Maria Efwa. He took his own drink and emptied it with one swallow. Then he took her head in his arms and tried to pour the seltzer through her lips. In a sudden jerky motion, she knocked the glass from his hand. She mumbled, "I'm sorry, Your 'xlency. So very very sorry." As she fell back full length on the couch.

He said, "I think you had too much to drink."

She got up and straightened herself to her full height. She said indignantly and yet clownishly, "I resemble those remarks." Then she fell back to the couch again, her skirt up to her slim dark sweet hips and he could see the crotch of her black bikini panties.

He felt a little wooziness. Thinking that last drink he had was lethal.

"Your 'xlency," she mumbled. "You wouldn't leave a lady in distress like this. Surely, you're much too chivalrous. Take me to my bedroom and put me in my proper bed. I'm at your complete disposal or perhaps it's your disposure." She giggled foolishly.

He took her up in his arms and stumbled toward the bedroom and lay her on her bed, as she mumbled, "Your Excellency, please undress me."

He fumbled clumsily with the buttons of her blouse, dispossessed her of her bra and stared at the dark sloping hillocks of her breasts all tense now and tumescent, burnished now and blisteringly swollen. He swallowed hard, and excitement beat madly at the temples of his forehead. He relieved her of her skirt

and slip. He hesitated, and she murmured, "My panties, please to remove them. You know I always did
sleep in the nude."

He slid her panties down along the round full slimness of her dark and gleaming thighs and legs. And she
lay there stretched before him as naked as a newborn
baby. He could not keep his eyes away from the scant
baby fat around her midriff and the tufted upside-
down pyramid that darkly curled sleepily between her
thighs. He stared at her from head to feet. So much
beauty was unreal, he thought. Extravagant. Ostenta-
tious. He must be hallucinating. He heard her mumbling, "Make love to me—with me, Jimmy Jay, Your
Excellency, whichever." And he disrobed hurriedly
and went toward her and took and slid her between
the lavender sheets. And now he *was actually* hallucinating, fantasizing, as he made himself believe that
she was for real Her Excellency Maria Efwa, there in
bed before him and had asked him to make love to her,
with her. The sweet special smell of her body made
him dizzy, as he began to get a funny feeling that was
tantamount to vertigo. He got beneath the covers with
her. And took her in his arms and felt his growing
hardness up against the middle of her, even as he felt
a growing dizziness. The bed began to dance beneath
him, as did the room, which danced around him, pir-

ouetting like a crazy carousel running wild out of control. He reached for her to keep from falling from the steepest precipice, just as he became totally enveloped in a great white world of nothingness.

The smell of bacon cooking had awakened him. He sat up quickly in a panic. The autumn sunlight came in thickly through the windows. Where in the hell was he? He scratched his beard, as had become a habit with him whenever thinking deeply, which was precisely when he found out he was beardless.

He leaped out of bed, as his head began to dance around again, and heavily. He came out of the bedroom. "What in the hell's going on here?"

Then he heard a pleasing voice say, "Breakfast is almost ready, Your Highness, Your Excellency." And she came out of the kitchen and stood before him in her cinnamon-colored see-through negligee. Her dark breasts honeycombed and muscadinely nippled, the darkness between her legs of her inverted tufted triangle. All of that darkening beauty belonged to her alone. So much lavishness was shameful.

She stared at him and smiled mischievously. "His Excellency is certainly in a proud and ennobled state this morning. If I hadn't known for sure you were Jimmy Jay, I certainly know it now." She began to laugh, raucously. "I'd recognize that pretty mole anywhere—"

His hand went up to the side of his nose.

She said laughingly, "I don't mean the one on your nose. I'm talking about that cute little darling mole on your member. I mean your member, of the wedding. Remember? We used to call him the member? Of the wedding?" She added, "Even though we never wedded one another."

It was only then that he realized the situation of his nakedness as he stood there before her protruding homely, and turgid. His face flushed warmly as he reached for the empty air to cover his extended rigidness. Ultimately, he ran back into the bedroom, as she followed him, and he snatched the sheet from the bed and wrapped it around the middle of him. She continued cracking up with laughter. "His Excellency, the ennobled member of the wedding, with the pretty darling mole. I shall never forget Him as long as I live." She was the devil in silken negligee.

They ate breakfast almost in silence. Finally, as she sipped at her second cup of coffee, she asked, "Well, do you want to tell me about it, Your Excellency?"

And he thought, Why the hell not? And the more he told her about it in its minutest detail the more relieved he felt. He didn't even bother to pledge her to secrecy. He knew it wasn't necessary.

They talked about old times and reckless times and foolish times, in and out of each other's lives. They had grown together and away from one another. Each of them had been married to some other person very briefly.

They talked about the time he took her to dinner at a fancy and expensive restaurant in downtown Manhattan. After they finished eating, he'd found that he'd left his wallet at home. He was flat broke, embarrassed, and perspiring.

"Not to worry," she'd said, nonchalantly, as she extracted two twenty-dollar bills from "titty city," as she called it, reaching in behind her bra.

"Titty city," he repeated now, ten years hence, and they laughed hysterically together. She was outrageous. She was self-possessed, as was Her Excellency Maria Efwa. But quite different was their self-possession. Tame, sedate, majestic was Maria's self-possession, as compared with Debby's, which was rebellious and irreverent.

When finally they ran out of conversation, little talk, chitchat, big talk, she said, "Well, what's it going to be? I'm unattached and I imagine so are you." She'd always been like that. As devious as the devil himself, or herself, but at the same time believed in bringing everything right down front. Bring it out into the open. Put it clearly on the table.

He cleared his throat, took a gulp of coffee that must have gone down the wrong way, as he began to cough fitfully, and his eyes began to tear. "Excuse me." Then he said, "Debby, it is a fact that I love you and that I always will love you. And I believe you love me too."

She responded, "So? So, what's the problem?"

He continued as if he was thinking out loud. "But I don't have the faintest idea where this present episode in my life will take me, and I have no right to complicate your life, while I stand around undecided. Obviously, I will be going back to Africa. At this point I don't know what I'm going to do with my life after that. I don't know if I'll make Africa my home for the rest of my life. I surely can't expect you to give up your career in the media. I understand that there's a chance you may become an anchorwoman on one of the national networks."

"There's only one question involved," she stated with finality.

"Which is?" he asked uneasily.

"Is there someone else?"

"But surely, I mean, the position as an anchor-woman. I mean—"

"I don't crave upward mobility so cravenly that I would sleep with Mister Charley."

He stared at her with a shocked expression. But why should it surprise him? "Surely you wouldn't have to—I mean—"

"You're a big boy now, Your Excellency. Such sleeping arrangements go along with the territory. Sometimes it's actually written into the contract. I'm not saying that every Black anchorwoman has had to make these kinds of compromises and sleeping arrangements. Some are luckier than others. But very little has changed, my dear, since the good old days of slavery." She smiled at him, ironically. "The question remains the same. And it remains unanswered. Is there someone else in your eventful life?" He was silent. She said, "I mean, you just told me you loved me, but are you in love with me? There is a difference, I suspect. The question is a simple one. Is there somebody else?"

He said, "The question is not a simple one, neither is the answer."

She said, "I think you just gave me the answer."

"It's very complicated. It might sound corny, but I think I actually fell in love with her, because she was so much like you."

She exploded. "Of all the bullshit rationalizations!"

He took her by the hand and walked her into the bedroom and stood her before the mirror. "Look at the lady in the mirror. You've seen her on TV. You've seen her in person. You said you were at the Armory that day."

Even as the two of them stood there staring at her image in the mirror, he knew that the only resemblance shared by Debby and Maria Efwa was entirely physical. They were merely look-alikes. Where Maria was always composed and proper, Debby was impetuous and passionate, excitable. The complete and total rebel.

She stared until her eyes were widening. "You are one flaky sonuvabitch!"

He argued, "I don't know what to say to you, Debby. She's your spitting image. Ways, temperament," he lied. "Everything. We've been thrown together so much these last few weeks. I just don't know, and I love you too much to lie to you. And it's further complicated by the fact that she's already married back in Guanaya to an older man, a man respected throughout the continent."

She sobbed, impulsively, "Jimmy! Jimmy! Jimmy!" And went into his arms again.

It was as if the night before was destined to repeat itself, but somehow altogether differently. There was no dizziness for him this time. There was only eagerness for both of them and tremendous expectations. Like the night before, he took her up in his arms and carried her lovingly to her bed and lay her down before him. And dispossessed her gently of her nightdress, her cinnamon-colored negligee. As before, she lay there in all her lovely nakedness. He stared at her and swallowed deep down to the bottom of his belly.

This time her entire body vibrated tremulously, as if his staring eyes were a member (of the wedding) and had stabbed into her profoundly down to the very tip of her convulsive womb. She moaned before he actually touched her. Now they lay together naked in her bed. The moment he entered her, they arrived at consummation and exploded simultaneously; she uttered a muffled scream, he groaned, as they both were overcome with spasms, tiny spasms, large spasms, long deep extended spasms. Then serenity and sweet fulfillment. And now the honeyed and salty smells and taste, of ocean waves and froth and sea and foam, floating, joysome, toward a peaceful shore. The sea was calm now, the storm abated, momentarily.

For love was good, as they'd remembered, and love was sweet and even sweeter, and love was love's blessed fulfillment, love was love's own *raison d'être*.

Notwithstanding, nothing had been settled between Jimmy Jay and Debby B. And they both realized it.

Like the man from France said (or the Frenchwoman just as likely), "*plus ça change, plus ça devient la même chose*" . . . "The more things change, the more they remain the same."

Now they lay there basking at the seashore on their private sunbaked beach. Breathing deeply into the essence of them all the feeling-good-about-themselves love smells, transported in another world of smug entrancement. Fully awake but dreaming. Blissful. The chimes of her doorbell could not possibly reach them, could not penetrate this transport. Seven more minutes of pounding on the door finally broke through the quietude of Eden's blithesome garden.

Ultimately, they heard, repeatedly, "Open up in the name of His Excellency The Prime Minister of Guanaya."

Debby Bostick said, "I can't believe that this is happening."

"Believe it," Jimmy Jay advised her, as he draped the bedspread around his naked body and trudged toward the door, where the banging continued unbated.

"Just a goddamn minute," Jimmy rumbled.

He finally negotiated the numerous locks, opened the door, and stared down into the nonplussed face of His Wife's (inevitable) Bottom, as Guanayan SS persons stood behind him, their guns drawn and at the ready.

Jimmy could not contain the laughter that quickly mounted in him and came from him in loud guffaws. He almost lost the bedspread that covered his stark nakedness.

HWB squeaked indignantly, "I say, Your Excellency, this is highly irregular. This is not a laughing matter."

24

LOLLILOPPI, MISSISSIPPI, NEAR-THE-GULF. Meanwhile, numerous phone calls had continued back and forth between the White House in Washington and the mayor of Lolliloppi, who was also chairperson of the White Citizens Council deep deep in the darkness of the 'Sippi delta. In fact, it was the only council remaining in that benighted state of unenlightenment fondly known throughout the recent world as "'Sippi," thanks to an obscure novelist by the name of John O. Killens, until the mayor was finally convinced he must assume the role of host to the fabulous African Prime Minister and his dignitaried entourage. The President, himself, after continued failure on the part of his numerous secretaries, Justice Department officials, State Department, the FBI, the CIA, took the bull by the horn or by his balls, whichever is your earthier preference in metaphors, and spoke directly to Mayor Rufus Hardtack.

"I don't give a fucking damn if he marries all of your funky steamy-tailed daughters, Olivamaki *is* coming down there and there'd better not be no fucking racial incidents, or heads will fucking roll! His Excellency is my good fucking friend, and besides, he represents the richest fucking mineral output on this fucking earth. It's more valuable than fucking gold or diamonds, or heads will surely fucking roll! Money! Rufus Rastus fucking Hardtack! Money! That's what I'm fucking talking about, or fucking heads will roll."

All the while the poor mayor of Lolliloppi was thinking, Could this really be the fucking President of this fucking USA with all that fucking "fucking" in his fucking conversation?

Also meanwhile, His so-called Excellency called an extra-private meeting of his own security persons (from Guanaya) and put them together with a few of those Harlemites of the Black Alliance, who had secured the 369th Armory on that memorable day that would go down in history and never be forgotten.

The idea was to send an advance guard a few days ahead to Lolliloppi to clear the way and to secure the place against untoward surprises. Jimmy Jay had told his entourage so many horror stories about "'Sippi" and the rest of dear old Dixieland that his cabinet members were a little nervous, perhaps even a *big* nervous and overly apprehensive, which would prevent them from conducting themselves with their legendary African dignity. And the fake PM would stand for nothing short of absolute undiluted unadulterated dignity.

"Follow the lead of your Harlem sisters and brothers," he admonished the Guanayan SS persons, gathered in his Waldorf suite. "They know what to look for. They know the landscape of the southern jungle. They know where the rattlesnakes and all the other wild beasts hang out . . ." He spoke directly to the Harlemites. "Most of you dudes are originally from down home anyhow." He almost said, "just like me," but he caught himself in time. "Take nothing for granted. Pile it on. Embarrass the hunkies! Disconcert the white-robed bastards! But always do it diplomatically and with gentleness and tact." He had forgotten who he was again and had resorted to the jargon of the streets. The Harlem sisters and brothers stared at him in honest wonder. His Excellency spoke their language like an honest-to-goodness down-home brother. He was truly one of them! One hundred and ninety-five percent!

He stared around at them into their worshipfully surprised faces. One of the very one of them who sat there staring so innocently back at him was probably the selfsame one who had called him a couple of nights before and knighted him for "martyr-dam." He listened sharply for the gravelly voice that would sound like a rusty knife scraping on a big blackboard.

"We will kill you and blame it on the American government in collusion with the Klu Kluck Klan!"

He would never forget that voice. The memory of it now made his flesh crawl. He questioned each of them, even one or two of the deep-voiced women, just to find out how their voices sounded. Was he becoming paranoid? Perhaps he had gone too far, he thought, with his jargon of the streets. Perhaps he had exposed himself. He tried to clean it up with "You cats know, of course, I attended Lincoln U. for four long years, which is situated just above the Mason-Dixon Line, and I spent a whole damn year up south here on Brother Piri's mean damn streets of the Big damn Apple. I got my third degree in Dixicology." He thought, I'm overdoing it again, but he laughed heartily. And they laughed with him, though in mild confusion. Even as he laughed he wondered, Which one is the hit man here?

A few days later, the advance guard literally descended upon old Lolliloppi. They had moved into

Lolliloppi County beforehand the most sophisticated antisabotage equipment known at that time, from a state just above the Mason-Dixon. Beginning at the airport of a nearby city, give away an inch or two, where the PM and his retinue would deplane, they swept across the airstrip of the little airport all the way out to the state highway with two prehistoric monsters that seemed that they might have very well been the amazing result of a cross-miscegenation between armored tanks and New York City sanitation trucks. The two mechanical monsters picked up everything on the highway between the airport and old Lolliloppi. And they stopped and inspected every time an alien object got in the path of these giant and voracious vacuum cleaners, which made the monsters blast forth like the sirens of fire engines going up Lenox Avenue during soapbox oratory at 125th Street. Even when they'd pick up a nail or a stick or a rock. Would they ever get to Lolliloppi? Mamadou Ben-Hannibala, né Robert Joseph Williamsburg, was the appointed captain of the advance guard. He was born in Birmingham, Alabama, and grew up on the streets of Harlem Town on Seventh Avenue, a.k.a. Adam Clayton Powell Jr. Boulevard, just about three blocks away from Smalls Paradise.

Mamadou Ben-Hannibala was ex–poet laureate of the Black Experience, all you unbelievers ask him, formerly and briefly a bodyguard for Malcolm X, did a two-year stretch at Howard University during the good old Stokely days, staunch leader of the Black Alliance, clear eyed, darkly clear, stockily constructed five feet eleven, had been a semipro football cornerback for the Harlem Detonation Squad for Black Liberation. Sorry. That was the name of the football team, during the glorious sixties.

The advance guard was convoyed into town by a special police escort made up of every squad car in the county, who had instructions to come back and gather around the monsters every time the sirens sounded off. They would drive back hurriedly, get out of their cars, and stand around and scratch their heads and stare wonderingly at these curious-sounding-and-acting people who looked so much like their own Negroes.

Big Mamadou Ben-Hannibala spoke with a strange accent, which sounded like an unearthly combination of West Indian, British, African, Pakistani, Harlem American, with a southern accent thrown in for good measure, or bad, all rolled into one, clashing and blending, mostly clashing. Mamadou Ben-Hannibala would complain, politely and growlingly, about everything encountered by the gleefully gregarious monsters. Big rocks, gravel, unfortunate pole kitten, pot holes.

Mamadou climbed down from one of the mechanical

monsters. "Hey, you, old boy, come over hyah. You, old boy. Don't stare around at the others. I wish to address my remarks to you."

The little sawed-off pink-faced white man came toward Mamadou. His face was drenched in sweat with circular stains of perspiration clearly evident, undignifiedly, under each armpit of his khaki shirt.

"You're the HCIC, are you not, old boy?"

"Suh? HCIC?"

"You're the Head Cracker in Charge, are you is, or is you aren't?"

"Yassah," the chief of Lolliloppi's finest replied. He was hopelessly confused by now. He was reddening by the seconds behind the ears, which were larger than Clark Gable's and lacked Clark Gable's sex appeal, his ears, that is, or that are, whichever. He'd never dreamed of such biggedy colored people in all of his born days. But he had had his orders from one on high. There must be no "nigger" incidents, or "heads will surely fucking roll!" He'd rather roll his eyes instead.

It was a hot day in October even for Mississippi and green everywhere lay over the land like summertime. "What in the hell is it that so despoils the atmosphere?" Ben-Hannibala demanded. "By Jove, we must've scooped a skunk." Ben-Hannibala sniffed haughtily at the atmosphere around him. "Mississippi is not always redolent with stink like this, I mean, hopefully."

The big bad chief said, "Nawsuh." He had a reputation to uphold of being the baddest meanest cracker in Lolliloppi County.

"We'll need to deodorize the whole damn county before His Excellency arrives. The Prime Minister has very sensitive and dainty nostrils, don't you know? That's the way it is with the aristocracy."

The big bad chief said, "Yassah."

"They told us Mississippi was aromatic with pleasant odors. What happened to all of those magnolia trees and honeysuckles? This is some strange-fucking-smelling fruit."

Meanwhile Mamadou Ben-Hannibala dressed in his miniskirted boubou with high glistening boots up to his knees, a white turban atop, riding crop in hand, was strutting and stomping around like he was imitating Charlie Chaplin doing an exaggerated imitation of Herr Schickelgruber imitating Charlie Chaplin, ad infinitum.

"You gentlemen will decidely have to clean up your act. You're not so deep down here in the delta bush that you have remained untouched by the civilizing influences of the twentieth century? I mean, you do have radios, tellies, running water, sanitation, and all the other ultramodern amenities? I mean, otherwise you wouldn't've presumed to insist that His Excellency visit your humble province." He lapsed back into his Alabama roots. "I mean y'all folks ain't ready yet for people of His Excellency's ennobleness."

The big bad chief shuffled his feet, batted his eyes, scratched his head, and muttered, "Yassah!"

Mamadou Ben-Hannibala stomped and strutted and goose-stepped again. "All right, old boy. Let's get the show on the road."

By the time they reached the Rob Lee Hotel, with the prehistoric monsters intact, the town was in an uproar. Naturally, the advance guard, under the leadership of Mamadou Ben-Hannibala, insisted politely and diplomatically on inspecting the proposed so-called hotel accommodations. Ben-Hannibala strutting and goose-stepping with riding crop and issuing orders even to those of the local police. "Make it look good, goddammit! Make it look good you buggering buggers."

They invaded the so-called presidential suite with every kind of antiespionage equipment that had ever been invented, and with some that had not been invented yet. They upturned everything, couches, beds, chairs, seeking out lurking and unfortunate bugs and buggers, took down pictures, pulled up carpeting. "Look sharp, boy," Mamadou Ben-Hannibala ordered. He tapped a local red-faced copper on the shoulder with his riding crop. They looked into the toilet tanks, flushed the toilets continuously, and the local policemen stood around, their mouths agape, and scratched their heads. Some of their heads were steaming by now, literally.

"Look sharp, lad," Mamadou Ben-Hannibala ordered, as he rapped a steamy-headed local copper on his shoulders. Rolling fucking heads or not, the steamy-headed one could take no more. He went to the water basin in the toilet, put his head under the water spigot, and soaked it to his heart's content.

When they had finished, the place looked like a cyclone had made a sudden visitation, with a bad tornado running interference. Then to add insult to injury, or the other way around, whichever, Ben-Hannibala had the unmitigated temerity to complain though tactfully. Ben-Hannibala strutted around with his riding crop. "This place needs tidying up a bit, especially before His Excellency arrives."

For weeks Lolliloppi had been preparing for the Grand Visitation, or "A Day," as one 'Sippi advertising genius dubbed it. People were converging into the little three-horse town from all over the Big damn 'Sipp, as some Black sisters and brothers were apt to refer to it, affectionately. The governor, lieutenant governor, state legislative people, White Citizens Councilors and Councilettes. Mayor Rufe had suddenly become the most popular politician in all of the Big damn 'Sipp. Letters and phone calls, telegrams poured in from all over, and even beyond all over, pleading for invitations to the Grand Visitation. Big white folks. Great big white folks. The word was out. Olivamaki was undoubtedly the most important colored man who ever was or ever would be. And the richest! A natural-born colored human bean! Mayor Rufe was being mentioned as gubernatorial material. A man like old Rufe might make it all the way to the White House.

First of all, Mayor Rufe, who was a churchgoing two-or-three-times born-again Christian, and a family man, had to get his own house in order. "Charity begins at home" had always been his motto. Therefore, he called the Hardtack clan together and read the riot act to them. He had first consulted the buddy of his childhood days of playing with themselves and with each other and smoking rabbit tobacco behind the old barn, Secret Service expert Carlton Carson, a dyed-in-the-cotton-patch Big damn 'Sippian.

"Here is the way it was explained to me, Rufe ol' buddy. These Africans ain't like our nigrahs. They human beans. They dignitarians. They look just like our nigrahs, but they're nacherl-born human beans.

You got to treat em like they're white folks. And another thing, they're really bugged by bugs. So, don't be bugging their living quarters with no bugs, cause their juju helps them to track them down, like hunt and destroy. Them boys is death on bugs and buggers. It ain't easy to figger the damn thing out, especially the human bean part, and particularly the buggery. But you can do it if you put your thinking cap on and keep it on. Hell, I been around them so much, I done just about got used to them. Course you know me. I still think there's a rotten fish in the woodpile in Denmark some damn where."

Which is exactly, more or less, how the mayor interpreted it to his family, especially to his pretty and retarded daughter, sweet-faced blue-eyed Evaline Gertrude, "or heads will fucking roll!" Obviously, the President's fucking fetish for fucking conversation was highly contagious. Mayor Rufe slobbered, pounded on the dining room table. "Treat em like human fucking beans and white folks!" And the same went for the police force and the fire department. "There must be no racial incidents, or fucking heads will fucking roll!" Evaline Gertrude had never seen her papa in such a mad state of excitement.

Announcements in the newspapers, on the radio and the television admonished the Lolliloppians that they must be on their best behavior, in the spirit and tradition of good old southern hospitality. "They look like our nigrahs, but they are human beans. You will know our nigrahs from the Africans by the long white robes the Africans will be wearing. They call them 'boobies.' If they should happen to visit our restaurants, the picture show, and other places of amusement, in their long white flowing boobies, they will not be members of the Klu Klux Klan. Heh-heh-heh."

All over the county, Black folks began to get their own "boobies" together. They started sewing on those white bedsheets. It looked like it was going to be difficult to tell the local "nigrahs" from the authentic African human beans, due to the outright treachery of their tried-and-trusted local "nigrahs." It was getting to be a helluva how-de-do when humble local nigrahs couldn't be relied upon.

Meanwhile and moreover even, the so-called city of Lolliloppi was becoming jammed with some of them un-Mississippian foreign accents, an entire week ahead of A Day, the time of the Grand Visitation. It became clear that Lollie's two so-called hotels could not provide adequate lodging. Tents were being thrown up on Main Street, heretofore all of three blocks long, which extended it several blocks longer, and all over every which a where. Big tents, little tents, wigwams, teepees.

Free enterprisers came by the hundreds from all over, from as far as Chicago and New York City. Hucksters, hustlers, whores, pimps, all in the spirit of free enterprise, which was what made America great, or words to that effect. Green and black and red Black Nationalist flags and pennants, African banners, Olivamaki buttons and sweatshirts, Guanayan flags, on sale up and down those happy streets. Main Street suddenly was as busy as Forty-Second Street in the Big Apple between Seventh and Eighth Avenues. A carnival atmosphere, like Merry Xmas and Happy New Year. It was something to behold. All of a sudden Black folks were in vogue. Crackers walked up to nigrahs and hugged and kissed them on the streets, *publicly*! Strange! Strange! Ripley was right.

One thing was certain. For bad or for worse, Lolliloppi, Mississippi, would never ever be the same.

25

The stewardess had cautioned them to fasten their
seat belts. Delta Airlines. They were in final descent over Jackson-of-the-Big-Sipp. There was no one
aboard the plane excepting His Excellency and his entourage and his own SS persons and good old Carlton
Carson and his henchpersons. Mississippi, he thought.
'Sippi! The Big Damn Sipp! A chill danced swiftly
across his shoulders. His stomach percolated. In a very
few minutes he would be home. Home! Fifty-three
miles from the place that birthed him. He was happy.
He was saddened. He was exultant. He was scared. He
thought of Brother Malcolm. "The chickens were finally coming home to roost." He smiled, remembering Louis Jordan. "Ain't nobody here but us chickens."
He reached out toward the beautiful one who sat beside

him, took her hand and squeezed it, and she returned him squeeze for warming squeeze. It was a pity Her Excellency was married and never forgot that she was married. He felt profoundly sorry for himself. But then there was always Debby Bostick, on the sidelines. Perhaps not always. She was not the kind to hang around forever. She didn't have to. All that beauty and intelligence housed in one great superstructure.

Thousands were out at the airport, white, Black, Red, men, women, and even little children. A kind of homecoming he could never have imagined or even dreamed of just six months ago. Against his will he felt his eyes filling up. Tears of sorrow? Tears of joy?

They were deplaning now, and the folks were cheering, and a great big band was playing DIXIE. Somehow it moved his fervent heart to laughter.

On the ground now, on the sweet Black Sippi earth now, it was almost like he remembered feeling when he first deplaned at Bamakanougou. Homecoming. From the Jackson airport they flew into Lolliloppi via a custom-made especially constructed bullet-proofed helicopter and came down in front of the Rob Lee Hotel where they would be stopping during their stay in Lolliloppi. Mobs of people thronged both sides of the street. As they deplaned from the chopper, an elderly colored gentleman dashed suddenly from the crowd and broke past the police security toward the ersatz Prime Minister shouting, "Jimmy boy! Jimmy boy!" And almost caused our hero to start a liberation movement in his trousers, an accident he narrowly averted, as the police dragged the old gentleman away, where they would keep him under lock and key until the Guanayan delegation had left old Lolliloppi. An incident that did not go unnoticed by crafty Carlton Carson, whose bulbous nostrils (à la Wallace Beery) were still on the lookout for the rotten fish in the Denmark woodpile or convoluted metaphors to that effect. Carlton Carson would visit old Jeb Robinson nightly in the Lolli hoosegow. He had a sudden revelation that the answer to the mystery of His Excellency was hidden somewhere here in Lolliloppi, not in fishy rotten Denmark. He sometimes thought his sudden revelations, his brainstorms, were sent to him from Up on High by the Big Man Up There. He therefore believed religiously in his sudden revelations.

During their brief sojourn in Lolliloppi, the Guanayan delegation went everywhere by armored chopper, even if it were no more than three doors from the Rob Lee Hotel. "Cawnt take no chawnces with these Hawnkies," Alabama-born Mamadou Ben-Hannibala was overheard to comment in the strangest accent ever uttered since prehistoric *Homo sapiens* graduated from signs to "ughs" to *this* and *that*.

The Biltmore Restaurant where they were to have dinner that first evening was four doors down the street from the Rob Lee Hotel. At precisely 7:30, they came down on the elevator from their penthouse executive-suite'ed apartment on the fifth skyscraping floor and in true military fashion led by Mamadou Ben-Hannibala, they sashayed across the lobby. Outside, Lolliloppi's finest had formed a tunnel of protection from the hotel to the restaurant. But instead, Ben-Hannibala convoyed them to the armored helicopter, and they got into the copter. White and Black folks stood on the opposite sidewalk staring wild-eyed as they heard the motor sputter and watched the blades of the copter turn furiously, lift from the ground only to, a half of a minute later, come to earth in front of the Biltmore Restaurant at Main Street and Fifth Avenue. At which point Mamadou and his folks formed their own tunnel of security from the copter to the entrance to the restaurant. The white folks scratched their heads, in panic. The Black folks smiled with admiration.

All during dinner, two white men of the famous LPD stood nearby lengthwise, north and south of the long rectangular table and tasted every item of the greasy down-home cooking, before it came to rest upon the dining table. Four Guanayan SS persons stood at attention, rifles at the ready, ringing the outer perimeter from all sides, north, south, east, and west. The more hours spent in old Lolli by the Guanayans, the closer the white citizenry verged on uncontrolled hysteria, the nearer Himself came to a nervous smashup.

Early on, it had become clear that the Grand Visitation would be overpopulated due to the fact that hundreds of counterfeit invitations had been printed and sold (sometimes on the corner of Main and Yazzoo) for fifty bucks apiece. In an act of divine inspiration and desperation, they had hurriedly thrown up a giant tent à la Bailey and Barnum, as His Wife's Bottom would have described it, and they moved the circus (change that to reception) way out on the outskirts of town. All of Lolli's finest were on duty, including the fire department, the FBI, the CIA, and the Secret Service. NBC, ABC, CBS, and all the national and local networks were in attendance at this Grand Occasion.

Coming down on the elevator that memorable evening with Maria Efwa at his side, in her elegant gown with her blouse of colorful kente cloth and a long flowing skirt of golden silk, the elevator was so jammed with security persons of all ethnicities and denominations, it got stuck between the fourth and third floors. The elevator twitched with a tension that was demon-instigated.

Obviously. Jujued, for days, perhaps from here, unto eternity.

The Chief-of-Police's voice, intending to be the voice of calm, said tremulously, "No cu-cu-cause to panic, folks, no cu-cu-cause at all to panic. Just a slight cah-cah-case of mal-fuck—I mean mal-functioning. Pu-pu-push the lobby button, Lee-roy."

Leroy pushed the lobby button, which had the effect of shaking the elevator up and down and sideways, somewhat like an airplane when it runs into a thunderstorm. Then it settled quietly into immobility.

Meanwhile, suspecting Caucasian skullduggery and even hanky-panky, four Guanayan SS persons formed a square ring around Her and His Excellencies, pushing those on the outer perimeter rudely further up against the wall, at the same time causing His and Her Excellencies to assume an ever-closer attitude of togetherness. His Excellency's face flushed painfully and broke out in a perspiration of embarrassment, as he felt his thumping thighs up against her soft and tender slimness and felt her sweet warm breath against his neck, and felt himself growing shamefully hard against the middle of her. He mumbled, "I'm sorry," to her. But the middle of him, full of mannish mischief as it was and always and forever was, felt no sorrow whatsoever. Grew resolutely even harder every ticktock of infinity. Her sweet face glowed with perspiration, as she whispered that she understood. At the same time, she tried to maneuver herself into a more uncompromising position, but it availed her naught, because the more she stirred herself the more mischievous Himself became down there where the tension was more furious than ever.

Panic in the voice now of the chief of Lolli's finest. "Try it again, Lee—roy. Pu-pu-pu-push the lobby button." Leroy pu-pu-pu-pushed the lobby button. This time the elevator shook like the ravings of a caged and enraged elephant.

Optimistic cries of "It's going this time!" "I knew we'd get it started!"

Just as it settled as before into a state of immobility and quietude, somebody screamed, "It's them Africans! Them African niggers! This damn thang is hainted!"

Meanwhile the tension grew more excitedly between Her and His Excellencies. It was as if the lines of communications had broken down between his mental faculties atop and his mannish mischievousness down under.

"Pu-pupupush the panic but—I mean the emergency button, Lee—roy!"

Leroy pushed the panic button.

"What's the matter in there?" A slow-syrupy voice came as if from out of nowhere.

"We stuck in here—between the third and fourth floors, Nicodemus."

"Rajah," Nicodemus responded, complacently. "Nicodemus to the rescue. Hold your water, folkses. Rajah."

The so-called Prime Minister thought to himself, I thought only colored folks named their children names like "Nicodemus." Her sweet breath was coming heavily now onto his nervous neck.

Ultimately, the elevator, huffing and puffing, shaking like Saint Vitus, made its way down to the lobby, due somehow to a combination of the white man's technology and the African's Juju, or whatever. In any event, when they reached the lobby, there were murmurs of ecstatic admiration all over the place as Her and His Excellencies glided across the lobby toward the entrance, where long black limousines outside were waiting, patiently. Excitement—Wow! Flashbulbs popping.

When they reached the mobs of folks outside there was a mix-up that verged upon becoming a racial incident. Across the street from the hotel the famous KKK had thrown up an impressive picket line, with signs that suggested bad forebodings. Signs that read

MAYOR HARDTACK HAS BETRAYED
HIS SACRED TRUST

TO WHITE SUPREMACY.
A NIGGER IS A NIGGER IS A NIGGER DON'T

CARE WHERE HE COME FROM.
THE KLU KLUX KLAN WILL RIDE AGAIN!

The Klansmen stood over on the opposite side of the street, white-robed and white-masked underneath their pyramidal white hoods, armed to the teeth and elbows with their rifles at the ready.

An odd excitement took over His Excellency's sensations that had naught to do with fear. His face creased into a smile of confidence. He reached out toward Her Excellency and took her warming hand in his own warm hands and whispered, "Not to worry."

His Wife's Bottom's eyes almost popped out of their sockets, as he recalled all the horror stories he had heard about the 'Sippis. Foreign Minister Mamadou Tangi smiled arrogantly and unperturbed. He heard Cool Horace Whitestick say, unmistakably, "The shit is 'bout to hit the fan."

At which point the two entourages separated. It had not been the mayor's intention that they should not be integrated. Mayor Rufe had organized a tunnel of policemen from the hotel to the limousines through which the entourages were supposed to walk, in safety in the spirit of togetherness. But Mamadou Ben-Hannibala had, as per usual, formed his own tunnel of protection that led inevitably to the armored helicopter. His Excellency's heartbeat quickened, as he heard Ben-Hannibala order, loudly and distinctly, "LIBERATION PLATOON! CLOSE RANKS!" As they moved in more closely around His Excellency's entourage. After they had deposited each of them into the helicopter, Her Excellency being first of course, followed by the Minister Primarily, they turned their attention to the famous Ku Klux Klan.

"LIBERATION PLATOON, PRESENT ARMS!"

"PLATOON, ATTENTION!"

"ASSUME THE POSITION!"

Whereupon most of the platoon knelt with their rifles aimed across the plaza at the famous KKK.

"LIBERATION SQUAD, FORWARD MARCH!"

About a dozen of Mamadou's persons (men and women) marched across the plaza to where the KKK stood transfixed. His Excellency watched the proceedings from the vantage of the helicopter thinking to himself, Old Mamadou Ben-Hannibala truly got his Juju working!

When Mamadou reached the other side of the street, he walked, militarily, up to the wide-shouldered six-footer who stood in the center of the group. Tapped him on the shoulder with his riding crop.

"I believe you're the Grand Dragoon of this motley collection of Neanderthals, Sire."

The wide-shouldered six-footer was speechless, temporarily. Finally, he answered, "You-you-you gu-gu-gu-got that right, buh-buh-buh-boy."

Mamadou Ben-Hannibala reached out with his riding crop and disengaged the hood from the red-faced white man, unmasking him before the world and Mississippi. "And you, Sire, are Rayfield Willingham of the Willingham Department Store, so-called."

Ben-Hannibala went down the line from red-faced white man to shocked red-faced white man, unmasking each of them and calling them by name and occupation. For the rest of their born days and lives they would always believe in Juju and witchcraft and Black magic and mojo and roots and so forth and so on. The last little biddy beady-eyed red-faced cracker squeaked the question. "But how do you know us all by name?"

"Elementary, my boy. We got you simple-assed crackers covered. We got you infiltrated. One of your stupid sapsuckers belongs to us. Plus, we got our Juju working."

Everywhere His so-called Excellency turned that evening he found dear Evaline Gertrude at his elbows. He thought he sometimes heard her mumbling,

"Or heads will fucking roll," but he knew he must have been mistaken; that is, until he thought he heard Mayor Hardtack mumbling, "Or fucking heads will fucking roll." The Big Tent reminded him of springtime and Barnum and Bailey at the Garden; Madison Square, that is. Music all over the place, B. B. King, Big Joe Williams, the Clancy Brothers, Lena, Nina, and Aretha. Black and white folks comingling freely, genuinely enjoying themselves and each other and at that moment he thought of Martin. He thought of Jesse and his Rainbow Coalition.

FREE AT LAST! FREE AT LAST!

He thought, at this moment, Blacks and whites were free at last, and even though it lasted only one-hundredth of a moment at this point in time and space, it will have been worth the trip for him. He wouldn't let the Klan incident outside the hotel spoil the trip for him. Guanayan flags hanging all over the place. Pictures of Jimmy Jay Leander Johnson hanging, not in effigy. Whites and Blacks dancing together in Mississippi! The irony of it caught him in the throat and shoulders, welling his eyes with shamefaced tears. He dried them slyly. Her Excellency's hand went out to him beneath the table and squeezed it warmly as if to tell him that she understood. Now it was time for the ceremonies to begin.

Speech after speech about how much progress the

races had made together, due to good old southern hospitality, which was traditional. Jimmy Jay realized that in his own way, Mayor Hardtack was serious, possibly sincere even. He actually believed that progress had been made. And perhaps it had. All the mayor's life he had been brought up to believe that Blacks were inferior to white folks. Jimmy Jay's trip back home made the mayor take another look at all those truths he had taken (from his mama's breasts) to be self-evident.

Then Big Joe Williams and Lena Horne came to the dais and sang together, and Jimmy Jay was overcome with a flood of memories. All the southern great ones gone but not forgotten, especially as the two sang:

I was born by the river
In a little tent,
And just like the river
I've been running home ever since.

Lena, sweet, petite, and beautiful Lena, dedicated her participation to Medgar Evers and Bessie Smith. Big Black formidable sweet-singing Joe Williams dedicated his to the great Sam Cooke and Bessie.

Jimmy Jay thought of Sam Cooke and Otis Redding and Ledbetter and all the other great ones.

It's been a long time coming, but I
know a change gon come.

He could not fight back the tears building in his shoulders up through his face and forming in his eyes. He was no longer His so-called Excellency, he was James Jay Leander Johnson, Mississippi orphan Black boy, listening to a jukebox in a country store. Sam Cooke wailing.

A long time coming,
But I know, yes I know
A change gon come.

His people had given so much beauty to this land and received so little in return. Indignities, rejection, death at an early age. Bessie Smith bleeding to death on a southern road because the hospital turned back the Empress of the Blues, because she was Black.

He remembered the handsome dignified Black man, Dr. Drew, at Howard U., who saved so many American lives with his contribution to blood plasma, only to lose his own life on another southern road because a white hospital refused him accommodations.

He took a silken handkerchief from his boubou and pretended to be sneezing as he slyly wiped his eyes and blew his nose. He stared out at the Black and white faces, dancing together, crying, shouting, jumping for joy. He understood Sam Cooke and all the others more than ever before. More than anything else he understood profoundly the deep faith of his people. It may be a long time coming, but now he knew, he understood, profoundly.

A change gon come, God was not through with Jesse Jackson yet.

Before he felt the touch of her hand, he sensed her reaching out again toward him beneath the table. Maria Efwa's hand took his in hers and they squeezed each other's warmly. It was as if they were on the same wavelength and always had been since time began. And amid all the shouting and the clamor, nothing else had meaning. A change was going to come, and they would share the change together.

Everywhere His so-called Excellency turned that evening he found ever-faithful Evaline Gertrude near him with those great big beautiful eyes that always seemed astonished, which made our hero extremely nervous. Jimmy Jay, a.k.a. His Excellency, was seated at the banquet table on the raised platform when he suddenly became aware that someone was playing footsie with him. He never knew he had such irresistible sexy ankles until this historic trip to the good old USA. He turned nervously to the left of him and realized that it was the dainty right foot of the angelic-looking daughter of Mayor Rufus Hardtack. She was seated between her papa and the Minister Primarily. Maria Efwa sat beside him on the other side. Himself broke into a cool damp sweat, which made the good mayor wonder at the perspiration pouring from the PM's forehead. Why would an African be sweating in an air-conditioned tent?

He reached again for Maria Efwa's kind of warmth and went again with her in a kind of 'Sippi dream sequence. He was brought back from his 'Sippi "paradise" (with Maria Efwa) by the old familiar rebel shouts that had always meant bad news for him and his kind of people. He thought his daydream had become a nightmare as he heard the familiar strains of "Dixie."

Out on the streets a couple of blocks away, the band was playing "Dixie." People who could not afford the price of a bogus invitation lined each side of the street, waving their confederate banners together with Guanayan flags, as the band swung into another tune, the people singing, shouting:

Colonel Reb's gonna shine tonight.
Colonel Reb's gonna shine.
Colonel Reb's gonna shine tonight

Out on the line.
When the moon comes up
And the sun goes down,
Colonel Reb's gonna shine.

Down the street came the unbelievable sight of a caravan of cars with police escort, and in the lead car Colonel Reb himself, the man of the moment on the U. of Miss. campus, standing tall and handsome. He was an academic, all-American halfback, 90 average in scholarship, dressed to kill in a confederate uniform, cap and all, and standing beside him in an open car was a lovely young southern lady, very white and very blond, "Miss Ol' Miss," the homecoming queen.

Now they were entering the big tent, as the rebel yells continued. Jimmy Jay could not believe what his eyes beheld. He thought surely he had gone back to his daydream changed to nightmare, nor could he believe his ears, as he heard them shouting:

Colonel Reb, we love you.
Colonel Reb, we love you.
We love you in the springtime and the fall.
Colonel Reb, we love you.
Colonel Reb, we love you.
We love you best of all.

Now the motorcade was coming up the middle aisle, Miss Ol' Miss and Colonel Reb with their arms around the other's waist and waving with the other hand. There's something incongruous about the picture before me, Jimmy Jay thought. His eyes were playing tricks on him. When he thought, But then, I'm in hot-weather sun country. He remembered words attributed to the venerable Sterling Brown by the equally venerable Margaret Walker. Together in Jackson, she was reputed to have said, "It's really a hot one today." To which Sterling is said to have responded, "Where in the hell did you think hell was except in Mississippi?" He remembered the words of his buddies, it seemed a hundred years ago, at the swimming hole outside Lolliloppi. He'd seen lots of swarthy white men in his growing-up days in 'Sippi, deeply tanned ones. But this young Colonel Reb was somehow different. The closer he came toward the platform the darker, deeper the tan, deepening every moment, a tan turning now to darkening brown, with broad nose and wide thick curvaceous sensual lips. Colonel Reb was a young handsome Black man all togged out in a confederate uniform, a contradiction in the flesh. The so-called Prime Minister thought to himself, ironically, Your Excellency, you just ain't ready yet. He watched them, mesmerized, as they came hand in hand up the steps to the platform. He made sure he was daydreaming, as the blond one held out her hand to him and curtsied, "Your Excellency!" in a breathless voice. He took her hand, kissed it, tremblingly. Then he turned to the nonplussed face of the handsome young Black man, who embraced him and kissed him briefly on each cheek, as the young man whispered. "Don't believe a word of it, Your Excellency. It's all as bogus as confederate money." Which did not rescue Jimmy Jay from his state of shock, as he watched the young confederate Black man take a seat beside Miss Ol' Miss. Mayor Rufus Hardtack was beaming proudly.

He leaned toward the Minister Primarily and whispered, "Each year the University of Mississippi selects the most popular senior on the campus. They take everything under consideration. Scholarship, athletic ability, service to the community, popularity, good citizenshipness, everything. And he is proclaimed 'Colonel Reb.' 'Man of the Year,' and he gets to escort Miss Ol' Miss to the homecoming game. It's a tradition that goes way back."

All His so-called Excellency could say was "That's nice." He remembered the old tradition. He'd stood on the streets many times and waved and enjoyed vicariously the feeling he imagined Colonel Reb was feeling, never dreaming of a Colonel Reb in blackface. He wanted to believe that he was the one who was dragging his feet. He simply wasn't ready for the so-called New South.

Mayor Rufe informed him, confidentially, "All these people here on the platform around you are founding fathers. They're real big shots. Course most of them out there in the audience is big shots too. Special invitations." Mayor Rufe had a habit of elbowing you in the ribs when he was making a point, a habit that Jimmy Jay did not take kindly to.

Then he remembered the words of Colonel Reb, man of the hour. "It's all as bogus as confederate money." The devil made him ask Mayor Rufus, "Where are the African founding fathers? The Black big shots?"

Sweat leaked suddenly from Mayor Rufe's beaming forehead. "They're a little late getting here. Excuse me a minute. Omma see what's holding em up."

Mayor Rufe went over to three or four of the Caucasian founding fathers already seated, gesturing to them frantically. They left the comfort of their seats and followed Mayor Rufe hurriedly toward the kitchen, which had been constructed several feet away from the Big Tent like an army mess hall.

Mayor Rufe ran into the mess hall shouting, "You're free! You're free! Or heads will fucking roll!" He ran up to the chef. "You're free! You're free! So, act like it or heads will fucking roll! Get over there and meet His Excellency. He wants to meet alla y'all, or fucking heads will roll!"

One of the cooks, a young Black brother, with dark wide eyes demanded, "If I'm free, where is my forty acres and that fucking mule?"

"You'll get them tomorrow! Get them tomorrow! Or fucking heads will roll."

The chef was a six foot roly-poly man, seemed in the last months of pregnancy around the midsection. "Like this?" the dark brown-faced man asked, skeptically. "Go out there like this? In this cook's outfit?"

Mayor Rufe looked around frantically. "Lend him yours! Lend him yours! Mine would be too little for him. Besides, I have to be out there with everybody. I'm the mayor, someday I might be president!"

All over the kitchen the erstwhile founding fathers were taking off their tuxedos and putting them on the cooks. There was laughter and shouting and applauding, as the Black cooks came up the steps to the platform dressed in ill-fitting tuxedos, some of them too long for short and some too short for long. You could see the chef's white apron showing beneath his tuxedo jacket.

Mayor Rufe went flush-faced to the lectern. "These are the rest of the founding fathers of the fair city of

Lolliloppi. And we want to ask our most foundering of father, Deacon Amos Roadhouse, to lead us in a special prayer. Ladies and gentlemen, Deacon Amos Andrew Roadhouse."

Amos Roadhouse sat there quietly for a moment, with Mayor Hardtack gesturing at him excitedly. Ultimately, Amos rose from his chair and ambled behind his pregnant stomach toward the lectern. He stood there, staring down at the noisy and expectant crowd, momentarily, waiting patiently for the noise and chatter to subside. He bowed his head and cleared his voice, menacingly.

"Lord, we come before you tonight, you who is ruler of the universe, with heavy heart and contrite spirit. You, who know every thought we ever thought of thinking, you above all things know I ain't nobody's founding father of this here Lolliloppi, Mississippi. You know it and everybody in the sound of my humble voice know it." He paused.

The mayor was shuffling in his chair, wiping the pouring perspiration from his plumpish face. His so-called Excellency heard the murmurs from the crowd below them and heard a smattering of "Amens" and "tell the truths." He fought hard to resist the temptation to get up and go to the lectern and put his arms around his brother. Great God Almighty! Glory halleluyah! He was in a trance again and he reached beneath the table and took Maria's reaching hand.

"Your humble servant, Lord, I ask from you a special blessing for this young man who has come thousands of miles across the ocean to bring us great tidings of peace and love and brotherhood. For he is blood of our blood and he is flesh of our flesh. We ask your blessing upon all who have come with him. We ask you to go with them and stand by them. We ask you to give this congregation gathered here tonight a new understanding that thou have made of one blood all the nations for to dwell in peace upon this earth. You knows, Lord, that Mississippi ain't near 'bout what it ought to be, and without your help, Mississippi ain't never gonna be what it oughta be, but with all of us pushing together, and with your divine guidance, Mississippi gon be what it ought to be, someday soon. And when our sojourn on this earth is ended, we ask you for a seat in thy kingdom, free and equal and unsegregated. We ask all this in the name of thy son Jesus, world without end, AMEN."

Like a man sleepwalking, His so-called Excellency moved bleary-eyed toward Amos Roadhouse, and took him in his arms and kissed him on both cheeks. "Thank you, Deacon. Thank you, brother. Thank you so much!" he said in a shouted whisper, amid the shouting and the weeping and amening from the crowd below. Jimmy Jay led him to his chair and then went back to his own. The old man sat there for a moment, then stood up and took off the tuxedo jacket, left it on the chair, and went back to the kitchen with his white apron wrapped around him. Shouting, stomping, crying, weeping, was the crowd he left behind him.

The moment was upon him. He felt everything had been said by the deacon. All else would be counterproductive, entirely anticlimax. He vaguely heard Mayor Hardtack introducing him. People were giving him a standing ovation, as he sat there in another time, another space. He heard the anxious mayor's voice. "Your Excellency."

He now moved toward the podium. He stood there quietly staring at the shouting madness. He keenly felt a sense of déjà vu. It had all happened before, perhaps in one of the dreams he had dreamed. He had stood beneath this tent on this platform before this very crowd perhaps a thousand years ago.

He was startled when he heard himself say, "It's all as bogus as Confederate money. I'm no Prime Minister, I'm Jimmy Jay Leander Johnson, born right here in Lolliloppi in the Big damn 'Sipp." They gasped, they smiled tentatively. Some of them fainted. Policemen dashed toward him from all over, pistols and guns drawn, as did the men of Secret Service. He could hear

Carlton Carson shouting gleefully, "I knew Denmark was rotten! I knew Denmark was fishy!" He was profoundly relieved when he realized he had not really spoken yet. Even the honest fantasy was bogus. Then he began actually to speak.

"Sisters and brothers, after Deacon Roadhouse, what is there for me or anybody else to say? I merely want to bring you greetings, especially to my African sisters and brothers from their sisters and brothers residing on the Mother Continent, but to all of you who, in the words of Deacon Roadhouse, have been made of one blood all the nations to dwell upon this earth in peace and brotherhood, and sisterhood. I want all of you to know that I feel a deep sense of homecoming here in this place that reminds me so much of Mother Africa, the sun, the earth, the sky, the bright green of your rain forest, the overall fertility, all this reminds me of Africa. Your struggle, your hardships, your determination to be free, through struggle." He listened to them cheering him. He made the same speech he had made at the 369th Armory in Harlem, a shortened version, much shorter, with variations on the theme from time to time. The special greatness of his people in this country, the contributions they had made to the greatness of the country, oftentimes unappreci-

THE MINISTER PRIMARILY · 563

ated. He spoke of Billie Holiday and her southern fruit. He agreed with Sam Cooke. It had been a long time coming, but he believed a change was going to come. He had finished.

And now the mad dash for autographs, with Mamadou Ben-Hannibala solidly in charge of security. Autograph-seekers had to run the gantlet of a long tunnel constructed by armed guards on each side, with somewhere along the middle an apparatus (similar to those at airports) to pick up any form of metal instruments. Black and white formed long lines, integrated, hundreds of them, perhaps thousands, mostly women. Some of them who had no paper for him to write on, went to the makeshift latrines and brought forth toilet paper, which proved to be too thin for autographing. Not to be outdone, some went back and took off their slips and bras and offered them up for His Excellency's signature. One handsome buxom blond woman who had neither slip nor bra, offered up her bare-assed baby boy for his pink backside to be autographed. "He already wet his diapers," the embarrassed young lady explained, gigglingly. Mayor Hardtack had been standing there next to him all along, pretending that they also lined up for his autograph. After all, there were signs around the town out there on the main stem, that read

RUFUS HARDTACK FOR GOVERNOR

and

ALL THE WAY WITH RUFE TO THE WHITE HOUSE!

Just as Jimmy Jay went to autograph the baby's pink backside, the pen slipped from his hand. And as he stopped to pick it up, the baby let go a jet stream of piss into the mayor's beaming face as if his little thimble-size pinkish pecker was equipped with gunsight and with time precision. The gathered crowd broke up with laughter. Mayor Rufe did not grasp the humorous aspect of it, at first. But after he wiped his face with his handkerchief, he too cracked up with laughter. His so-called Excellency laughed so hard he had to sit down. He apologized. "I'm sorry, Mr. Mayor, but—" and he went off into gales of laughter again, especially when the young mother of the baby said, "Just think, Honeybunch, you may be able to say one day that you pissed in the President's face!" After which the autographing party ended.

Mamadou Ben-Hannibala's booming voice announced, "That's it for the night, folks. His Excellency is exhausted. That's it, folks. That's it. Sorry about that. Perhaps something can be arranged for tomorrow. We'll announce it on the radio and television."

During most of his stay in 'Sippi, he felt as if he were under house arrest, as indeed he was. He had risked everything, risked unmaskment, even, to come down to his own hometown to spend his few days in a two-by-four hotel, overrun with bugs. They spent most of the time fumigating the place of antiquated listening devices. He wanted to be out on the streets among his people, listening to the stories they had to tell. When he got back, he would compose and sing folk songs to the grandeur of his people. As it was, he had to sit in all day and listen to Cool Horace rave about a foxy sister by the name of Lottie Jefferson. "Man, she was a natural fox. Pretty as a speckled peach from Georgia. Sweet, petite, and ready for Freddie, which was me, Cool Horace Frederick Whitestick. I mean she was a little piece of leather, but she was well put together. I sure would like to see that chick one more time, and she's right here in this little old one-horse town. Goddamn old Rose!"

Sandwiched in between his ravings about fine Miss Lottie Jefferson were His Excellency's meetings with the press, interviews on television, always fearing instant recognition and exposure by some sister or brother from his bygone days of yore in the times of his great innocence, no harm intended. His great nerves were shipwrecked and going down slowly, more swiftly than the great unsinkable *Titanic*. His right eye was developing a twitch. Were it not for Maria's soothing glances, he would have been in terrible shape. The next day after the Grand Visitation a couple of Hollywood bigwigs flew into town. Now and then he thought of Debby Bostick.

Over lunch and heavy drinking they offered the PM a $5 million contract for a three-picture deal to be paid in five installments over a five-year period, so that the tax hit would be softened, though the three movies would be shot within the year.

Jimmy Jay turned the offer down with the proper indignation of an authentic African Prime Minister, as his heart beat wildly. He thought perhaps they could hear his poor heart thumping, palpitating! Five million dollars to become a movie actor, a star! A thing he'd dreamed of all of his remembered years. Five million green ones! He'd never get a chance like this again. He reached for his drink and tried desperately to keep his hand from shaking, in the little country tavern room. He thought of the fact that in less than a couple of weeks he would be back to singing jive highlife and calypso songs at Club Lido in little old Bamakanougou.

He took another drink and shook his head, negatively. "I appreciate your offer, gentlemen, but you see I have a country to serve. I suppose I should be flattered, in American terms, but in African terms, I feel insulted." His indignation was not faked.

They thought he was angling for more money. The one with the bulbous nose and thick glasses and the Havana cigar said, "All right, Your Excellency, you're a hell of tough negotiator. Okay, how about ten million dollars? We can fix it so you'd hardly have to pay any tax at all."

The cigar smoke was almost mesmerizing Jimmy, that and the $10 million offer. Jimmy was flattered, tempted, and insulted, simultaneously. His mind was leaping crazily about.

"You did not understand me, sir. I said I have a country to serve. And no amount of money could sway me from my duty." He sounded phony even to himself.

The more sensitive thin-faced Hollywood one said, "I can understand your POV, Mr. Prime Minister. Your duty to your country, etcetera and so on. A very admirable sentiment. A man of rare integrity and so forth, unheard of in these days of rugged individualism and rabid opportunism."

"Then you do understand where I am coming from, sir," Himself said, gratefully.

"Oh yes indeed," the sensitive thin-faced one replied. "But we can arrange a coup and get you overthrown. That way you will no longer owe your country any duty."

His Excellency stared at the thin-faced one, incredulously.

Thin Faced said, "Furthermore, why should you limit yourself to a little insignificant country like Guanaya, when you can have America and the whole world at your feet? And who knows how long it'll be before that combanium is exhausted? You can be the biggest movie star that ever was."

"Okay, twenty-five million," the cigar-smoking Holly bigwig offered.

They talked until they ran out of conversation. The bigwigs would not accept a negative answer. Cigar Smoker said, "Who're you kidding, Your Excellency? Every cockermamie person on this earth has his price."

The bogus PM said, "Obviously you haven't named it yet."

They talked a little longer. Finally, Cigar Smoker said, "Obviously we haven't. Perhaps it ain't money. Whatever it is, we'll find out. We always do. No man in this world is that principled. We've cracked tougher ones than you. We'll make you another offer over breakfast."

Later that night, he brought up the question with the Guanayan delegation.

The Foreign Minister said, abruptly, "What is there to discuss? Your agreement with us stands until we return to Bamakanougou."

His Wife's Bottom said, "Twenty-five million dollars is a lot of money."

Jimmy Jay resented both of their attitudes. "I merely mentioned it, because I thought you should know of the latest development."

Mamadou Tangi said, "And you hoped we could find a way for you to accept their offer."

"I hoped nothing of the sort. I just wanted you to know." Thinking to himself, why had he brought the question up?

Which was the Foreign Minister's second thrust. "Why did you bring it before us then? We didn't have to know about it."

Really, why had he? What was his motive? Perhaps the Foreign Minister was right.

Maria Efwa came to his rescue. She knew him better than he knew himself. "He simply wanted us to know how loyal and committed he was to us and Africa."

"Thank you so much," Jimmy Jay said sincerely. He went toward Maria Efwa, like a man sleepwalking.

He pulled her to her feet and took her in his arms and kissed her fully on her lips. And he thought surely that she kissed him back. Or was it his imagination? Wish fulfillment? Fantasizing? Hallucinating?

They came at him from all sides the next morning. Two others had flown in from Hollywood. They took turns at the Minister Primarily.

"Why don't we cut out the bullshit? Every damn body has his price. Thirty million dollars and you can even have Her Excellency Maria Efwa, as your leading lady, or Raquel Welch or anybody. You can have some of the most beautiful women in the world, before, during, and after the movies have been produced. We can guarantee it. Put it in your contract."

Another one asked him, "Why should you let all of your obvious irresistible sex appeal go to waste? You're like Paul Robeson, Harry Belafonte, Sidney Poitier, Muhammad Ali put together and multiplied. The most beautiful women on earth are dying to get into bed with you."

The thick-lensed cigar-smoking owl-eyed one giggled. "You could even make it with the President's daughter."

Jimmy Jay said, smilingly, "I thought we were discussing beautiful women."

The cigar smoker shouted, "I love it! I love it!" Then

he said, "Thirty-five million fat ones for three pictures to be made in one year, payments to be made over a five-year period, so that your taxes would be minimal."

Jimmy Jay's head was doing a somersault now, swimming around and around, or was it the little dinky dining room? His opportunistic mind had his conscience in a half nelson hold. Jimmy Jay Leander Johnson, a.k.a. His Excellency the Prime Minister of Guanaya, got shakily to his feet. "Gentlemen, this conversation has been very revealing, but I see no point in further discussion. You'll excuse me, surely, for, as I said clearly to you in the beginning, I have a country to serve." He turned and walked dignifiedly out of the dining room with his bodyguards in tow.

That night he felt like celebrating. He had learned some things about himself anew. He had come to grips with himself, and he felt victorious. He took Cool Horace aside and said, "Let's sneak out of here tonight and find Miss Lottie. Perhaps she also has a foxy friend."

"Oh?" Cool Horace signified. "What about Her Excellency?"

"I'm surprised at you Horace Frederick. You know Her Excellency has a husband."

And so, Jimmy Jay Leander sans beard and Cool

Horace Frederick Whitestick sneaked. They searched all over Lolliloppi for the mythical Miss Lottie. "She's fine as elderberry wine!" He'd never seen the Cool One so excited since the phone booth time at Sutphin Boulevard in Jamaica.

"Miss Lottie, she used to live here, but she moved over on Jefferson Davis Street over yonder in Bluebeard Bottom. Seven Fifty-Six, I think the address is." Okay, over to the Bottom. "She's fine as blackberry wine," Cool Horace boasted. "I mean I'm turning on just thinking about her."

In the dark backyard a dog was barking. "Yessir, she used to live here a few years ago, but now I b'lieve she's over in Tybee on Tallyfarry Street." They went from place to place, where Lottie *used* to live. Horace Frederick was breathing heavily now. "You'll see, she's really fine. She'll be worth the trouble we took to find her." Meanwhile they had stopped at a couple of joints and had several stiff ones. For after all, they were celebrating. Weren't they? Also, they got the feeling that they were being followed by a car with its lights turned off.

Finally, the PM said, "It's after midnight. This is our last stop. If she isn't here, we're going to sing 'Lottie Doesn't Live Here Anymore.'" Cool Horace agreed, reluctantly. The car behind them had turned on its high beam lights. Suddenly the highly beamed car speeded up and came alongside the one Cool Horace was driving and began to bump up against it like they do in the "moom pitchers" and on the Tee Vee.

"Hey," Jimmy Jay said. "What in the hell's going on?"

Two white men got out of the high-beamed Cadillac and came toward them. "What're you niggers up to riding around here in the dark?" Drawn guns were gleaming in the moonless night.

At which point Cool Horace gunned the motor and shot off down the unlighted street. When it's darkness on the delta, it is black dark, truly. Now his own high beam lights were on, as he turned at the next intersection on two wheels, brakes squealing, into an even darker narrower alley. He remembered the Lolliloppi alleys. He'd lived in several of them. The darkness seemed to close in on them from both sides, and Jimmy could not help from mumbling, "Was this trip necessary?" He was leaking sweat now from all over.

"Don't you worry 'bout the mule going blind," Horace stated with assurance.

Just up ahead at the end of the narrowing block high beam lights from two Cadillacs lit up the darkness, effectively blocking off the narrowing intersection. "The mule is blind as a frigging bat" was Jimmy Jay's contribution.

Crackers started climbing out of the two Cadillacs, endlessly, like circus clowns out of a Model T Ford in the Big damn Tent. But Jimmy understood they were not there for Horace's and His Excellency's entertainment. Else why would they have guns and shotguns? Repeat: "Was this trip necessary?"

One little biddy cracker came toward them, shotgun at the ready. He drawled, "Your time is come. Your race is run. Where's that smart-assed nigger that knew all our names? It don't matter nohow. You ain't gon live long enough to say them xcept maybe to Saint Peter."

Jimmy had often wondered how he would react faced with a situation like this. Would he fall upon his knees and plead for mercy? Would he put a puddle in his underwear? Would he start a liberation movement of his bowels in his trousers? He was proud that he did neither. But a frightening calm settled over him. He thought of the little children of Birmingham. He thought of Emmett Till, Medgar Evers, Mack Parker, Martin, Malcolm, Chaney, Goodman, Schwerner. He thought of Fannie Hamer. Nobody lived forever. Especially in Mississippi. He remembered Martin's speech at the mountaintop. The calm in his voice scared even Himself. "What's the problem, brother?"

The little biddy mousy cracker said, "I ain't no brother of yourn, and you and that other nigger only ones got a problem, the way I sees it. Course y'all ain't gon have no problems very long." He could hear the other crackers giggling. "Cause I hear tell dead folks they don't got no problems. Not even niggers."

One of the other crackers growled, "Aw to hell with all that who-shot-John, Gus. Let's git the damn thing over with."

They aimed all their guns at Jimmy and Horace. The Cool One's hands went up to protect his face. Little Gus said, "All right, brothers, READY—AIM—FU—"

At which point the silence was broken with the blasting of sirens making enough noise to wake up the dead. The alley lit up like the middle of the day. All the policemen in Lolliloppi County seemed to be in the alley. Uniformed policemen piled out of four squad cars. The chief of police came running toward the gathered Klansmen. He was the one with big ears like Clark Gable but without Clark Gable's sex appeal. "All right, boys, the picnic's over." Jimmy had never been so glad to see 'Sippi cracker policemen in all his born days. He'd never known there were so many in the county. He thought perhaps they'd gathered from adjoining counties. Sweat poured from him like he was raining from the inside outward.

Little Gus said, "We was just having a little fun, chief."

The chief with the big ears said, "You know better than that, Little Gus. These niggers are with Olliemackey's group. We can't treat these niggers like niggers, or fucking heads will roll. Now y'all clear out of here and gone on home."

The Klansmen backtracked, grumbling, protesting, got into their cars and drove away. By now Black folks were standing on front porches in the dark all up and down the alley. The chief walked over to Jimmy Jay.

"Whatchall doing out here this time of night anyhow?"

Cool Horace had finally found his voice and cool. "I'm from this neck of the woods, my own self, chief. We were looking for an old lady friend of mine, name of Lottie Mae Jefferson. She ain't old at all, but—"

The chief said, "Lottie Mae Jefferson? Why one of her younguns keeps house for us and looks after our chilluns. De-beau-rah Jefferson. You jest git in your car and foller me."

Cool Horace said, "Yassah. Thank you Sah." Jimmy Jay understood it was the dialogue of survival. The chief got into his squad car and took off up the alley, sirens blasting, with Jimmy Jay and Cool Horace in pursuit. It was the strangest sight the inhabitants of Spareribs Alley had ever witnessed. His Excellency thinking, skeptically, what if they were being led some-where out of town to a Klansman midnight picnic? And they would never be seen or heard of ever again. He thought, against his will again, of Chaney and Good-man and Schwerner.

In front of the three-room shack now, the proud chief floodlighted the front porch. "This is the place all right. Y'all be good boys now, and don't forget to tell Mayor Rufe what I done for you."

Cool Horace said, "Yassah."

The chief raced his motor and took off down the road with the other squad cars following behind him.

They walked up the front steps to the porch and knocked on the door. They heard somebody walking from the inside. The hanging naked-one-bulbed porch light came on, dimly. A woman's voice from inside de-manded, mischievously, "Who dat?"

Cool Horace answered, "You dat." An old southern game Jimmy Jay had clearly forgotten.

The woman's inside voice said, "Who dat said you dat when I said who dat?"

A big fat woman opened the door and stood there filling the door with her space. She had to weigh three hundred and fifty pounds, at least.

Cool Horace took off his hat. "Sorry to bother you so late, lady, but we're looking for Miss Lottie Mae Jefferson."

The hefty soft-faced woman stared at Horace suspiciously. Then recognition lit her face. "Horace Frederick, you bring your butt on in this house. Who's that pretty gentleman you got with you?"

Horace stood there transfixed, tongue-tied, and incredulous. "I'm looking for Miss Lottie Mae Jefferson."

"Who you think you talking to? Come on in here, you trifling scound. Somebody told me they seed you in town."

So this was the fabulous sweet petite little Lottie Mae. "A little piece of leather well put together." Jimmy Jay and Horace came in sheepishly. "Have a sit-down and make yourself at home." She called out toward what Jimmy imagined was the kitchen. "Debeau-rah, bring the gentlemen a couple of bottles of beer." She turned back to her company. "De-beau-rah is one of my oldest daughters." She sat down in a chair, and it gave way under her weight. Two of the legs collapsed. Suddenly the little room was crowded with children, all sizes and ages. There must've been ten or fifteen of them, underfoot and all around them. "Mama! Mama! What's the matter?"

She tried, unsuccessfully, to raise herself as the chair

cried out for mercy. "These chairs they sell you these days ain't a bitter count. I deswear before the good Lord up on high." Deborah and the older children and Jimmy and Horace were around her now, trying to help her to her feet. Even some of the little ones were there around her feet, pulling and puffing. Lottie broke out into laughter. "Lord, Jesus, have mercy! I do declare!" She was on her feet now and had settled cautiously into another chair. She stared at Jimmy Jay. "Frederick, where you get this pretty thing from? Look like a moom pitcher star. His face sure do look familiar." She aimed her question at Jimmy Jay. "Ain't I seed you on that television mess? Seem to me—"

Jimmy Jay said, "No ma'am I—"

Cool Horace said, "He's an old buddy of mine from New York City. Name's Roger Bakefield. Me and him work for that African Prime Minister."

She laughed her hearty laugh again. "That's where I seed him. On that television mess. Honey you look just like that pretty Prime Min'ster. All you need is to get you a beard." She laughed again. "Lord Jesus, have mercy!" The children were all between her legs, climbing up into her lap. "Go 'way. Shoo! Scat!" she said to them good-naturedly. "Can't you see I'm entertaining high-tone company?"

The Cool One was overwhelmed by the heft of the

formerly petite woman of his fondest memory, his "little piece of leather so well put together," and the children running hither and thither all over the place.

Uncool Cool Horace could not avoid exclaiming, "Lottie Mae, what in the world have you been doing with yourself?"

"Keeping busy," she answered, as she shuffled toward the kitchen.

Likewise, Jimmy could not avoid commenting, "With all these younguns running around here, what in the hell you think she's been doing? She ain't hardly had time to get out of bed."

When they arrived back at the hotel, they were faced with the outrage of his delegation.

"We had no idea where you'd taken off to."

"Something could have happened to you," Maria Efwa declared, vehemently, "down here in Mississippi with the Klu Klus Klan."

Mamadou Tangi said, "A totally irresponsible thing to do. It is clear that you do not take our mission seriously."

Even Barra Abingiba agreed. "Hey, man, that wasn't cool at all."

What could he tell them? "You're absolutely right. It was a foolish caper, and certainly unworthy of the Prime Minister of Guanaya."

"You still think the whole thing is a joke, don't you?" Maria Efwa stated angrily.

The bogus PM said, "Well, isn't it? I mean, what else is it? I mean, after all—"

"And you're simply incapable of taking us seriously? Is that it? A little African country like Guanaya."

"That simply is not true, and you know damn well it isn't."

She said, "In any event, Your Excellency, Mister Casanova, your New York lady friend called you. You're to call her back as soon as you return, no matter how late the hour. She sounded rather desperate." Maria sounded rather sarcastic.

He went straight off to his bedroom. "I'd better call her right away then." He was relieved to escape the heat of their wrath. At the same time, he was apprehensive.

Before she even said hello, she said, "What in the hell have you been up to down there, gallivanting all over Mississippi. Have you suddenly gone out of your mind?"

He said, "What's happening up there? Her Excellency said you sounded desperate."

Debby retaliated with, "Her Excellency is aware of your existence all right, you flaky bastard. Believe me when I tell you. She's got the hots for you. I could feel the heat wave all the way to New York City."

He said, "Come on, already. Tell me now, what's happening?"

"Thos sons of bitches broke into my apartment while I was at work. All of my papers scattered all over the place. Dresser drawers pulled out. Desk drawers on the floor. The whole damn place plundered and ransacked."

"What?!"

"Nothing stolen. Bastards wrote with crayon on my mirror in my bedroom, 'DID HIS EXCELLENCY GIVE YOU A GOOD FUCKING?'!"

"Are you sure they didn't take anything?"

She demanded, "Is that all you can say to me? Am I sure they didn't take anything? They took me. I feel like I've been raped, violated . . . I feel unclean."

"Who do you think they could have been?"

"Think. Who else could it be except the FBI or the CIA or some lower species of the animal kingdom? Who else could have known that you visited with me? Who taps the goddamn phone?"

He thought he heard her weeping, blowing her nostrils. He said, "Keep cool, baby. We'll be coming back to town tomorrow."

"What the hell good is that going to do me? Will you be moving in with me as soon as you get back?" He could hear her crying, unrestrainedly now.

Against his will he could not keep himself from thinking, Perhaps she's putting on an act to get me involved with her more deeply. From his experience with her at the Lenox Terrace apartments he had to conclude she was a devious woman. Or even perhaps she was working for the State Department. Perhaps she'd written the letter in the *New York Times*. He hated himself for being so distrustful of her. They had been through so very much together.

He heard her shouting at him now. "Go screw yourself!" as she banged down the telephone.

He dialed her back immediately and listened to it ring six or seven times before she answered.

"You can go politely straight to hell, you bastard!" She banged it down again.

He lay back on the bed and felt a migraine coming on. What could he do? What could he do? He heard a soft rap on his door. Two even softer raps.

"Who is it?"

A soft voice answered, "Maria Efwa here."

He felt a thumping where his heart had been. "May I come in?"

His heart began to skip about, as if it might leap out of his chest. He was speechless, momentarily.

Then he mumbled, "Of course," as he left the bed and went toward the door to open it. Before he reached the door, she entered. He thought perhaps he had fallen asleep and was in a dream he hoped he would not awaken from. He stood stock still, transfixed, as he watched her moving toward him, gliding, like a moving picture in slow motion, a Tee Vee instant retake. He couldn't believe his happy eyes.

"May I sit down?" she asked him.

"Of course!" He dragged a chaise lounge toward her. "Please be seated."

He watched her, as she lowered herself onto the lounge, kept his eyes on her as if he thought if he looked away, when he looked back, she would have disappeared. His sweet dream would have evaporated. He sat away from her on the side of his bed. He got up again. "Can I get you something? Tea, coffee, something stronger?"

She said, "No thank you. I shan't be here that long. I just wanted to know if Her Ladyship was all right. She sounded so upset."

He told her briefly of her conversation with "Her Ladyship." She said sympathetically, "You are really in a mess."

He said, "*She* is in a terrible mess. And there's nothing I can do about it."

She rose from the lounge. "I suppose I'd better be leaving now. I thought perhaps there was something we could do to help her."

He left the bed and went to her. "You're such a beautiful and compassionate woman!" He took her in his arms and almost squeezed the breath out of her and kissed her fully deeply on her plentiful and curving lips. He thought she kissed him back, for a fleeting moment. He heard her sighing, breathing deeply. Then she pulled away from him. "How can I make you understand that there can never be anything romantic between us? *I am a married woman!*"

He answered, "By not visiting me in my bedroom at this time of night."

She went out and slammed the door.

The following morning, they left town for the Big damn Apple.

26

Back in the Apple, they really felt like celebrating. They had conquered Mississippi and had emerged unscathed. The only thing left was his speech at the United Nations General Assembly. It was Tuesday. A party was planned for them on Wednesday. The executive suite exuded euphoria, which made the Minister Primarily uptight with suspicion and foreboding. To him, euphoria was a bad omen. Good feelings were a forecast for catastrophe. With only a few days left, something bad was bound to happen. Somebody would recognize him without a shadow of a doubt, and then, disgrace, shame, not only for him but also for the little nation of Guanaya and for all of Africa, and its peoples. He lived now in growing dread of his discovery. If Debby Bostick saw through his bearded disguise, others would do likewise.

It was just a matter of time. And time was running out, and swiftly.

The party was to be held at the Malaga Mission in Mount Vernon in Westchester. Guanaya was still in the process of setting up an embassy and mission in the USA. As they drove up the oval driveway to the Mission mansion, complete with police escort and a slew of security people, front and back, Guanayan and otherwise, he heard them strike up the Guanayan national anthem. Maria Efwa reached for him and took his hand and squeezed it.

As they debarked from the limos, there was cheering and loud applause. It seemed that hundreds were standing on the portico, cocktails in hand, smiling, cheering. Blacks all over the country had watched, breathlessly, their courageous journey into darkness of the 'Sippi delta. On the television, in the newspapers, on the radio. Overnight Jaja and his entourage had become national heroes to African Americans. It was an event that might be compared with SHERMAN'S MARCH THROUGH GEORGIA.

As he moved quickly up the walk with "his lady," he recognized some of the great ones. But he hoped they would not recognize Jimmy Jay. He could not suppress the feeling of great pride that suffused him, as he came up the walk with the beautiful Her Excellency. He could hear the aahs and oohs and murmurs. Ernie Crichlow, Belafonte, Feelings, Louise Meriwether, John A. Williams, Rosa Guy, Bill Forde, Paule Marshall, Jimmy Baldwin, Killens, Angelou, Bambara, Loften Mitchell, young Arthur Flowers, Nunez-Harrell, Conner-Bey, Ramona, Carol, McMillan, all the up-and-coming young ones, and then his heart flip-flopped as he saw her, the smiling very lovely one, he once loved, the one he used to call "the Princess of the Black Experience." Surely she would recognize him. She, of the happy darkly shining happy smiling eyes. One of them would surely recognize him. His heart stopped beating, momentarily, as he heard someone call out "JIMMY JAY!" Was it the princess? Was it his imagination?

Standing now at the head of the reception line beside Her Excellency and the rest of his entourage. Belafonte before him now in a warm handshake, staring at him long, intently. "Excuse me, *please*. Your Excellency reminds me so much of a friend of mine. It's really uncanny, I mean, the resemblance. We used to work together."

His (so-called) Excellency smiled and responded shakily, "We all are from the same root source." He sought to temper it with irony and humor. "After all, it's a known fact, all Negroes look alike."

"I'd like to discuss with you a concert tour of your great country, Your Excellency. Perhaps you can spare me a brief moment during the evening."

"Definitely. I should be delighted." He was also greatly relieved.

Could it be that Harry actually did not recognize him? He had done a brief gig with the Belafonte Singers. Harry had sponsored him at the Village Gate. He exuded perspiration now as the famous one continued to stare. But finally said, "Later, Your Excellency." And moved along.

He had been standing in the line almost half an hour when it happened. Suddenly she appeared before him like a figment wrought purely out of the strength of his tremendous wish fulfillment. Debby Bostick had been coming before him off and on in recurring flashes ever since the experience at the Lenox Terrace apartments. All during his sojourn in Lolliloppi she would come before him, night and day, like a welcomed and recurring dream, sleep and wake. And now, when his mind was all at sea and rudderless, all of a sudden, here before him was the dream and beside him the reality. Maria Efwa and Debby Bostick. But who was who and which was which?

"Your Excellency, I wonder if it would be an imposition to ask you for an interview? Just a half an hour of your time before you leave us. I'm just a poor working media slave."

He said, shakily, "I'd love to if I can work it in. Check with my secretary tomorrow morning. I'll tell her to expect your call."

She did an outrageously flamboyant curtsey. "Thank you so very much, Your Excellency."

"That was obviously the one," Maria Efwa whispered, after the media slave had departed.

"The one and only," Jimmy answered, mischievously. "Perhaps," he said hastily, "I should have said, 'the two and only.'"

Maria Efwa said, "Doesn't it get confusing sometimes. Remembering? All those broken hearts you've left behind you."

"Especially when who and which are so very much alike. Beautiful, determined, lovable, faithful, irresistible." Then he added, "Please don't make it more difficult than it has to be. Promise? Please?"

Her Excellency said, "I promise."

He said, "The only way you could keep the promise would be to suddenly become invisible."

The line was breaking up now and she walked rapidly away from him. The rest of the evening was like a continuing existence in fantasia. Music, people, familiar faces, voices, smiling, staring, on the brink of recognition. So many had been friends of his. How could they help knowing who he was? Did a beard make that much difference? He was a nervous piece of wreckage from the fear of recognition.

He was amazed at the number of white folk at the party, especially the women.

"My name is Norma Dingleboffer, Your Excellency. I work for the United States Information Agency."

She had an uncommonly handsome face, wide blue eyes, and skin of burnished ivory, as were her gleaming breasts, which were very much and heavily in evidence showing far below the usual cleavage. One could say accurately she was doubly double-breasted. It was impossible to look her in the face and not be totally aware of their formidable thrust. Indeed, it was the most prominent feature of the slender-waisted woman. She almost seemed afflicted. The kind of tits that came into a room a half a minute before she entered. He started to ask her, were they real? As Jimmy Johnson would have asked her so many experiences ago, it felt like years. But he remembered he was the dignified His Excellency, Prime Minister of the Independent People's Democratic Republic of Guanaya.

He stared down into her face and had to stare away again. Her décolletage extended downward to her navel almost. He said, "And is that why you're here tonight? Are you gathering information for the Agency?"

"Indeed no," she assured him. "I'm gathering information for myself. For example, what do you do when you're not ministering primely? I'm an Africanist. I'm making an empirical study of folkways and mores of the African male. I'm an anthropologist. My specialty is the African male. What are his intellectual drives? What are his sexual drives? I believe absolutely in the efficacy of experimentation. I'll go to any lengths to discover and uncover." She was rambling now like a truck out of control, breathing deeply, downhill all the way then uphill again. Her bust was thrusting at him, threatening. And he actually felt threatened. She had obviously imbibed heavily.

"Let us go somewhere in this palace so that we can experiment."

He said, "Lady! I *am* the guest of honor."

He remembered being pulled away by another fantasy of his wish fulfillment. "Come, Your Excellency. There is someone here whom you must meet." Debby Bostick turned to the empirical anthropologist. "Please excuse us."

"That bitch pulls that shit every time she gets a chance," Debby Bostick hissed. "Come now," she said, "we have things we must discuss, and it isn't anthropological. Here, over here in this little alcove, Jimmy Jay, Your Excellency."

The alcove was so constructed that they could almost be hidden from the view of the hundreds of other guests. "You must have reconnoitered the joint ahead of time," Jimmy Jay observed. They sat on the softly cushioned ledges of the alcove opposite one another.

"The interview?"

She said, "Well, I finally met my rival face-to-face. Her Excellency is beautiful. Undoubtedly a formidable adversary."

He said, without thinking, "So now you see the problem."

She said, "So what's it going to be, you coldhearted sonofabitch? I suppose what happened the other night at Lenox Terrace meant nothing at all to you."

He said, "That was not of my own making. You—"

She said, "I suppose you've checked Her Excellency out, and now you're making up your mind. How do I rate in comparison with her, I mean, beneath the sheets?"

He was slowly definitely getting pissed. "You know I really have no basis for comparison. I've never shared Her Excellency's bed."

"Please," she said, sarcastically. "You're talking to me, Debby Bostick. I've known you almost all my life. Remember?"

"I'm talking to you and I'm telling you I have not been to bed with Her Excellency, although I don't see how it's any of your goddamn business. Her Excellency is a—"

"A lady," Debby Bostick finished for him. "She is a woman, just like any other woman. She pees, just like every other human being. And she doesn't piss Scotch and soda."

"Her Excellency doesn't know I exist, romantically. I tell you, she's a very loyally married woman. I've never gotten out of line with her."

"So, what's the problem? As if I actually believed your mouth is a prayer book."

"The problem is—me. I know that I love her, and I don't know whether or not it's because she reminds me of you."

"Have you made up your mind? Are you going to stay in Guanaya, hanging around her like a sick cow? Somehow that doesn't fit my picture of you. Am I supposed to believe that you're going back to Guanaya and hang around like a young sick calf, waiting forever for whatever?"

He looked away and up into the face of Her Excellency Maria Efwa. She reached a slender hand out to him. "Come now, the banquet's about to begin, and you're expected to make a speech." She took him by the hand to lead him away. She turned back to Debby Bostick. "Please excuse us. I'm sure there'll be time for your interview. Somehow he'll be able to work it in."

Debby was speechless momentarily. She mumbled, "Thank you very much." The one thing she was certain of was—Her Excellency was aware of His (so-called) Excellency's existence, romantically and otherwise.

Another thing was clear, when the Malagans gave a party, they really did it.

Meanwhile Maria Efwa was speaking with His (so-called) Excellency in an almost scolding tone of voice. "You can't afford to give all of your time to one person, especially at an affair like this. You're the guest of honor."

He had to fight to control the smile struggling to dominate his face. His whole heart felt like laughing hysterically. Could one so humbly born as James Jay Leander Johnson dare to think that Her Excellency could possibly be jealous regarding him and Miss Debby Bostick? "Should I dare to have the slightest hope that Her Excellency is jealous?"

"Everyone has a right to hope and fantasize to his heart's content. It's a constitutional right in the Independent People's Democratic Republic."

He spoke rapidly. "In my blessed fantasy, you and I are lovers. We fall madly in love. Nothing else matters.

If King Edward could give up the British crown for his lady love, can humble Jimmy Jay do any less in manifestation of his love for the most beautiful woman on this earth?"

They reached the head of the long rectangular table, overloaded now with delicacies of every kind and ethnicity. He had overheard a couple of old Englishmen talking earlier. "By Jove," one said to the other, "the bloody Blacks really know how to give a bash."

"Well," Her Excellency said, "here we are. Your Excellency, may I have the honor of introducing you to the president of Malaga." The two African heads of state embraced one another and kissed each other's cheeks. "A pleasure I have looked forward to for the longest time."

The tall regal though elderly president of Malaga stepped back and looked at the bogus PM admiringly. "The very spitting image of your father, as they say here in America."

All along the line of tables a chant had begun. "Jaja! Jaja! Long live Jaja!"

President Bakadou El Salvadou held both hands up for silence. The chanting ultimately subsided. The president said, "His Excellency will speak to us briefly, but first things first. Let us first taste of this legendary cuisine, which even a hundred years of British colonialism could not corrupt."

His (so-called) Excellency lifted his glass. "Long live Malagan culinary distinction!" And fell back into the chair at the head of the table amid round after round of cheering and applause.

"Hear! Hear! Hyah! Hyah!"

"Right on! Right on!"

He was quietly getting inebriated. Tables were piled high with African delicacies, British, French, Italian, Guanayan, and especially Malagan. All the while in the midst of the bedlam he was thinking, If both Maria and Debby love me, I must really be worthwhile. Beautiful, devious Debby, with a mind as sharp as a guillotine and equally as quick, and as deadly. Lovely, majestic Maria Efwa, Her undisputed Excellency, with a quiet saber-sharp all-encompassing intelligence. If they both loved him—well. It came to him now that it was not just their physical loveliness that bewitched him; it was the beauty of their intelligence that kept him off balance. Whereas Debby B. was glib, Maria Efwa was articulate. Debby was dazzlingly brilliant; Maria Efwa was quietly profound, self-assured! Hers was a blessed assurance. "It doesn't matter whether or not I'm His Excellency or just plain old Jimmy Jay from 'Sippi." They loved him for himself alone, he hoped. For some reason, the image of Jesse Jackson came to mind. He felt like getting up and shouting to them all, "*I am somebody!*" But he hadn't had that much to drink. He sat there eating now with Maria Efwa on one side of him and the president of Malaga on the other. What would he say to them in his speech? Now he was mumbling to himself, "I may be Black, I may be born in Missi-damn-sippi, I may be Jimmy Jay Leander Johnson, I may not be the Prime Minister of Guanaya, but *I am somebody!*" Perhaps that was the profounder lesson to be learned from this entire charade, that everybody is somebody.

Maria kept her large darkening worried eyes on him. What was he mumbling about? Almost an hour had passed since they sat down to eat. The chanting had begun again.

"Jaja! Jaja! Long live Jaja!" . . ."Jaja! Jaja! Long they live Jaja!" And now the Black Americans had picked up their version of the chant.

"We want Jaja!". . . . "We want Jaja!" . . . "We want Jaja!"

He thought, perhaps they wanted him for their dinner.

President El Salvadou rose in his melon-colored princely robe and raised his hands for quiet. And when quiet was maintained, he quietly introduced the man of the hour, His Excellency Jaja Okwu Olivamaki.

His (so-called) Excellency rose and moved labori-ously to the podium, as an almost ominous silence settled upon the audience. It seemed he could not hear a glass clink or a knife or fork or spoon or a piece of china come in contact with each other. He stared out over the crowd, and the first face he saw at a table to the side was that of the cigar-smoking mogul from Hollywood. Seated right beside Cigar Smoker was his buddy Carlton Carson of the good old SS corps. A premonition created a nest of hornets in his stomach. His eyes wandered nervously around the room. He saw a lovely young woman disguised as Her Excellency who sat there within arm's reach of him. Debby's dark face was so beautifully intent, it almost caused his eyes to tear. She was weepingly beautiful. Their eyes met, held, remembered, then his own eyes moved along back again to Cigar Smoker and Carlton Carson. He knew that Carlton Carson was still in constant contact with the old man who had yelled "Jimmy" out at the 'Sippi airport and had been incarcerated temporarily. But what did he have in common with big Hollywood Cigar Smoker?

Someone passed a note up to him. He glanced at it briefly, frowning, and he made a swift decision. He reached for his vodka and tonic, took another drink, took the paper his speech was written on out of the pocket of his boubou and tore it up into shreds, deliberately, and let it fall floatingly from his hands onto the podium, scattering like falling snowflakes.

"Mister President, Madame El Salvadou, His and Her Excellencies, distinguished guests, and I believe that all of you and each of you are just as distinguished as the other. I had prepared a written speech, but tonight I have decided to speak to you from my heart." He was staring now directly at Hollywood Cigar Smoker. He held the note he'd just received up before them. "But more about this later." He cleared his throat and took another drink. He looked around at the working crews of television networks. He was on nationwide television. *Live!*

"Sisters and brothers, I wish to address my brief remarks here tonight to the American people, but most especially to those truly great American people of African descent." His remarks were greeted by applause. "As you know we have just completed an invasion of Lolliloppi, Mississippi. So many people tried to persuade us not to make the trip, feared for our safety. Even your President Hubert Herbert Hubert advised us not to take the trip. But stubbornly we refused to be dissuaded. We went, we saw, we conquered. We invaded them with brotherhood and sisterhood. Assaulted them with African humanity, bombed them with civilized civility, redundantly, continuously. And we found they were a bunch of paper tigers." He had to wait several minutes for the applause to die away, the stomping, whistling, cheering, hand clapping. "I'm reminded of a story I read in one of Brother Killens's novels. It seems that way back yonder in 1954, the Supreme Court of the USA handed down a mischievous decision outlawing segregation in the public schools of America. *Brown versus the Board of Education.* When a brother deep deep in the cotton on a Mississippi plantation heard about the Supreme Court decision, he didn't stop running till he reached the Big House." He paused, as the audience laughed in anticipation. "You know, of course, I'm a student of Dixicana. I have my PhD in Dixicology and Afro-American folklore. Anyhow, when old Jesse heard the news he ran toward the Big House. He usually always went around the back as was the custom in those good old days, when Negroes were happy with plenty of nothing and nothing was plenty for them and all the so-called darkies was a-weeping when Old Massa got the cold cold ground that was coming to him. But this time old Jesse started directly across the front yard where Mister Charlie and Miss Anne were seated à la Willie Faulkner and Tennessee Williams beneath electric fans hanging from the ceiling on the front porch. It was one of those hot spring days in Mississippi. Mister Charlie said, 'What's the matter with you Jesse boy, running like that in all this heat?' He considered Jesse to be one of his truly good friends, one of the hardest-working cotton-picking cotton choppers in that part of the state, or in any other parts. Jesse shouted, 'The Supreme Court done spoke! The Supreme Court done spoke! Ain't going around to the back door anymore. Coming right straight up to the front door from now on.'

"Mister Charlie said, 'What you say, boy?' Jesse turned to Miss Anne sitting there with her mouth agape. 'That's another thing. Ain't no more calling you Missy Anne. You just plain old common Annie from here on in.' Mister Charlie lost his cool, which was a rare occurrence with him. Against his will he heard himself shout to his best Black faithful friend Jesse, 'Nigger, don't you know you're in Mississippi?' Jesse shouted back, 'That's another thing. Ain't no more Mississippi. Ain't no more Mississippi. It's just 'Sippi from now on!'" After the laughter and the applauding died away, His (so-called) Excellency assured them, "But don't you worry, we are not deceived by that rare display of sisterhood and brotherhood, but, hopefully, a little taste of freedom will go a long way. One thing is sure. It ain't no Mississippi. It's just 'Sippi from now on.

"Getting this note a few minutes before I began speaking sort of gave to me a new perspective on what I would speak to you about tonight, other than to tell you that we Africans think you Afro-American-and-Caribbeans are some of the greatest people on this earth.

"And thus, I am reminded of a story told me by my friend Professor Samuel Yette." He looked out over the audience. "I believe I saw him here tonight over there with John O. Killens. He told me the story of the preacher who had lost his bicycle, and against his will he was forced to conclude that one of his congregation had liberated it. Another preacher advised him, 'If you really feel that way about it, why don't you preach on the Ten Commandments next Sunday, and when you come to the part about thou shalt not steal, perhaps the brother's conscience will be stricken, and he'll put your bicycle back unnoticed.' The aggrieved preacher thought it was a good idea. A week later, the other preacher saw him riding his bicycle. 'Well,' the other preacher said, 'I can see that suggestion worked.' The preacher on the bike said, 'Well, yes and no.' . . . 'Why what do you mean? You obviously have your bicycle back.' 'Well, but you see it was like this, I started out with the Ten Commandments, but by the time I got to the part that said thou shalt not commit adultery, I remembered where I'd left my bicycle.'"

He paused until the laughter had subsided. "It just goes to show you how a word or note or something can put you back on the right track, can give to you a clearer perspective. Like this note here from a Hollywood bigshot that reads, 'Every man on earth has his price, Excellency, and we think we know what yours is. May we have breakfast with you on tomorrow?'"

He tore the paper slowly into shreds. Then he told them about the Hollywood offer that orbited up to $35 million, which he had rejected. There were gasps throughout the audience. He stared out toward them, until his eyes locked with Hollywood Cigar Smoker.

"Listen to me, Hollywood and all of corporate America. There will be no breakfast with you on tomorrow. You could never meet my price. My price is the liberation of First World people throughout this earth, including especially the people of 'Sippi and South Africa and the Caribbean and Central America, South America, the oppressed wherever they may find themselves. Hollywood, can you pay the price? Can you give me freedom for Ireland, the Lebanese? Will you remake *Gandhi* and *The Grapes of Wrath*? Will you make *Youngblood* and *And Then We Heard the Thunder*? *A Measure of Time*? *The Man Who Cried I Am*? *Go Tell It On the Mountain*? Will you do the lives of King and Malcolm? and Fannie Lou and Rosa Parks? No! Liberation can be achieved only through struggle. Frederick Douglass understood this, as did Old John Brown of Kansas. And Chaka and Fidel. Our great Black ancestors understood this fundamentally, those Black and unknown bards of long ago,

when they sang" (and he began to sing in strong and lusty baritone, a cappella, with his hand up to his ear, à la Robeson).

My old master promised me—
Raise the ruckus tonight,
When he died he'd set me free,
Raise the ruckus tonight.
He lived so long, his head got bald,
Raise the ruckus tonight.
He got out of notion of dying at all.
We'll raise the ruckus tonight.

In the midst of his singing, he realized he was giving himself away. Surely Belafonte would recognize him now, and many many others who had heard him at the Gate and other places in the Apple. But somehow he couldn't stop. His voice became even bolder and more robust than ever. He challenged. "Everybody join in the singing. You know the song. It's from your great ancestors:

Get on board, little children get on board,
While the moon is shining bright.
Get on board, down the river road,
We're gonna raise the ruckus tonight!

They repeated the chorus over and over again. They sang till they were exhausted, and he fell back in his chair, breathing heavily, almost entirely out of breath. They were standing on their feet now, cheering madly, old, and young, prissy ones, bigshots, dignitaries, muck-th-mucks, and everybody. Even the Big Time Cigar Smoker from Hollywood. Even Carlton Carson of the Secret Service.

Jimmy Jay got to his feet again and held up both hands to them for silence, and quietude ultimately descended. "I just want to say a few more words to you, to all of you. In the words of the Duke of Ellington, I think you're beautiful, you're wonderful, and I really do love you madly!" He'd given himself away again.

He sat down again and got up almost immediately. He was ready to leave. He was flying high and not from alcohol, he thought, but high on love. He was surrounded now by Guanayan and American SS persons and some from the Black Alliance who had been with him in 'Sippi. The NYPD were clearing the way. He would not let these good feelings give him a premonition of negative forebodings. Somehow Belafonte got through to him and embraced him and whispered to him, hoarsely, "Jimmy Jay! Jimmy Jay! All the way with Jimmy Jay! I thought all along the resemblance was uncanny. But after the singing, there

was no question about it. No matter, I still want to come to Guanaya for the concert tour. Talk with you before you leave, baby, I mean, Your Excellency?" Jimmy Jay saw Debby Bostick trying to get to him, unsuccessfully. He called out, "Let her through. Let the lovely lady through!"

She was escorted to him and she went into his arms. She murmured, "Oh I love you. Yes, I love you, you sonuvabitch! Love you love you love you!" He hugged and he kissed her. He whispered, "We have an interview for tomorrow. Call me early."

They were alone now in the back of the long black limo, heading toward the lights of the city. The high-beamed lights were burning big holes in the blackness of the night. Her Excellency was nestled in his arms. "I love you too," she told him. He said, happily, pleased with himself, apprehensively, remembering the time-old proverb that PRIDE COMES BEFORE A FALL. "Now now, you made a promise you would not make it difficult for the two of us. You do remember?" he asked teasingly. Half-serious, even sincere, almost, at least, perhaps. The tension building, ever building. His thighs began to quake and tingle. He, the "Cool One," more nonchalant than Horace White-stick. The essence of sophistication.

She said, "I don't mean that kind of love. My love for you is neither physical nor romantic. It's the kind of love that all the people have for you. I love your sensitivity, your superior intelligence, your wit, your zest for life, your daring, your—"

He was so high and happy he could have shouted aloud for all the world to hear. He was afraid to feel so joyful. Was it a bad omen? He muffled his voice. He said, "Oh shut up your blasted babbling." And took her deeper into his arms and kissed her on her pliant lips profoundly, and he thought hopefully that she kissed him back, profoundly. The entire affair was shocking, to say the very very least.

Later, back at the Waldorf, with the world locked out of their lives, they all relived the party, reveling in its grandeur and audacity.

"You were magnificent, Your Excellency," His Wife's Bottom told him ecstatically. HWB was beginning to believe that Jimmy Jay really was His Excellency the Prime Minister of Guanaya.

"You were out of sight!" Barra Abingiba slapped his palm.

Even Foreign Minister Tangi grudgingly conceded, "You were indeed magnificent, Jimmy, although there were a few anxious moments. Nevertheless, you were great. I'd say you were actually profound."

Maria Efwa smiled happily up into his face, as she bounced a glass of wine up against his glass of vodka and tonic. She was in a strange and dangerous mood, and he picked up the strong bizarre vibrations. She said, "They all loved you madly, and I love you madly too."

He laughed nervously. "Which leaves me speechless and in an awesome state of trepidation." Jimmy Jay was serious.

They drank far into the evening, toasting this, that, and the other, especially themselves. Until Mamadou Tangi said, "Well, I think we've done enough tippling, for now. We have a rather heavy schedule for tomorrow. And you, Sire, and Her Excellency have your speech to prepare for the United Nations General Assembly."

"You are absolutely right, Your Esteemed Excellency," Jimmy Jay responded, jestingly. And bowed flamboyantly and took Maria Efwa by the hand and guided her down the corridor to her bedroom, after she had bid them all goodnight. Now they stood at her bedroom door as she fumbled in her pocketbook for her key. The vibes here now were devastating, overwhelming. She found the key and reached it to him, her slender hand atremble, a gesture so unlike this very

very independent woman. "Kind Sir." She curtseyed. His hand trembled as he took the key.

"Perhaps, for a brief moment, a cup of tea or coffee before we say goodnight? I mean, to unwind ourselves?" she suggested. They were in her bedroom now.

Jimmy Jay said, "Parting is such sweet sorrow." Then he said gruffly, in a trembly voice, "We're making it very difficult for ourselves."

Unexpectedly she said, "Yes! Yes! Jimmy! Jimmy! Jimmy Jay! How I do love to say that name!"

He took her into his arms and his mouth sought her mouth feverishly, when suddenly she froze, her entire body going rigid, even as she shivered. It was as if he made love to a mannikin in Macy's window on a wintry evening. He thought, at first, he'd apologize and beat a swift retreat. He was that awesomely respectful of her. But his wanting for her was too strong and swept away before it all manner of resistance. He kissed her cheeks, her nose, her chin, her eyes. He sought desperately her lips again. But at first she kept her even alabaster teeth fiercely clenched, then slowly she opened her ample rich curvaceous mouth to receive the almost violent thrusting of his eager tongue, as her own tongue withdrew from the conflict, darting from side to side in an attitude of unrelenting self-defense. But too late were her defenses, and finally her inexperienced tongue reached

out to be caressed by his. It was like an Indian wrestling match, in which neither wished to be the winner,
or both, perhaps, it didn't matter. He felt his hardness
growing, pulsating up against the throbbing middle of
her. He was ashamed of himself. Actually. Truthfully.
Abashed with guilt was Jimmy Jay, as if he took advantage of an innocent and nubile maiden.

She shouted softly, "Please, Jimmy. Jimmy! Jimmy!
I cannot handle this. I am a faithful married woman.
Please leave me now or I shall scream for help. I mean it!"

It was all as if she'd said, "Undress me, Jimmy! Please
undress me!" As he fumbled at the buttons in the back
of her dress. She beat both fists against his palpitating
chest and shoulders.

"Damn you, Jimmy! Damn you!" It was the sweetest strangest case of déjà vu he had ever in his life
experienced. He somehow knew all along she would
say, "Damn you, Jimmy! Damn you!" Then finally
she would unloose the collar of his boubou, and that
they would undress each other. Ultimately, they would
stand facing one another, and her loveliness and majesty would take his breath away. She was a work of art,
a breathing piece of African sculpture, of ebony come
alive and glowing.

He looked away and stared at her in full-length
profile in a floor-to-ceiling mirror. Her long slender

roundish legs, her shapely buttocks reaching high up on her back and beamingly curvaceous, so slimly roundly and divinely formed, and as tight and tender-looking as a brand-new baby's backside. Her rounded fulsome glowing ebony breasts with red burgundish undertones and overtones, so sweetly and blackthornly nippled. And all that formidable intelligence housed in such devastatingly stunning architecture. Maria Efwa was an incredible creation. He thought the African Gods must have looked upon her and smiled and said, "That's good!" That is damn near perfection.

Somehow, he knew he would take her up in his happy arms and lay her, trembling, down beneath the sheets. He knew the bed would be four-poster. She was naked in his arms now, as he had known and even dreamed of, and he'd known that it would be as if he'd never made love before. A rookie and an amateur. All else had been screwing, fucking, fornicating, but this was making love, a holy thing of inspiration. It would inspire in him an articulateness that he never knew existed. As if his tongue had been divinely lubricated. It was as if the African princess-goddess inspired him clear out of his element. Between her legs she twitched and throbbed. It had never been like this before. Her toes were tingling. She was tightly wet between her thighs, as she felt a sweet and undeniable love potion pouring magically from the middle of her. Her body glowing with excitement, which she fought against, in vain, even now at this final moment. Cool, slim, aloof; it was as if she had waited since remembered time for him to light her candle. To pour fuel into her lonely lamp. Stirring the hot flames of her sleeping passion.

Penetrating her was deliciously difficult. At each thrust, back and forth, like he was out of his mind, he began to murmur, as if he were suddenly possessed with tongues, religiously Jujued was Jimmy Jay. Again, he felt he was on automatic pilot now, as the words poured forth from him effortlessly. "Dear African princess, you are the River Nile, in its passionate and compassionate journey from Lake Victoria down north past Khartoum past the ruins of ancient Thebes past Cairo all the way to the Mediterranean. You are the Niger making its way back from deep in the delta at Bonny on the Gulf of Guinea past the mangroves making its torturous way back up past Onitsha past Bamako and Segu all the way to the nearby south of Timbuktu and beyond. You are the loveless Transvaal of South Africa. You are the subtle sleepy Congo. Your deep dark sultry eyes have known the loneliness of the Bedouin in his desert tent. Your sloe-shaped soulful brilliant eyes have laughed, your lovely eyes have cried. You are the majesty of Mount Kenya. You are the chill of early desert mornings. You are the heat of midday Timbuktu. You are Africa incarnate, and I love you as I have never loved another. I love your physical you, your spiritual and your intellectual you. Nor is it possible that any human being could ever know a greater or a profounder love."

All the while the thrust continued. Now gentle were the thrusts, serene relaxed, then quick excited, almost violent, as if they were the last ones on this planet earth. The little sucking sounds of tender thrusting now, in and out of her vulva, he thought, were like the faint and gentle slapping of ocean waves, eternally, against a distant shore. He looked into her lovely face, so beautiful with knowing, yet with innocence aglow, now suddenly a mask of tender seriousness; an overwhelming sincerity suffusing her sweet face, enhancing its beauty beyond the borders of imagination.

Reaching now, desperately, toward the final conflict, when recklessly they went for broke and for life's sweetest treasures, as he felt a growing quaking in each of their bodies, and saw her dark head shake from side to side, now the quaking came in spasm, quick and rhythmic spasms, like the countdown at Cape Kennedy, and now there was no rhyme or reason. There was only love's impassioned reaching for the crisis and the climax, the highest peak in all this earth, and ultimately the Great Blast Off, as they both fell from the earth, launched into infinite space, floating weightless and serene. Oh! If they could just drift out there forever and never come back down to earth.

She lay there biting at her fist, apparently to keep from screaming. As tardily she sought reconciliation. Belatedly she sought atonement, desperately.

"Oh, my husband, please forgive me! Dear God, I had no control over this whatever, this sin I have committed against you, my great and wonderful husband." And deeper was the guilt because she could not really feel regretful. "It was the happiest most beautiful moment on this earth for me!"

He, who was an arrogant and self-proclaimed agnostic, perhaps even atheistic, a skeptic and a cynic, Second Coming Doubting Thomas, a backslider, an unbeliever, and an infidel, felt now an overwhelming moment of sacredness, a washing away of all skepticism and cynicism. He thought he now believed in saints, angels, and miracles divinely wrought. And what had he done to deserve such a blessed visitation, revelation? He lay there thinking, this place, this Waldorf of Astoria, stood alone on holy ground. This room, this bed, this canopied four-poster. He believed, credulously, in the legends of Saint Jeanne d'Arc d'Orleans, Saint Harriet Tubman of the Eastern Shore.

Time stood still for him now. Everything was momentary, ephemeral, and at the same time firmly ensconced in stone like the pyramids. Hours, days, weeks, months, years, centuries, were nonexistent. The millennium was then and now and premature and coming on like hurricanes and eternally forevermore. His heart sang as he thought, Sweet Mystery of Life, at last I found you. At last he knew the secret of it all.

He wanted to tell her that neither was he in control. But to her he whispered huskily, happily, guiltily, overcome with feelings of shame and solemn expiation, all mixed up with joyousness, "Hush! Hush! Hush, my dearest!" It was such a tender moment for him that his eyes began to fill.

As she cried herself to sleep.

27

The next day was work. Like the man said, THE PARTY WAS OVER. A meeting with Belafonte. Mr. B. had called about two thirty before day in the morning, directly following a midnight visit at Mr. B.'s on West End Avenue from crafty Carlton Carson of the US SS, questioning him about the Minister Primarily. "Is or not there a connection between His so-called Excellency and James Jay Leander Johnson of Lolliloppi, Mississippi? Didn't he used to work for you?" . . . "Prime Minister Jaja working for me? Preposterous! You must be kidding." . . . "I saw him talking with you at the party." . . . "His Excellency spoke with lots of people at the party. What does that prove?"

Actually, the job was going to Carson's head. Since assuming his appointment as chief of Secret Service, he had become a man beset with sudden brainstorms, holy-rolly visitations, divine revelations. Crafty Carson suffered greatly from these sudden strokes of genius (as he saw them), with which these days he was often stricken. Giving him sometimes dreadfully painful headaches, which he endured stoically, since he deemed them heavenly endowed. He believed the Good Lord spoke to him through these sudden so-called brainstorms. At these rare and rarified moments, his poor mind could hear the thunder, his brain could feel the sharp-bladed edge of the terribly swift lightning. He thought his brains caught fire sometimes. Also sometimes he blacked out momentarily (whited out?), came back a half a second later and went immediately into action like a robot programmed and motivated by a God-sent brain wave, of which he retained no remembrance. Belafonte said, "The cat has flipped out completely. What did you do to the dude? He was snorting like a dragon. His eyes were leaping like a madman."

His Excellency's interview with Debby Bostick was an exercise in futility and frustration. They simply got nowhere very swiftly. The rest of the time had to be spent with His (so-called) Excellency and Maria Efwa working together on his historic speech at the United Nations, *supposedly.*

All morning long their eyes had avoided one another, as if they had committed some mortal sin together. It was like this during the usual tea-and-crumpet get-together of the delegation to discuss their program for the day. At breakfast they hardly spoke to each other, except to bid a stiff good morning. When she would come into a room, he felt a bulging knot doubling up his stomach like the great knot of his Boy Scout days pulling tighter in the middle from both ends like a great tug-of-war. He swallowed solid his saliva deep into his troubled belly and thought the same knot had reached up into his throat to choke him for his evil ways. He found difficulty breathing. Was this what true love was about? A couple of times he tried deliberately to catch her eye, darkly brilliant, to let her know he suffered too. Which would have made him feel even guiltier if he but understood himself. He was a selfish bastard, he thought, wishing her to share his suffering. Perhaps she understood more profoundly her great impact upon him. For her brown-to-black sloe eyes avoided him as if he were too ghastly an abomination for her to gaze upon. He felt the jaw muscles just beneath his ears pulsating.

The Foreign Minister watched them worriedly.

Ultimately, they got together by themselves, ostensibly to talk about his UN speech. Obviously, he could not make the same speech over and over again, like the one he made at the Armory, or in 'Sippi or the other night in Mount Vernon. Surely, he could not do his singing act at the august United Nations. They talked around the question like boxers sparring for an opening shot at the other's chin, avoided looking into the faces of each other. But it was there between them and it could not be kept eternally at bay. The world had changed for them forever. Everlastingly.

Finally, she blurted out, "What're we going to do?" Like a lone voice in a wilderness of unquiet desperation.

"Well," Himself answered shakily, "we could agree upon a premise and sketch a rough outline, you know, a first draft. Then we could—"

"Oh, you know that's not what I'm referring to. I mean what we did last night." He could tell that she was agonizing. She repeated anguishly, "You know what I'm talking about."

"Yes, I do know what you're talking about." His face burned with guilt and shamefulness. Even as he thought to himself, What in the hell do I have to be ashamed of? If there were guilt or shame, well then, they both must share them equally. So, what was there to talk about? He made himself feel angrier than he actually felt. He forced himself to be indignant.

"It was not a trivial thing with me, Jimmy, I don't

know how you feel, but never before have I been un-faithful to my husband. It goes against everything I— I mean—" she stammered.

"Nor is it trivial with me, Your Excellency. It was just the excitement of the moment. The trip to 'Sippi, the party, the drinking, the euphoria, the celebra-tion, the ambience. Like I say, the excitement of the moment." He even sounded phony to himself. Even his voice to him was fraudulent.

"Don't you 'Your Excellency' me," she said angrily. Then she said, despondently, "Is that all it really meant to you, Jimmy Jay? A moment's excitement?"

"Dear Maria Efwa," he answered in a trembling voice, "it meant everything in the world to me. But what can we do about it? You're married to a human legend, an international institution. You belong to your people. I wish we *could* think only of ourselves. I don't know what I'll do with my life now that all of this is coming to an end. Perhaps I'll go back and be just a jive folk singer at the Club Lido. You're the Minister of In-formation and Education and Culture. You're married to a living legend. Me, I'm nothing. As the great Nat Cole used to sing, THE PARTY IS OVER.

It was so unlike Her Excellency, he thought, who had always held both hands on the controls. It was an essential part of his image of her, which he did not wish to relinquish. He had her always in the driver's seat. The Supreme Navigator. She almost sobbed uncontrollably, "You're everything to me, Jimmy. Don't ever say you're nothing. You're everything I want out of this crazy life. I've watched you grow from a jive folk singer, as you are want to regard yourself, to a man of stature and of daring and of great dignity, even as I felt my heart growing fonder of you day by day, even as I fought against it. And I never knew till last night that making love could be like that. Making love. Now I understand the metaphor."

"Maria Efwa, I swear to you, I've never made love before last night. All else before was fornicating. Last night we made love *with* each other. There is nothing I'd want more than anything else than to spend the rest of my life with you, but you're so much greater than that. You're not only the most beautiful woman on this earth. You're a spiritual and intellectual happening that comes once in a lifetime, perhaps once in a century. You're a colossus, you rank up there with the pyramids, the Temple of Artemis at Ephesus, the lighthouse at Alexandria. You're the eighth wonder of the world. You're the grandeur of the Sphinx. You're the Great Wall of the Chinese people. You're—" He thought, where were the words coming from that were pouring from him like the rapids in their overflow, Niagara Falls? Words he had never known before. Had he been bewitched? Or was he suddenly possessed? Or had he been inspired? Of one thing he was sure. She brought out the very most in him. Like a maestro who wrought music from an ordinary instrument, a music unparalleled up to the very moment.

She said, unheedingly, "I never dreamed it could be like this. That I could love two men at the same time. Because I do love my husband. I respect him. I adore him. I revere him. You could even say I worship him. But there's a different kind of love I have for you. And I need the love I have for you." She sobbed. "And I despise the love I have for you." She shook her lovely head in anguish. "No, I don't. I'm glad I love you. I need to love you terribly. And it makes me feel like a trollop, because I can't help feeling what I feel for you. It's like a terminal disease."

His eyes began to fill, with tears of joyousness and sorrow. His face, all through his shoulders, over-flowed with a great gladness that such a lovely great one loved him in all his unworthiness. The bogus Minister Primarily, the dude from Lolliloppi. At the same time, he was overcome with a deepening dis-tress that their love must come to naught but frustra-tion and unhappiness. He tried desperately to speak calmly to her. "Dearest Maria, if there ever were such

things as angels, you would certainly more than qual-
ify. Don't you ever call yourself a trollop." Then his
voice hardened. "And now we'd better get down to
the immediate question of the United Nations speech.
We'll discuss this question later on."

Later that night, led by Maria Efwa, the entire group
discussed the thrust of his speech in detail. Foreign
Minister Tangi raised some crucial points, as did His
Wife's (inevitable) Bottom, but on the whole, they
agreed upon the premise and the thrust, as proposed by
Maria Efwa. Then they discussed the future of Jimmy
Jay Leander Johnson, *aka* His Excellency, so-called
prime minister of the Independent People's Democratic
Republic of Guanaya. After kicking the question back
and forth as if he weren't present (he felt like Ellison's
INVISIBLE MAN), the suggestion was made by Her
Excellency Maria Efwa and agreed heartily upon by
the rest of the cabinet, that Jimmy Jay be appointed the
co-chairman of the Ministry of Information and Education and Culture, sharing the responsibilities (the creative and artistic aspects, books, films, radio, TV, etc.)
of the office with Her Excellency. At which point the
phone rang with the information (in Hausa code language, triply encrypted), that the real Prime Minister
Jaja had just flown in to Kennedy under heavy security

and secrecy and would be arriving at the hotel within the hour. He would speak for himself at the UN. THE MASQUERADE WAS TRULY OVER.

It seemed that all along they had hoped that the real Jaja would be able to make his own appearance before the United Nations, but had not mentioned it to Jimmy Jay in case it had not proved to be possible. But all subversive problems had been cleared up on the home front. There was no further need for the bogus Minister Primarily.

Things were happening much too quickly for Himself. Like the brightness of noonday in Bamakanougou just before a tropical storm. The sun is shining dazzlingly bright. Blazing, blinding. Then suddenly raindrops begin to fall down through the sunbeams. Back home in 'Sippi, they used to say the devil was whipping his wife. And if you put your ear to a seashell you could hear her weeping. Back in Bama in Guanaya the thunder rumbles from afar, the lightning flashes, and suddenly a torrential downpour, without warning.

Jimmy did not know how he felt now that the great charade had ended. He had taken off his beard forever. All during the following days he glanced secretly in the mirror, every time he passed one, and nobody was looking. He didn't recognize himself. The transition had occurred too swiftly. The man, the real Jaja, had come in looking good and hale and hardy, and especially he looked ready. Perhaps a little weary in the eyes. He thanked Jimmy Jay properly and profusely. But it was clear that now he was ready to take charge. TCB. The meetings with the President, the 'Sippi trip, the party in Mount Vernon, the love night with Maria Efwa, the return of the real Jaja. Quick. Quick. Quick Quick. Decisions to be made. New positions to assume. Himself *had* to talk with Her Excellency. So much to say, so little time, the way things were.

Jimmy told her the next morning, within the hearing of the others of the delegation, "We have to discuss this co-chairpersonship." But they knew why they had to talk, alone. Their excuse to the cabinet was that they had to go more fully into the question of co-chairpersonship, the pros and cons, the significance of such a transition, the implications, alone at breakfast.

They were seated downstairs at the Waldorf in one of the several breakfast rooms. "Well, what's it going to be?" she asked him. "We can't go on like this, pretending that it didn't happen."

He said, "I don't understand."

"If I go back to him, of course you know I'll have to tell him," she said.

"What do you mean, *if* you go back?"

"How can I look him in the face and say, 'My husband, I'm in love with another man'? 'I've made love with another man'?"

His heart beat stethoscopic thunder in his frowning forehead. He repeated, "What do you mean, *if* you go back?"

"After the other night, after all this time with you, it seems like years, the length of time we've been together. Things can never be like they used to be. I can't live a lie with my husband. He's too good a man. Do you know he gave up the practice of polygamy just for me? He went against a national tradition just for me. My husband is a saint."

He stared into her anguished eyes and looked away again. He could not stand the agonizing torture in the dark eyes, the mesmerizing color of smoky topaz, that had become so dear to him. He wanted them always to be happy eyes. And he blamed himself for her agonizing. He said, sadly, "Your husband is a saint. And his wife is an angel. I thought we had settled that already."

She stared him in the face unflinchingly. "Do you wish to marry me, or don't you?" She had not meant the words to come from her in this kind of juxtaposition. She had only meant to ask him if he truly loved her.

He was in temporary shock. His face and shoulders were aflame. "You haven't thought this through thoroughly, Your Excellency. You're already married."

She said, "What do you think caused these sleepless nights? These red eyes?" She paused. She plunged headlong into the quicksand. She didn't want to stop to think. She demanded, "Yes or no?"

Jimmy Jay said, "I want you more than I want my own life, but obviously, you have not weighed the consequences."

She stared at him. She shook her head, almost as if she sorrowed for him his enormous ignorance, his colossal lack of understanding. "Do you think it just began for me the other night?"

"I didn't know," he stammered. "I-I-I didn't dare to hope, or even dream. I thought, I hoped. It was driving me crazy. I couldn't sleep either."

"Well now you know," she said. "Now you dare. What's it going to be? Just how daring are you, Jimmy Jay?"

He thought his ears must be deceiving him. "Are you sure? I don't understand. You're like a different person. The big decision's up to you. You're a leader in your country, a legend in your own time. So is your husband. I've seen how your people look upon you. They adore you. They look up to you. Of course, I'd love to marry you. But, how can we? I mean, you also love your husband. You just said so."

A single tear spilled from a bright and darkening eye. "I have wrestled with that question for a long time, almost ever since I met you, and watched your growing and your change. And you never lost your sense of humor. You never took yourself more seriously than you took the crazy job that we imposed upon you. I thought you were a jive chicken, I mean turkey, as you say in your country. But I realize now, you have no idea of how great you are. It isn't just the way you look, your physical beauty. You're much much more than that." The tears were spilling freely now. "I do love my husband." She took a handkerchief from her pocketbook. She wiped her eyes and blew her nose. "I respect him. I revere him. I worship him. But my love for you is different. I am *in* love with you, excitedly, turbulently. I love you and I'm glad I love you. I love to hear me say I love you. With my husband our love is calm. It is the great gift of peace and serenity. He is a haven in a time of stress. With you, I never knew such excitement existed, or was possible. My husband is like a lighthouse in a tropical storm at sea. You are the storm itself. I want the storm, Jimmy Jay. I want the tempest. I want the thunder and the lightning."

"My husband" . . . "My husband," he thought, as

he stared into her anguished face, wondering to himself why it was that most women, even great ones like Maria, hang on so desperately to that which no longer existed. The myth of holy matrimony, inviolate and inviolable, eternally. Why did she continue this charade with this human antiquity? Was it respectability? She had loads of it. Certainly it was not for security or protection that she could not let go. She was an independent woman, economically, intellectually. So why not psychologically? Why did "*My husband*" have such a powerful hold on a woman like Her Excellency? Father image? True, he was old enough to be her father, "My husband" was, but she had a father of her own. She had never wanted for affection or protection. Was "My husband" a status symbol, a fashionable adornment, a woman felt naked if divorced or dispossessed of? Was it like the ownership of a television set that once was a luxury but had now become an absolute necessity like food, clothing, and shelter? He thought, what was it with womenfolks?

Breakfast was extending irresistibly toward lunchtime. The waiters were politely clearing the tables and their throats, readying the dimly lighted dining room for a lunchtime clientele. He was aware that one of the waiters stood unusually close to their table, as if to overhear their conversation. They were the only couple left.

Her Excellency invaded his sorrowful stream of consciousness, heatedly. "I'm tired of being a legend, tired of being dignified and proper," she stated. "I'm sick and tired of living up to other people's image of me. I want to be me. Right now, I don't know who I am. I want to live, Jimmy Jay. And I want to live with you." He caught the waiter staring directly into his mouth as if he wanted to do some fancy lipreading. Jimmy Jay stared back.

Jimmy Jay said quietly, tremulously, "I love you. I'm in love with you. And I want to do what you want to do, wherever such a commitment takes me. But you must do some heavy thinking."

The cadence of the happenings quickened even further. Jaja had prepared his speech in flight. Now they discussed what was to become of Jimmy Jay as if he had no actual existence. Ellison's Invisible Man again. He thought indignantly, what if he didn't want to co-chair the Ministry of Information and Education and Culture? What if he wanted just to go back to his job singing at the Lido? What if he preferred to remain here in the States? They didn't really require his service any longer.

The stewards were busily packing and preparing for their departure back to the old "countree." He seemed again to be living through a dream sequence, as he watched the real Prime Minister move about the quarters as if he had been there all the while. Jimmy felt left out. *Perdido.* He felt like there should be some recognition that he still existed.

All through the night before he had heard them arguing back and forth from his isolated room the great debate about the PM's speech and the cobanium. They went at each other hot and heavy. He even heard Maria Efwa's voice raised in anger. He thought, the least they could have done, in recognition of his contribution, was to call him in and seek his counsel. But they never called. Not even Maria Efwa called. And that was more than hurtful. He had played his role successfully. With dignity. It was as if they no longer considered him a Guanayan, or even an African for that matter. He was getting pissed off. Moment by moment. With all the activity around him, he felt like he was in the way. Excess baggage. A supernumerary. Perhaps most of all he was losing Maria Efwa.

Now they sat together there this morning ignoring him, discussing the essentials of the United Nations speech. And he was losing Maria Efwa. That was the greatest loss of all.

Sensitive Maria Efwa could feel Jimmy Jay's growing resentment, his angered indignation. She looked at him and said to Jaja, "You really do have something to live up to, cousin. James Jay Leander Johnson has made a tremendous impression on behalf of the people of our country. He has truly been magnificent."

Jaja looked around at Jimmy, as if he had just become aware of his existence. Jimmy felt like he imagined a french poodle must feel when being admired, having just left the doggie beauty parlor. Jaja said, "I'm well aware of his contribution." The real PM came over to Jimmy Jay as if he were about to stroke the gleaming luster on his fur. If he'd had a tail, he would have wagged it. The real Jaja took the fake PM's hand in a warm handshake. Jimmy stood up for the gentleman. And they embraced each other cheeks to cheeks. "I'm aware that we owe you a debt of profound gratitude. And we will find a way of expressing it to you some time soon. Perhaps the co-chairpersonship?"

Jimmy Jay said, "It was really nothing at all." He had never known how to accept extravagant praise even for a job well done. He'd always been essentially a shy person. But he'd learned to disguise his reticence with extravagant bravado.

28

Meanwhile Brainstorm Carson of the US SS was getting his act together. Carefully putting the pieces of the puzzle into place. He'd made a couple of trips back to 'Sippi and had finally gotten it out of the old man in the cell at Lolliloppi that the so-called Prime Minister was in reality none other than Jimmy Jay Leander Johnson, the-used-to-be-called "Hot Shot," who had caddied for the President out at Ye Olde Golfe Course in the Big 'Sipp Near-the-Gulf. Carson had in his possession a picture of Hot Shot (many copies made), and it was clear that all you had to do was to put a beard on the lower part of Hot Shot's face, and he immediately became the Prime Minister of the Independent People's Democratic Republic of Guanaya. He was breathing hard now; he was hot on the trail. He was brainstormed out of his skull. Thought exploding in his mind like firecrackers on the Fourth of July. He paid Belafonte another visit. He got no help from those quarters.

He was like a dog who had just caught the fresh smell of the rabbit. It made no difference whether or not his brainstorms made sense. When a brainstorm struck our man of the Secret Service, he went immediately into action. The more "nays" he received, the more suspicious he became. Clearly Brainstorm Carson was not as stupid as he seemed to be. Perhaps his down-home homespun inane facade was an act to throw the sophisticated up-South people off their guard, so to speak, and notwithstanding.

He even took the Hot Shot picture down to Washington to the President. While the President had to admit there was a strong resemblance of his erstwhile Lolliloppi caddy, sans beard, to His Excellency, the cock-and-bull story that Crafty Carson had woven out of 'Sippi cotton was too far-fetched for the President, who had also gotten to like the bogus PM.

"How in the fuh-fucking hell could somebody like Hot Shot be smart enough to pull a fuh-fuh-fucking stunt like that?"

Brainstorm Carson was puffing and huffing like an old hound dog who had the smell and, President or no, was not about to let it go. "I tell you, Mr. President, there's something fishy in the rotten woodpile in Denmark somewhere. My nose don't never lead me wrong."

"Your fuh-fucking responsibility is to see that nothing untoward happens to His fuh-fuh-fucking Excellency. Forget about that fucking woodpile in Denmark and every fucking where else. His fuh-fucking security is your only fuh-fuh-fucking responsibility, and don't you fucking forget it . . . So, take your fucking nose out of that rotten fucking woodpile. If anything happens to him, I'll hold you personally responsible, I guaren-fucking-tee you!"

Brainstorm Carson caught the next plane back to New York City. There was something up there he was overlooking. Deborah Bostick, Belafonte, Art D'Lugoff, notwithstanding. Mamadou Ben-Hannibala of the Black Alliance including. But what fucking was it?

He sat down at his desk in the security room in the Waldorf staring at the record of the coming and goings of His Excellency and his entourage. There was nothing strange here. Nothing out of the way at all. No matter, the storm in his so-called brain had blown up a whirlwind. And he noted that there *was* the time when His Excellency and the Vice–Prime Minister had left the hotel before day in the morning in a taxi. Where had they gone? Carlton began to breathe like he was having an asthmatic seizure. His brain was burning. He circulated pictures of Hot Shot around to all the cabbies who had been on duty that morning. His stubborn perseverance finally hit pay dirt.

"Yeah," the pudgy-faced cabbie said, "I remember that face all right. I'll never forget that face. He was clean shaved just like this here pitcher here. Then he put on his beard, and right away he changed to Prime Minister Olliemackey."

Brainstorm Carson began literally to jump up and down, breaking wind in his excitement. "I knew it! I knew it! I knew it!" Then he calmed down momentarily. "Are you sure? You sure this is the man you took out to Jamaica? You absolutely positive without no shadow of a doubt?"

"There ain't no doubt about it. I'd swear to it on a stack of Holy Bibles. That's him all right. He talked so much he gave me a headache, and when he got where he was going, he put on his beard and became the Prime Minister of Africa. But he sure did give a big tip." Brainstorm Carson was trying to control his excitement. Breathing hard like he had just run up a long steep hill. "Well, if what you say is true, you have just helped to expose one of the biggest international frauds in history. You have saved the fair name of America."

The fat-faced cabbie said, "Do I get a ree-ward?"

"There ain't no ree-ward. Sorry," Carlton Carson answered.

"Do I get my pitcher in the papers? Do I git on television?" The anxious cabbie was overweight, built in big chunks like a baseball catcher. He seemed to squat eternally. Most of his weight had taken up heavy housekeeping in his face and in the lower regions of his body. If he weighed 240 pounds, 189 of them resided from his hips on down. He was sloppily constructed.

The Great Brainstorm said, "I guarantee it. You'll be on the day after tomorrow morning news. The *Today* show. Johnny Carson. You'll be the most popular cabdriver in the Big Apple. Only one thing. You can't say nothing to nobody about this till after it hits the fan tomorrow at the United Nations."

"The one thing I can keep is a secret," the flabby cabbie said excitedly.

The cabbie was gone now, and Great Brainstorm sat behind his desk brainstorming crazily, his heart thumping like thunder in his chest, thoughts crowding one another in his mind like the traffic on old Broadway just at curtain time. How would he carry it off? Should he get back to the President with this new development? The poor gullible good-hearted President would probably forbid him to take any action.

To hell with it. He would do this one on his own. God had given him the brainstorm.

Then he thought it over, then thought perhaps he'd better not risk going against the specific orders of his personal friend the President, the Great God notwithstanding. He could hear the voice of the President clearly now. "His fuh-fucking Excellency's security is your only fuh-fuh-fucking responsibility. And don't you fucking forget it."

He dialed the direct line to the President in the White House. He listened to it ring exactly a dozen times, which was his rule and habit. His mind strayed away off somewhere in the wild blue yonder, perhaps way up there in "them Green Pastures." He'd loved that moom pitcher. And just as he was about to say, "Fuck it," and hang up, he heard the President's first personal secretary on the other end. He came back down to earth instantly. "This is Carlton Carson, Marybelle. Can you get the President on the line for me? It's an emergency. You mights even say it's urgent even." He was drenched with perspiration. His mind was leaping all over the place as if invaded by a swarm of locusts.

Marybelle said, "The President is involved on the highest level. Triple A-One Priority. His orders were for him not to be disturbed under any circumstances short of Doomsday Emergency. He's interviewing a young thing for special secretarial work. Cute little thing. With scarlet ribbons in her hair. Somebody must've given her the message. And you know how that is. You know how conscientious he is about things like that. It might take him all night long. Top secret and that kind of stuff." She paused. "Would you have a message I might pass along to him?"

"No thank you, Marybelle." Brainstorm Carson hung up, thinking:

"Fuck the fucking President!"

29

It was a decision arrived at after much discussion, that Himself should not accompany the delegation to the United Nations. SS persons would be all over the place. CIA, FBI, Secret Service, G-persons, T-persons, men and women. Someone might notice his strong resemblance to the real Jaja. There was no sense taking chances at this late hour. Of course, Jimmy Jay heartily agreed, or seemed to, or pretended to. Even so, it was extremely hurtful to him. He felt left out, adrift and rudderless, like a man without a country. His mind accepted the wisdom of it, but his feelings were as if they lived on another planet altogether. What hurt more than he was willing to admit, even to himself, was the fact that Maria seemed wholeheartedly to agree that he be left out of everything. It didn't matter whether it was true or not. It was the way it made him agonize. He couldn't give her up as easily as she seemed to be able to give him up. The poor boy from Lolliloppi suffered bitterly. Felt profoundly sorry for himself.

Just as the real PM was about to leave backstage for the widest broadest most far-reaching stage on this crazy planet earth, Brainstorm Carson came backstage with his favorite fat-faced cabbie. The real Jaja had just risen from his chair in which he had been seated chatting with his cabinet members. He was resplendent in his long silken burgundy boubou underneath a jaunty Touré chapeau. He wore the golden map of Africa as an amulet around his neck. The real PM was splendor personified, and effortlessly.

Brainstorm Carson was momentarily intimidated by so much magnificent Blackness in the flesh. So much awesome majesty, but only momentarily. For he was, after all, a red-blooded American patriot of the first water, and the Mississippi River itself ran in his bloodstream. He stood now before the awesome Jaja.

Even though he sensed a disturbing difference between this PM and the one he had become accustomed to deal with, he nevertheless turned to his favorite flabby cabbie. "Is this the man you drove out to Jamaica?"

"Without a doubt," agreed the flabby cabbie.

"You absolutely sure?"

"Sure as I am of the nose that's on your face."

The simplistic mention of Carlton Carson's nose made the SS chief's heavy nostrils flare and glow suddenly like a red light at the intersection. Brainstorm Carson possessed a proud bulbous nose that reminded, especially his New York colleagues, of bagels, two of them, situated contiguously in the middle of his pudgy face. He was breathing now heavily through his bagels, puffing, snorting like Porky Pig, for whom there was a strange resemblance. "Sir," he said to the real PM in a trembly voice, "you are an imposter. You are none other than James Jay Leander Johnson of Lolliloppi, Mississippi, better known as Shot Hooter, I mean Hot Shooter, and I hereby place you under arrest for commonist subversion, fraudulent impersonation, and attempt to overthrow the constituted government of the Uniney States. I am duly bound to Miranda you that anything you say may be used against you in a court of law. I fur—"

Meanwhile up in the tense expectant gallery, a Black uniformed security person tapped Jimmy Jay on the shoulder and said in a strangely foreign accent Jimmy could not identify, "You're wanted on the telephone."

Jimmy Jay's heart sank. He could actually feel it

diving toward his stomach like a belly buster. "Wanted on the telephone?" he mumbled.

"So to speak," the Black security person with the familiar face and the strangely unfamiliar foreign accent said. The Black security person definitely looked like someone he had seen before. Jimmy Jay was puzzled. Round-faced, Black, and formidable. "You might say 'the die is cast.'" Familiar Face and Unfamiliar Accent then added "Or you might say the shit is about to hit the fan."

Jimmy Jay quipped grimly, "Or you might say, as the Queen would, that the excrement has come into sharp contact with the blasted air conditioner."

Familiar Face said, "You got it, H.E." Now his voice sounded like the one who had offered him marty-dam.

Jimmy Jay felt tremendous shame, saw abominable disgrace, he heard the clanging of prison cells closing in around him. The Tombs? Sing Sing? Leavenworth? Atlanta? Just when he thought he was, at long last, home free. His premonitions had deserted him. PRIDE COMES BEFORE A FALL. All the signs had been there for him. The era of good feelings, the euphoria, Maria's love. Positive signs, which must all be always read by him as negative presentiments. He felt a churning in his stomach. Perhaps his heart was down there acting up. But then he felt it thumping in his forehead, leaping loudly in his eardrums, as if his heart were geared with amplifiers.

The Big Familiar Stranger led him down seemingly unending stairs and then through an endless maze of corridors. He thought a couple of times of running down one of them for his worthless life. But he had not gotten over the illusion and the aura of His Excellency's Prime Ministershipness. And he deemed it definitely undignified for an African Prime Minister to be running down corridors. Besides, the brother had a gun in his holster. Would a brother shoot another brother in the back? He preferred not to be empirical at this moment in his swiftly fading youth. This was not the moment for experimentation, he decided. Finally, they entered a room just as the real Jaja was speaking with a righteous indignation.

"Is this some sort of an example of the so-called American sense of humor? Is this supposed to be a joke?"

"Well here he is," Familiar Face stated, importantly.

The sloppily constructed cabbie stared wide-eyed at Jimmy Jay and then at Jaja and said, "Wait a minute."

Great Brainstorm demanded, "What do you mean, wait a minute?" Then he looked from Jaja to Jimmy Jay and back again, and he repeated, "Wait a minute!"

The flabby cabbie said, "This here's the guy what

I was talking about." He indicated Jimmy Jay. "Not the udder guy." Then he said, "I dunno who is who or which is which."

Jimmy Jay's departed mother's favorite son had gotten it together by this time. "Your Excellency, you are deserving of an apology from this dastardly ruffian, whoever he is."

Great Brainstorm said, excitedly. "You know who this bastardly ruffian is. I is, I mean, I am Carson of the Secret Service."

"Sir, I have no idea who you are. Perhaps some crazed crackpot, more than likely."

The frightened flabby cabbie said, "Crazed crackpot?" He turned to Carson. "You mean you ain't who you claimed you was? You mean you been imposting me?"

Jimmy Jay laid it on with a heavy trowel. "Sir, whoever you are, you are perpetrating an international scandal that will be an embarrassment to our great government and its wonderful President. If His gracious Excellency is willing at this late moment to accept your apology, you should consider yourself a lucky individual and be eternally thankful to His most esteemed Excellency."

Even crafty Carlton Carson, of the famous brainstorms, saw the wisdom of Jimmy Jay's remarks. He could still hear the last orders the President had given him. "The fuh-fucking security of His fuh-fuh-fucking Excellency is your only fucking responsibility." Before he knew what was happening, he found himself on his knees pleading His Excellency's forgiveness. "I apologize to Your fuh-fuh-fucking Excellency from the bottom of my fuh-fuh-fucking heart." Obviously, the President's fuh-fuh-fucking fucking was contagious.

The sloppily constructed cabbie said, "Does this mean no TV for me, after you promised me, and after I told my fu-fucking wife and all my fuh-fucking friends to keep it a fucking secret?"

Jaja said, magnanimously. "In that case, old chap, I imagine we can forget about the entire matter."

"Thank you very very very much, Sir, from the bottom of my humble fuh-fuh-fucking heart." Carson kissed the PM's hand, quite slobberly. Meanwhile the flabby cabbie was pulling at the jacket of the repentant Great Brainstorm. Carson turned to the excited and disappointed cabbie. "Will you get the hell out of my fuh-fuh-fucking sight?"

Jimmy Jay had already split the scene unnoticed, after a wink from the big fellow of the famed Familiar Face, just as he connected the familiar face with one of the members of the Black Alliance who had made the trip to 'Sippi with him. He made his way back to the gallery.

Jimmy Jay felt funny (peculiar) completely out of sync seated up in the gallery of the UN Assembly. The place was jam-packed with people. The entire hall was taut with tension, expectation, apprehension. Thousands were outside the building in United Nations Plaza, formerly First Avenue. Picket lines. Demonstrations. New York's Finest all along the avenue interspersed with the thronging people. Plainclothespersons, FBIs, CIAs, SS persons. Picket signs that read:

COBANIUM FOR PEACE, NOT WAR
FOR CONSTRUCTION, NOT DESTRUCTION

Also signs that read:

BLACKIES, GO HOME!
CLOSE DOWN THE DAMNABLE UNITED NATIONS!
GET THEM UN COMMIES OUT OF OUR COUNTRY!

Jimmy felt acutely now he should be down there with the delegation. He should be there with Maria Efwa. It would take him much longer to get used to the idea that he was no longer center stage. He was a spectator, no longer an actor or an activist. And Maria Efwa was lost to him forever.

When the crowd saw that the Prime Minister and his delegation were arriving onstage, the folks stood up, as if by signal and started shouting:

"LONG LIVE JAJA!"

"LONG LIVE JAJA!"

Which conduct was unheard of in the UN and certainly was not to be condoned or tolerated. Uniformed guards ran from place to place trying vainly to quiet the crowd. It was an impossible chore. This continued for more than fifteen minutes. Downstairs at the entrance to the Assembly you had to go past a security apparatus like out at the airport. They apparently thought somebody would try to highjack the United Nations, Jimmy Jay thought amusingly.

When relative order had been restored, the language interpreters at their stations, electronic equipment adjusted, the secretary of the General Assembly, in a softened voice, quietly introduced His Excellency Jaja Okwu Olivamaki, Prime Minister of the Independent People's Democratic Republic of Guanaya. And the disorder began all over again.

"LONG LIVE JAJA! LONG LIVE JAJA!"

Ten or fifteen more minutes of cheering and applauding with the real Jaja standing at the podium in front of the microphone clapping his own hands, applauding the beautiful audience, reciprocatingly.

Someone from the gallery yelled, "Sing RAISE THE RUCKUS TONIGHT!" The audience laughed and applauded. Someone else yelled, "Sing WE SHALL OVERCOME!"

He shook his head. He started to tell them, "I can't sing. I'm not a singer." But then he remembered Jimmy Jay, a man of various and varied accomplishments. A MAN FOR ALL SEASONS.

A distinctly Dixified voice shouted, "Sing ALL THE DARKIES AMA WEEPING." And a fight broke out up in the gallery with shouts of "Hunkie motherfucka!"

When bedlam was frustrated or quiet was restored, whichever, His Excellency began to speak. He was a little shaken by the previous occurrences backstage. But now the descending and respectful quietude, and His Excellency began to speak in a clear and resonant voice, combining the sounds of Africa with Harlem Town and jolly London.

"Sisters and brothers. I address you as sisters and brothers, because I believe in the sisterhood and brotherhood of humankind throughout the entire universe. It is in this sense that I speak to all the people on this earth, and bring you greetings from the people of the Independent People's Democratic Republic of Guanaya, and pledge to you that the natural resources of the little country I serve will be used only and entirely for peace and prosperity and the pursuit of happiness for all the peoples of this earth."

There was a smattering of scattered and restrained applause, as the Prime Minister continued.

"Every nation in Africa stands at the crossroads of history at this very moment and must answer the burning question for themselves. How can we as nations make use of the revolutionary technology of the West, and still maintain our African humaneness, our system of values, which has always been revolutionary, a process always in becoming, developing, evolving.

"So that even as we associated ourselves unreservedly with the dreams of the Reverend Doctor Martin Luther King and Mister Malcolm X and Medgar Evers and Robeson and Du Bois and Jesse Jackson, the dream they all shared with each other for an America in which freedom is in the very air we breathe, even as we share the revolutionary dream of Osagyefo Kwame Nkrumah for a United States of Africa, we must deal seriously with the question of Western technology vis-à-vis our innate and revolutionary African humanity."

All during this part of his speech his audience was in a quandary. There was a gradual building of murmuring applause. Muted shouts of "Like it is!" and "Amen" and "Right on." The people wanted to applaud him at the end of every other word or sentence.

At the same time, they did not want to miss one iota of the full impact of the words he spoke. They had waited for the words so very long. It was somewhat like the days of Jesse Jackson. Even more so.

Now his voice softened, and one could hear the quiet and dramatic tension in it. "We have considered very carefully, and sometimes even painfully, and heatedly, the genuinely generous offer from the United States government of invaluable technical assistance, and after much agonizing and soul-searching, debating almost violently the pros and cons, the answers did not come easily. Momentous decisions that shape world history never come easily.

"On the one hand, there was a serious and convincing argument for accepting from the United States government such a generous offer of partnership to extract the cobanium ore from the earth of the Northern Province as expeditiously as possible. On the other hand, there were those in our cabinet that argued persuasively against such a partnership for fear that we might gain the world's great wealth and riches and lose our African soul. Somehow the offer of Guanayan citizenship to all Black people on this earth got into the heated dialogue and was earnestly discussed." He could hear the awesome murmuring quiet now, a quiet that was tangible. "We will deal with this question when we get back home. We will call a national referendum and a plebiscite on the question. And back to the question at hand, i.e., the cobanium in the Northern Province, we have decided that, with all due respect to the United States of America and its magnanimous President, nevertheless we have reached the decision to rely on our own Guanayan technicians to extract the cobanium out of the Northern Province at our own rate of speed, as we listen to the beat of our own indigenous drums and drummers."

The impact of the PM's words cast a tomb-like silence on the entire Assembly. Then gradually the growing understanding kept pace with a growing crescendo of agreement and a thunderous applause. Whistling, stomping, standing, wildest cheering, men and women embracing, hugging, kissing one another, weeping for joy, shaking each other's hands, high fives, low fives, slapping palms. What was the matter with these crazy African Americans? What happened to their patriotism?

"LONG LIVE JAJA! LONG LIVE GUANAYA!"

"LONG LIVE JAJA! LONG LIVE GUANAYA!"

At which point our patriotic hero, proud protector of the North American Republic, who had just experienced another sudden and divine revelation (like Saint Joan of the famous Arc, he had seen a vision like Moses when his stick became a snake or was it the other way around?), a brainstorm which exploded in his so-called brain like a stick of nitroglycerin, charged upon the stage screaming, "This man is an imposter! This man is an imposter!" Followed by the flabby cabbie demanding, "What about me? What about me? Am I gonna be on television? I got my rights in this here mess."

Brainstormed Carson seized the mic still shouting that His Excellency was an imposter. His brainstorm had suddenly convinced him that, since he had never seen the PM without a beard, and the so-called PM at the UN podium wore a beard, then obviously he had to be the real PM pretending to be James Jay Hot Shooter Johnson, of Lolliloppi, near-the-Gulf, since naturally the beard he wore had to be phony, or else how could he be the real PM pretending to be Jimmy Jay from Lolliloppi? It was plain to Brainstormed Carson as the bageled nose on his friendly face, since Jimmy Jay could not possibly be His Excellency. It made a helluva lot of sense if your name was Carlton (Secret Service) Carson. It made no sense at all if your name was something else. It made no difference anyhow. When a brainstorm struck our man, he acted. His so-called brain was programmed that way. He reached for His Excellency's elegant beard, with the firm conviction that if he tugged at it even gently, it would come off, or at the very least become in obvious disarray. Jaja pushed our patriot firmly away from him, which made Carlton Carson surer than ever that international hanky-panky was afoot. Ultimately, he seized hold of Jaja's beard again, convinced religiously of the glorious rightness of his cause. He tugged away, but nothing happened. Our born-again Christian patriot pulled harder with no better results. Suddenly another brainstorm struck him, as if a flash of lightning came in sharp contact with a second streak of lightning, which caused a growing and frightening suspicion in Brainstorm Carson's befuddled and enfeebled mind that the PM's beard would not be disconnected from his chin without the aid of shears or shaving equipment. No matter, Carlton Carson persevered. Now he was fumbling around in the PM's beard, understanding by now, reluctantly, that the hair of the beard was more or less permanently attached to His Excellency's formidable chin. Brainstorm Carson panicked. More than that, his mind flipped out and went along its merry way. He began to jump around and giggle.

"Just a little joke, he-he-he, Your Excellency, he-he-he, sir. A little example of the great American sense of humor." Giggle giggle he-he-he—

The dignified Prime Minister of the Independent People's Democratic Republic of Guanaya pushed the

SS patriot away from him forcibly. "Are you out of your mind? Have you completely lost track of your senses?"

The President had just rushed in out of breath from a top-level meeting into the presidential TV room when Carson had charged upon the stage. He could not believe what his eyes beheld on the wide screen at the White House. Neither could the audience at the General Assembly, where bedlam again had been set in motion. He reached for his direct line to the UN. "This is the President speaking. Get Carlton Carson out of there. What? The fucking President of the fucking USA. Get that fool out of there on the fucking double!"

Meanwhile the Guanayan SS persons had sprung into motion. Almost simultaneously, so did the SS of the USA. To make a long story short or the other way around, it was a proper mess. Hell and bedlam breaking loose as if they were in collusion. Screaming people swarming from all over toward the center of disturbance, the great eye of the hurricane. From the gallery, from the mezzanine, from especially all over. They leaped from mezzanine to mezzanine, from one floor to another. The Guanayan security persons pulling Brainstorm Carson leftward, the SS of the US pulling him to the right. A riot at the United Nations! Shades of Lumumba and Adlai Stevenson. Not since the murder of Patrice had there been such an uproar at this august body. Even so, the Lumumba incident was subdued, by comparison.

When the smoke cleared and the storm abated, our Secret Service hero had been secreted away, some say, to live out the rest of his faithful patriotic life under the bountiful aegis of Saint Elizabeth of the DC. Some say he was on a funny farm that wasn't very funny. The President went on a worldwide hookup and apologized to His Excellency and to the people of Guanaya and to the nations of the world. The Assembly was adjourned, to give them adequate time to get themselves together, to renovate the quarters, which seemed to have been victimized by a typhoon in collusion with a tornado. Members of the UN insisted that His Excellency be invited to speak to the opening session of the next Assembly.

Demonstrations against American embassies broke out all over the world.

About 1:30 a.m., two nights later, a heavily secured back-and-front caravan moved through the city to John F. Kennedy Airport. In one of the long black limousines (one in which things were visible from the inside but invisible from the outside) near the middle of the convoy were Her Excellency Maria Efwa and the erstwhile bogus Prime Minister of the Independent People's Democratic Republic of Guanaya.

There was a sense of urgency in her usually calm voice. "You're going with us. You simply must go with us. We need you. Africa needs you. I need you. If you're not going, neither am I." There was a note of hysteria in her voice he had never heard before, nor could he have imagined it.

Trying to envision a world without her almost brought him to the brimming brink of tears. He fought hard to keep the tremor from his voice. "I've been in love with you ever since those first days you spent at my bedside in the hospital back in Bamakanougou, which is where it all began, even before." He made himself smile. "The first time ever I saw your face, in the words of the great one, Roberta Flack. I was mesmerized. I thought you were a Juju priestess working her magic. A magic I was helpless to resist."

She said excitedly, "You and I co-chairpersons of the ministry. How beautiful it would be—how wonderfully we could work together!"

He said firmly, flatly, "It could never work. Sure, they love me back in the old country, but how about the Great Africanization Program? How could my appointment to the ministry be justified? Of course, I *am* an African, but I'm an African with the stigma and taint of four hundred years of Americanization. I'm an African American whether I want to be or not. You cannot live in a ruthless jungle for four hundred years without being infected by some aspects of jungle fever. And what about your legendary husband? Your commitment to him and to your country? You belong to Africa. It's so much greater than just you and me. You know that better than I do."

Maria was not accustomed to pleading. "Come with us, darling. We could figure something out. Something for you and also for our country. You could make a contribution."

The big Guanayan jumbo jet stood there in a private isolated section of the airport silhouetted glowingly like silver in the moonlit darkness. Slim and streamlined like a giant metallic suppository. The door to the limo opened. Maria Efwa stepped out of the car with those long slimly rounded dignified legs of hers. She turned back to him and said in a husky unfamiliar voice, "Of course. You didn't really think I had forgotten my commitment to my country, did you? And my husband?" She made herself smile at him, mischievously. It was a face-saving gesture, as he understood it. She was on the verge of tears. "I was merely testing you, to see how profoundly you actually understood the meaning of unselfish. I—" Her voice choked off. She bent toward him and kissed him quickly on his lips, her tear-stained eyes spilled gently now upon his cheek; her wide sloe-shaped eyes, narrowing now, seemed at half mast.

He stared back at her wordlessly. He did not trust himself to speak. It was the most courageous act he had ever committed. He would not spoil it now with tears. She stood for a moment staring down into his face. She parted her rich curving lips. Her mouth worked vainly for the words of good-bye to come forth. Finally, she said, shakily, "Safe journey."

He did not trust himself to speak.

She turned and walked majestically away toward Guanayan Airways.

And never did look back.

Epilogue

Legend has it that on a certain evening in the week a folk singer by the name of John Henry Leanderson will make a guest appearance at the Village Gate or the Vanguard without prior notice. And sometimes, only sometimes, he will sing, with a faraway whimsical smile in his eyes and on his face, as if he is enjoying a private joke with himself, he will burst into singing, robustly:

My old master promised me,
Raise the ruckus tonight,
When he died he'd set me free,
Raise the ruckus tonight.
He lived so long,
His head got bald,

Raise the ruckus tonight,
He got out of notion of dying at all
Raise the ruckus tonight.

And oftentimes people will join in the singing at his request and go away with a smiling in their hearts and stomachs, and rack their brains as to when and how and where and whether they have ever heard him sing that song before.

And legend has it further that later on, that one James Jay Leander Johnson was wedded to the one and only Deborah Bostick. And that one day, in a burst of optimism and Pan-Africanistic romanticism, after a furious exchange of correspondence between New York and Bamakanougou, the newlyweds took off for the Independent People's Democratic Republic of Guanaya, where they would live out their turbulent and eventful lives together.

They are still there, by last report. She is in charge of national television, and he is a national TV personality. They, of course, work wonderfully, though sometimes nervously, under the aegis of the Ministry of Information, Education, and Culture and Her Excellency Maria Efwa.

As to the cobanium, the Guanayans extracted it from the earth by themselves at their own rate of speed in cadence with their own indigenous drums and drummers. His Excellency Jaja adopted a slogan, some say taken from the Black Panthers of the USA: "Power to the People!"

The road to "People's Power" was not easily achieved, has not been smooth all of the way. There have been roadblocks, and ruts and great New York–styled potholes all along the highway to stability. There have been great and white destructive foams on this stormy sea of independence. Some of the leadership labored under a grave misapprehension. They thought that "People's Power" was meant only for certain people. Gentlemen in high places were discovered with bountiful bank accounts in the banks of Switzerland. Certain leaders with their spouses were found asleep in beds made entirely of the rawest purest gold purchased in jolly London Town, clandestinely.

They were dismissed in disgrace from the country's leadership. Some were placed in confinement. Solitarily, there to ponder deeply in profound atonement their shameful misdeed, their betrayals of the trust.

Jaja was firm and steadfast.

The people's power overcame, ultimately. Their latest venture was to irrigate successfully the Great Northern Desert. Their land there, once entirely unproductive, is now arable. The food supply is more than adequate, if not in great abundance yet. Some exported, practically nothing is imported now. No more seven years of drought and famine.

LONG LIVE JAJA.

LONG LIVE MARIA EFWA.

LONG LIVE DEBORAH AND JIMMY JAY.

LONG LIVE THE INDEPENDENT PEOPLE'S DEMOCRATIC REPUBLIC OF GUANAYA.

GOD AND ALLAH BLESS THE PEOPLE.

About the Author

JOHN OLIVER KILLENS was a major influence on African American literature. He was a legendary novelist, playwright, essayist, professor, mentor, and activist. He insisted that every time he sat down to the typewriter, he was out to change the world. "There is no such thing as art for art's sake. All art is propaganda although there is much propaganda that is not art."

Born January 14, 1916, in Macon, Georgia, Killens attended Edward Waters College, in Jacksonville, Florida; Morris Brown College, in Atlanta, Georgia; and Howard University and Terrell Law School, in Washington, DC. He also studied at Columbia University and New York University in New York City.

He was one of the founding members of the Harlem Writers Guild, with Paule Marshall, John Henrik Clarke, Rosa Guy, and Walter Christmas. Other members

included Lonne Elder III, Ossie Davis Louise Meriwether, Audre Lorde, Loyle Hairston, Sylvester Leaks,
Godfrey Cambridge, and Irving Burgess, among others.
He encouraged poet Sarah Wright from Philadelphia to
join the workshop and Maya Angelou from California
to come to New York and focus on her writing. Angelou
and her son stayed with the Killens family in Brooklyn
when she first moved to New York City.

John Oliver Killens died October 27, 1987, on a
stormy Tuesday evening. It so happened that the following Sunday, November 1, the New York City Marathon
was held, and for the first time in its then-eighteen-
year history the first-place male winner was a Black
man, Ibrahim Hussein from Kenya. Ironically, in his
essay "Wanted: Some Black Long Distance Runners,"
Killens insists that, "We Black folks, as a people, have
produced some of the most magnificent athletes the
world has ever known, but have produced very, very
few long distance runners. We've raised a whole lot of
hell in the hundred- and two-hundred-yard dashes.
Long distance running [however] requires planning,
pacing, discipline, and stamina and a belief in the ability to win everything over the long haul." Interestingly,
for the thirty-four years since his death, the New York
City Marathon has been won by Black men; the one
year it was not, 1993, it was a Mexican, Andres Espi-

nosa, who came in first place. Not to be outdone, Black women have also been winning the marathons.

With his life of literary activism, John Oliver Killens *was* that long distance runner, along with his beloved wife, Grace, leaving us a body of work that spans three centuries, from his fictionalized biography of Pushkin, *Great Black Russian: A Novel on the Life and Times of Alexander Pushkin* to *Great Gitten Up Morning*, a biography of Denmark Vesey; *A Man Ain't Nothin' But a Man: The Adventure of John Henry*; *Youngblood*; *And Then We Heard the Thunder*; *Sippi*; and now this new gift, *The Minister Primarily*.

HARPER
LARGE PRINT

We hope you enjoyed reading
our new, comfortable print size and found it
an experience you would like to repeat.

Well – you're in luck!

Harper Large Print offers the finest in
fiction and nonfiction books in this same larger
print size and paperback format. Light and easy to read,
Harper Large Print paperbacks are for the book lovers
who want to see what they are reading without strain.

For a full listing of titles and
new releases to come, please visit our website:
www.hc.com

HARPER LARGE PRINT